# FOUR MINUTES

## J C LAIRD

ISBN: 1539728145
ISBN 13: 9781539728146
Library of Congress Control Number: 2016917925
CreateSpace Independent Publishing Platform
North Charleston, South Carolina

# CHAPTER 1

Dana actually felt it—a gritty movement in her throat under his thumbs, a faint, almost audible vibration as the cartilage of her trachea was fractured and crushed. Dana stared up at her abductor, and watched her left hand release his shirt and fall limply to the floor, there to join the other that had once been striking at her tormenter. Her legs had stopped their thrashing, her feet their pounding. The killer was still leaning forward with crushing pressure, gasping and groaning, his spittle leaking down onto her face in long strands. But her throat no longer hurt. Nothing hurt. Dana just wished she could move her head away from his drooling spit. Her mind wandered....

After almost three miles into her training run, Dana couldn't resist the beckoning green oasis of the San Miguel Cemetery and its promise of a tranquil respite from the hot New Mexico sun. The cemetery covered several acres and was shaded by large cottonwoods, oaks and evergreens. Two loops around the manicured grounds and she would head back to the motel for a hot shower and something to eat. Dana turned in at the doublewide, heavy metal gate.

It was a beautiful spring afternoon, a gentle breeze rustling the new foliage overhead as her long smooth strides carried her in and out of shaded swaths of roadway. Dana's cadenced pace, steady breathing, and the rhythmic sound of her jogging shoes on the asphalt lulled her into memories of the gentle swells of the rolling Pacific near her San Diego home.

Lost in her reverie, Dana failed to notice the kneeling man by a shaded grave as she navigated the first loop around the tranquil necropolis.

But the man had noticed her.

Norman knelt and placed the colorful bouquet in the brass vase next to the flat rectangular grave marker. The flush-with-the-ground metal plate couldn't have been over eighteen inches by thirty-six inches in size. He frowned in disapproval, preferring the old-fashioned marble and granite above-ground tombstones. Different sizes, shapes and colors with witty and pithy inscriptions had always been the traditional way of doing things. The trend to the more uniform flat metal markers laid out in long, even rows... just didn't seem right, almost sacrilegious. And its terse inscription—Nicole Anna Bartholomew, Born April 3, 1969, Died June 6, 2001—was so cold and sterile. Norman could have chosen so many more informative and clever epitaphs if he'd had his way. But he'd had no say in the proceedings....

Norman's attention was drawn to the female jogger completing her second lap of the grounds, now heading back up Canna towards him. Nicole, her immediate neighbors, and Norman were shaded by a large cottonwood standing sentinel nearby. The approaching runner dashed through a long swath of bright afternoon sunshine, her long, ground-eating strides gobbling up the distance between herself and Norman. As she flashed by with arms and legs pumping rhythmically in balanced counterpoint, the brunette gifted him with a quick smile of acknowledgement before turning onto Lombardy.

The attractive, sinfully clad runner reminded him of his mother. Norman's breath hitched in his chest. There was always something about any particular woman that reminded Norman of Nicole. Their eyes, hair, height, build, legs, asses or tits... the way they dressed, or didn't dress.... Norman scrunched his eyes shut, gritted his teeth, and clamped down on the images that were trying to surface in the cesspool of his mind.

Norman returned her smile and watched the long slim legs—book-ended by red, nylon running shorts and complementary colored running shoes—carry the young woman away from him. The matching red athletic halter top, although fitted to support and restrict the movement of her breasts, was not completely successful. Her ponytail, extending through the rear hole of her baseball cap, swayed back and forth rhythmically as she ran. Norman thought the ponytail poking out of the cap's opening was sexy.

Norman imagined his old psychiatrist, Dr. Benjamin Tolliver, would have opined that it stood for some kind of phallic symbol in Norman's mind, or some such psychological bullshit. But the good doctor had no reason to touch upon such an obscure subject as hats and pony tails over a decade ago. Norman's smile had disappeared, replaced by something entirely different.

He pulled his gaze and reverie away from the disappearing runner and looked back at the grave marker. Norman squatted on his haunches, forearms resting on his knees. "Well, Mama, I have to get going; it was nice chatting with you. I'll see you in two or three weeks—if I'm not too busy. Maybe I'll have something a little more interesting to tell you by then."

Nicole hated it when he called her Mama. Norman grinned as he stood, gazing off in the distance at the pony-tailed jogger who was just now reaching the wrought-iron gate at the front of the property. He glanced around the peaceful cemetery. The office was well to the rear of the acreage. It appeared he was now alone in the immediate area—no people or parked cars within view. Relatives and friends were too busy on this beautiful day to be visiting dead people—their "loved" ones. Norman snickered at the thought.

He unzipped his pants and urinated on the grave before him. When he was finished, he spit on the marker for good measure. Norman's handsome, pleasant face had been transformed into a sneering mask, dark with hate. "Fuck you, Nicole."

Nicole's son quickly hopped into the black Nissan Maxima parked nearby, fired up the engine and headed towards the front. Norman didn't want to lose sight of the red-clad female runner. He stopped at the gate and looked to the left, breathing a sigh of relief as he spied the woman running south on Coulson Drive, still striding smoothly, almost effortlessly, through the bright midday sun.

She must live nearby, he reasoned. The temperature was in the mid-eighties, she hadn't been carrying a water bottle, wearing a fanny-pack, or one of those backpack water thingies with the tube to suck through. Unless the woman was ignorant to the dangers of dehydration, she wouldn't be clipping along at her pace for too long without water. And considering her sleek physique and brisk gait, Norman figured she knew what she was doing.

She was approaching Bullock Avenue. There were only three houses on Coulson north of Bullock and she had already passed them, but an older subdivision began south of the intersection. Norman turned, halved the distance between them, and pulled over to the curb. He didn't want to arouse suspicion, but he wanted to see where she was going.

He was surprised when the woman turned left and headed away from the homes. Norman pulled out from the curb and drove slowly towards the intersection. There were no houses between this juncture and the next main drag, California Avenue, just the fenced south boundary of the vast cemetery. A little farther up and on the opposite side of the street was Socorro High School, Holy Redeemer Lutheran Church, and a Valero gas station. Once you got to College Avenue… apartments. On the other side of the intersection was an apartment complex. Businesses and office buildings dominated California north and south. After the apartments there was an assisted living home and not much else for some distance. Norman turned, sped up and passed his prey, pulling into the gas station at the corner where he parked and waited.

After several minutes the woman arrived, but instead of crossing the street she stopped at the station's convenience store. Norman's heart lurched in his chest, but the perspiring woman was intent on her trek and didn't seem to recognize Norman's car. He had parked some distance away from the store's entrance and was confident she'd be unable to see much through the vehicle's tinted windows.

In the air conditioned cocoon of his Nissan, Norman watched the woman walk up to the door breathing deeply. He could see the sheen of perspiration on her skin, the bright sunlight provocatively highlighting her blatant temptations. He again gave thanks for the tinted windows of his car as she glanced around the parking lot from behind her sunglasses before entering the store. Her gaze had slid by his vehicle without hesitation or apparent recognition. Norman exhaled and leaned back in the seat. He hadn't been aware that he was holding his breath.

It was a busy little gas station/convenience store, and with all the in and out foot traffic it was a good five minutes before the young woman emerged, chugging down a Gatorade. The runner stood several feet to the left of the door gazing idly at the vehicles coming and going, their drivers pumping gas, many "paying at the pump" with credit cards, others entering the mini-mart to pay. She received several admiring glances from passing men before she finished her drink and tossed it into a nearby trash bin. With her ponytail swinging back and forth, she headed out, resuming her run north on California Avenue.

Norman was a little surprised. Nothing but businesses and offices in that direction until you got to Tamarack Street after another mile. He searched his mental atlas and recalled that a Comfort Inn shared that intersection.

Would this bitch ever stop running? She was starting to piss him off and, coupled with an increasing anticipation, the resulting emotional brew was becoming nearly uncontrollable. Norman's heart was thumping in his chest and his mouth was dry from a rising excitement. A waning part of his mind was trying to warn him about taking a victim in New Mexico, let alone this close to his home.

But the tall and tanned brunette had inflamed him. Norman knew he should wait for his upcoming trip to Montana before exacting his next round of retribution, but reason was beginning to lose the battle. It was unlikely he'd find a more worthy candidate in Bozeman than this gorgeous man-eater in her skimpy red outfit. Who knew how many men he'd save from being used and abused by this little slut? Norman's blood was roiling. He'd better concentrate on the task at hand and not go off half-cocked, as strong and overpowering as the familiar urge was becoming. He watched the receding woman with the bouncing ponytail for a minute before he started his car and pulled out.

Norman would leave it to fate and take a calculated risk. He picked up speed, again passing the tiring woman whose pace had slowed somewhat in the heat, and drove directly to the Comfort Inn at California and Tamarack. He pulled around to the opposite side of the building from the office and parked. Quickly donning his blond custom made wig and mustache from the glove compartment, plus an Albuquerque Isotopes baseball cap from under the seat, he exited and walked around the corner towards the office, slipping on a pair of aviator sunglasses as he went.

In the office he furnished a driver's license and credit card in the name of Nicholas Franklin Bertrand, filled in a fictitious vehicle and plate number, and registered for one night. The young, heavy-set Hispanic woman behind the counter seemed bored with the whole thing, going through the motions perfunctorily. He signed the registration form, almost forgetting to use his alias instead of his real name.

The woman, 'Juanita,' according to her name tag, handed him a room key card. "You're in room #213, Mr....," she glanced down at the signature "... Mr. Bertrand," she said. She nodded at the hallway to Norman's right. "You can take the stairs or the elevator. A hot, complimentary breakfast is served between 6:00 and 9:00 in the dining area..." she nodded to the left... "Checkout time is 11:00. The pool is open till 10:00, opens again at 9:00 in the morning. There are several restaurants north on California and east on Tamarack if you're hungry. There's also a pizza place, Papa John's, that delivers." Having finished her spiel, the clerk silently dismissed him and went back to playing at a computer terminal behind the counter.

Norman kept glancing out the window, wondering if he was wrong about his jogger's destination. He bit his lower lip and hoped his reasoning and intuition were correct. He gave the clerk his most charming smile as he picked up a USA Today paper off the counter. "I'm just going to relax and catch up on my reading before I head up."

The clerk looked up and smiled at him absently. Norman sat in a plush chair by the window, wishing he had the time to find a different colored shirt to wear.

He licked his lips and tried not to keep looking at the motel's wall clock as it ticked its way towards five minutes. Norman jerked as a flash of red caught his eye passing the window. The jogger breezed in the front door at a fast walk and headed for the hallway before reversing course and ambling back to the counter, still breathing deeply. She glanced at the woman's name tag. "Excuse me, Juanita, what restaurant would you recommend around here for some good New Mexican food?"

Juanita didn't appear to be too overjoyed at having to be working on such a beautiful day. Still seated behind the counter in front of a computer monitor, she managed a quick glance and a forced smile at Dana before answering flatly, "Little Anita's."

The runner waited patiently for several long seconds. "And Little Anita's would be located where?" she finally asked.

Juanita seemed a little put out by the continued interruption. "Just up the road on the right," she answered without looking up from the computer screen.

"Thanks for the information, you've been a real help," the slim brunette replied with just a hint of sarcasm.

Norman, hidden behind his newspaper, listened to this exchange with a grim smile. Now he knew where the woman would be eating dinner.

Norman waited a few minutes after the young woman left the lobby before leaving himself. He drove his vehicle across the street to the apartment complex, found a parking space that afforded a view of the front of the motel and waited. Norman reached over, opened the glove compartment and pulled out a pair of binoculars. He leaned back in the seat and tried to relax.

Less than an hour later Norman put binoculars to eyes as the woman left the Comfort Inn. The jogger had changed into a white blouse and a dark blue skirt that ended above her knees, modestly showcasing her slim, tanned legs. A pair of high heels accented them even more. She looked cool and crisp in the still, hot desert air. A short walk across the asphalt lot and she folded herself into a parked vehicle. The late model, maroon Honda Civic pulled out and headed north on California.

The black Nissan followed—a shadow unnoticed.

# CHAPTER 2

Norman followed the Civic at a discreet distance. That her destination was Little Anita's was confirmed when she pulled into the restaurant parking lot. He looked at his watch; it was almost 7:30. He couldn't erase the image of her long, lithe body from roiling dangerously through his mind. Norman had to control himself somehow. That weak, but persistent warning voice was still in his head, still cautioning that this was too dangerous. But the way his luck was holding, this was meant to be; he'd come up with something. Norman's smile became smug and lopsided. He was omnipotent, had been for the last ten years. He quashed that still, small voice of sanity—just as he had silenced all those women during the past decade.

At the restaurant he parked two rows past the Honda. His vision partially obscured by several parked vehicles, Norman stared as the woman gracefully exited her car and walked towards the entrance. Her hair was no longer pony-tailed, but now tumbled past her shoulders in thick, lustrous waves. She looked so good that Norman actually groaned aloud. He could imagine the smell of her. His hands trembled. This woman had the same narrow-waisted hip swagger as Nicole when she had been younger, when she had... Norman ground his teeth together—this bitch would pay, and she was going to be worth every minute of it. He chuckled at the thought as he watched the woman sashay into Little Anita's.

Norman preoccupied himself by eyeballing the parking lot, and could see no noticeable security cameras in the immediate vicinity. Yes, he thought to himself, this unexpected opportunity was meant to be. That was why everything was going his way. He scowled as an assortment of cars pulled in, their occupants happily heading into the popular eatery to feed their fat, middle-class faces. With an effort Norman unclenched his jaws

He waited, trying to calm himself. It was nearing sundown, but wouldn't be dark for another hour. If the night didn't cloak him, or if other people were in the immediate area, he'd have to come up with a Plan B. That feeble, but insistent voice in his head was screaming faintly that Plan A wasn't a good idea either. Unfucking believable.

If he pulled this off, he'd have to take the bitch to his place outside Magdalena; a big gamble. He'd have to be careful. If the cops stopped him for any reason, his ten-year run of luck would come to an abrupt end. But Norman was confident that his fate was ordained by providence, and wasn't dependent on the whimsical winds of luck—as long as he didn't test the limits of that fate by being too careless, he reminded himself.

It was a large restaurant. If Dana remembered correctly the architectural style was described as Mission Revival—patterned after the structures of the early Spanish settlers—with stucco walls, recessed windows, and a flat roof with its surrounding parapet. The inviting interior with its muted lighting, continued the illusion with an eclectic mix of heavy wooden furniture, colorful murals, iron work, and Spanish knick-knacks and bric-à-brac. Even her waitress, with her floor length black skirt and white peasant blouse, helped catapult Dana back into another world and time.

The restaurant was doing a steady business, and the background hum of conversation, subdued clinking of glass and silverware increased Dana's good mood. The dim, cozy atmosphere enhanced her positive state of mind—that and the fact she was famished. She couldn't resist ordering a combination plate which included a tamale, enchilada, chile relleno, refried beans and Spanish rice.

Her waitress who had introduced herself as Belinda, was smiling and shaking her head. "Somebody must be hungry. What would you like to drink?" she asked.

"How about a local beer? I'm from San Diego; I've never been in New Mexico before—I might as well try something new." She impulsively extended her hand. "And my name is Dana," she added.

"Well, welcome to New Mexico, Dana." The young waitress paused from writing on her pad to shake Dana's hand, her own smile widening. "As for the beer, you're in for a treat. We have something from a micro-brewery in Albuquerque—Chama Brewery—called 'Sleeping Dog Stout'. It's popular around here."

"I'll try it," Dana enthused. "Hell, I'm celebrating. My divorce is final, I'm on vacation, I'm running a marathon in Boston, and I plan on surprising my sister in Detroit with a long overdue visit."

Belinda grinned and continued. "Congratulations on all counts. And I'll also give you separate portions of red and green chile on the side for you to try. You're in the chile capital of the world, so you might as well at least taste the real thing. As for dessert, I'll bring you a New Mexican sopapilla, a fried pastry to die for and best eaten with honey."

Dana laughed. "You're the boss, bring it on." As the waitress turned to go, Dana stopped her. "Wait a sec, Belinda, there's a big 'M' painted on the mountain to the west. If the name of this town is Socorro, what does the 'M' stand for?"

The waitress paused, rolling her eyes upward. "Ha, that would stand for Magdalena, a little village in the mountains maybe twenty-five or thirty miles to the west off of US-60. Not much there—a café, an ice cream parlor, a few quaint shops... just a quiet little burg with a few ranches scattered around the area."

"Thanks, I guess I'll scratch that off my list of touristy things to do," Dana replied.

An hour and a half later, she finished her second pint of Sleeping Dog Stout, her "doggie bag"—a Styrofoam container holding the leftover portion of a very healthy sized dinner—sitting next to her purse on the table. Belinda returned with her credit card and dinner check. Dana added a big tip to the bill and signed it. "Thank you, Belinda, for a very pleasurable dinner." She tapped the Styrofoam box. "And I already have my lunch for tomorrow."

"Thank you and, if you have time before you leave town, please visit us again," Belinda said.

"I just might do that." Dana smiled, picked up her purse and left-overs and made her way out.

It was early evening, and the temperature had dropped after sunset. There was a gentle breeze that wafted the tantalizing aromas of the restaurant to those anywhere nearby. After the bullshit of her and David's prolonged divorce, Dana was finally unwinding and feeling like an unfettered human being again. The two mugs of Chama's finest hadn't hurt either.

The ambient lighting from Little Anita's and the highway, struggled to illuminate the dark edges of the world as she made her way to her car. Dana pushed the button on her key-fob, unlocking her car door when she was thirty feet away. She was almost to the safety of the waiting Honda when she heard a masculine voice call out, "Excuse me, miss..."

Dana jumped, her hand impulsively reaching and clutching the car's door handle as she glanced over her shoulder at the dark-haired man approaching, seemingly hesitant and unsure. He paused, a car length away. It had been a superb day, but even with two mugs of beer adding to her euphoric mood, caution still prevailed. She quickly unlocked the car door, her thumb on the panic button of the key-fob.

The stranger was still talking "... didn't I see you earlier today at the cemetery?"

Dana suddenly recognized him. "I was out jogging," she said. "You're the man with the flowers at the cemetery." She slid into the driver's seat, shut and locked the door. She felt more secure now and rolled down her window to talk to him. He was a hunk, and she was in a good mood.

He walked up to the car with his hands in his pockets, a small embarrassed smile tugging at the corners of his mouth. "Yes, that would be me. My mother is buried there. I try to get by a couple times a month to put new flowers on the grave." He was standing next to the driver's door now.

Dana smiled up at him as she put the key in the ignition.

"I'm impressed. Many people nowadays forget about their parents or relatives once they've passed away. My own parents—"

Dana would not have believed anyone could be so quick. His hand was a blur, out of his pocket and shooting through the window before her mind even registered what was happening. His fist was like a hammer, the short downward chip clipping her solidly on the chin, her head whipsawing sharply from the force of the punch.

White stars on a dark background exploded before her eyes. She could sense her body listing, then falling to the side, her face now resting on the Styrofoam box smelling of enchiladas. Dana was floating, semi-conscious, only vaguely aware of the world around her. She stubbornly clung to consciousness, knowing intuitively that her life might depend on it. But the darkness was slowly closing in....

Strong hands roughly pushed her by the buttocks and legs until her body was scrunched up against the passenger side door. The man grabbed her arms, pulled them behind her back, and tightened something painfully around her wrists. Her ankles were also bound together. A wide strip of gray adhesive—duct tape she thought—was slapped over her mouth. There were words coming from the man, but they were just a fading background noise as the darkness finally enveloped her completely.

Dana regained consciousness a short while later as the car came to a stop and her body rocked forward. Through half-open eyes she could see the Comfort Inn Motel sign out the driver's window, the view partially blocked by her assailant's profile. Her jaw ached, and she was nauseous, but at least she was alive. She closed her eyes as the man's head turned towards her.

The voice was calm and matter of fact. "I'll only be a minute, sweetheart. I have your room key, and I will collect and pack your things for you. You'll be using the express check out on their TV channel, a nice feature I've found. Don't you worry; I'll take care of everything."

The shadow donned a baseball cap and sunglasses and leaned over and adjusted her body until her back was more exposed. "Even though you're trussed up good, I don't want to take any chances..." he chuckled deep in his throat. "... or mess you up any more than I have to. Not yet, anyway."

Bracing himself on her hip with one hand, he slammed his fist into her kidney twice, three times, with sledgehammer-like blows. Dana's eyes flew open as a soul numbing pain flashed through her. Her diaphragm froze in shock and her lungs refused to work. The curtain of darkness descended once more over her.

As the car bounced over the uneven roadway, the passage of time and the erratic rocking brought her back around again. Not only was Dana's lower back wrapped in a nauseating girdle of pain, her ankles and wrists were throbbing from their restraints. Crumpled awkwardly against the passenger door, the pain in her neck was excruciating, and she was having trouble breathing through her nose with the tape sealing her mouth. Dana had no idea how long she had been out, but she kept silent with her eyes closed, realizing that feigning continued unconsciousness while trying to think was a matter of survival.

Dana's abductor was talking, but whether he knew she was conscious or was speaking to himself, she didn't know. She thought the latter since he had already been rambling when she came back to her senses.

The man's voice was deep, disturbingly calm, continuing, "… and when we're done, I'll pick up my car tomorrow and have Hector take care of yours; he knows several good chop shops in Mexico. You won't need it anymore." There was a humorless chuckle, followed by silence.

Although her eyes were closed, she could imagine—literally feel—the man's predatory gaze traveling over her. This accurate sensation was followed by a hand groping her exposed thigh below her hiked skirt. Dana managed not to flinch only by a supreme effort of will. She gritted her teeth, motionless and silent as his hand caressed farther up her leg.

Her captor's breathing quickened, followed by a low growling deep in his throat. But even worse was the agonized moan, almost a whimper that followed. His hand abruptly left her leg. "It won't be long now, Nicole. Soon, it'll be fun time—your very own four minutes," he whispered.

Dana wondered who Nicole was and what four minutes he was talking about, but there was only silence now from her captor. As she felt and heard the car turn onto a gravel surface, pain and fear forced tears from her tightly shut eyes. She had to control herself, not only from fear of detection, but because she would have trouble breathing if her nose became plugged.

The car came to a stop. As the driver's door opened, Dana watched through slit eyes as the amorphous shadow exited the vehicle into the night. The interior light failed to work; the man must have disabled it. Footsteps came around to the passenger side, and the car door abruptly opened, freeing her head from its cramped position against it—the night air cool against her flushed and tear-streaked face.

Strong hands pulled her roughly from the vehicle, hoisting her up and over her kidnapper's shoulder. She grunted as his shoulder cut into her stomach, and air forced through her mucus clogged nose. "Welcome to my humble abode, you fucking bitch," the man said. "You should feel privileged. Out of twenty-six, you're only the second one I've ever brought home. Other than the first one, the other cunts got theirs on the road. You were just irresistible, I guess." The shadow laughed into the darkness—a brittle and breathless chortle.

Little grunts escaped her as she bounced along on his shoulder while he strode towards his "humble abode." Her tears fell to the desert floor as she wondered about the other twenty-five and what the ominous words "got theirs" meant.

# Chapter 3

Dana continued to fake unconsciousness, keeping her body limp, arms dangling and swaying at the man's waist. Eyes open now, she tried to observe as much as possible as her head bumped gently against the small of his back in counterpoint to his stride. Her head was throbbing in pain and her fear was almost overpowering, but she realized that knowledge of her surroundings, however slight, might help in any escape attempt.

Her captor stopped at the front door and fumbled with the keys in his hand. By the light of the full moon Dana realized that they were in a large, covered flagstone patio. She was only able to see to her right and everything was upside down, but tucked away in the shadows was a café table with two chairs and a ristra of dried red chile peppers hanging from an overhead beam.

The door open, they entered, and the man flipped on a wall-light switch. He carried her across a dark-brown, travertine tiled entryway and through what appeared to be a Southwestern styled great-room, turning on lights as he went. They crossed a kitchen and came to a stairway— but downward, not upward. Dana had read somewhere that basements were unusual in this part of the Southwest. The hardpan made basement costs prohibitive; the cement-like clay just below the soil layer so hard that even plant roots had trouble penetrating. Much too expensive an option for the average home construction. But apparently not so for her kidnapper.

The man was breathing more heavily now. He had been carrying Dana over his shoulder for several minutes. As for Dana, his broad, muscled shoulder had been cutting into her midsection and, with the tape over her mouth and a partially plugged nose, she had the frightening sensation of suffocation. It took all of her willpower to keep from struggling in panic and giving away her state of awareness. She had to be ready to make a break whenever the opportunity presented itself.

Her eyes involuntarily blinked as light flooded the room, revealing a sparsely furnished basement. Seconds later she was dumped unceremoniously onto a wooden chair, her kidnapper grunting with relief. Dana kept her eyes closed and remained limp, sagging back in the chair as she continued to affect unconsciousness. Dana felt fingers fumbling at her mouth. Abruptly and painfully the tape was ripped away. She managed to keep from flinching.

She heard the bastard humming to himself as he grabbed her by the hair and pulled her forward. She was now bent double, her head at her knees. From the side, he cut the tape binding her wrists, then knelt and sliced away the tape at her ankles. He yanked her back to an upright position, leaning her back in the chair.

Her abductor stood in front of her with his hands on his knees and gazed into her relaxed face. "It's more fun when you can put up a fight. I want to see the terror in your eyes as your struggles weaken, and their agonizing surrender as you slowly leave this world. Then, that exquisite finale—those beautiful, sublime four minutes—experiencing what I'm doing to you with the finality and terror that only the knowledge of your death and absolute helplessness can bring."

His voice had become a snarl, his breathing becoming more rapid—but not from exertion. He stared at her for a long second. "But I'm wasting my poetic breath right now. Let me get you a little water to wake you up, then I can—"

Dana's eyes flashed open as she simultaneously lashed out with her right leg, catching her abductor in the crotch. The man grunted, his eyes wide in pain and surprise as he grabbed himself. She kicked with her left foot and caught him with a glancing blow. He staggered back several steps, his handsome face contorted in a grimace of pain. Dana bolted out of the chair and ran for the stairs. She heard him roar in anger as she frantically scrambled up the stairs, tripping, regaining her footing, stumbling again and clambering on, her panicky breathing loud in her ears. Almost there—

The man caught her at the top. He lunged, grabbed her ankle, sending her sprawling onto the cold tiles of the kitchen. Dana rolled onto her back and kicked out at her attacker. In a fury he swatted her wildly bicycling legs aside as she tried to scrabble away from him on her backside. He lunged between her legs and was atop her.

The killer was astride her, his weight on his knees as he leaned forward, his hands at her throat exerting an ever increasing pressure. He was sitting high on her, almost on her chest. Dana planted her feet and pushed with her legs while arching her back. The throttling pressure on her throat eased as her attacker was caught by surprise. He was nearly upended, but quickly regained his balance and settled more weight on her chest as he regained the hold on her throat. Dana bucked again, and again, but he was ready and his weight was too great.

Her teeth clenched together, her neck muscles straining in resistance, she stared up at her attacker, her eyes slits of determination. The face glaring at her was a twisted caricature of itself, its owner bending farther forward, leaning ever more weight on his hands—and her throat beneath them. She tried clawing at his face, but the distance was too great. Her fingers pried at his throttling grip but failed. Finally, she resorted to a wild pummeling at his arms and chest with her fists.

Dana's vision blurred as her eyes tried to focus through her tears. Her mouth yawned wide in an attempt to breathe—a breath so close, yet so far—distantly aware of her legs and feet thumping spasmodically on the tile floor, her overwhelming urge to swallow thwarted by the fingers crushing her neck. One of her hands gripped a fistful of his shirt. The other continued to beat feebly at his arm. More weight and pressure. The pain in her throat was excruciating, her lungs screaming in their need for oxygen.

Dana actually felt it—a gritty movement in her throat under his thumbs; a faint, almost audible vibration as the cartilage of her trachea was fractured and crushed. Dana watched her left hand release his shirt and fall limply to the floor, there to join the other that had once been striking at her tormenter. Her legs had stopped their thrashing, her feet their pounding. The killer was still leaning forward with crushing pressure, gasping and groaning, his spittle leaking down onto her face in long strands. But her throat no longer hurt. Nothing hurt. Dana wished she could move her head away from his drooling spit. Her mind wandered....

With one final shudder, he released her and leaned back. Dana could see a dark splotch on the front of his pants; the man had ejaculated. Disoriented, she looked around the room—before, below, above and behind her. The man was standing now. They weren't struggling anymore. *Why wasn't she fighting? Why wasn't she running?*

She felt/saw/heard/smelled the killer grab her under the arms and drag her dead weight across the floor to the head of the stairs. Still she didn't resist as her attacker pushed her over the edge and into the stairwell with his foot. Dana's body flopped and tumbled down the stairs and back into the basement. Strangely, she felt no pain mingled with her alien, swirling senses. Dana lay acquiescent on the cold floor until the man followed her down, still breathless from his exertions.

Strong hands grabbed her by an arm and dragged her across the floor to an old leather couch along the far wall of the basement. He lifted and set her on the couch, arranging her in an upright position. He put a throw pillow behind her neck to prop her head up.

*Why couldn't she move or speak?* Overwhelmed with strange, alien perceptions of the world, Dana could still hear, feel and smell—as well as see—but on an eerie, primal level. A distant roaring was sounding in her head, faint but growing. And the lighting in the room had intensified. Maybe a concussion or head injury? Maybe she was in a coma... but no... she was still weirdly cognizant of everything. Her thoughts were chaotic; confusion enveloped her.

Although her eyes were staring lifelessly ahead, she watched the man drag a wooden chair across the floor from the other side of the room and place it in front of her. He sat, his knees between her splayed legs, leaned forward and stared into her vacant face.

When he spoke the sound subtly reverberated, echoing from everywhere. He stared at her driver's license in his hand before gazing into her blind eyes. His smile was malevolent, his voice calm again. "Dana, Dana, Dana... did your parents want a boy and got you instead? Is that why you're stuck with such an ambiguous name? No matter..." He continued to talk, her confused terror slowly growing with his words. He paused and leaned forward, his handsome, sneering face up close, manic eyes only inches from her blank ones.

Dana's senses were mixed, jumbled, juxtaposed. Her paranormal sight was now slightly blurred, mixing nauseatingly with the metaphysical senses of touch, smell and sound. She could see odors, smell sounds. She could hear the weight of her body on the couch, could feel the smell of his sweat. Her senses were becoming a mishmash of swirling, slowly dissipating soup.

The killer began talking in staccato-like bursts, his breathing becoming more and more rapid, spittle peppering her, his words a horrifying barrage. He paused, frowning. Dana knew her empty stare was fixed over his right shoulder, her mouth sagging luridly open. He leaned forward, one hand resting on her smooth thigh just below her hiked, rumpled skirt, the other reaching and gently closing her mouth. His fingers lingered at her lips. "Nicole, my mother, always said that you'd catch flies with your mouth hanging open like that. But don't worry; I'll open that hole back up when I'm ready to fill it with something." His scornful chuckle would have brought chills to Dana if she had still been capable of such a thing.

He stood and retrieved several items from a table nearby, along with a wooden-handled broom. This last item he broke in half over his knee. He peered at it critically and muttered to himself, "This should do." He placed his collection on the floor by the couch and returned to the chair.

Dana was silently screaming, terrified at his words and what they meant. *Please,* she thought, *somebody come and wake me from this nightmare. Stop this madman from doing these things—*

Leaning forward and resting on his elbows the madman continued. "Well, Dana, I know you're in there, screaming in the darkness. I read somewhere that after the lungs stop processing oxygen and the heart ceases to pump it—in short, after you die—there's still enough oxygen remaining in the brain tissue for it to survive several more minutes. You've read the stories. If someone dies, but you can revive them within a few minutes, they are A-Okay. After four to six minutes, the oxygen starved cells begin to check out and irreversible brain damage will begin. As the minutes tick by, it's a slow 'fade to black', until you're totally kaput—usually ten minutes max. They call it hypoxia."

"So, what's it like in there?" The smirking nightmare shook his head. "Hell, Dana, of course everything's on the fritz now. Your central nervous system is shut down and those synapses aren't firing in the ol' brain anymore, are they? Are you screaming in terror, in the darkness, waiting for the last of the oxygen to run out, waiting for the brain cells to begin dying, teetering on the edge of that long journey into the great abyss? When your brain starts gasping, and you realize the approaching, ultimate death of you—not to mention what I am doing to the poor body you're slowly relinquishing—will you go silently insane?"

Dana was aware of herself sitting and gazing off into nowhere, permanently acquiescent, her blue skirt hiked midway to her hips, her white blouse ripped open from her struggles with her killer. Powerless and reduced to sensing events in a primal, fundamental way, her mind was a swirling hodgepodge of memories and sensory perceptions. The distant roaring was louder, the lighting in the room ever brighter. She could hear herself screaming, the sound amplified nails on a chalkboard. *Oh, my God, can I really be dead somehow? Am I some kind of ghost? Is my soul trapped inside my dead body? Why is it still here…?*

She saw the man licking his lower lip, staring at her. He leaned forward again. "I know you're in there Dana. You remember—you know what's happening. I bet it's like a sixth-sense or something…."

Dana could see, feel, hear and smell her body, in some paranormal way, listing to the side. She could see pictures of women, maybe two dozen, tacked to corkboard on the wall behind him. They looked dead, their vacant expressions staring out into the room. The corkboard and its grotesque collection slanted to the side as her body sagged. *Oh my God. Was she going to become one of them? Was she already one of them?*

The killer roughly grabbed her slumping body, repositioned it on the couch and adjusted her flopping head slightly so that her dark eyes were fixed on his—as if insisting that she concentrate on him and his task. His hands were on her bare thighs now, running up under her skirt. He was panting, drooling. "You're trapped in there, you filthy whore", he yelled. "I am the god of your body now!" He was ripping, tearing at her clothing. "I will make you pay in ways you never imagined, and all you can do is watch from inside, unable to hide—even death unable to save you from me."

The cries of Dana's fading sentient being mingled with the roaring in her mind, whether from the growing thunder or the sounds of her killer—she knew not. The abhorrent, ghastly acts now being committed upon her lifeless body brought a horror that was total and absolute. She screamed into the dark void, pleading for the last of her reality to die and spare her any more psychic agony.

But Dana had been a well-conditioned marathoner—it took longer than four minutes for her ultimate end to arrive, closer to ten. The killer would have been pleased to know that the last sensations imprinted on those final, dying cells were that of dirt being shoveled over her body.

# Chapter 4

Howie looked up from his lackluster chore of wiping the dark wood surface of the bar's countertop. It was a good hour before the lunch crowd came in although the word "crowd" was certainly a misnomer. Even with its decent location on Central and 3rd Street, Howie's Bar and Grill had suffered a considerable loss of business during the recent recession. His only morning customer to date was his regular, Julio, who was sitting at the end of the bar, already half-in-the-bag. Howie would have to boot him out soon. He didn't need another drag on business.

He inventoried his small refrigerator, checked the grill, and was getting ready to tap a new beer keg under the counter when the door opened and a junkie staggered into the bar. The woman collided with one of the small, half-dozen tables along the far wall, knocking over the table's napkin holder, salt and pepper shakers and condiments. Grabbing onto a chair to steady herself, the muttering, crying woman reeled towards the back of the room.

Howie mentally cringed. Damn, just what he needed—a junkie O.D.'ing in his bar. That ought to bolster the bar's rep and increase his clientele. From behind the counter he headed after the woman. She had managed to zigzag to the farthest table in the rear without further damage and had collapsed onto a chair.

As he neared her, he noticed that the young woman's clothing was classy, albeit tousled, the shirt-tail of her expensive red silk blouse hanging loose outside her black skirt. Now, Howie figured he was dealing with a hooker, as well as a junkie, although the high-end prostitutes usually plied their trade several miles to the east on Central, between Stanford and Broadway. And he had to admit, most hooker-junkies didn't look as good as this woman did, despite her wild and disheveled appearance.

This woman was a real mess. She sat in the chair, holding herself and rocking back and forth, her eyes wide and bloodshot, black mascara streaking her cheeks. Mucus from her runny nose was mixing with her tears and dripping from her chin, spotting the table. She was shuddering uncontrollably, shaking like an out of balance clothes dryer, hugging herself ever tighter—seemingly in a frantic attempt to keep herself from disintegrating—spittle now joining the drops of tears and mucus on the table.

Howie had meant to order her out, even physically escort her if need be. But now, looking at her he hesitated. "Lady, are you okay?" he asked. What a stupid question, he thought.

The dark-haired woman was oblivious to him, kept rocking like a metronome and mumbling to herself. It sounded like a monotonous monotone of "no... no... no..."over and over again.

"Lady, do you want me to call someone?" Shit, he was sounding dumber and dumber.

And all he was getting in response was the "no... no... no" amidst the rocking, tears, snot and drool. Screw this, he thought, it was time for 911; he didn't want her dying in his bar. He fumbled in his pocket for his cell phone.

Howie hadn't even punched in the 9 when a strong hand grabbed his upper arm from behind, the cell phone dropping to the floor with an expensive and costly clattering. The barman spun around. "Dammit, Julio, look what—". He froze, staring not into the glassy, unfocused eyes of the local drunk, but into the smiling, mahogany hued eyes of a stocky man of indeterminate age. Julio was no longer in the bar.

The stranger was equal to Howie's six foot height, but was wider at the shoulders and thicker in the chest. His craggy face reminded Howie of a closed fist; a Caucasian version of a younger Danny Trejo, the Hispanic actor of 'Grindhouse' and a few other action flicks that Howie liked—sans the mustache, of course. In fact, one of the actor's earliest roles had been a bit part as the bartender in the '96 movie 'From Dusk Till Dawn' and—

The meat-hook of a hand gripping his arm was becoming painful and helped refocus his attention. Despite the man's smile, Howie was a little intimidated. But the subdued and blubbering "no... no... no's" coming from behind him gave him a sense of righteousness. "Listen, buddy, I have to call 911, I think this hooker-junkie is O.D.'ing. The police—"

The smiling stranger let go of his arm and produced a Detroit Police Sergeant's I.D. badge from the pocket of his denim jeans.

It was on a long chain which he slipped over his head, the badge coming to rest against the front of his light-blue chambray shirt. "No need to call anyone, I'll take care of her." His voice was deep, but surprisingly gentle considering his imposing presence. "I'm Sergeant Jack Kroner, and this woman called me. I'm a friend of hers, and I'll take responsibility for her care."

Howie was eager to be rid of the woman. "Fine by me. My name is Howie Elwood, I own this place. You think she'll be okay?" he asked.

Sergeant Kroner looked at the shivering and quaking woman with concern. Her pallor had taken on a decidedly gray hue, a sickly sheen of perspiration covered her skin and wet strands of disheveled hair were plastered to her forehead. He wasn't sure what was wrong with her, but he knew it wasn't drugs. His best guess, based on past experience, was that his friend was several steps beyond hysteria, in the midst of the crash and burn phase. The officer ignored the barman's question. "You'd better get us a couple shots of your well-whiskey, with beer washes." Shaking his head, he reevaluated. "Better make those doubles, Howie."

"Yes sir," the bar owner replied. His stepfather, an Army colonel, had instilled in Howie a deep respect for authority, in-graining in him the use of 'sir.' He headed off to get the drinks.

The over-sized cop pulled up a chair and sat next to the rock-ing, murmuring woman. With one hand he grabbed her forearm; with the other he gently clasped the back of her neck and pulled her head onto his shoulder, whispering and murmuring as he rocked her gently.

He held her and spoke all the soothing words that came to mind, telling her that all would be okay in every way he could think of, trying to calm her in an effort to find out what had caused this trauma. Gradually, the shivering and trembling abated and her mumbling ceased. She eased back in her chair, eyes closing, and her breathing slowing. He let go of her neck and arm as soon as he was sure she could stay upright on her own.

The off-duty cop grabbed a handful of napkins out of the holder and dabbed at her face. She was coming around, now appearing no worse than your typical drunk. He turned and called to the barman. "Hey, Howie, bring me a glass of water and a couple of wet washcloths with those drinks."

A minute later the nervous bar owner delivered their order to the table. The sergeant took out his wallet and emptied it—the total coming to just over a hundred dollars—and handed the money to the bar owner. "I'd like to reserve your bar for the next half-hour. This is to cover your expenses. If it's not enough, I'm good for the rest of it. Okay?"

Howie stared at his only two patrons for several seconds, then took the money. "Yes sir." Curious, he squinted at the woman. "Is she going to be okay?"

"Not to worry, she'll be as good as new in no time."

Howie left and put up the CLOSED sign on the door and went back to tending his nearly empty bar.

Sergeant Kroner's big hands continued to minister tenderly to the woman. He finished cleaning her face with a wet washcloth, rewetted it from the water glass, and dabbed at her forehead and the front of her neck. He lifted her damp hair from her nape and placed the second washcloth there. "Better, Ryan?" he asked.

The woman took a deep, shuddering breath, opened her eyes and looked around her. "Where is this? Jack, I remember..." Sudden panic widened her eyes.

He covered one of her hands with his and slid a glass of whiskey towards her. "Calm down, Ryan... drink this."

Ryan grabbed the glass and gulped down the double shot. She winced and started coughing, but took the beer that was proffered next and managed to drain half the mug before coming up for air. Her eyes were still pinched shut, but the choking had stopped. A slight blush suffused her fair complexion.

Her benefactor had slugged down his drinks at the same time. Jack cleared his throat and resolved that the next time—should there ever be one—he would avoid the cheap bar whiskey and order something a little more expensive. This stuff tasted like kerosene smelled and made his eyes water.

Once Ryan had blinked away her whiskey induced tearing, her eyes appeared clearer. Those questioning, chestnut colored eyes now focused on the grim faced man next to her. "Jack... oh, my God... what's happening to me—" Ryan gagged, jerked forward and vomited on the table.

Jack helped her to the women's restroom where Ryan went through a round of puking, his strong hands holding her shoulders as she knelt on her knees and heaved into the commode.

When they finally made their way back to the barroom proper Howie was standing there, hands on hips, glowering at them. Jack looked at the mess Ryan had made on their table, helped her to a seat at one near the front of the room and walked back to Howie. He took a Visa card out of his wallet and handed it to the barkeep. "To cover the cleanup and..." he turned and peered at Ryan "...to reserve your bar for another half hour. Take out whatever you think is fair and add a big tip for yourself."

Howie's expression melted as he took the card. "Okay, you got it."

Ryan was staring out the window. Her complexion was still sallow, and holding her head up appeared to be an effort.

Jack sat down. "You weren't making much sense on the phone when you called. I know you told me no doctors or hospitals, but I think you should get checked out. I don't know what's wrong with you, but you don't look well."

Silence and a blank stare was her only comment. Jack could hear the faint sound of traffic from the street, and the clink of glasses from the bar area as Howie tended to his duties, acting oblivious to the two of them. There was a slight echo to the sounds, and the dimness of the bar—illuminated by the sunlight filtering in from the front windows and the neon beer wall signs behind the bar—only added surrealism to the moment. Ryan's eyes flicked from the window, to the room and back to his face—like a skittish rabbit on the verge of bolting in fear. Jack could almost see the eddy of fragmented thoughts and questions swirling in her eyes, striving to coalesce into a semblance of order.

"What happened?" Jack whispered. "What's going on?"

Her elbows on the table, Ryan propped her head on her hands. With eyes downcast and her dark hair hanging and brushing the surface of the tabletop, her voice whispered papery thin in the stillness. "He killed me. The madman killed me. Then after I was dead... he did things... horrible things—"

"Stop it, Ryan. Calm down. You're okay. I'm here, everything's okay. We're in Howie's Bar and Grill. You've had some kind of hallucination. What caused this? Did somebody drug you?" He rapid-fired staccato sentences at her out of concern—and immediately regretted it.

Ryan's head snapped up, pure unadulterated terror on her face. "Not now, not now! I don't know how or what... there's so much... I need to sort it, to think... what he did... oh, God... just take me home, Jack. Don't ask anything. I promise I'll explain it when I understand it. Just take me home. I think I'm going to be sick again."

Jack hurried and retrieved his charge card from a smiling Howie. He didn't wait for a receipt; he was sure the bar would make a nice profit during the lunch hour. But more importantly, he had a lot of unanswered questions for Ryan, and it was going to be difficult to wait for the answers. Ryan was one tough cookie—intelligent, beautiful, but hard as nails. He had never seen her like this. Whatever had shaken her this badly had to be some very serious stuff.

He was a little slow. By the time he returned to the table Ryan had thrown-up again.

# CHAPTER 5

It was a tsunami of biblical proportions. It stretched to her left and right, tapering in perspective until land, sky and water met at a single, disappearing point in each direction. The liquid mountain towered upward, a massive concave wall of water, blocking out the horizon and all but the sky directly overhead. Ryan stood frozen before the impossible gray flood, paralyzed by the impending assault. As its shadow slowly consumed her and its crest loomed above her, Ryan could see a myriad of dark shadows swirling and swimming in its bowels.

Now the monstrous wave was crashing down on her, thousands of tons of water crushing her, the churning shadows fragmenting into thousands of memories, shattering into bits and pieces of her life. Ryan struggled as the debris swirled around her, pinned to the ocean floor by the monstrous weight of memories of her and her sister.

Each fragment, each piece that touched her was a small electric shock, bringing the fragmented memory into sharp focus. Places, people, things. Playing hide-and-seek in their backyard when they were five. Tent camping at a KOA campground with her parents. Christmas morning, in the dark, crawling under the Christmas tree with a flashlight. Checking the names on all the gaily wrapped presents and dividing them into their respective piles of "ownership." Later, in high school, trying out for the cheerleading squad. Their parent's funeral. Thousands of memories whirling around her in the grayness, touching and coming into focus briefly before fading away. Dana and David's courtship, their divorce. The tears, laughter, sorrow and joy of her life. Staccato, machine gun bursts of memories overwhelming her.

But new, strange memories and hazy pictures alien to her life were now juxtaposed with the old in the swirling brew engulfing her. A hodgepodge of alien, horrific images and sensations bombarded and shocked her before disappearing back into the churning deep.

Ryan couldn't breathe. She struggled for air as a larger, darker shadow touched her, shocking her into a brilliant light. Something, someone was crushing her. A man was atop her, pinning her down, choking her. Ryan struggled for freedom, for air; failed and gagged. A man's crazed face filled her vision and her mind; his words and spittle raining down on her—a slimy wetness congealing in the water. She continued to fight, thrashing, struggling for breath. But failing... weakening... weakening... fading... dying... dead.

But Ryan didn't die. She stopped breathing and her heart stopped beating. She could no longer see, feel, hear or smell. She could no longer struggle. But she knew—she was aware. It was as if all the pores in her body took the place of her senses, soaking up information somehow and feeding it to her still alive brain. She was inside and outside her body, could "see" from both places simultaneously. There was no physical pain—only psychological, psychic terror. And the knowledge that she was dead; her mind knowing within a few short minutes that, it too, would slowly begin to die, the light inching its way to a final blackness. But this wasn't good enough for the monster atop her.

Foul, disgusting words flooded her mind, from his mouth flowing through her, into her. Now he was biting, ravishing, pushing things up into her body through every opening, her mouth, everywhere, more going in… Ryan couldn't stop screaming in horror, disgust, terror; her screams silent and unnoticed—because she was dead. Eventually, mercifully, her mind began to die, but her screams wouldn't, couldn't stop. The monster continued to desecrate her body all the while talking, talking, talking… images became hazy, darkened. She could sense movement. Fading now… the last sentient awareness as the final few cells expended the last of their vital oxygen, was the sense of dirt falling on her—as she screamed and screamed her way into the final, great abyss—

Ryan bolted upright in her bed, gasping and gagging, another scream catching in her throat. She was drenched in sweat, her tank-top clinging to her, hair plastered wetly to her head. Propping herself up on her elbow she leaned over the side, dry heaves wracking her body. Gulping convulsively, she brought herself under control and flopped back down onto the bed, breathing heavily, eyes squeezed shut in horror and an over-whelming grief. Escaping tears slowly tracked down her cheeks.

Ryan didn't leave her house for the next three days. She called Lonnie, her friend and business partner at Madigan's Gym, giving him the truthful excuse that she wasn't feeling well and wouldn't be in to work or train for the next few days. Jack phoned to check on her, but she continued to put him off, telling him she was okay and would call him when she had things sorted out.

For two more days she lay bundled in the blankets and silence of her darkened bedroom. She left her sanctuary sporadically to go to the bathroom, only to return to the safety of her makeshift cocoon. Her phone rang several more times, but she ignored it, letting her voice mail answer. She shut off her cell phone.

But Jack had been right, Ryan was as tough as they came. She bent but didn't break. By the afternoon of the second day Ryan had survived all the fragmented memories, horrendous images, psychic pain and death that had deluged her unprepared mind, and had even been able to sort and compartmentalize much of it—as best as was humanly possible, anyway. Analyzing the flood would have to be done at a later date, slowly and carefully.

She lay in the tangle of sheets and stared at the smooth stucco of her bedroom ceiling in the gray morning light. She still didn't understand what and why her mind had been overwhelmed with bits and pieces of memories from childhood onward, not to mention the horrific images of the ghastly attack on her. Was she to be the victim of a violent, future attack and this was some kind of psychic premonition? Ryan shuddered as she recalled the graphic details of her abduction, attack and defilement. Her stomach roiled queasily. Dear God, never had she experienced anything like that in her life. She would rather kill herself before allowing all those desecrations to be committed upon her body—

Ryan jumped out of bed and walked quickly to the drawn curtains, throwing them wide and opening the window. Shafts of afternoon sunlight brightened her room as she stared at the billowing curtains, the fragrant scent of honeysuckle faintly wafting through them. It was a pleasant distraction from the stale smell of cigarette smoke.

Ryan returned and sat on the edge of her bed and stared with distaste at her nightstand. She had used a cereal bowl for a makeshift ashtray, but couldn't even remember when she'd bought the cigarettes… maybe when Jack brought her home the other night. And she had been doing so well, too—hadn't had a smoke in almost five years. She took a Marlboro out of the half-empty pack, stared at it, put it back. Her throat was sore and her mouth tasted like a garbage pit. She stood up, but this time it was for more than to go to the bathroom. Ryan was hungry.

Her stomach rumbled, reminding her of its neglect. Barefoot, she padded down the hallway to the kitchen in her bra and panties, put on a pot of coffee, made herself a large omelet, sausage, eggs and toast and poured a glass of juice. She wolfed down her food standing up, put the dishes in the sink, poured a cup of coffee, and headed for the shower. The normally fastidious Ryan grimaced; she realized that she'd been wearing the same underwear for the last three days. She stripped as she headed for the shower, the coffee temporarily forgotten on the counter behind her.

An hour later she was back sitting at the kitchen counter sipping her reheated coffee. Ryan felt much better, all things considered. She'd have another cup of coffee, let her damp hair dry a little more, change out of her bathrobe into her sweats and head for the gym. But first she wanted to call her sister again in California.

Something was nagging at Ryan. It wasn't so much the visions of the attack on her, but all the family memories mixed throughout. When she thought about it, the memories always included both of them, never just Ryan. Now, Ryan was wondering if her twin may have been subjected to the same mental onslaught as she had.

They had never been "psychically" close as identical twins were wont to be, instead having been the product of the very rare phenomenon called polar body twinning. Doctors theorized that polar body twinning occurred when the mother's ovum split prior to fertilization, the resulting pair fertilized by two separate sperm. The result was semi-identical twins, both having the same genes as their mother, but acquiring different genes from their father. Ryan didn't understand it any more than the medical profession did.

Although they looked nearly identical, their personalities differed dramatically, and they had never been any closer than normal sisters would have been. But now, Ryan felt the overwhelming need to talk to her sibling to see if she had experienced anything. Maybe Ryan just had to confirm her own sanity to herself, to know that she had not succumbed to an unexpected nervous breakdown, mental aberration or an insidious brain tumor.

She'd tried calling Dana a half dozen times during last forty-eight hours, but had only succeeded in screaming at her sister's voice mail.

Now, it was time to phone Dana's ex-husband, David, as much as Ryan detested the cheating, lying son of a bitch. Sweet, naïve Dana had still viewed the world through "rose-colored glasses" at the age of twenty-four when she and David had married. She refused to believe the obvious for the four ensuing years until finally, bitterly, she had pulled the plug on the whole sham of a marriage.

Ryan walked over to her kitchen junk drawer and rummaged through it until she found her old address book. She had deleted David's number from her cell phone when Dana left him and filed for a divorce. She picked up her land-line, walked over to the kitchen table and sat down. Crossing her long legs, she leaned back and tried to relax.

It wasn't only because of her dislike for the asshole. Ryan was anxious to get in touch with Dana. All the joint memories interspersed throughout Ryan's nightmare had to have some kind of meaning. At the end of that horrible hallucination the madman had been spewing a steady stream of invectives during his non-stop tirade. It was hard to remember everything, but there was something he had said. Ryan couldn't quite remember; she'd have to keep working on it. She took a deep breath and dialed his number. Seconds passed. She was getting ready to hang up when her ex-brother-in-law answered.

"Hello, David, it's Ryan... yes... I know, it's been a while... yes, the divorce... listen, David... please... David, just shut up for a second and listen to me!" she finally snapped, her voice rising. Her former brother-in-law had a tendency to run off at the mouth, probably an offshoot of working for a long string of insurance companies.

With an effort, she clamped down on her emotions. "I'm sorry for yelling, David, but I've been trying to call Dana, and she's not answering her phone. I've had a few personal problems and I really need to talk to her." That certainly wasn't a lie, she thought. She listened patiently for a minute. "I know we've had our disagreements, David... yes, I know... please, just check for me..." her voice trailed off as she fell silent, letting the idiot interrupt and ramble on.

When he paused for air, she continued. "Please, just go over and check on her. Maybe the neighbors know something. And you could check with the temp agency she's been working for..." She listened for another minute. "... I appreciate it. Have her call me as soon as you get hold of her. Thank you, David, and again, I really appreciate your help in this." She disconnected and grimaced with distaste. David was an asshole, but at least he was going to check on Dana for her.

Ryan's nerves were frayed, and she felt an overpowering urge for a cigarette. Instead, she headed for her bedroom to change— better to work off some of her tension at the gym. Plus, she needed to get back to the real world.

And she had a little explaining to do.

# CHAPTER 6

**Strengthened by the** food and refreshed by a good scrubbing, Ryan grabbed her gym bag and cut through her utility room—mentally noting the full laundry hamper—entered her attached two-car garage and hit the wall switch-pad to turn on the light and open the overhead door. Her gleaming midnight-blue, Ford Shelby Mustang GT500 greeted her silently, her pride and joy—a definite morale booster. It had been a parting gift from Senator Mosby three years prior, the last of her sugar-daddies, a term she still found a tad distasteful. She preferred using the word sponsor, a more appealing synonym for the derogatory label.

She carefully backed out of the garage, stopped in the driveway, and keyed the remote control. While she waited for the garage door to close Ryan spent a few more seconds admiring her one-story brick ranch, tastefully landscaped with shrubs, the large front yard accented by two flowering dogwood trees. It was modest, but attractive, located on a quiet cul-de-sac. It was her first house—a sound investment she had reasoned—financed by her previous employment.

Ryan had always been a pragmatist. She'd tried the minimum wage waitress gig her first year of college and decided the tips weren't going to do the trick. Mona, an acquaintance and seemingly well-to-do junior at school, suggested that with Ryan's face, body, intelligence and personality, she might want to look into "The Service"—a discreet escort agency catering to a well-heeled clientele. Ryan had, and the rest was history, as the saying went. She afforded herself a tiny smile as her mood continued to regain its balance. She relished the throaty purr of the 540 horsepower Shelby designed Mustang as the Ford slipped through the twilight shadows of early evening. Ryan pointed it in the direction of Madigan's. She needed to talk to Lonnie.

She parked in front of the nondescript building on Figueroa, its only distinguishing feature the big, red lettered sign in the large window, Madigan's Mixed Martial Arts, and the black silhouette of a figure in a crouched, fighting pose next to it. The gym was usually open until 10:00 p.m., so the door was still unlocked. Of course, Ryan had her own set of keys.

An old building and an old gym, it was defined by the lingering odors of liniment, wrapping tape and sweat accumulated over the years, now forever permeated into the very fabric of the structure. Ryan breathed in deeply of the familiar and not unpleasant mixture. For the uninformed, it came as a surprise that the gym was the premier training venue for mixed martial arts fighters in the state of Michigan. There was a waiting list for up and coming fighters who wanted to sign on, both men and women.

Lonnie and Ryan had bought out the old owner, Jimmy Madigan. Lonnie had worked for Jimmie while still in college and, being the astute businessman he was, had continued on after graduation. Coincidentally, Jack had taken Ryan to Madigan's for self-defense lessons when she persisted in her dangerous, but lucrative, profession. Already acquainted with Ryan through the university, it wasn't long before Lonnie approached her with a business proposition in exchange for help in the financing—and their partnership was born.

Relying on the gym's reputation and stable of good fighters, Lonnie had kept the best trainers and promoted the best fighters, using his business acumen to further his and Ryan's investment. Within two years their fighters had laid claim to three of the weight classes in the UFC and were competitive in several others. Ryan was more of a silent partner and had invested for financial gain, but she enjoyed the physical challenge of mixed martial arts, and was actually proficient at it. She even did a little bookkeeping to help out in the office.

It was after eight o'clock, but there were still a half dozen fighters training. Two women were in the ring sparring, both in headgear and eight ounce, open-fingered gloves. Ryan recognized one, Maria, a young up and coming Latina. As she watched, Maria suddenly charged her taller opponent, picked her up and slammed her to the canvas. The two rolled and grappled on the mat. Elizabeth "Lizzie" Matrone, a middle-aged, thickset trainer, was leaning on the edge of the ring and yelling through the ropes. "Nice take-down, Maria... side mount, side mount... now get top control... that's it, that's it... go for an arm-bar."

The trainer redirected her attention to Ryan as she approached. "Hey, Ryan, I haven't seen you in here for a few days. You wanna go a few rounds with Maria?"

Ryan shook her head. "Ha-ha, Lizzy, thanks but no thanks," she said. "I'm just going to hit the weights and the heavy bag for a while. Is Lonnie still around?"

"Yeah, I think he's in the office doing paperwork." Lizzie switched her attention back to the women in the ring.

Ryan went to the vacant women's locker room and changed into her athletic bra, tank-top and nylon shorts, tying her hair in a loose ponytail with a rubber band. She grabbed her gym bag and headed for the weight room. For the next forty-five minutes did non-stop circuit training with the free-weights and machines. Ryan was breathing heavily and covered in a patina of perspiration when she laced on the gloves and moved on to the heavy bag outside near the ring.

The hanging, five-foot long training bag was soon absorbing punch after punch, kick after kick. Ryan jolted the bag with left hands, right hands, backhands, jabs and hooks. Her long legs fired out front kicks, side-kicks and spinning back kicks. Harder and faster the punches and leg-strikes came. Soon she was grunting with every powerful blow to the bag. Instead of slowing, the thudding hits increased. Seconds turned into minutes and still she pummeled the bag mercilessly, never wavering in her assault.

Two of the male fighters heading for the locker room stopped to watch the grunting and snorting fighter. Ryan was tall and sleek, her body toned and sculpted; there wasn't a useless ounce of weight on her anywhere. But today their fascination was directed at the tireless ferocity with which she was lashing out at the bag.

The women in the ring had finished and were now standing, leaning on the ropes, and watching Ryan. Lizzy had walked around from the far side of the ring and was standing with her arms crossed, staring.

Her tank-top sodden with sweat, flying arms and legs glowed with her body's moisture. Unnoticed, her ponytail had come loose. Her dark hair glistened wetly in the light, droplets of sweat flying from her head as she spun and turned violently. A jumping, spinning back kick thudded heavily into the bag, then another, her head snapping around and throwing off another light shower of perspiration that even reached the two mesmerized men.

They both stepped back reflexively. The shorter fighter turned to his friend. "Son-of-a-bitch, remind me never to get in the ring with her—she's nuts." They both continued to stare, mouths slightly gaping.

Like some kind of groaning automation run amok, she continued to fire punch after punch, kick after kick. Finally, Ryan looped one last roundhouse right accompanied by a bellow of rage and dropped to her knees in exhaustion, weakly holding onto the bag to keep from collapsing.

Concerned, the two men started towards the kneeling, gasping woman, but were stopped by Lonnie who had also been standing nearby and watching for the past several minutes. "Hang on guys. It's okay, I'll check on her. You two hit the showers. I need to close up soon."

The two smiled tentatively, glanced again at the panting woman, gave Lonnie a nod and started to leave. Shorty spoke again, "You got it boss, see you tomorrow. Hope she's okay."

Lonnie walked over, reached down and helped Ryan to her feet. "What the hell was that all about?" he asked.

Ryan was bent over, hands on knees trying to catch her breath. She finally stood, her chest still heaving. "Just releasing a little pent up aggression, I guess."

"Shit, Ryan, I hope you never get pissed off at me," he said.

"I need to talk to you, Lonnie. Let me take a quick shower, and I'll see you in the office."

Lonnie watched in admiration as Ryan walked away, amazed as always—in a somewhat academic way—at the rare combination of beauty, power and speed. He wondered what she needed to talk about, but based on her frenzied attack on the heavy bag, it couldn't be good. He was suddenly nervous. Lonnie headed back to the office to wait.

Ryan finished rinsing off in what was her second shower of the day. Supporting herself with her hands against the tiled wall, she continued to let the steaming jets of water cascade over her for several more minutes. Her arms were still rubbery and her legs ached, her right foot even more so from a misplaced side-kick. Slowly, her muscles relaxed, and the coiled knot in her stomach began to unwind.

She only had two close friends, Jack and Lonnie. They were the only two she could conceivably confide in, the only two who knew her and her history. She would soon find out if they were close enough to believe her. If the whole episode hadn't been so vivid and soul-wrenching, she wouldn't have believed it herself.

Lonnie looked up from his desk and the seemingly never-ending paperwork as Ryan walked in, limping slightly. She was toweling her damp hair, but was still eye-catching in blue jeans, t-shirt and tennis shoes. He shook his head; the big, white-lettered inscription on her red t-shirt read: Women Who Behave Rarely Make History. "Ryan, Ryan," he sighed. "Why can't you wear a 'Madigan's t-shirt? The gym can always use the promotion. And besides, as part-owner you have a vested interest."

Ryan plopped down on the top of her desk, across from his—a desk much neater and much less used. "Sorry, Lonnie, I was in a hurry and just grabbed this."

He looked at her dangling feet. "Hurt your foot?"

"Just a little, hurried one of my kicks, I guess."

"What was the reason for that little manic exhibition out there? You could have hurt yourself." He glanced again at her foot and reconsidered. "More than you already have, anyway."

Ryan was staring down at the floor. Several seconds passed before she looked at him again. "Lonnie, I think something might be wrong with me."

His smile disappeared. "More than your foot? What did you hurt?" Her friend started to rise.

Ryan put up her hand and stopped him. "No, no, it's not like that—"

"Are you sick?" Lonnie was still standing, concerned.

"No, three days ago I had a vision or premonition, a night-mare of things happening to me... my death, I think... a very horrible one...."

Lonnie sat with a blank look on his face. "What...?" he asked stupidly. Then he grinned; this was obviously a joke. Ryan was one of the most rational people that Lonnie had ever known. It was unlike her, but he decided to play along. "A premonition, Ryan? A vision? A nightmare? No, wait, it happened during the day, so it would have to be a daymare." He grinned. "You'll have to be a little more specific, not so obtuse and ambiguous—"

Ryan inhaled sharply. "What? What did you say?" Ryan interrupted.

"I said a premonition, a day—"

"No, at the very end."

Lonnie looked at her vacantly for a long second. "You mean about your being so obtuse and ambiguous—"

"Ambiguous... that's what he said... ambiguous." Ryan looked bemused. Her mind raced backward, sorting through the myriad images, words and fragments. Her mind reflexively tried to shy away from the terrible visions and sounds, but she forced herself to look and hear again.

Finally, she found the thread. It was after the murderer had strangled her and carried her to the couch. He was sneering at her, talking to her and she was somehow hearing through her dead body. The madman said she was ambiguous... no, that wasn't right. She searched and latched onto the moment, his mocking voice seemed to echo in her mind. "Dana, Dana, Dana... did your parents want a boy and get you instead? Is that why you're stuck with such an ambiguous name? No matter..."

Ryan didn't realize she had risen to her feet during her bizarre, trancelike recollection. As the shocking truth hit her, she staggered back into an end table, knocking over a framed picture and trophy. She managed to remain on her feet, both hands covering her mouth, her eyes wide in shock.

Lonnie was around his desk and next to her immediately, all traces of levity gone. "Ryan, what is it? What's wrong?"

Again, she held up her hand. "I'm okay, Lonnie. Just give me a second." Ryan clenched her teeth, her jaw muscles working. Finally, she took several deep breaths, her eyes refocusing. She carefully set the picture and trophy back up and returned to her seat on the corner of her desk. She stared at Lonnie.

"Dana is dead," she breathed.

"Dana? Your sister? Your twin sister?" Lonnie asked stupidly, trying to follow the abrupt change.

Ryan looked at him patiently. Her boyishly good-looking business partner and good friend was not processing very well, even worse than she was. "Yes, Lonnie, Dana—my only sister— you know... the one living in California?"

He was bewildered by the turn in the conversation, but this track he could fortunately follow. "Oh, my God, Ryan, I'm so sorry..." He took a tentative step towards her, stopped "... when did this happen?"

"Sit down, Lonnie, I'm okay and you need to stay seated." She said it loudly and as firmly as she could, false bravado attempting to hide the tremor in her voice. It was apparently successful. He looked confused, but returned to his seat, his nylon sweat suit whispering as he sat. She continued. "And as for when, it was three days ago."

Lonnie was processing better now; three days ago was when Ryan had called in sick. He knew Ryan and Dana hadn't been that close, especially for twins. For this to put the normally stoic Ryan Sanders out of service for three days had to be somehow extraordinary. "How did it happen, Ryan?"

"She was murdered—strangled."

"Oh, my God... I'm so, so sorry..." he shook his head in disbelief. "... did they catch the killer?"

"No."

Lonnie couldn't read her expression, nor catch any inflection in her monotone. "Where did it happen, where's she at... I mean where's the funeral going to be? Do you need to take off for a while?" He figured that once the police investigation was complete Ryan would be headed to California if not before.

"He buried her. I'm not sure where. There were trees, but not like around here; I'm not familiar with them. The house was different, too—stucco siding, I think, and with a flat roof. Not much grass, large open areas. Maybe somewhere in the Southwest," she intoned. Although she was looking directly at Lonnie, it seemed she was eerily looking through him, somewhere else.

He was confused. Or maybe it was Ryan who was confused. Either way, he wasn't following the conversation well. "Ah... Ryan... what do the police say? Do they have any leads?"

"The police don't know about it." Now, her attention was back, and she was looking at him—hard at him.

Lonnie was flustered. He absently began rolling a ballpoint pen back and forth on his desk with one hand, the other picked up and started kneading a green squeegee ball designed to relieve stress. He wasn't sure where this conversation was going, or if he even wanted to go there. But this was his friend.

"You're saying Dana was murdered—strangled—three days ago. You don't know by whom. She was buried, maybe somewhere out west. And it hasn't been reported to the police? Dana lives in California, 2500 miles from here. How did you find out about this; who told you?"

Ryan's expression had turned bleak, almost pleading. "I told you I had terrible visions, premonitions..." her voice trailed off.

"But... but, you said... ah... that those were nightmares, I mean daymares... sorry, but I thought they were about you," Lonnie stammered.

"I was wrong," Ryan whispered.

Lonnie's face was a blank. He was no longer connecting the dots.

"Dana told me," she said, her voice barely audible.

The pen stopped rolling, the hand stopped its unconscious squeezing and his eyebrows lifted. "Dana? I'm not sure I understand what you're saying. How... if she was... but, I mean... how..."

"It was after."

"After?"

"After he killed her. After she was dead. While he was doing things to her... after she was dead... after she was dead..." Ryan's eyes were squeezed shut in anguish, tears coursing down her pale cheeks. "My visions weren't my nightmares. They were hers," she sobbed.

This time when Lonnie dashed around the desk and grabbed the crying woman, she didn't stop him.

# CHAPTER 7

Howie delivered Jack's cheeseburger and fries with a smile. The unexpected visit by the junkie hooker and the big cop four days ago had resulted in a nice lunch hour profit for Howie. And thanks to a large gratuity that would soon appear on Jack's charge card, any inconvenience caused by the ill woman was largely forgotten. "So, Sergeant, how's that woman doing, the one you took out of here? She a hooker, bad drugs or something... you arrest her or what?" Howie asked.

Jack leaned back in his chair. His dark eyes flicked coldly up at the man from the sunken craters in his roughly chiseled face. The fault line of his mouth cracked and threatened a smile before settling back into its pre-quake lines. "She wasn't on drugs and she's not a hooker." At least not any more, he amended mentally. "She was just a little emotionally upset over some personal things."

The barkeep looked properly dismayed. "Oh, I'm sorry, I hope she's okay—"

Jack interrupted. "It's okay, Howie, just keep the grill warm; she'll be here in a few minutes." He looked away, picked up his cheeseburger and took a bite, mentally dismissing Howie. The owner took the hint and left to tend to his other customers: two late lunch couples sitting at tables, and three early happy-hour drinkers at the bar. It appeared the bar owner handled the place by himself—a sign of the economic times, Jack supposed.

He looked out the window at the gray, overcast day and the downtown vehicle traffic passing by on the street. He took a gulp of his coffee. Jack was currently assigned to Vice out of the 10th, working the graveyard shift. He could never get accustomed to sleeping during the day and relied on large doses of caffeine to combat his slumber shortage. He had taken the table where he and Ryan sat four days ago. Jack had called several times over the last two days and left messages, but respected her privacy. She'd finally called last night, apologized and suggested today's meeting.

Jack, the rough and tumble no nonsense Sergeant in the 10th Precinct, had known Ryan Sanders for nearly six years, ever since he had busted—well, almost busted—the young college student for prostitution back in '07. A task force, including Jack and other members of Detroit's 8th Precinct Vice Squad, had taken down a high-end, wide ranging "escort service." It primarily operated in the Renaissance Center, Hart Plaza, Cadillac Square, and the more affluent areas of Detroit—as well as the city of Ann Arbor and the state capital in Lansing. More importantly, their clientele had included influential members of the business community and, even more newsworthy, high ranking state politicians and several Washington politicos.

Ryan, with her intelligence, charm and stunning good looks, had been one of the most popular escorts for—what was simply and accurately named—"The Service." Among other things, she had cultivated a feigned innocence and naivety that, when utilized, appealed to a number of the more jaded of her well-heeled and well-connected "escortees."

Ryan learned the things that worked, and she learned them well. For the two years she had been employed by The Service, she was one of the highest paid and most sought after escorts. Fortunately for her, Ryan decided to go independent and carve out a much more profitable niche in a growing trend among a few college students—the use and reliance on "sugar daddies," or as Ryan preferred to call them—"sponsors."

Jack's cell phone rang, breaking into his reverie. Its caller-ID said it was Ryan. He answered brusquely, "You're late, Ryan."

"Well, hello to you too, Jack," came the feminine voice from the other end. "There was a bad accident on I-75. I had to detour around; I'm running about ten minutes late. Cut me some slack, okay?"

"I guess I'll survive. I'll have Howie rustle up a burger and fries for you," he said.

"Better make that a tossed salad. I have to start eating a little healthier."

"Right. See you in ten." The call ended, Jack yelled out to Howie, "You can start that burger and fries now." A salad? Not going to happen, he thought. She should know better than to let him order. His thick fingers swirled several of the cooling fries in ketchup before they disappeared into his maw, followed by a huge bite of his burger. A swig of his Coke and he went back to his musings.

With a throaty rumble, the dark-blue Shelby pulled off the freeway onto the service drive. Ryan hit the gas, turned onto Twelve Mile Road and headed for Cooper Street. She'd bypass the accident and get back on the freeway there.

Ryan found an oldies station—she didn't really like any of the rap crap and new age stuff—and tried to relax. She wondered how Jack would take her explanation for the meltdown the other night at Howie's. She had known the big cop since her junior year at the University of Detroit—the year that The Service went down in that scandalous investigation.

Ryan continued reminiscing. Even though she had been out of the active loop for several months, she had been brought in for questioning because of rumors of her past association with the escort service, and the possibility she might furnish information about their current dealings, employees and clientele.

Sergeant Jack Kroner had been assigned to the task force during this period and was involved in the investigation of The Service and their eventual prosecution. Jack knew Ryan had been connected, but as far as any criminal prosecution was concerned, he had nothing but inadmissible, circumstantial evidence. She'd been interrogated by Jack several times, but Ryan coolly and calmly bobbed and weaved her way through the interviews, admitting nothing, nor incriminating herself or others.

Despite her interrogational tap dancing during their interviews at the police station, the Sergeant had remained professional and had always treated her with respect, despite her "alleged" profession. By the time all the scandal and hoopla died down she had formed a grudging admiration for the rough looking Sergeant. And as impossible as it seemed, she got the impression that—behind his gruff, no nonsense attitude—a grudging respect was reciprocated by the cop.

Ryan's attention snapped back to the present as the red Mazda in the lane next to her started to drift closer. It was one of those small, four cylinder jobs that the owner had modified by mounting a spoiler on the back and installing those enlarged tailpipes, making the car sound like a rumbling eight cylinder—a poor man's muscle car. Sure enough, the driver was some young kid, a cell phone plastered to his ear, gesturing wildly with his free hand as he talked.

The Mazda continued to pull closer to her. Ryan finally laid on her horn. The teenager jerked the car back into his lane. "Idiot. That's all I need," she hissed. "You put a dent in my car—"

Calm down, Ryan told herself. Why was she so nervous? Jack would believe her; he would help her. And even if he didn't, it wouldn't stop her. She pulled back onto the freeway. Another five minutes and she'd be there and find out. Ryan let her mind drift back to the days of yore—a chapter that had been closed for several years. Ironically, a chapter still connected to the present by the man she was on her way to see.

Needless to say, when the raid went down there was a tremendous amount of resistance, interference and pressure from high up the food chain to derail the investigation and prosecution of the escort service. There were careers, reputations and marriages to be protected and saved, not to mention the potential jail time to be averted.

The "Madame" of The Service, Cindi Muldoon, plea bargained her criminal charges all the way down to "lewd and lascivious conduct"—plus the more serious charge of income tax evasion—in exchange for testifying against several members of her stable. Others were offered immunity from prosecution for rolling over on their co-workers.

It took months before the scandalous feeding frenzy abated. Shocking testimony, lurid details and "he said she said" accusations kept the public entranced. A number of lesser political and business scapegoats were eventually thrown under the bus to appease the citizens and the press.

Ryan had managed to fly under the radar during the whole sordid mess. Even after all this time, Jack still couldn't believe she had emerged unscathed. Neither could Ryan. None of the other women turned on her and, even more astonishingly, neither had any of her former clients. Jack firmly believed that powerful men shielded her, or more likely, she had the goods on the big rollers and they couldn't afford to have her go public.

True enough, she mused. But Ryan had also posited to her friend that maybe there really was something to that "honor among thieves" theory. Maybe honesty and loyalty counted for something—even in the immoral world that Ryan had surfed in. Ryan preferred to believe that altruistic viewpoint anyway as opposed to anyone's fear of the detailed journal she had kept of her activities. She shook her head and smiled at the big palooka's continuing confusion and disbelief.

Ryan parked her car on Stanford, just around the corner from Howie's. She grabbed her purse and headed for the bar and grill, still sporting a smile. In the reality of Jack's world, she was an oxymoron, an anomaly. He had trouble getting his head around the fact that people like her were even possible. After The Service, Ryan had gone into the much more lucrative area of sugar daddies—older, financially secure men who showered her with gifts and took care of her monetarily. This in exchange for her being theirs exclusively, at least whenever they needed her— or in the case of the married ones—whenever they could get out. Of course, this all had to be worked around her University studies, both undergraduate and graduate. But obviously she had been more than worth it.

As Ryan opened the door to Howie's, her smile faded. She paused momentarily in the building's small vestibule and took several deep breaths, composing herself and rearranging her smile.

After The Service fiasco, Jack looked the other way regarding her transgressions and had come to her aid on several occasions, at least when she was working the Detroit area. He became her unofficial protector and, somewhere along the way, her friend. Ryan knew that Jack had never married and had no children. He said he'd seen too many police officers fail in their marriages, the stress and the temptations that occurred on the job often proving fatal to permanent commitments.

Why he'd chosen to take her, a young college student with the unusual, part-time employment under his wing and, in effect jeopardize his career, was just as big a conundrum for her as she was an enigma to him. Although she was too old to fit the picture, maybe Jack viewed her as the daughter that he'd never had.

On several occasions over the course of her remaining college "working" years, she'd been roughed up by a few of her former clients. They were unable to take no for an answer, including her last sugar daddy, and had objected when she made the decision to quit the profession upon the completion of her graduate studies. Jack, unofficially of course, had addressed the problems with firm, man-to-man talks. Only one of the men needed to be hospitalized.

# CHAPTER 8

Jack gazed out the window at a young couple walking by hand-in-hand. Three smartly dressed women—he guessed secretaries on their lunch breaks—laughed and gestured animatedly to each other as they ambled in and out of his vision. Cars crept by in the bright sunshine, unknown people heading to unknown destinations. Jack often wondered—

His attention was snagged by a strikingly attractive woman walking past the window. It took a second for his idling mind to register that it was Ryan. She disappeared from view for a moment before entering Howie's Bar and Grill several seconds later, whooshing in the front door of the building accompanied by a rush of warm summer air and sunshine.

If Ryan's rollercoaster life had presented a riddle for Jack before, he was in for a revelation—a rude awakening. He would discover the bogeyman under the bed was real. Worse, Ryan was going to offer Jack a hand grenade; one she had already pulled the pin on.

Jack watched Ryan stop just inside the door, scanning the room for him. She looked a hundred percent better than she had on their first visit to Howie's. Ryan's shoulder length black hair gleamed in the light. Long, thick eyelashes enhanced her ebony eyes, subdued red lipstick glistened wetly and pale blue eye shadow reflected the color of her blouse. Her form fitting navy blue slacks belled slightly at the bottom before stopping at the surface of the floor. Jack had always wondered how women could get the length of their slacks so exact; his pants were always a little too short or a little too long.

Ryan spied Jack at the window table and hurried over, her high heels clicking on the hardwood floor, a sound that was always somehow sexy and suggestive to Jack. A faint and fragrant cloud of perfume emanated from her as she slid into her chair. She set her small black purse on the windowsill and smiled warmly at him. "Well, big guy, where's my lunch, I'm starving and—"

Howie interrupted her question by presenting her with a heaping plate, displaying a half-pound cheeseburger and a mountain of fries. He set the overflowing platter down in front of her with a flourish and added a Diet-Coke from his other hand. "Ta-Dah," he chimed in. Grinning hugely, he turned and headed over to the other tables.

Ryan stared at the food in front of her. "Jack, this doesn't look much like a salad."

"Hey, you need your strength, and besides, you're getting too skinny." Jack knew the last part was a lie, he figured that God had sculpted Ryan from His master blueprint for perfect people.

"And anyway, the Diet-Coke will help cancel out the burger and fries," he chided.

Ryan threw him a look, but dove into her burger. Jack watched as she silently waded through half her plate before she came up for air. He waited patiently. Finally, she sipped her Coke, sighed and leaned back in her chair. "Granted, that was much better than a salad. I think I'll get a doggie-bag and take the rest home with me."

Jack cut through the small talk. "What happened, Ryan? What's going on?"

She leaned forward, the smile gone from her lips, her dark eyes searching his rugged face. "What all did I tell you the other night? I was a little out of it."

"Yes, to put it mildly. You were talking crazy. You kept saying that some madman killed you and was doing horrible things to you after you were dead. Nothing made sense. If I didn't know you better, I'd have said you were on drugs and hallucinating. You have a few blanks to fill in, Ryan."

Although her eyes were locked onto his, she hesitated, biting her lower lip.

Jack leaned forward, arms resting on the table. "Spit it out Ryan. I've known you since... well... since your college days. There's not much about you that I don't know." That wasn't quite true either, but decided to let that sleeping dog lie. "I want to know what's going on."

Ryan broke eye contact and looked down at her plate. "Okay, pal, if anyone deserves to know what happened and what I'm going to do, it would be you." Ryan looked up and took a deep breath. She pursed her lips and exhaled, slowly, as if blowing bubbles. Another breath and she began. "As you know, my sister, Dana, and I were never really close, as far as what you might expect from identical twins—half-identical, anyway." She paused and took a sip of her soda. "Four days ago she was murdered. Those hallucinations I was having weren't mine. They were Dana's... and they weren't hallucinations—she was calling, screaming out to me."

Fifteen minutes later Ryan was still talking and Jack was still listening. He didn't laugh and hadn't interrupted with questions or comments. She figured her story was shocking him into silence—the tale the second half of a one-two punch—the first being her emotional breakdown of the other day. Jack always said that Ryan was an anomaly in his reality. If so, that anomaly was taking another sharp turn and heading far out into left field. She wondered if Jack would follow.

"It was like a dam had collapsed, a floodgate opened. In those few minutes after she died a thousand images spewed out. Not just his knocking her unconscious in the parking lot, but bringing her back to his house, killing her and doing those things...." Ryan stopped and tentatively touched her throat as if to make sure no throttling hand was clutching her there. Her face had paled, but she continued... "but images from the past, even our childhood, everything all mixed up. But this perverted killer... it wasn't just like pictures or images, I was there with them—I was Dana. I could see, hear, feel, smell and taste everything Dana was experiencing. My God, Jack, her brain—her mind—was still alive. I could feel her terror, her horror, her screaming inside...

see, hear, feel and smell the beast…" Ryan had paled even more and now convulsively gulped several times.

Jack reached a big hand across the table, engulfing her slender fingers in his. He eyed her for several seconds before speaking. "Easy, Ryan, I don't think ol' Howie would be too happy if you puked on his table again. He might think you didn't like his food."

Ryan took a sip of her Coke and smiled weakly, returning the squeeze from the big paw holding hers. Another sip and she continued. "It's impossible to explain what it was like. Everything she was reaching out in horror with… it was like feeling the sounds, smells, touches, tastes… I can't describe exactly how it was visualized in my mind."

Perplexed, she shook her head. "It was like looking at a lake bottom through the calm surface of clear water. Then, as the minutes passed and her brain began to die the water's surface began to ripple, like something was stirring the waters. Slowly, the water roiled and everything started to blur and become indistinct; the feelings, the sensations, the images became fainter and more disjointed. Slowly, her mind darkened—cell by asphyxiated cell—until she was mercifully spared any more horror. The last fleeting sensation was of dirt falling on her. That, and the fading, echoing sounds of her screaming."

Jack released her hand and leaned back, exhaling loudly. Despite the wild tale from the normally stoic and even-keeled Ryan, Jack wasn't smiling, and his ruddy complexion had paled a shade. "My God, Ryan, but you said there was never any psychic bond between you and Dana. Why now?"

"I don't know, Jack. Maybe it took something like this to make the connection, to break down the barrier between us. As I've said before, Dana and I were never close, not like identical twins are always portrayed. Apart from the physical, we were about as opposite as two siblings could be. She was born two minutes before me. Dana was always the delicate, feminine one—quiet and reserved. She liked frilly dresses, dolls and tea parties. I was the polar opposite. Independent, out-spoken, a regular tom-boy; I went for pants, toy cars and Lego building block sets. My knees were always skinned up."

Ryan smiled at the childhood memories; a pleasant change from the haunted look of her former account. "My mother had a favorite baby story that compared our different personalities. After Dana and I first began to crawl, she would put Dana in the middle of the bed, followed by me. Dana would crawl to the edge, turn around and carefully inch backward until she could dangle her feet over the brink, then lower herself down. As for me, I would barrel forward at full speed and my mother would have to stop me before I plunged over head first."

"Dana was married, but getting a divorce, wasn't she?" Jack asked.

"Yeah, the divorce was final just a couple of months ago," she replied. "Dana was innocent and naïve. Hard to imagine, but when they married she was twenty-four and still had faith in the inherent goodness of people. Dana believed in true love, love at first sight, and all that malarkey. It didn't take long for that cheating bastard she married, David, to disillusion her and crack those rose-colored glasses of hers. Thank God, they didn't have any children."

"When was the last time you saw her?" he asked.

"In California, at our parent's funeral, two years ago. It was a closed casket affair; the car accident was pretty bad. We exchanged Christmas, birthday cards and short letters afterward, but that was about all. Last I heard she had a temp job at an insurance agency and had taken up jogging. Good at it I guess; she said she qualified for the Boston Marathon." Ryan's eyes were blurring and welling up with tears. "She suggested that she might stop and visit later this year on her way to Boston."

Jack's voice was rough with emotion, but gentle. "So, where do you go from here, Ryan?"

His beautiful young friend blinked back her tears. "She passed a lot of information on to me; I guess some of it could be used as clues. If you were to help, I might be able to track this sicko down." Her eyes searched his chiseled but strangely handsome face.

The seconds ticked by in silence as Jack toyed with a cold French fry. He gazed at the dark-eyed enigma before him. "I'm not sure what I can do. What do you want?"

Sergeant Jack Kroner had no idea the endgame anticipated by Ryan Sanders was radically different from the one he envisioned.

# CHAPTER 9

Norman wiped the steam off the bathroom mirror and stood gazing at himself. He'd never known his father, but he must have been a big man whoever he was to have passed on this extra-large stature to Norman. Nicole had been only 5'6" and was a strikingly good looking woman, at least when Norman was younger—another fine set of genes passed on to him. If Norman had been allowed to go to public schools, he was sure he would have been a star football or basketball player. Probably popular with the girls too, with his thick black hair and dark good looks. Norman flexed his muscled arms, did a couple of poses, and admired his toned body, still pumped from the strenuous workout just ended. He had a full array of free weights and weight equipment set up in his rec room, which he used on a regular basis.

Norman shaved, slapped on aftershave and donned a thick terrycloth robe. He ran a comb through his damp hair and padded out to the kitchen, grabbed a beer from the fridge, slipped on a pair of flip-flops waiting by the French doors, and stepped out onto his tiled, rear lanai. He sighed contentedly as he sat down on a patio chair and put his feet up on the chair opposite. Norman took a swig of beer and set the bottle on the table. He gazed westward at the last remnants of a gorgeous sunset—the final swirls of orange sinking below the horizon. He pulled a cigar and lighter from the pocket of his robe and fired up, inhaling the thick aromatic smoke.

Norman contemplated his next little out-of-state foray. He figured in a few weeks he'd head up to Montana, maybe Butte or Bozeman. It was time for another state to get saddled with an unsolved homicide. But he had to be careful. His escapades, as enjoyable and necessary as they were, had been getting a little too close together. He needed to keep them apart, not only in time, but in location. And those fugues; they seemed to be getting longer. Norman needed to keep the upper hand on Nicole. He exhaled a cloud of cigar smoke. "No, Nicole, I've got you down and I'm going to keep you down—I'm not through with you yet."

He gazed out in the dwindling twilight towards the small shed a hundred feet away. His eyes wandered to two old juniper trees fifty feet to the left. Between the two trees were the two graves of the only two women he had taken on his property. The first one, and then that Dana chick a few weeks back. He preferred not to kill them here—too close, too dangerous, but sometimes he couldn't help himself; the urges had been so over-powering. He had to be more careful, had to be stronger....

Dana Ryan Sanders, the name stuck in his head. She had been a good one, probably the best. He shivered in the cool, early evening air. When the sun set in the high desert, the temperature dropped. There was usually no cloud cover to hold in the heat, and it rapidly dissipated. Norman decided to head inside. There was something he needed to do.

Norman retrieved the heart-shaped locket and chain from the pocket of the coat he'd thrown on a chair and headed for the basement, turning on the lights as he went. Basements were somewhat of a rarity in New Mexico. Not only was it a non-traditional building style, the hard clay layer just below the surface of sand and soil usually made it labor intensive and cost prohibitive. Norman had to use a pickax when he dug the graves; the clay was as hard as cement. But thanks to Nicole's penchant for buying State lottery tickets—plus her good fortune in picking a winner—the cost of his sparsely furnished, but very functional basement didn't pose a problem.

In one corner of the room was an old trunk, the kind with leather straps and a key operated hasp. The key was long gone. He'd discovered the trunk in his mother's garage after her untimely, but provident, "accident." He grabbed a wooden chair from an equally old and scarred kitchen table nearby, sat down, opened the trunk and gazed at his small, but growing, collection of souvenirs. Norman opened the delicate silver locket and looked at the enclosed picture of Dana once more. He still found it odd for someone to carry around a picture of themselves, especially in such a personal thing as a locket. He shook his head; there was just no accounting for people's idiosyncrasies.

Norman closed the locket and placed it inside and began gently fondling his collection of memories, reminiscing. The varied assortment included several pairs of colored, frilly panties, not including the thong, two bras, several necklaces, two pairs of earrings, nylons and a garter belt, a pair of red, high heel shoes, and a small black purse. He kept his souvenirs small and light for logistical reasons as well as personal; the two biggest—the shoes and purse—were from the two women he had taken here in the basement.

Norman picked up the purse and leaned back in the chair. He hadn't bothered to go through it yet; it had belonged to Dana— tall, strong and full of fight. Now was a good a time as any. He'd put the locket inside with the rest of her stuff. He unsnapped and opened the purse, held it near his face and inhaled deeply of the faint scents still emanating from it: traces of old perfume, cosmetics and soft leather. Norman stood, took his chair and moved over to the wooden table and sat, dumping the contents on the aged surface.

Almost tenderly, he sorted through the woman's belongings: cosmetics, keys, papers, receipts, small address book, pens, gum, trinkets and assorted other personal memorabilia of a life now gone.

There was a nice faux-leather wallet he opened and began inventorying: credit cards, gas card, driver's license, a small change compartment with... let's see... thirty-six cents... and forty-seven dollars in cash. Not a big spender. There was a section with several plastic photo sleeves containing pictures. Norman idly flipped through them. They appeared to be family pictures, the people dressed up for the most part, a couple taken at a beach somewhere, children playing—

Norman stopped, and straightened in his chair, staring. He pulled the driver's license out of its compartment again and peered at the photograph and name: Dana Ryan Sanders. He looked back at several of the pictures, two children playing, two young women posing together. His eyes widened and his jaw slackened as awareness came to him. "Shit, there's two of them. That dirty little whore has a twin sister." That explained the locket.

He gently ran his fingertips over the images of the two smiling women. Norman glanced at the address book. The feral look of madness brightened his eyes. "I wonder if sis's address is in there...."

# Chapter 10

Ryan finished creating her lunch—a turkey, low-fat cheese and fat-free mayo combo sandwich—poured a glass of skim milk and plopped down at the kitchen table. It was a beautiful, sunny day, and the view of her backyard out the bay window was pleasant and serene. Her eyes surveyed her humble abode as she munched away on her modest lunch.

She was so glad she had made the leap and purchased the small single-story house. It was only 1925 sq. feet, but was more than adequate for her. The kitchen was a little on the small side, but had a breakfast nook by the bay window. The home had three bedrooms, one of which she used as a combination study/exercise room.

Maybe she'd just have a quick workout at home instead of heading into Madigan's for one of her full-scale rituals. A Bowflex machine, treadmill, and a heavy bag hanging from the ceiling comprised her exercise area. A small desk with her computer and an adjoining bookcase defined her makeshift study area. Proudly displayed on the wall over her desk were her framed college diplomas. Several pictures of Ryan in various fighting poses adorned the other walls, including one of her and Lonnie standing out in front of Madigan's MMA Gym.

A little exercise and she'd have a long hot soak in the bathtub. The large bathroom off of the master bedroom was an even bigger perk than the kitchen. She loved it. The roominess of the area and the Jacuzzi garden tub made all the rituals a woman had to go through to be presentable almost worth it. Almost.

The living room was cozy and tastefully decorated. The second bedroom and bathroom were seldom used, except when Jack occasionally slept over. He lived in an apartment on the other side of Detroit in Devonshire Heights. When he was working the graveyard shift and, depending on his assignments—which sometimes necessitated his working with the precincts in her area—he crashed at her place for convenience. Ryan kept a spare key in one of those fake rocks camouflaged among the others to the left of her front entryway.

She took a sip of her milk and gazed out the window. The large back yard was enclosed by a chain-link fence, the yard dominated by two good sized oak trees which provided much needed shade in the summer. The grass was green and well kept. She paid Jerry, a teenager from down the street, a nice stipend to take care of it, which included keeping her rose bushes pruned. The boy did a good job; the yard was beautiful. She wondered if the birdbath and feeders needed filling—

Ryan's reverie was interrupted by the doorbell. She glanced at her sundial shaped wall clock with the Roman numerals. It was one thirty—probably Jack and the sketch artist. She put her dish and glass in the sink and walked hurriedly to the front door. As she opened it she was greeted by a flood of sunlight, followed by an unsmiling Jack and a younger, shorter and thinner young man with a small handled carrying case.

"Hello, Ryan, this is Johnny Adams," Jack said, nodding at the grinning young man next to him. "We work together down at the 10th. We're both off-duty today, and Johnny's agreed to help us with a sketch of the guy who you think might be stalking you." This said with a perfectly straight face.

Ryan opened the door wide, stepped aside, and ushered them in. "I'm pleased to meet you, Officer Adams. I really appreciate your doing this for me."

The young officer was still wearing a stupid grin, obviously impressed with Ryan and making an awkward effort not to stare at her in her blue shorts and t-shirt. "It's my pleasure ma'am. Sergeant Kroner has helped me a lot, ever since I got out of the Police Academy last year. But you should make a report on this guy if you think he's stalking you."

Ryan smiled at him sweetly. "I'm not really sure yet; it may have only been coincidences when I saw him at different places. Maybe I'm just jumping to conclusions. I thought that if I had a picture to show my coworkers at the gym, they could alert me if they saw him hanging around. Jack said you were really good, but if it's too much trouble… and I don't want to take up your off-duty time—"

"No, no, Miss Sanders, I'm glad… happy… to do it for you… and Jack, of course… no problem, ah…"

Ryan touched him lightly on the arm. "Johnny—I hope it's okay to call you that—I'm so grateful to you for doing this. You don't know how much this means to me." Ryan exuded sincerity. "Would you like to sit in the living room or at the kitchen table?"

The blushing officer glanced into the living room with its rich leather couch and loveseat, fronted by a long low coffee table inscribed with a medieval print of the old-world known in ancient times. He was obviously tempted by the inviting area, but opted for the practical. "Let's use the kitchen table, the lighting is much better," he said with just a touch of wistfulness.

Jack had remained quiet and stoic during the whole exchange, watching Ryan ply her charms on the young officer. The two men sat at the polished wooden kitchen table, and Johnny opened his case and began setting out large pads of paper, pencils, chalk and erasers.

The flustered officer continued, "You know, Miss Sanders… Ryan, I mean…" he glanced over his shoulder at Ryan, who was standing behind and to the side of him, "… if you made an official report we could use the Department's computer graphics software to do this. It would be quicker and easier—"

Ryan placed her hand gently on Johnny's shoulder and gave it an almost imperceptible squeeze. "Maybe when I'm a little surer about this guy, and besides, Jack says you're a real artist and put the computers to shame," she added.

Officer Adams, one of Detroit's finest, blushed again and fiddled with his pencils as Ryan hovered nearby. "Would either of you like coffee, snacks or anything?" she asked. When both men declined, Ryan sat down and watched patiently.

The young officer began, "Okay, Miss Sanders, let's start with the general shape—"

"Ryan, please call me Ryan," she interrupted. She smiled shyly and tentatively touched his forearm. "Officer Adams, I just want to say again how much I appreciate your doing this for me, on your own time and all."

"I'm glad to do it Miss San... I mean, Ryan. And you can call me Johnny if you'd like." The sandy haired officer cleared his throat, tried to compose himself and started over. "Let's start with the shape of his head...."

For the next thirty minutes Ryan described the man from the images she had received from Dana. The sketch artist transcribed her descriptions to the pad in front of him, outlining, and shading in the eyes, nose, chin and cheeks. Finally, he roughed in the thick head of hair on the pencil portrait of the man who had materialized on the paper before him. Minor changes here and there and it was nearly an hour before the drawing was finished. Ryan smiled appreciatively; the young man had been meticulous in his attention to detail. He had wanted to please her. Most men did.

Finished, he turned the paper toward Ryan. "What do you think?" he asked.

She pulled it closer to her and studied it. "That's him; that's the man I saw in my..." she caught herself in mid-sentence "... I mean around town several times. Maybe following me," she corrected.

Staring back at her was a handsome young man, completely devoid of any hint of the appalling things he was capable of doing, and had done. Ryan shuddered, her lips a compressed thin line as she remembered the defilement and desecration she had seen him perpetrate upon Dana.

Officer Adams was busy putting away his gear, but Jack noticed Ryan's reaction, her distress. "I'll take that that cup of coffee now, Ryan, if you don't mind." His interjection broke her attention to the picture.

Ryan pushed back her chair and stood. "Sure, coming right up. What about you, Johnny, you want anything?"

Johnny's blue eyes flicked up, oblivious to the fleeting distress that had passed through hers. "No, I have to get going; my wife has a long 'honey-do list' for me. That's why I brought my car."

Ryan and Jack walked the officer to the door. Ryan shook his hand and, leaning in, kissed him lightly on the cheek. "Thank you so much, Johnny. Jack certainly has good taste in friends."

Officer Adams turned crimson, a seemingly common occurrence. With an effort he regained his composure and managed a professional tone. "Now, Miss Sanders... Ryan... if you see this guy following you again, please come down to the precinct and file an official report."

"Yes, sir, I promise," she said.

Still red faced, Johnny turned and faced Jack. "I'll see you tomorrow at the station. You're on duty, right?"

"You got it, bro. And thanks again for your help. I owe you one," Jack answered. He smiled warmly and shook the young man's hand. "See you tomorrow."

As they watched him leave, Jack grinned and said to Ryan out of the corner of his mouth, "Well, it appears you've made another conquest."

Ryan just smiled sweetly and waved at the departing officer.

They walked back to the kitchen table, their expressions turning somber. Ryan continued on, averting her eyes from the drawing of the killer lying on the table as she passed. Jack paused and gazed down at the charcoal drawing. The dark eyes stared back.

An involuntary shudder passed through him.

# Chapter 11

"Have you heard from David yet?" Jack asked. He and Ryan were sitting at the kitchen table, both sipping an afternoon cup of coffee.

"Yeah, at least the creep is following through on his promise," she replied. "After he couldn't get her by phone, he went over to her apartment—nobody home, locked up tight. He talked to several of her neighbors and even called the temp service she worked out of, Work Solutions." Ryan paused and took another sip of her coffee and frowned. "Bottom line, they said that Dana—still depressed by her shattered illusions and her divorce, I'm guessing—threw a few clothes in her car and said she was planning to take a month off and do a little traveling. Sort of like a 'walk about'—"

"A what?" Jack interrupted.

That elicited a crooked smile from Ryan. "A 'walk about', like in the Crocodile Dundee movies…"

Jack still looked puzzled.

Ryan shook her head and rolled her eyes in mock exasperation. "The hero in the movie was a guy called Crocodile Dundee, because he killed one—a crocodile that is—single-handedly with just a knife. He was an Aussie who'd take off on foot in the Australian outback for days and weeks if he needed to get away and think. Dana liked all those romantic movies with the happy ending bullshit. Anyway, she said she needed to get away for a while, but nobody knew exactly where she was going. Probably not even Dana herself."

"She never hinted to you that she might do something like that?" Jack asked.

"I told you before, Dana and I drifted apart after I left home. She wanted to stay in San Diego. Then she met that bastard David, got married and... well, we didn't stay in touch all that much. I should have, I know, but our lives went in different directions. You'd think identical twins—half-identical, anyway— would have done a better job at staying close." There was no smile gracing Ryan's face now. "It's been over a month since she left, and nobody has heard from her. David filed a missing person's report with the San Diego Police."

"I'll follow up with the locals there and keep tabs on their investigation," Jack replied. "I don't suppose you're going to add your info to their reports?"

She gave him a look. "Yeah, right. I can just imagine how they'd view my 'psychic visions' and how I received them."

Jack thought it best to change the subject. "What about the terrain, trees, and foliage that you saw but weren't familiar with?" he asked. "Did you come up with anything on that?"

Ryan felt horrible in doing it, but she decided to lie to her longtime friend—at least for now. "No, not yet. It seems they're native to many of the States west of the Mississippi." Guilt washed over her. She decided to change the subject before her expression betrayed her. Her hand touched Jack's shoulder, "Did you get a chance to check on any similar sex murders in other states? Did you get any copies of reports?" she asked.

Jack took a deep breath and exhaled slowly. "Sit down, Ryan," he said.

She sat. Ryan couldn't read the expression on the rough, chiseled face gazing at her. "What is it?"

"I haven't done any checking yet. Do you even know what you're asking of me, Ryan?"

Judging from his tone, she thought it best if she remained quiet.

Jack continued gruffly, "Yes, I have friends in the 'cold case' bureau, and yes, there are State and Federal databases that track unsolved homicides and sex crimes, including cross referencing with other states. But, Ryan, times have changed. You can't just request information and reports without a reason, without a paper trail. It's called 'invasion of privacy,' with descriptive and ominous words like 'privileged' and 'confidential,' among other things. Police investigative use only. In your case, there's no official report, crime, or investigation. There is no legitimate reason for me to do this. If I were to get caught, my ass would really be in a sling."

Ryan looked at her friend, studied him. "Jack, I would never want you to do anything to jeopardize your career. But if you only knew what he did to Dana, what he did to the other women. Yes, he talked about them while he was 'with' Dana. Jack, I will find him—with or without your help." Ryan gave him a small, sad smile, looked away, then back at him with a tentative look in her eyes, her lips slightly parted. She reached and put her hand over his and gave it the gentlest of pressure.

Another wave of guilt washed over Ryan. In college with The Service, and later with her several "sponsors," she had learned an important lesson. There was more to it than a beautiful face and a sculpted body. You needed to study, learn and apply the resulting knowledge to reap the commensurate rewards. Ryan was a fast learner; it didn't take long for her to grasp the nuances of "love." Not just the stylish clothing, fragrant perfumes, or her expertise in the bedroom; she discovered there was much more to it than that.

Ryan considered herself a courtesan, and to that end she had carefully refined her use of all the senses—sight, sound, smell, touch and taste. She learned to read and be sensitive to the mood, temperament, and desires of her clients. She crafted her tones of voice and their inflections to the needs of the moment. Over time she was able to intuit when a gentle touch to the arm, the resting of a hand nonchalantly on a thigh, or a gentle stroking of her slender fingers along the nape of a man's neck, would be the most effective. Ryan took the nuances of her mannerisms—her repertoire of looks, gazes, smiles, expressions and gestures—and learned to summon them at will, fashioning them to fit and in-fluence her individual consorts. When and how to laugh, giggle or chortle, when and how to sigh, murmur and whisper. When to be bold, shy, demure, coy, nervous—any number of manner-isms—and how to present them most effectively. She became a connoisseur in the art of love.

Ryan cultivated her garden of charms and became the consummate actress. Her refinement and staging of the senses could drive her clients to a near frenzy before they ever got near a bedroom. Ryan was proof of the axiom that it wasn't just the package itself that was important, but how you offered that package. The presentation was all important, and it soon became obvious the power it helped afford her over men. The fruits of her garden could influence them to her way of thinking and doing. In short, Ryan learned how to manipulate men.

And now she was doing it to her best friend. Maybe he knew it, she couldn't tell. That he was conflicted was obvious. His jaw muscles clenched as he gritted his teeth, his lips pressed together, his eyes brown agates in their deep sockets. But he didn't remove his hand from hers.

He wavered. All men did.

Finally reclaiming his hand, Jack leaned back in his chair and sighed. His expression was one of sadness and melancholy as if facing disaster from an untenable and unavoidable position. "Ryan, I'll have to check databases for unsolved homicides, cross-referenced with sex crimes. I will need as many details as you can give me on Dana and... ah... what he did to her. With a little luck I'll be able to narrow down the list and locations." He looked away.

Ryan paled and unconsciously averted her eyes—not only in shame at her actions—but at the memories she was now forced to face again; memories she continually tried to wall off from her consciousness. She took a deep breath and began. For the next half hour she described the images that had been transmitted by Dana—paranormal images of what Dana had experienced after her death and had convulsively transferred to her twin—images and feelings reflecting all the five senses. Ryan was as descriptive as possible for Jack. On several occasions she had to pause to control her breathing and maintain her composure.

When she finished, the tough, cynical, battle tested cop—mentally and physically hewn from metaphorical granite—stared out the window at the green landscape of her backyard, his expression reflecting the darkness of a rolling thunderstorm, his eyes sparking pieces of flint. "I understand, Ryan." He finally looked back at her, his gaze softened now to a profound sadness… and something more.

Jack's voice was barely audible. "Okay, Ryan, I'll do whatever I can."

# Chapter 12

Lieutenant James Bocher was scowling and staring at the document in front of him. Considering the mess of paperwork scattered around his desktop, this was somewhat of an achievement. At the moment his ulcer was making its presence known; he would need a big swig of Mylanta as soon as he took care of this. He should have realized the pepperoni pizza he had for lunch was going to cause him grief. But pizza, among other things, was a weakness of his. Shit, eight more months and he was out of there. Thirty-five years was long enough. What was left of his hair had gone totally gray, his pot-gut was causing him grief, and his wife, Agnes, wanted to retire to the warmer climes of Florida.

Emphatically poking the transfer request in front of him with his forefinger, he spat out at the Sergeant standing in front of his desk, "So what the hell is this, Kroner? You actually want to add the 'Monroe Murders' to your plate? The Monroe Task Force isn't exactly the most popular assignment on the Department. What's your angle?"

Jack wasn't a very good liar, but as the old saying went, "necessity was the mother of invention." The Monroe "cold case" had been a long standing—and currently dormant—thorn in the Department's side for several years. It presented Jack with the best opportunity to make clandestine inquiries regarding Ryan's haunting problem, without technically violating Department procedures.

He continued with his ruse. "Lieutenant, multiple homicides—seventeen separate sets of bones identified at last count—occurring almost twenty years ago poses a unique challenge. I think my experience in homicide would be invaluable in the investigation. If I remember correctly, forensics has only been able to establish the identities of five of the women. There's still a lot of investigation and boots-on-the-ground footwork to do, not only to identify the remains, but to come up with possible suspects—of which we currently have zero. Besides—"

"Enough, Kroner," the Lieutenant interrupted. "Seventeen suspected prostitutes killed over a period of three years nearly two decades ago, and their bodies all buried in a remote section of Monroe County. No suspects, no leads, no glory—"

"But Lieutenant," Jack interrupted, "if I was instrumental in breaking open this high profile cold case, there would be glory involved."

The Lieutenant squinted up at Jack; his glasses were buried somewhere on his desk under the scattered paperwork. "Well, that slant I can understand, although you've never struck me as a glory hound, Kroner."

As his boss absently rubbed his chin, mulling it over, Jack could almost read his mind. *Kroner was a pretty good homicide detective, and should the inconceivable happen in the apparent dead end investigation… well, the Department could always use the positive publicity.*

The Lieutenant came to a decision. "You realize, of course, that the State Police are in charge of the investigation here, but the F.B.I. is overseeing the whole shebang, right? Besides, what's your case load like, Sergeant?" he asked.

"I don't mind working with the State boys, or…" Jack inserted the appropriate grimace of distaste "… the shit stirring F.B.I. As for my case load, I have two active investigations—the Higgins and Morrison homicides—plus two cases coming up in Circuit Court. If I could get my active cases taken care of…" he paused for emphasis "… I should be good to go."

Bocher sighed in harmony with his leather swivel chair as he leaned back and rubbed his gurgling stomach. "Okay, Kroner, Corporal Davidson has been pissing and moaning about his stint on the Task Force for some time. He thinks it's beneath him somehow, so you'll be taking his spot. I'll reassign your active cases to him, but you'll have to bring him up to speed. Of course, your court cases you'll have to follow through on. I'll make the call to State." He gazed longingly at his bottom desk drawer where his Mylanta was secreted. "Get with Davidson and let me know when everything is squared away. As of now consider yourself reassigned, pending your getting all your ducks in a row along the way. Now beat it, I have work to do."

"Thanks, Lieutenant, I'll take care of my end."

As soon as Jack closed the door behind him, his boss opened the drawer, removed the bottle of Mylanta and took a big swig. *Damn ulcer*, he thought. He'd be glad when he was outta here and relaxing on a nice sandy beach in Florida.

Breathing a sigh of relief, Jack headed straight for his desk, plopped down in the chair and stared at the blank screen of his computer. A twenty-year veteran, he felt as guilty as hell with the lying and subterfuge. He was conflicted; he considered himself a moral person and obeyed the rules as best he could. The only times he had occasionally strayed from the path was when it involved Ryan, and now he was sticking his neck out even more. But he knew her; she would continue on with her vendetta against the unknown killer, with or without him. And if she somehow did find him....

Jack shoved the disquieting thoughts aside. He didn't really have any interest in the Monroe murder investigations, even less in working with the State Police or FBI. But an old, multiple homicide investigation with the prostitution/sex angle and possible interstate implications... well, maybe he could use it as a pretext for doing a little research into Ryan's problem... without getting himself fired in the process, he hoped. He turned on the computer, oblivious to the bustling squad room around him, but still managing an occasional response to the hellos and wisecracks of his fellow officers.

He looked up the investigative case number for the Monroe Task Force and jotted it down on his desk blotter. As an official member of the interstate group investigating the old Monroe murders, Jack now had a legitimate reason to access the various databases for unsolved homicides. And since several of the bodies—all female—had been identified as prostitutes, Jack could inquire into sexually related homicides.

He decided to work through the smaller databases, TLOxp, Accurint, and NIJ before working up to the biggies—the "triple eye": the Interstate Identification Index, and wrap it up with the granddaddy of them all, the FBI's NCIC: the National Crime Information Center. He sighed, leaned forward, and pecked away at the keyboard. Considering his caseload and the time available to him, this little extracurricular activity would take him several days. Plus, if he came up with anything, he would have to contact the various State agencies to obtain the individual reports. Time to get cracking.

His thoughts drifted back to Ryan. Jack's fingers picked up the pace.

# Chapter 13

Ryan and Lonnie stood leaning on the ring apron and watched as the two welterweights grappled on the mat. The white guy was plastered with tattoos over the upper portion of his body and sported spiked, orange hair. He was sure to draw attention in the future, even if he wasn't the best fighter in the ring. But it appeared he had potential. He was currently in control with a top mount over the black fighter beneath him and was pounding away with fists and forearms. No sooner had the thought flitted across Ryan's mind than the black guy freed a leg, arched his back and reversed positions on his tormenter, smoothly transitioning into an arm bar on his adversary. Tattoo boy was tapping out within seconds.

Lonnie shook his head. "Things are not always what they seem, I guess." He glanced at Ryan next to him. "Let's talk partner. I've been wrestling with a few things—no pun intended." He smirked as Ryan groaned.

They paused as Bernie, one of the Madigan trainers, yelled at the fighters from the other side of the ring. "Nice move, Jamaal. But you, Frankie, you orange haired dunce, how many times do I have to tell you to watch out for that move from that position? Next time, I'll just let 'em break your arm."

Lonnie took Ryan by the upper arm to guide her. "Let's talk in the office." They made their way across the gym, nodding and greeting to several of the men and women who were training that afternoon.

The sounds of the gym were muffled when he closed the office door behind them. He sat down at his desk. "How long have we known each other, Ryan?"

Ryan gave her own desk a cursory glance, opting instead to fall with a comfortable whoosh onto the old leather couch along the wall. "Since my sophomore year in college... what, about nine or ten years ago? Right around the time I started my meteoric rise in the lucrative courtesan business, anyway." She grinned and gave her friend a playful look. "Don't tell me you regret never having taken advantage of my services."

Lonnie leered and then sighed. "I was a struggling college student. Your fees—although I'm sure they were commensurate with the benefits offered—were way out of my league."

"Why, Mr. Lonnie Allemande, for my best friend I would have worked something out."

Ryan couldn't suppress a grin. Sandy blonde hair and intelligent blue eyes, together with boyish good-looks and a charming personality—applied in large doses—made Lonnie a "babe magnet," as he liked to put it. He never had a problem landing women. Indeed, he was somewhat of a cock-hound, a skirt-chaser, a male chauvinist pig—any number of clichés fit his male profile. The only redeeming feature in that regard was his penchant for honesty. Lonnie was always upfront with his potential conquests when it came to his objectives concerning women. But Ryan wasn't going to be judgmental concerning his character flaws, considering a few questionable ones of her own that he willingly overlooked.

Lonnie's blue eyes now reflected a more serious expression. "If that would have happened, I don't believe the best friend thing could have been possible. And besides, loving you from afar—to coin a phrase—has allowed us to remain friends, and for you to…" he gestured with his arm, encompassing the room and alluding to areas beyond "… be part owner of the prosperous and ever growing Madigan's Gym; soon to be Madigan LLP and involved in, not only fight management, but fight productions." He ran his hand through his curly blonde hair. "But that's not what I want to talk about."

Ryan had become somber as she stared at her friend. Lonnie never judged her and had always been there when she needed a shoulder to lean on. Plus, he was one smart cookie, helping her several times in a few of the more difficult college business courses. When the Madigan Gym opportunity arose, he hadn't hesitated in offering her a chance to get in on the ground floor. The source of her investment money hadn't been a moral problem for him. Lonnie's comment about "loving her from afar" bothered her a little, causing a ripple of sadness to pass through her heart. But he was smiling, and his expression was innocent and unassuming. He appeared at peace with their status. Hell, it was only an expression, and she had heard a rumor—

"You're planning to go after this guy," he said, interrupting her musings. It was a statement, not a question.

Blunt and to the point, she thought. Despite the wild story she had related weeks prior, he had never doubted it and believed her at face value. "Yes, and I will find him, Lonnie." Ryan could also be blunt and to the point.

"No police involvement, I suppose."

Ryan chuckled sarcastically. "Other than you and Jack, I doubt that anyone would take my crazy story seriously, especially the cops. Dana's worthless ex-husband is taking care of her affairs on that end. But we know the investigation in California will be a dead end. She's buried in another state, and I plan on finding out where."

"I suppose Jack's helping you?" Lonnie asked.

Ryan paused as she considered her answer. Jack and Lonnie weren't exactly drinking buddies but, although being from different worlds, they got along well. As a matter of fact, it was Jack who suggested Ryan enroll in a self-defense course, and had steered her to Madigan's after being roughed up a few times by clients. Ryan had known Lonnie worked at a gym while in college, but hadn't really paid any attention to which one. So she was more than pleasantly surprised when Jack brought her to Madigan's and, ta-dah, there was Lonnie. And as fate would have it, Ryan had taken to mixed martial arts like the proverbial "duck takes to water," and the rest, as they say, was history.

"Yes, he is," she finally replied.

"I'm a little surprised; he could get his ass in a sling for any off-the-grid assistance," he said.

Ryan let the comment ride.

Her friend was scrutinizing her closely—her dark look, cold eyes and clenched jaw. "You don't plan on tracking this guy down just to turn him over to the police, do you?" Several seconds passed in silence before Lonnie continued, "Does Jack know?"

Still no comment from Ryan.

"Ryan, I don't care how tough you think you are, you need to rethink this. From what you told me, this maniac is a sadistic serial killer. Looking for revenge might get you hurt, or even killed. It may even get you in a jam with the police. It's not worth it. Investigate it if you have to and then let the police handle it. I don't want anything happening to you."

Ryan rose from the couch, her expression still dark. "You didn't see what he did to Dana, or hear him bragging about what he did to the other women. And he even had pictures of his victims tacked on the wall… I'm sorry, Lonnie, I can't promise you anything. And other than info gathering, I'll keep Jack out of it." The clouds lifted from her face and a smile brightened a bit. "Don't worry about me; I can take care of myself."

Lonnie watched Ryan turn to leave. He hoped she was right. He knew that no one was going to dissuade her from this quest; she would go after the killer with or without his or Jack's approval or help. He decided to shelve the problem for the moment and change gears and subject matter until he talked to Jack.

"Hold on a second, Ryan," he called before she reached the door. "Enough of this serious stuff for now. I've been thinking and, as I've said, it's time for us to take the plunge into the fight promotion side of the business. I have an idea about putting together a fight package at Cobo Arena early next year, and I want to run a few preliminary ideas by you to see if, in your opinion, the project would be financially feasible. Let's head over to O'Malley's for a couple—I'm buying. But if you could do me a favor first and dash in the women's locker room and catch Maria before she leaves to see if she wants to join us."

Ryan had stopped and turned, her hand resting on the doorknob. She was staring at her friend, eyebrows raised.

"What?" Lonnie questioned. He glanced down at the desk top, uncomfortable. "She's one of our best, already 6-0, with three KO's and two tap-outs. Teresa Foster was the only one that managed to go the distance with her. I figure Maria will challenge for the bantam weight title in the next year or two. She might be able to give us ideas—"

Ryan interrupted, shaking her head and sporting a wide grin. "Lonnie, Lonnie, you sneaky son-of-a-bitch, you're dating Maria, aren't you? But, what…" Her expression turned pensive and thoughtful. "Let me see now, you're pretty intelligent and pragmatic—for a man. Maria is a hot fight commodity, with the potential for a lucrative future for herself and us. And you're well aware of the pitfalls and dangers of an employer/employee dalliance, especially since the negative consequences would be not only emotional, but financial as well for everyone involved, including myself. So, for a smart man like you to take a risk like that, when there is no shortage of women for a self-described 'babe magnet.'…"

She let her comment trail off. Ryan couldn't remember ever seeing her friend looking as uncomfortable and at a loss for words when the subject was a woman. He shifted uneasily in his chair.

"Oh, my God, Lonnie; this girl has gotten to you," she tittered. "The mighty Lonnie Allemande, heaven's gift to the female sex, has been brought low by a little brown-eyed Latina. I can hardly believe it. And don't even try to deny it."

Her friend was blushing and looking at her with a sheepish grin. "I won't, and it's hard for me to believe, too. I got blindsided; she swept me off my feet somehow, and I still can't figure it out. Maybe, it's because she's the only woman I ever met that could kick my ass—present company excluded, of course. And she just might demonstrate that ass-kicking ability on me if you don't hurry and catch her before she leaves."

Ryan was unable to suppress a grin as she entered the women's locker room. It was still hard to imagine that her slick-talking friend had met his match. She had just assumed that Lonnie would never change—a perpetually over-sexed adolescent trapped in a man's body. Ryan saw no one in the locker room, but headed towards the showers in the rear to make sure. She called out, "Hey, Maria, are you still in here?"

From the back came a voice. "Yeah, hold on, just finished showering. I'm coming."

Ryan reached the end of the aisle and turned the corner to be met by Maria just emerging from the shower area. She was toweling off her hair, her caramel-hued body still wet and glistening. Unselfconscious in her nudity, Maria brushed by Ryan and opened a locker at the end of the nearest aisle and continued to towel off. "What's up, Ryan?" she asked.

"Lonnie sent me in to see if you wanted to stop at O'Malley's with us," Ryan replied. "He wanted to talk to me about putting on a fight program at Cobo Hall Arena next year."

Ryan regarded Maria appraisingly. Maybe 5'4", she was buff and toned, narrow-waisted and slim-hipped. She was tight, even her small breasts seemed to resist jiggling when she walked. Ryan noted her firm butt with admiration. "She could crack a walnut with her ass" would be Lonnie's sexist way of describing Maria's caboose.

Maria fastened her bra, slipped on a matching pair of red panties and shimmied into her jeans. She smiled and looked at Ryan. "And you're wondering why he wanted me to tag along while you two discussed business?" she asked.

If Ryan had been a switch-hitter, Maria would have been high on her to-do list. But Ryan had taken a couple of swings from the left side of the plate while in college and found that it just didn't appeal to her all that much. Too bad, she mused. Maria not only radiated a youthful vitality but, with her dark good-looks, the Hispanic beauty also exuded a smoldering sexuality that only the most jaded could miss. Obviously, Lonnie had missed neither.

Ryan murmured, "I can understand why Lonnie was smitten by you. I just never thought I'd live to see the day, I guess." She shook her head in admiration. "You are one hot tamale, Maria."

Maria, finished with her jeans, stopped and looked blankly at Ryan with raised eyebrows. "Huh, what did you say?" she questioned.

Ryan hadn't realized that she'd spoken her last thought out loud. Time to back pedal. "Lonnie wants you to come along because he figures you might be headlining a fight card by next year, and we'd be interested in representing you."

Maria pulled a Madigan's t-shirt on over her head, poked her head out the neck and grinned at her. "Thanks for the compliments, Ryan, including the hot tamale reference. Yes, I heard you. Not racially insensitive, are we?" Fortunately, Maria's grin belied any serious belief in her comment. "So, I guess Lonnie told you about us?"

Ryan could feel her face growing warm. "Yeah, just a few minutes ago. I'm still trying to wrap my head around the idea. I'm sure you know about Lonnie's past rep?" Ryan decided this was a delicate area, but one that needed to be addressed.

Maria gazed at her thoughtfully. "Ryan, you don't have a thing for Lonnie, do you?"

Ryan was caught off guard for a long second, before replying, "No, Maria, Lonnie and I have been good friends since college, and we decided long ago to never take a chance on ruining that. I just wanted to make sure you knew—"

Maria stopped her with a laugh and a raised hand. "I'm aware of his sexist, whore-mongering, bed-hopping days of yore. And he's also aware that those days are now over. I made it clear that if he crossed me I'd kick his ass."

Now, Ryan was laughing. "Lonnie alluded to that 'ass-kicking' thing before I came in here."

"By the way, why won't go a few rounds with me in the ring?" Maria asked, changing the subject.

"Because I'm six inches taller and twenty pounds heavier; it wouldn't be fair. And besides, I don't want to jeopardize the gym's future investment by injuring you."

"Excuses, excuses," Maria lamented. "I prefer to think it's just because you're afraid of me." She finished running a brush through her dark, still damp hair. "Let's go get those beers. I'm sure Lonnie's getting a little antsy with us two in here gossiping."

# Chapter 14

O'Malley's was an Irish themed pub on Jefferson near Wyandotte. With its friendly "Cheers" type ambience, subdued lighting, dart boards, dark wood and dark Irish beer, the bar entertained a loyal core clientele, supplemented by a steady stream of curious newcomers.

Ryan, Lonnie and Maria were nursing their way through a pint each of "Beamish Stout," a dark and chocolaty Irish brew that required sipping—at least for them—because of its infamous, potent un-beer-like kick. And they did, indeed, talk of Lonnie's expansive ideas concerning his ambitious fight promotion plans.

He had been enthusiastically outlining his business ideas since they'd first arrived, and Ryan was impressed. They were solid on the surface, Ryan thought, and this could well be the first giant step in expanding Madigan's from a respected training facility into the more lucrative arena of fight promotions. She had to muzzle a smile; Lonnie's animated speech and gestures were out of the ordinary, even for him.

Lonnie paused in his presentation, took a long swig of the lethal brew before him and leaned forward, resting his forearms on the table. He stared at Ryan, his boyish grin morphing into a more sober expression. "Ryan, you're a knowledgeable businesswoman and partner, due to my extensive tutoring, of course." He conceded a brief grin before continuing, "You are a hell of an MMA fighter. In the few years since Jack first brought you to the gym, you've become more than proficient at mixed martial arts. You've taken to the discipline like a 'duck takes to water,' You're an excellent boxer and grappler, and you already have an amazing grasp of Muay Thai and Brazilian Jiu-Jitsue. I think you'd do well if you got serious and turned pro. And you would be fighting under the Madigan's banner, which could only help the gym and—"

"Hold on, pretty boy," Ryan interrupted, "I have no interest in turning pro. I'm quite happy being a businesswoman and don't relish getting smacked around in the ring."

"But, Ryan, you're a physical anomaly, almost a freak of nature—no offense intended—when it comes to your reflexes relative to size. What, you're maybe 5'10, 140 pounds?"

"Close enough."

"You literally defy the laws of physics," he continued. "The length and weight of your arms, legs and torso should dictate a longer span of time to move from point A to point B. But when you fight, it's akin to watching a shorter, lighter fighter's reactions. It's amazing. You could—"

Maria punched him playfully in the arm. "Hey, put her in the ring with me. I'll show you fast, she said."

Lonnie turned and kissed her scowling, but happy, face.

Ryan grinned at the lucky couple, relieved that she was temporarily off the hook in having to come up with a reply to Lonnie's blossoming arguments. She had no interest in turning pro, or even fighting as an amateur in club settings. She enjoyed the physical workouts, the sense of achievement and, she had to admit, the knowledge that she could kick the asses of most of the men who crossed her path. Ryan imagined a psychiatrist would have a field day with that little nugget of information, considering her history and all....

Wistfully amused, she sipped her beer and continued to study the two lovebirds sitting across from her. Maria, talkative and animated, sat close to Lonnie and often made contact with him in small, but affectionate ways. She'd gently shoulder-bump him when one of them said something humorous or witty—an "aw shucks" sort of push and, whenever possible, a light touch to his hand or forearm to emphasize a point in the conversation.

For Lonnie's part, he couldn't take his eyes off Maria. It was as if he were trying to memorize her every feature and expression, all the nuances in her dark, luminous eyes. Lonnie was in love. As far as Ryan knew—unless there had been a big high school romance—this was the first woman who ever subjected Lonnie to the big "L". And considering his sexist track record during the intervening years, this had to register as a "10" on his emotional Richter scale.

Maybe it was the "Beamers" making their effects known, but a growing sense of melancholy was beginning to envelope Ryan. Two young studs made plays for Ryan during the evening, but she'd politely rebuffed them both. She preferred to remain alone. And therein lay the problem.

At twenty-eight, she was still on the outside looking in at that illusive thing people called love. She was sure that her choice of "employment" during her college years had permanently impaired her chances at any emotional balance or happiness. She had really liked a couple of her regulars over the years. Senator Griswold for one, who, in another place and time—assuming he didn't have his wife and children in that other place—might have developed into something more. She liked to think so, anyway. Then there was that sweet, nerdy young man who wanted to save her, to rescue her and take her away from her "profession"... but always, always, that ill-defined something seemed to elude her. Ryan had dated a few men since those days, but no one stuck. She was damaged goods, and she knew it. There was no sense moping about it. She—

Her reverie was interrupted by a hand touching her shoulder. She looked up at stud #1—she thought his name was Braxton—who she had rejected earlier in the evening. He was now leering at her stupidly in the throes of alcoholic lust.

"Hey, baby, you ready yet for numero uno, the big kahuna, to show you a fun time tonight?" he slurred.

Both Lonnie and Marie's attentions were quickly redirected towards the big man looming over Ryan in the crowded bar.

Ryan smiled benignly up at him. "Like I said earlier, Braxton, not tonight. I'm just out with friends for a couple of drinks and private conversation. Besides—"

The man, seemingly oblivious to Ryan's gentle rebuke, leaned over unsteadily and began whispering in her ear; one hand still on her shoulder, the other now covering hers on the table.

Ryan's expression didn't change as the drunk continued to breathe beer-sodden sexual musings into her ear. Unnoticed, her free hand slid over and covered his gently, almost affectionately, on the table.

Alarmed, Lonnie started to rise, but was restrained by Maria's hand on his arm. She shook her head, smirking.

Suddenly wide-eyed, Ryan's suitor pulled his head back and reluctantly began to kneel, until he was on one knee, akin to a beau proposing marriage to his beloved. Of course, his pained expression belied that romantic image. Ryan had gripped the thumb of the hand she was covering and was twisting it slowly and severely backward. Her other hand, now free, joined the first in gripping his, adding even more leverage. Mr. Braxton was now on the verge of falling over as the excruciating pain on his wrist and arm increased.

Maintaining her grip and pulling the sharply twisted wrist almost lovingly to her breast, Ryan leaned over and murmured into the captive man's ear. After a long second he nodded emphatically, his face still contorted in pain.

Ryan leaned back and released his hand, her expression never changing, her lips a thin line of distaste, her dark eyes smoldering coals. The grimacing man rose unsteadily to his feet while massaging his injured wrist. He teetered slightly and glanced warily at Ryan before heading for the door—bumping into several people as he hastily made his way to the exit.

Lonnie stared at Ryan as she resumed sipping her beer.

"What was that all about? What did you say to him?" Lonnie asked.

"Well, young Braxton couldn't take no for an answer, and was making several suggestions as to what we could do sexually—in a rather lurid effort to change my mind." She paused, glancing around the room.

"And?" Lonnie prompted, a little exasperated as her silence lengthened.

Ryan's eyes refocused on him. "Not much else. I just wanted to make sure I had gained his undivided attention before I suggested discreetly that it was time for him to leave. And if he didn't—or said one more word to anyone—I was going to rip his arm off and shove it so far up his ass he'd be able to brush his teeth from the inside."

Lonnie's jaw dropped. Maria giggled.

Ryan sat in the quiet semi-darkness of her spare room, seated in front of her huge, roll-top desk staring at her computer. Her computer stared back, waiting. Besides the illumination from the blank screen, the only other light was furnished by a small, brass desk lamp sitting to the right, and behind the monitor. The faux mahogany desk was made for housing this technology, but still had various sized drawers, shelves and slots—as well as the corrugated roll top—to make it an authentic looking replica of its nineteenth-century ancestors. Ryan loved it.

She kept a laptop in her bedroom for lazy-time use. But she spent most of her home computer time here; she loved to sit in front of her wooden monster. Unfortunately, tonight sitting in front of the desk was as far as she had progressed. Ryan's fingers rested on the keyboard in front of her but remained motionless, the sign-in screen patiently awaiting her key strokes.

With an effort Ryan shook off her wistful and confused longings of the night before at O'Malley's; feelings spawned by Lonnie and Maria's budding relationship. Her fingers began searching across the keyboard. She had work to do—a killer to track down. Revenge would be a more than sufficient emotion for the foreseeable future. She didn't need to feel anything else. Dana had given her a flood of clues to work with—pieces of a jigsaw puzzle she needed to fit together. Once she fit those pieces together someone would pay a very steep price for their depravity. But the whole process was painstakingly slow.

The deluge of images sent by Dana were all jumbled together, no chronological order and many with no apparent relevance to each other. Some images were obvious, others less so. It was as if Dana's mind literally exploded, the explosion aimed directly at Ryan. Days had already turned into weeks, but she had mentally sorted through everything as best she could and had some semblance of order. She would put it all together, and once she gleaned all the information from Jack's "covert" police investigation, she'd be heading out for an extended vacation. Ryan just needed to figure out where in the hell she was going.

She opened her picture files and reviewed her Google collection. She had browsed the Western states, perusing the geography, fauna and flora of each, trying to match as much as possible the pictures with the images received from Dana. Ryan felt these forwarded memories of Dana's were more recent somehow than those accumulated during earlier periods of Dana's life. At least she sure as hell hoped so. If not, she'd be royally screwed.

She leaned forward and studied the photos and captions beneath them—Ponderosa Pine, Desert Willow, Pinion Pine and Alligator Juniper, a shrub-like tree described as a "scrub oak" and several pictures of cacti with long scientific names. Clicking to another page, she studied buttes, mesas, rolling plains and distant mountains. Another click and she was looking at examples of Southwestern architecture—adobe, stucco, Pueblo, Spanish, flat roofed, tiled roofed and tin roofed, interior designs and layouts.

Ryan sighed, closed her eyes and leaned back in her chair. She tried to relax and review the myriad impressions she'd received, the patchwork collage of mental pictures, trying to determine if they came before, during or after... Ryan opened her eyes and leaned forward, looking, matching and comparing. She decided that the only states that could support the majority of the pictures she'd collected were Arizona, New Mexico, southern Utah and Colorado, and maybe northern Texas.

Next, she reviewed her license plate "collection." Ryan hadn't been able to discover any particular vehicle license plate numbers in the deluge of often indistinct images swirling around in her mind. But she could make out blurry colors on a number of vehicle plates; the primary color being yellow. So, she checked on the current registration plates and their colors in all fifty states. The only two using predominately yellow plates were New Hampshire and Alaska. That didn't jibe with her Southwest theory; especially if Dana had been making her way to Ryan for a surprise visit... of course, people driving cars with those plates could have been on vacation....

Frustrated, her slender fingers flew over the keys; she'd check a little further in the states potentially containing the terrain, architecture, fauna and flora she had identified. It took longer than she anticipated. None of the State Motor Vehicle Departments currently issued standard yellow license plates. But the registration plates in each state had changed in style and color over the years. Plus, she had to take into account all the "personalized" plates issued....

Ryan gradually made her way through her short list, checking the history of each state's registration plates. She eliminated Colorado right off the bat; no yellow license plates ever issued. Utah had one used back to 1928, but she considered that a real stretch. Arizona was a possibility; they had a personalized plate that was yellow. Ryan hesitated, and instead of typing in New Mexico, she zeroed in on Texas—bigger state, a lot more people and cars, probably many variances in license plates over the years. She patiently traced the registration plate history in Texas back to the beginning: no yellow one's ever issued. So much for that idea.

Back to New Mexico. She typed in her search, and as she scanned the state's registration plates Ryan's eyes widened. Their current plate was turquoise, but until 2008 it had been yellow with red lettering. Plus, there were five other personalized plates that were yellow, bringing the total to six. Bingo! It was New Mexico. She knew it, she felt it. Everything fit, everything made sense. She hoped.

Ryan's euphoria evaporated as she researched a website on New Mexico. It was the fifth largest state at over 121,000 square miles, with a population of only a little over two million thinly spread out across the state, primarily in small villages and towns. There were a handful of true urban areas. Even if Ryan determined the state Dana was murdered in, she had no idea how to narrow it down any further.

# CHAPTER 15

Ryan whisked into the lounge of the Marriott Hotel, trailing behind her an alluring hint of an exotic perfume. She had just grabbed and misted it on after a hurried shower, dabbed on a little makeup and threw on a change of clothing before heading out. Despite her rushed departure, more than one head turned to follow the tall, dark-haired woman in the belled black slacks and lavender blouse entering and strolling up to the bar in her high heels. Ryan glanced into the mirror behind the counter, sighing in relief at having remembered to run a brush through her hair before dashing out the door.

Jack had called late, almost ten o'clock, and wanted to meet for a drink after he got off duty at eleven. He said he had information on her "case" he wanted to pass on, as well as information from the San Diego Police Department in California. But something in the tone of his voice made her uneasy. She had known Jack for a long time and, although he was difficult to read, she could occasionally guess when something was bothering him.

Still, she was having trouble containing her excitement; any new information would bring her closer to—

The young bartender was looking at her expectantly, waiting for a reply to a question she'd missed while in her reverie. She smiled sweetly and took a stab at a logical answer to an assumed question, anyway. "I'll just take a whiskey sour and..." she scanned the room "...just have the waitress bring it to the table over in the corner." She nodded in the direction of the table she'd selected. "Oh and please have her bring a Bud Lite also; I'll be meeting a friend shortly. Just run a tab for us." She headed for the table and the barman departed to mix her drink, a little miffed that the attractive woman had ignored his compliment on how her good looks had brightened up the place.

Ryan had no more than taken the first sip of her drink when Jack walked in. In blue jeans and a Detroit P.D. "PAL" sweatshirt, he stopped near the entrance and slowly panned the room looking for her. His thick, dark hair was wet and slicked back; he'd obviously taken a shower before leaving the P.D. locker room. A couple walked by him heading for the exit which only accented Jack's size. Ryan knew he was a good six feet tall and guessed his weight at somewhere around two twenty. But he was far from being an Adonis. Thank God he had a neck, she mused. Broad shouldered, heavily muscled, but thick waisted, the lack of a neck would make him look like a giant fireplug.

His weathered features added an extra dose of masculinity and, although he appeared menacing to some, this perceived aura of danger appealed to many women. His personal philosophy that cops were a bad investment in the serious relationship department—coupled with his often emotionless, near inscrutability—zeroed out all but the most determined women. Still, Ryan had seen her friend in the company of some real lookers on occasion.

Jack was making his second scan of the dimly lit lounge, so Ryan raised her arm and waved. That caught his attention, and he ambled over, surprisingly light of foot for so large a man. He grinned sheepishly as he pulled out a chair and sat. She could now read the smaller lettering on the sweatshirt: **P**olice **A**thletic **L**eague. Jack was active in his Department's P.A.L. organization. The kids just loved the gentle giant.

"Thanks for the beer," he said. Ignoring the glass, he took a gulp from the bottle before continuing. "I'm sorry for dragging you out on such short notice, but I wanted to fill you in on a few things. And, by the way, you look pretty damn good for it being a spur of the moment thing."

"Aw, Jack, you really know how to turn a girl's head," she replied, laughing. "So, what's up? What did you find out?" She leaned forward eagerly.

Now, Jack's smile faded. Ryan had a feeling his expression was related somehow to his tone of voice on the phone. "I got a call from Lonnie," he said.

Shit, thought Ryan; she needed to smack her business partner up side of the head.

Jack continued, "Lonnie's under the impression your quest for Dana's killer isn't a matter of bringing the psycho to justice, but is strictly a matter of revenge. You plan to kill him." He took another sip of his beer, measuring her.

"Lonnie said I said that?" she asked.

"No, not exactly, but he inferred it from conversations with you."

Ryan needed to stall; Jack would never help her if he knew her true intentions. "Jack, how long have you known me?" she asked.

A faint smile crept back onto Jack's creviced features. "About eight or nine years, I guess. Ever since I brought you in for questioning on that prostitution bust."

Ryan winced. "Jack, please, it was an investigation into my being employed as an escort in The Service. Prostitution is such a common, vulgar word. I much prefer escort, consort, companion, or better yet—as I had moved on and up by the time you brought me in—a courtesan."

Now, Jack was really grinning. "Okay, a 'courtesan.' And your point?"

"Other than when you were grilling me during those interviews, in which I gave slightly evasive answers, I've always been straight with you and everyone else, haven't I?" she asked.

"Three interviews and you tap danced your way through all of them; I was never able to trip you up, even once. And I always thought I had a pretty good interview technique—"

Ryan interrupted, she was picking up steam. "I never rolled on any of my coworkers or my former employers, never blackmailed or scandalized any of my later sponsors—please don't use the term 'sugar daddies'—and I've never intimated that I would ever use any dirt for a shocking expose or a tell-all memoir. I was honest and upfront with everyone I was associated with in the business—barring those police interviews. I mean, hey, I didn't want to go to jail. And I've continued to be upfront with everyone since I closed that chapter of my life almost four years ago." Within reason, Ryan mentally amended. She looked at Jack with raised, inquisitive eyebrows.

Jack was studying her but still didn't look convinced.

Ryan plowed on. "Yes, I used my face and body to bankroll my education and get my start, but I walked away—the rest I'll do with my brains. After what I've gone through, do you think I'd jeopardize everything now?" Before he could reply, Ryan continued. "Jack, I know you're taking a chance in helping me and I appreciate it, but I'd certainly understand if you changed your mind." She looked directly into his eyes as she finished. "Believe me, Jack; I'd never do anything like that and endanger your career."

When she saw his expression and body relax, she knew he had accepted her ambiguous answer—accepted it because he wanted to. And Ryan hadn't actually lied to her friend. When, and if, the end game occurred, she'd make sure that Jack wasn't around when she executed the killer—slowly and painfully.

Since he seemed satisfied, Ryan decided it would be best to refocus on the primary subject. "So, Jack, you mentioned you had more information?"

Jack signaled the waitress with his hand—pointing at their table—indicating another round of drinks. He swung his attention back around to Ryan. "I had the San Diego P.D. fax me the missing person's report on Dana. It seems your little phone call to her Ex prompted him to get on the ball. Officers interviewed her neighbors and the temp agency she worked for. It turns out no one has seen her for a month and, since she'd told everybody she was taking off for a few weeks, nobody thought anything about it. At least until you bugged David about not being able to get in touch with her."

They paused as the waitress deposited their drink orders on the table. After she left, Jack continued. "You said that the terrain in her images looked like the Southwest. I fibbed a little to the local department there, telling them you said she might have been on the way to visit you here, and suggesting that they put out a B.O.L., that's police vernacular for 'be on the lookout, for her vehicle along the routes between California and Detroit. I'm just giving you a heads up in case San Diego calls to verify that with you."

Jack was already moving on to his next subject. "Here's some interesting information for you. I've been keeping my computer humming, checking Federal and State data bases, especially the NCIC— the National Crime Information Center. They have a central depository on file of all the crimes reported by state and local agencies across the nation. Of course, its effectiveness is dependent on the agencies submitting crime statistics to it. Still, using the details given by you, I narrowed down my search to unsolved, suspected necrophilia sex crimes. I further restricted the search to the Southwestern States. Initially, I came up with eight. I expanded my search to all states west of the Mississippi and added six more. The results were interesting."

He paused for a second. Ryan smiled inwardly; the big guy was looking for an "attaboy" and, all things considered, he deserved it. She matched his smile with one of her own. "Jack, you've been a busy boy, and I appreciate everything you're doing. I hope you're not going to get yourself in trouble with this."

"I don't think so; I got myself transferred to the task force investigating the multiple Monroe homicides here in Detroit from almost two decades ago, so I have an excuse to surf the NCIC database and do follow-ups. I just need to make sure I actually do a little work on the Monroe cases, too."

Ryan wasn't sure she had ever seen Jack quite so animated. It might not have been noticeable to the casual observer, but for her his stoic demeanor had certainly been compromised. He was enjoying the investigation—the chase. She had to suppress a smile.

Jack was talking again. "Anyway, I've pinpointed thirteen possibilities—thirteen bodies, or the remains of bodies, that fit the specific profile parameters I plugged in and using the details you provided." He leaned forward. "Two each in Texas, Oklahoma and Arizona, one each in Utah, Nevada, Colorado, California, Idaho, Wyoming and Nebraska. Granted, I'm sure that there have to be other, as yet, undiscovered bodies, but do you notice anything unusual about that list I just mentioned?"

Ryan thought about it for a few seconds. She knew the answer, but shrugged her shoulders, feigning defeat.

Jack gave her a hint. "What state, regionally central to the states I mentioned, is missing from that list?"

Ryan mentally visualized a map of the United States. "New Mexico," she replied. She volunteered a puzzled look.

His smile slowly turned back into his more serious, taciturn expression. He pointed his forefinger at her. "Let's say you're an intelligent, calculating serial killer. Even if you were suffering from a sexually compulsive behavior, would you not at least try to conduct your crimes away from your home state, spreading them out to diffuse any local suspicion?"

"Down, boy, down," she admonished. "You said yourself there could well be other bodies fitting the profile buried somewhere. For all we know, there could be several victims buried in New Mexico waiting to be discovered." Ryan felt bad for raining on the big guy's parade. She threw him a bone. "We'll have to double check and make sure everything fits, but you could be onto something." Of course, Ryan was already pretty sure everything fit; she just had to slow him down a little while she figured out the next step. And maybe Jack could help with some ideas on the next step.

So, before her friend could reply, Ryan decided to encourage him to continue on with his current train of thought. "Let's assume you're right. New Mexico is a big state; how and where would you even start?" She sipped her drink, trying to keep her hopes in check.

Jack didn't need any encouragement; his animated expression said it all. "Okay, let's think about this logically. These unique homicides began occurring approximately ten years ago—at least based on when the first body was found—but not in New Mexico. If I'm right, and the killer resides in that state, the onset of the killings may well have been preceded by some unusual event or circumstance, something that initiated this decade long rampage. And since we know something about his uniquely sick methodology—thanks to you—the initiating event would probably be related in some way." He stopped for another swig of beer.

"If you're right, Jack, that would give us an approximate time line for the start of those… events," she said, suppressing a shiver. "I'm following you so far, go on."

He leaned forward and dove back in. "There aren't many big cities in New Mexico. After Albuquerque's half million, there's only a couple that even approach a hundred thousand. Most of the people live in small towns or villages scattered across the state. But if there were some related newsworthy event it would be carried in one of the larger newspapers. And if there was a crime or trial involved, there might be a record of court proceedings, again conducted in one of the larger cities. There might have been police investigations, in which case there would be police reports somewhere. Off hand, I'd start looking in Albuquerque, Santa Fe or Las Cruces for a paper trail. I'd go back ten to… say… fifteen years ago. This would allow for the possible delay between the causal incident and the onset of the killings, or more likely, the fact that several of the initial homicides may have gone undiscovered." Jack paused for breath, leaning back with a well-what-do-you-think smile on his face.

Ryan was duly impressed. "Nicely thought out, Mr. Investigator. But how come you know so much about New Mexico?" As soon as she said it, a light bulb went off in her mind and she answered her own question. "Your grandmother was Indian—I mean Native American—wasn't she? I didn't realize she was from New Mexico. When you told me your father met her on a reservation, I assumed it was one of the many in Oklahoma, or maybe the Navajo or Hopi in Arizona—"

"Acoma Pueblo," Jack interjected. "One of the smaller pueblo reservations in New Mexico, of which there are nineteen. I'll give you a little more history sometime." But it was apparent his thought processes were in a groove, and that groove was not in his personal history.

He got back on track. "I have an idea on how we can pull this thing off. I go to my Lieutenant and say I've received some detailed information from an anonymous source…" he grinned conspiratorially and nodded at Ryan "… and using those details, I did a little checking and came up with the information I just related to you. If I do this right, I might end up working directly with the Feds on a multi-state task force." He finished his beer with a flourish. "I've got to get going; I have court in the morning. Give me a call when you check things out." He dropped two twenties on the table and headed for the door.

Ryan watched him go. It was an effort to keep her smile from faltering; her spirits had done a sharp U-turn following his last comments. She was sure Jack had visions of arresting and bringing a sadistic serial killer to justice, and the glory that such a result would bring. And Jack deserved it; he was probably the finest man she had ever known. Unfortunately, Jack's visions did not coincide with hers. She would protect him if she could, but the die was cast. Nothing was going to stop her. She was just going to have to delay Jack from getting the police involved.

# Chapter 16

Norman finished packing the second, smaller suitcase, having decided to stick with the original plan of a "vacation" to Montana. His American Airlines flight was scheduled to depart Albuquerque at 10:20 in the morning. He would have preferred an earlier flight, but it was a two and a half hour drive just to get to the airport from his remote home outside Magdalena. It was one of the downsides to living out in the boondocks, but one he could easily live with. Still, he'd have to leave for the airport at 6:00 a.m. That Dana cunt had been an unexpected bonus—albeit risky—temporarily easing the constant pressure. His compulsions could never be completely sated. He had been looking forward to this Montana trip and the gratification of slowly snuffing the life out of some deserving bitch. And, of course, the ultimate pleasure of escorting them into the void after their death.

He grinned humorlessly. He was going to modify his original plans somewhat—extending his vacation to capitalize on an even bigger bonus. Montana, yes, but he would not be returning home immediately. Instead, he would catch a commercial flight out of Billings to Detroit.

The thought of finding Dana's twin, Ryan, was exhilarating. It reminded him of that old Doublemint Chewing Gum commercial: "Double your pleasure, double you fun"… damn… he couldn't remember how it went, other than it ended with the word gum—to rhyme with fun. He was becoming agitated just thinking about escorting that twin bitch into her slow, terrifying post mortem death passage. And Norman would enhance that last horrifying trek with a few final defilements, ensuring that her last, fading memories would be of the basest of acts committed on her body and departing soul.

A frown temporarily clouded Norman's handsome features. His forays were coming closer and closer together, the impulses harder and harder to resist. True, the more whores he ushered into the abyss and the more horrific he could make that trip for them, the better. Still, it wouldn't do much good to get caught. It was inevitable, of course, but—as the old saying went—the more, the better.

But the disturbing blackouts. They seemed to be increasing, and the things he was doing to the whores during them were pretty creative. Nothing wrong there, he supposed. Still… there was a nagging shadow, a feeling of contradiction. Norman wasn't ignorant. He remembered once when he was twelve Nicole had allowed him to watch television; a reward for doing a good job of "pleasuring" her. He shivered, a tremor coursing through his body. And there had been that movie he'd watched—*Psycho*, by some guy named Alfred Hitchcock.

Could his mother really be lurking in the darkest corners of his mind? That was bullshit. It was only a fucking movie. Mommy... Nicole... was long dead. He had killed her when he'd thrown that old radio—playing those crappy "oldies" that Nicole liked—in the bathtub with her. Maybe his psychiatrist at Fort Bayard, Dr. Tolliver, believed in weirdo shit like that, but Norman was smarter than the good doctor and all those other people at the hospital. Norman squeezed his eyes shut. Still, those thoughts were like shards of glass piercing his brain.

Instead, he concentrated on the anticipated Montana trip, and the timely victim who would be sharing her death plus the next four minutes with him—maybe longer, if he was lucky. He smiled wistfully. He wished he knew exactly how long he had to play and talk with them after those first four minutes. Plus, there was the bonus trip to Michigan to look forward to. His headache started to abate. Time to hit the weight room and sweat out the rest.

There were still a couple of hours of sunlight left when Norman emerged from his exercise room after a strenuous workout, his muscles pleasantly fatigued. Clad in his nylon sweat suit to keep from cooling off too quickly, he made his way into his Southwestern style living room, dominated in one corner by a kiva fireplace. He enjoyed the ambience of the kiva, or Bee Hive, as he'd occasionally heard it called. The rounded front with its distinctive arched firebox door ran from floor to ceiling and blended in naturally with the stucco interior. And the smell of burning pinion and cedar in the winter almost made cold weather worthwhile.

He paused briefly as he glanced out the large picture window opposite with its western view of his property, covered with pinion, juniper, scrub oak and scattered ponderosa pine. Norman skirted the long sofa with its Native American motif and two matching lounge chairs before stopping in front of a locked cabinet of roughhewn oak. Dominating the wall above the cabinet was an impressive three foot by four foot painting of a Sioux village with several Indians on horseback. Norman reached behind the corner of its heavy frame and produced a key to the gun cabinet and opened it.

Inside was Norman's very modest gun collection: A Mossberg .12 gauge shotgun, a Kimber .300 Winchester Magnum w/scope, plus two handguns— a .45 Glock semi-automatic, and a Smith & Wesson stainless steel .357 magnum. The shotgun was for knocking down walls and most anything else, the Kimber for hunting, the Glock because it was light, accurate and almost never jammed, and the .357 because it had been Nicole's—or more accurately—Norman's unfortunate, unknown and unnamed father. He took the Glock, a box of shells, eye protection glasses and sound muffling "ear muffs" and headed out the back door. Better safe than sorry was his motto.

Norman had his own shooting range set up on the back forty and he liked to keep in practice. Other than sniping the occasional coyote, deer or jackrabbit that made the mistake of crossing his path when he was armed, he didn't have much practical use for the guns—when it came to people he preferred the "hands on method," so to speak. He chuckled to himself at the thought. But

Norman was of the opinion that if you were going to do something, you should do it right.

He stood behind the waist high bench, loaded the gun's magazines, slid one into the .45 and racked a round into the chamber. With his glasses and ear protection in place, he began by firing ten quick rounds at the silhouette target twenty yards away. Norman had the paper targets custom made—they were all female. It helped him concentrate.

When he was done, he painstakingly cleaned the weapons and secured them back in the cabinet. He decided to relax with a couple of beers and watch the sunset. He grabbed his laptop from the kitchen counter, tucked it under his arm, removed the last two beers from the fridge and headed out to the patio. He pulled up a chair to the small café table, opened the laptop and turned it on. With paper and pen he had jammed into the pocket of his nylon sweat pants, he decided to recheck a few numbers he had culled from the PC the night before.

Putting pen to paper was completely redundant and unnecessary, of course, since his car was equipped with a Garmin GPS, and he made sure that all of his rentals were similarly equipped. Plus he'd have his laptop, although, to date, he had resisted getting one of those I-Phones or their kin. Phones were made for talking was his take on the whole damn thing. He made do with a simple flip phone. Of course, when Norman was on the road taking care of business he used disposable cell phones purchased at a local Wal-Mart, but never a store in the same state where he would be enjoying himself. Norman looked down at the figures on the plain white paper. Maybe he was being old fashioned and just wanted to relish the hands-on aspect of this planned enterprise.

He leaned back in his chair, sliding down slightly as he stretched his legs out in front of him and crossed them at the ankles as he relaxed. He sighed and took a swig of beer. The sunset was going to be spectacular. Sunlight, penetrating and reflecting through the scattered cloud cover at different levels, was going to be awe inspiring.

Life was good.

# Chapter 17

"**Let's get out** of here," Elisha said. "This place is dead. I bet Benegens would be better than this." The pretty blond looked from one to the other. "Well?"

Nahni threw her lot in with Elisha. "I'm game, there's nothing going on here. Granted, there aren't a lot of guys in here tonight, but you'd think someone would have hit on us by now." She looked at each of her friends, critically appraising their short, body-hugging dresses, finally glancing down at her own considerable cleavage, enhanced even more by a pushup bra. "If these dresses haven't gotten results by now, we must have stumbled upon 'Gay Pride Night' at the Sheraton." Nahni turned to the third member of their group. "So, Amy, what do you think about blowing this place and trying something else?"

"I think I'm going to stay for a while, guys," Amy replied. This comment met with unified looks of disbelief. "What?" she asked, palms raised questioningly. "I'll meet up with you two at

Benegens in a little while. I'm going to give that good-looking, shy guy at the end of the bar a little more time."

The three friends had driven in their own cars, rendezvousing at the lounge at the Sheraton Hotel for drinks, and to start their evening of bar hopping and socializing. The three had graduated from Montana State University the previous month and were planning to take the summer off before embarking on the next phase of their futures. Elisha, bucking the tired, passé platinum blond typecasting, was starting medical school in the fall at the University of Michigan. Nahni, a voluptuous brunette of Hawaiian ancestry, had been accepted into the Columbia School of Law. Nahni, meaning "beautiful" in Hawaiian, was an apt name for the mocha-hued knock-out. Amy, a natural blond with a hoped for future in the business world, was going for her Master's Degree in Economics at State, right there in Bozeman. A little depressing that she wasn't going somewhere else in the fall, or that her chosen profession wasn't as exciting as theirs, but still…

Elisha and Nahni were staring at the man in the dim light of the bar, the one who was apparently going to break up their little group.

"Hey, you two," Amy hissed. "Quit staring, are you trying to embarrass me?"

They turned their attention back to Amy. Nahni spoke first. "Are you sure about this? I would kinda feel bad, leaving you here alone and all."

"And what makes you think that Mr. Shy Guy is going to overcome his nervousness and make a move?" Elisha added.

Actually, Amy wasn't sure he would. But maybe three beautiful women sitting together at this table had cowed the few unattached men in the lounge. Obviously, there were no "players" in the room this evening. The three college friends were akin to a trio of exquisite paintings on display in a drab setting, breathtaking to look at but too beautiful to touch. Who knows, Amy thought, maybe if she were by herself... and if that didn't work, another drink and she'd make a move on the guy.

"Listen, you two, I'll probably be meeting you at Benegens in an hour. If not, it just means I'm successfully cultivating a new relationship this evening." Amy picked up her glass. "A toast—may we all meet the man of our dreams tonight."

The three clinked glasses and laughed.

Minutes later her two friends finished their drinks and left, numerous pairs of eyes following them discreetly and longingly. Amy ordered another drink from their pert, bouncy server. "Your friends coming back?" the girl asked

"No, just me for now," Amy replied.

The waitress picked up her friend's empty glasses, wiped the table and left to get Amy's rum and coke. Sitting alone, Amy suddenly felt uncomfortable. She glanced at the handsome, dark-haired man at the bar. He, like the other unattached men in the lounge, had watched her friends leave, and was now shyly glancing her way.

Amy picked up her purse and walked—nonchalantly, but sexily she hoped—to the women's restroom. Once there she rummaged through her purse and retrieved her lipstick and makeup. Blessed with a near perfect complexion and years of practice in the art of maquillage—a term Elisha had humorously contributed to their college vocabulary—it took little makeup to return things to flawless.

Miraculously still alone in the restroom, Amy stepped back from the mirror and surveyed her appearance with a smile. She ran her hands down the sides of her crimson dress, smoothing out nonexistent wrinkles. The satin-like fabric clung to her curves like a fitted glove. Spaghetti straps supported a bodice revealing a modest amount of cleavage. Amy tugged at the hem of her dress, a hem that ended at mid-thigh. High heels accented her shapely legs.

Satisfied that she was "the best that she could be," she took a deep breath, straightened her posture and pulled her shoulders back, accenting breasts already enhanced by her new, pushup bra. Another deep breath and she headed back to her table through the sparse evening crowd.

Amy sat down for a long minute, sipped her drink and gazed around the room feigning nonchalance. Another deep breath. You only live once she thought. She picked up her drink and casually walked over to the bar. The young, well-dressed gentleman was smiling at her nervously, shyly, his obvious timidity so very endearing. Well, she would introduce herself... this just might be a night they'd both remember....

Norman came out of his temporary fugue, his breathing almost normal, drying perspiration on his body causing a slight chill. From his vantage point on the bedroom chair, he stared at the nude body of the blonde on the bed. She was lying on her back near the edge, one arm and leg draped over the side, her foot on the floor. Norman admired this side view of her shapely leg. Nicole's legs were beautiful, too. That's what Norman first noticed about the woman—he couldn't remember the pretty blonde's name now—but she'd been wearing that tight, short skirt at the nightclub… and when she sat down… you could almost see…

Norman leered. All were whores, one way or another. They were all Nicoles'. Sometimes it was the legs, sometimes the breasts or their ass. On other occasions it was the eyes, the lips or their complexion. Hair, hands or feet could fan the smoldering fires within him into an all-consuming blaze. Every woman reminded Norman of Nicole somehow, someway. Nicole had been his mother, and his lover. He loved every woman. And he hated every woman.

Norman rose and walked across to the bed with the red satin sheets and the pale white body, picking up his wristwatch from the nightstand as he went. He glanced at it and did a quick computation. He figured the woman had been dead for nearly twenty minutes, no chance that her brain was functioning or aware on any level now—he didn't think, anyway. Norman was sure she'd already gone screaming in terror into the eternal dark.

He glanced down at his flaccid penis. It had done an admirable job, more than once in fact—although things had gotten a little hazy a few minutes into his frenzy. Maybe it was one continuous non-stop, euphoric ejaculation, he mused. Nicole would be proud on that score. She always seemed to be "needy," and he had sometimes been forced to perform multiple times during the day and night.

Norman shook his head violently and refocused on the woman. He had borrowed several items from the cluttered bedroom dresser to make sure he plugged all the fucking openings in her body. And Norman was thorough. From some of the things he'd read, men's sexual fetishes covered most everything, and Norman tried to make sure he corked up all the holes—time permitting, of course. He snickered at the end of the ballpoint pen peeking out of one ear, and the two dimes partially visible in her nostrils. He stared at her sightless blue eyes—almost the same shade as Nicole's—and at her chewed nipples.

He always left the blank, empty eyes untouched. Norman liked to gaze into them as he relished and exercised his ultimate power and control, imagining them as a still functioning gateway to the imprisoned, dying soul—the powerless and fading mind relegated to enduring the justice he was bestowing upon them.

Norman's gaze traveled over the slowly cooling body and noted the blood between her legs, a dark shadow on the satin sheets. He gazed at the end of the broken towel rod protruding from her cunt, and guessed that he'd rammed it up a bit too far... if there was such a thing as too far for Nicole, he snickered.

He reluctantly pulled himself away from his abject admiration of his accomplishments. It was time to get dressed; he didn't want to overstay his welcome. But when he sat down on the bed next to the body to put on his socks and shoes, her lifeless head lolled to the side. The yellow urine slowly leaked out of her mouth and onto the bed sheets, despite the fact that he had closed her slack mouth after filling it. Damn, thought Norman, he always relished pissing or shitting in their mouth as a grand finale—after he rammed something down their fucking throats, of course.

He didn't know if he could manage another piss before he left. He quickly repositioned the woman's head correctly to save the remainder of his contribution. Norman sighed. Earlier he had wolfed down a stuffed burrito with hot sauce at a Taco Bell. Too bad it hadn't worked its way through him yet, it would have been a nice touch. It was too late anyway; the little bitch had already made her four minute trek into the great beyond—she was no longer around to appreciate any more of his thoughtful details.

When he finished dressing, he picked up his coat and pulled out his blond wig, fake mustache and rolled up fisherman's hat from his pockets and carefully donned them. One never knew what exterior cameras these apartments used. Norman retrieved the young woman's nylons from near the headboard—he had used them to strangle her—and brought them to his face, inhaling deeply of their scent. He shoved them in his pocket. They would be an excellent memento of the evening.

His Budget rental car was parked—leased under a fake name, of course—on the other side of the apartment complex. It was a beautiful night; the walk would do him good. Although he tried to be careful, he never worried too much about leaving trace physical evidence behind. As anyone who ever watched CSI or any of the myriad police shows knew, you could have all the print, hair, blood and DNA evidence you wanted, but if you had no one to compare them to you would be out of luck.

Norman had never been arrested for anything. He was not in any local, State, or Federal police databases, and he had no intention of running afoul of the law and having that happen. If it did, well, then the jig would be up, so to speak. Of course, there was that little stint in the mental hospital after Nicole's accident. There might be blood tests on record somewhere. But, if so, that was before DNA databases—plus his juvenile records would be sealed, even if there was a reason to check them.

And his little escapade tonight occurred in Bozeman, Montana, almost 1100 miles from his home base in Magdalena. He tried to spread out his conquests. This had been number twenty-seven, and they covered eight different states. Within the next day or so, the city of Bozeman would find they had a rather gruesome murder on their hands.

Norman stopped at the door and looked back at... Amy... Amy, that was her name, he remembered. The pretty blonde with the sexy legs would never have to worry again about going night-clubbing and hooking up with a guy. She had hooked up with her last one. Hooked up after she was dead, anyway, Norman chuckled. He blew a kiss at the pale body and walked out, locking the apartment door behind him. He headed out into the night; there were things to do, places to go, people to see.

And Norman had to catch a plane to Detroit.

# CHAPTER 18

Norman, aka Nicholas Bertrand, decided to try out an American Airlines Airbus A321 for his flight to Detroit. No matter what airline he was flying or who he was flying as, he always flew first class. What good was money if you didn't use it? With only two seats on each side of the wide aisle per row, there was plenty of elbow and leg room. A wide fold down armrest/divider separated the two seats. Each leather, swivel seat sported its own reading light, power-port for laptop connections, video screen for in-flight movies, and a Bose sound system with headphones. As an added bonus, there were only a dozen other people flying first class.

Norman was playing with the electronic reclining and adjustable lumbar systems when the blonde stewardess in the starched white blouse approached and addressed him. "I'm sorry sir, we'll be taxiing for takeoff in a minute. Please keep your seat in its upright position and fasten your seatbelt." She smiled pleasantly at Norman. "My name is Sally; I'll be your hostess during this flight. Shortly after takeoff I'll be taking your drink and dinner order. Would you like me to get you a duvet and pillow for later?"

Norman struggled to get his seat back to its upright position and fumbled with his seat belt, finally getting it secured on the third try. "Yes, ma'am… I mean… I'm sorry about the seat… and dinner sounds good, too." Norman couldn't look the stewardess in the eye and felt himself blushing. He was self-conscious and nervous around women. It was something he had learned to live with—up to a point. "Do you have a menu?" he mumbled, looking away from her smile and out the plane's window.

Sally leaned across the aisle seat—it was vacant—and pulled a small menu out of the leather pocket just below the video monitor on the seat in front of him. "Here you go, Mr. Bertrand. I highly recommend the salmon."

The woman's perfume and nearness sent a nervous jolt through Norman, startling him and causing him to jump. He took the menu from her. "Sorry… you surprised me… um… thank you… er… Sally," Norman stuttered, blushing again with a sheepish look.

Sally returned to the front of the plane where she and the other first class hostess, Miriam, finished up their preflight checklist. Having completed their tasks, they settled into their seats and buckled in. "Miriam, you see that guy sitting in A12 with the black polo shirt?" Sally asked.

Miriam looked towards the back. "Sure, how could you miss a handsome hunk like that? Is he some kind of athlete or actor?"

Sally laughed. "I don't think so. He's about the shyest, most timid guy I've run into in a long time. The guy wouldn't look at me and was blushing almost the whole time I was talking to him. What a combination, macho good looks and painfully shy. I'd like to know the story behind that."

After takeoff Norman took Sally's advice and ordered the smoked salmon with baked sweet potato and asparagus, adding a glass of wine upon her suggestion. He even splurged and ordered a piece of apple crisp with a scoop of ice cream for dessert. She brought him a soft blanket and pillow.

"Why don't you put your seat back and relax, Mr. Bertrand? If you fall asleep, I'll wake you when we're making our approach to Detroit," she said.

"Okay... um... Sally... that sounds good, and... ah... thank you for everything," he murmured, almost inaudibly. He reclined his seatback, adjusted the headrest, and pulled the duvet over him. Sally reached across again and helped him adjust the pillow behind his head. Her nearness made him giddy. He gulped involuntarily.

"There you go, Mr. Bertrand. Pleasant dreams."

Norman closed his eyes and imagined the pert young blond beneath his throttling hands, and what he would do to the temptress after she was dead.

*Little Normie peered through the wooden slats of the closet door into the well-lit bedroom. His Mommy— no, no, no, it was Nicole now he must remember—had adjusted the slats so he could see out. Normie rubbed his cheek, remembering the sharp slaps of her palm against his face whenever he forgot to call her Nicole. He didn't understand why he wasn't supposed to call her Mommy anymore.*

*And he must remember to watch his teeth when he was feeding. Mommy...
Nicole... said it hurt when he wasn't careful, and he needed to be careful.
Not only because it hurt when she hit him, but because he loved his Mommy
Nicole, loved the softness of her big chest—breasts she called them—and even
though there wasn't any milk anymore, he loved to suck and have her snuggle
his head to her. She said if he was careful, he'd never be too old.*

*He was six years old, a big boy now, and needed to start learning how
to do things. Normie squinted out into the dimly lit room and watched the
man walk up to the bed. He didn't have any clothes on. Neither did Mommy
Nicole, who was lying on the bed waiting for him, her legs spread apart. Both
had a patch of dark hair between their legs and the man had a pee-pee like
Normie, but his Mommy Nicole didn't. He would have to ask about that.*

*The man, one of Nicole's many friends, was doing things to her, playing
with her chest and the dark hair between her legs with his hand. He started
sucking on her chest like Normie did. Maybe he was trying to feed, too. He
must not know she didn't have milk any more. She was making moaning
sounds and Normie was becoming alarmed, except it didn't sound like a
hurting kind of moaning. He needed to pay attention to what the man was
doing, Nicole said. Normie had to learn how to do things right. But he
needed to be quiet while he was watching from the locked closet. Once, he had
made some noise while moving around in the large walk-in and she used the
Whiffle Ball Bat on him.*

*Normie hated the Whiffle Ball Bat. He thought that Mommy and him
would play games with the bat and ball when she brought it home from the
store. Instead, she used it to spank him when he was bad. And the hard,
hollow plastic bat really hurt bad when she hit him. So, he had to be quiet.
And he had to pay attention. She would kinda test him when the men left.
He had to learn where and how to touch her. He really didn't know what he*

*was doing, but he did know when he did things wrong cause she hurt him. And when he was really bad, she'd lock him in the closet after whipping him. She said when he was a little older it would just be him and her. She wouldn't need any other men, so he had to learn how to do things right.*

*Now the man was on top of his Mommy, moving up and down. Normie hoped he wasn't hurting her. Nicole said he'd be able to do things like that to her someday, but for now he just had to watch and learn. And when the men were gone, she'd show him herself, "hands-on," she'd laugh at him. He didn't know if he liked all these things, but he did know she'd hurt him if he didn't do them. Besides, he wanted to make her happy. Normie wanted his Mommy to love him—*

Norman squirmed in the plush seat of the Airbus. If only he could escape the dark, haunting memories, but there would never be freedom. The years passed slowly and agonizingly along the twisted, shadowed labyrinths of his tortured mind.

*Now he was sixteen, still spending much of his time in the bedroom closet. Norman hated her. Nicole used to be beautiful, but the men, alcohol and drugs made her ugly. And as the years passed and her mind deteriorated even further, she stopped taking care of herself. Her waist had thickened, her breasts and butt sagged, and her complexion became blotchy and sallow. She bathed infrequently, neglected her hair and hygiene. She smelled. None of her men friends had been around for a long time. Nicole said she didn't need them anymore because she had her little Normie.*

*Normie looked down at his dinner plate, his "processed" Chinese food still warm and foul. Tears filled and overflowed his eyes, coursing over his pale cheeks unnoticed. She still locked him in the closet. Their little single wide trailer afforded very few places that could be secured anymore. He doubted his dark little world could hold him if he truly wanted to get out—but he feared* her, feared what she would do to him. Nicole was his whole world now, all he knew. He knew nothing else.

Nicole used to read to him sometimes when he was little, but no more. Normie was never allowed to go outside the trailer anymore, either. When he was little, Nicole promised her Normie that he would be the only man in her life when he got older. She spoke the truth. It was just the two of them now. And she only wanted him to do stuff to her, with her, all the time. She never seemed to get enough and, even though Normie tried to do everything the way she wanted, whenever she wanted, sometimes it just wasn't right. It just didn't make her happy, and she would beat him with the Whiffle Ball Bat.

Nicole could never get enough of the sex stuff, and she kept acting crazier and crazier. Normie didn't get a say-so in anything—he was just supposed to do it. But last month she had brought him a "special" dinner. If he cleaned up his plate, she said, he could watch TV with her as his reward. His dinner was a glass of her urine and a plate of warm feces. Nicole cackled, something she had been doing even more of lately, giggling that it was a good steak dinner with a couple of beers—she had just "processed" it a little for him. Now, she managed a special processed dinner for him every week or so, plenty of variety too.

Normie was sitting cross-legged in front of the slatted door, looking out and waiting, his "dinner" sitting untouched next to him. He scooted back into the farthest corner of the big closet and waited. He wasn't hungry—yet. Normie didn't know what time it was, but he figured his Nicole would be coming for him soon. She would have him do things to her again and again, all the while hooting and cackling. Normie began sobbing. Part of him still wanted to do those things for his Mommy, just as much as he hated Nicole for making him do them. Love and hate, lust and loathing were a devastating whirlwind in Normie's sixteen-year-old mind. Normie curled up into a fetal position in the darkest corner and cried silently—waiting.

Sally sat down in the seat next to the moaning, sleeping man and began shaking him by the arm. Groaning and crying out loudly in his sleep, the handsome Mr. Bertrand had disturbed and alarmed the other passengers in first class. He was obviously in the grip of a powerful nightmare.

With a start, Norman opened his eyes and looked around him wildly, finally focusing on the concerned face of the stewardess next to him. He bolted upright and grabbed her hand resting on his arm, glaring at her. Sally flinched back and yanked her hand away. It wasn't so much the man's painful grasp, but the fire in his steel-gray eyes. Eyes that burned into her. Eyes that showed no shyness or timidity, only a feral, savage, uncontrollable need.

"I'm so... sorry, Mr.... Mr. Bertrand. You... were having a nightmare and yelling out... in your sleep," the flustered hostess stammered.

Norman looked away, closing his eyes and clenching his teeth in effort. When he looked back seconds later, sanity had regained a foothold and his expression had softened and regressed, his eyes now only a gray shadow of the madness of before. "I'm sorry... Miss... um... Sally... I was having... a... a... nightmare... and you startled me. I didn't mean... to scare you or... the passengers."

He was again the meek and subservient Norman in the presence of an intimidating and terrifying being—a woman. They would always dominate, abuse and terrify... unless they were dead. Norman had to remember, no sleeping on planes, trains—or anywhere publically—in the future.

Sally returned to the galley, still slightly shaken. Miriam was filling her cart for another round of drinks for the passengers. She glanced up at Sally. "Are you okay? Everything all right with the hunk in A12?" she asked.

"Yeah, he was just having a bad nightmare, a really bad one. When he woke up he had this crazy, wild look and grabbed my arm."

Miriam laughed. "Handsome and shy, wild and crazy. What a combo. You going to put the moves on the guy?"

Sally wasn't smiling. She stared back down the aisle and shivered. "Not a good wild and crazy, more like an insane wild and crazy. Looks aren't everything. I think I'll pass on this one."

Miriam followed her friend's gaze to the man in A12. That had to have been one helluva nightmare, she thought.

After the plane landed, Norman grabbed his carry-on bag from the overhead compartment and joined the other passengers making their way along the aisle. Sally, another stewardess and one of the pilots stood by the exit, bidding the passengers farewell as they deplaned. "Thank you for flying American, have a wonderful day," they chorused, pleasantly out of sync, smiling and nodding as the passengers exited.

As Norman passed them he looked away and mumbled his thank you, but not before he saw Sally's awkward smile and her own averted eyes. Norman was mentally fuming. He would have to be a more careful in public—especially around women—no matter how difficult it was. It was easier to just avoid them when possible unless he was ready to exercise his ultimate power over them.

Norman walked briskly down the concourse follo,
the posted directions to the baggage pickup, mentally runnin₂
through his immediate itinerary. He'd get his luggage, pick up
his rental car at the Avis counter, and check into his room at
the Hyatt. Maybe he'd still have time to scout out Ryan's home.
He slowed his pace when he came to a restaurant along the concourse, Diego's Mexican Cantina. Norman found it highly im-
probable that the Hispanic food in Detroit was as good as back
home, but the idea of finding out was making his mouth water.
He briefly debated about stopping and grabbing something to
eat, but the thought of getting things squared away and his visit
to Ryan won out. Norman picked up his pace again. There would
be time for other Mexican restaurants.

# Chapter 19

Ryan sat on the edge of her bed staring at her suitcases. It wasn't even noon yet and her plane didn't leave until six, but she had been filled with nervous energy all morning. She had to switch planes in Chicago, but gaining a time zone flying west would still put her in Albuquerque by 10:30 pm. She was packed and ready.

Ryan had cleared her desk at Madigan's, catching up on all her neglected paperwork. Lonnie said she was good to go; he could easily hold the fort for two weeks or so. Maria, who rented an apartment on the East Side, had happily agreed to house-sit for Ryan—watering her plants, overseeing the yard work, cleaning and dusting. Having someone in the house while she was in New Mexico furnished Ryan with peace of mind. She had already dropped off the keys to Maria the night prior.

Ryan leaned forward, resting her elbows on her legs, her head in her hands. Guilt and its related depression had blanketed her. She hadn't told Jack she was leaving, and an unusual confusion gripped her. Ryan had used her friend, as she did anyone when necessary, to accomplish her ends. But she didn't want to take a chance on him doing anything further that might get him into trouble. Besides, he would try to talk her out of it, and want the police to handle it somehow. Even if they did find the maniac, the legal system would let him slide with an insanity plea, and he'd be allowed to spend the rest of his days in an institution, getting his three square meals a day, blissfully medicated at the taxpayer's expense. Well, Ryan would spare the people that expense. She would make sure justice for the killer was a little more painful—and final.

Jack was going to be very disappointed in her for running out on him, for not at least including him in her plans, even if he disagreed with her. But her two main reasons were still valid: she did not want him to get into any trouble, and she didn't want him to interfere or try to stop her in any way. His impending disillusionment bothered her; it bothered her more than she liked to admit. Ryan couldn't remember the last person whose displeasure in her had been more than a temporary blip on the radar of her life. Her parents when she had left home, of course. And Dana. Dana hadn't been happy when Ryan had struck out on her own. As for others, she usually didn't give a damn, not for very long anyway.

Maybe she should call him. He couldn't do much now; he would understand. No, he wouldn't Ryan realized. He was a cop. For Jack, that took precedence over everything else. Still, she couldn't stop thinking of the hurt and disappointment she would cause by leaving without a word of warning or explanation. Hell, now she worried about hurting him, as well as disappointing him. What was going on here?

She tried to block it from her mind. She wanted a cigarette. Ryan jumped to her feet and walked down the hall to the kitchen. She fumbled around in the junk drawer until she came up with a stray swizzle stick. She put the hard plastic straw in her mouth and gnawed at it. Not very feminine, she thought, but better than a cigarette.

Ryan glanced at her wall clock. Screw it; she'd call him. He wouldn't be happy, but it was better than just disappearing on him. She grabbed the wall phone and called his cell. Jack had finally given up his land-line to keep "technologically current," as well as reasoning that he was never home much, anyway. After six rings it went to his voice mail. Strange, she thought, he was technically on call 24-7 with the Department. She disconnected and dialed his number at the P.D. It was answered by a Corporal Mulky.

"Yes, Mr.... I mean Corporal Mulky, may I speak to Sergeant Kroner? My name is Ryan Sanders, I'm a friend of his."

"I'm sorry, Ms. Sanders, Sergeant Kroner is on vacation; he'll be gone for the next two weeks. Can I take a message?"

Ryan was stunned. All she could manage was, "Vacation?"

It sounded as if the corporal was trying to stifle a laugh on the other end of the line. "Would you believe he entered a big chess tournament up on Mackinaw Island? I think that's where they were holding it, anyway."

"Chess tournament?" Ryan was still behind the curve.

"Yeah, you know how those crazy Russians are. Chess is part of their genetic makeup."

"Yes... yes, that's true. I'll try calling him on his cell." She slowly hung up the phone. Ryan's mind was grappling with the information. Jack was an excellent chess player and occasionally entered tournaments, doing well in several. With a point rating of over 2100, he had an Expert ranking with the U.S. Chess Federation. Maybe chess was in the genetics of Russians.

But Jack had never mentioned the upcoming tournament to her. She couldn't believe he hadn't told her. And even worse, his omission hurt. Yes, Jack could be enigmatic at times, the rare man that Ryan sometimes had trouble figuring out. He was, after all, one of the oddest ethnic mixtures that she'd ever come across. His grandmother was a Native American, his grandfather Russian—Ukrainian, actually. Definitely an unusual heritage, details of which she would be interested in hearing one day. But no excuse would mitigate the disappointment she felt. And here she had been worrying about hurting him.

Ryan yanked open the refrigerator door in frustration, looking for something to appease her oral fixation; she would not succumb to temptation and have a cigarette. She spotted a pitcher of iced tea and set it on the counter. It sounded good on a hot day and she could chew on the ice. Ryan poured herself a glass and headed out her patio door onto her shaded veranda, plopping down in the cushioned chair by her glass-topped patio table. Ryan looked approvingly at her gas barbeque sitting next to the brick wall of the house in all its black and chrome glory. She'd only used it two or three times so far, but it had been on sale at the local Wal-Mart, as had her patio set, and she couldn't pass up a good deal.

Ryan absently fingered the single strand of expensive silver pearls circling her slim neck. The valuable South Sea cultured pearls had been a gift from Jackson Bederman, her first sponsor. Ryan also had a matching string of gold pearls. He was the CEO for Cyntex Technologies, a not unattractive middle-age executive with a rocky marriage and a severe midlife crisis. He had enjoyed showering his beautiful consort with gifts, and Ryan, in return, made Mr. Bederman feel as if he were the most virile and important man in the world.

The incongruity of the pearls and the inexpensive barbeque were, for all practical purposes, lost on Ryan. It was just not something that occupied her thoughts. That she had used an amoral life of relative opulence to intentionally achieve a life of less abundance would seem backwards to most, but not to her. Ryan was a pragmatist. She knew what she wanted; she just used an unusual and novel way of getting there. Ryan beamed with pride at her barbeque as she fingered the pearls.

She should ask Lonnie and Maria over one afternoon for a cookout. Maybe Jack... Ryan frowned; she was still pissed off at him. And the heat and humidity were not making her mood any better. She was in the shade of the patio overhang, but it wasn't helping much. Ryan figured the temperature had to be around eighty-five degrees, but the worst part was the humidity. She guessed it was as high as the temperature; it was like being in a steam bath. As if to emphasize the point, a bead of perspiration trickled its way down her chest between her breasts. Her formerly crisp, lavender blouse was sticking damply to her. And her belled, black slacks and color coordinated lavender high heels were becoming increasingly uncomfortable.

Ryan's backyard was beautifully landscaped with a green expanse of manicured lawn, populated by two large oak trees and several smaller poplars, the perimeter nicely balanced by blooming shrubs and a variety of rose bushes. Everything was green and lush. Even her shed in the back corner of the yard had a neatly cultivated border of brightly hued flowers surrounding it.

Huey, a shy fifteen-year-old who lived at the end of the court, took care of mowing the lawn. But Ryan had splurged and had a company, with the imaginative name of "The Lawn Ranger Landscaping Company," come in twice a month to do trimming, pruning and whatever else they did to keep things green and growing.

Usually the scene brought a sense of serenity to Ryan. Today the green abundance, sweltering in the bright noonday sun, brought to mind a tropical rain forest. She imagined that her long, waved and curled hair was gradually straightening in the humidity. Ryan wasn't a masochist. She opted for a hasty retreat into her air-conditioned house until it was time to leave.

Although the cool interior of her kitchen was a blessing, her mood didn't measurably improve. Ryan was back to thinking about going on a "search and seizure" mission for a cigarette when the doorbell rang. Just what she needed, a couple of Mormons or Jehovah Witnesses wanting to convert her. What the hell were they doing out on a day like this? These had to be true believers, but Ryan was way too edgy to be discussing theology with anyone at the moment.

She took a deep breath and composed herself, formulating a polite but firm excuse as to why she didn't have time to talk to them. She'd be gracious and accept their pamphlets and that would be that. Ryan opened the door armed and ready to deliver her polite spiel and stood face to face with—Jack Kroner. She froze, her mouth slack, her mind blank.

Her grinning friend looked at her expectantly. "Are you packed and ready? I figured we could grab a bite to eat on the way to the airport. Maybe talk over our battle plans. We have until six." Jack's eyebrows raised in a questioning look.

All Ryan could think of was that she was suffering from early onset Alzheimer's, probably a world record at the age of twenty-eight. Had she completely forgotten something? She continued to stare, mouth open. Finally she managed to blurt out, "Jack... the chess tournament... what are you doing here? Why didn't you tell me?" Realizing she had things out of order, she started again. "I mean... how did you know I was... leaving... I mean flying...? I'm sorry I didn't..." Ryan's questions finally ground to a halt. She wasn't sure what the right order was, or even how to proceed.

Jack decided to show mercy. "I knew you weren't being entirely straight with me, so I wasn't too surprised when Lonnie called me the other day with your plans. A couple of calls to the TSA and Southwest Airlines confirmed the rest. The hard part was getting the vacation approved. I didn't have time to go through the Department's contractually sanctioned procedure with the City. The Lieutenant wasn't too happy with me. But here I am, so all's well that ends well." Jack paused, looking at her. "Is it okay if I come in, or should I continue talking from here? It's hotter than hell out." He was wearing a short-sleeve, blue chambray shirt and blue jeans, but seemed crisp and fresh in the hot sun. He didn't appear uncomfortable at all.

Ryan finally regained her power of speech. "Yes, of course, Jack." She stepped back and moved out of the way as he brushed by her in a draft of warm air.

Jack was talking again before he even made it to the living room. "Of course, in conversations with a couple of the more talkative officers, I alluded to competing in a chess tournament up in Mackinaw. I figured nobody would believe me if I said I was flying off with a crazy woman in search of a suspected but unknown serial killer, information on said mystery killer received by the crazy lady's dead sister—post mortem, no less."

Ryan began, "Jack, I'm sorry but—"

The big man put up his hand and stopped her. He wasn't smiling now. "You are not going by yourself. I am going with you. We'll worry about what to do when and if we find him. And I'll be pissed off for a long time for your not telling me. End of discussion. Now, where are your suitcases? I'm driving."

Ryan's mind was swirling with emotion. Should she object, protest, argue? Would it do any good? Would she even want it to do any good? All she could manage in the way of a feigned protest was a frown. "They're in the bedroom on the floor next to the bed," she conceded.

Jack returned her frown and headed for her room.

The realization she was relieved, and glad that Jack was going, made it impossible for her to keep her smile to herself, but she managed to suppress her budding grin until his broad shoulders were disappearing down the hall. Ryan didn't want the big lug to get a swelled head.

# Chapter 20

Jack finished loading their luggage into the back of his maroon Ford Escape. He hadn't purchased the Hybrid model; he figured buying the smaller SUV in lieu of the larger versions was enough of a concession to the environmentalists. Both Jack and Ryan piled in, Jack firing up the engine to get the air conditioning going.

"I see we're flying Southwest Airlines," Jack said. "I suppose that's because we're flying to New Mexico; they kind of go together, don't they? By the way, I was lucky to get a seat at the last minute."

Ryan gave him a sideways glance, ignoring the last comment. "True. Plus, they don't charge for your luggage. I couldn't see paying the extra cost in baggage fees that the other airlines charge. And since you volunteered to drive, head on over to Valet Connections in Taylor; it's on Sibley near Northline. We can leave your car there—it's only thirty-five dollars a week—and their shuttle will take us to the airport."

Jack just shook his head. He would never understand this woman. He pulled out of her driveway and headed towards the neighboring city of Taylor.

The drive to the airport was accomplished in relative silence. Both Ryan and Jack wanted to maintain an air of righteous indignation at the perceived subterfuge of the other, although in reality, both were happy with the final outcome. But neither wanted to give the other the satisfaction of knowing that fact.

Even after parking at the Valet Connection, getting ferried to the airport and checking their bags, they still had over two hours to go before their plane departed. Jack suggested they give Diego's Mexican Cantina at the airport a shot, on the theory they might as well familiarize their stomachs with a little Southwestern cuisine.

After being seated, their waitress arrived to take their drink orders. "Just water and an iced tea for me, please," Ryan said.

Jack leaned back in his seat and sighed. "I'll have whatever lite beer you have on tap, in the biggest serving glass permissible," he added.

The waitress jotted down their orders on her pad. "Coming right up, iced tea and a really big beer." She was smiling and didn't seem perturbed at all with Jack's request.

Ryan couldn't help but grin herself. She remembered that Jack didn't like planes. No matter what the safety statistics in comparison with other modes of travel, he was the tense, white-knuckled, armrest-gripping, teeth-clenched, eyes-shut air traveler when the plane was taking off and landing. Jack would relax somewhat when they gained cruising altitude.

The only explanation he could give was his feeling of helplessness, the complete loss of control or response in the event of an "accident." In a car mishap he could maneuver to avoid it, or at least minimize its potential seriousness. If a ship sank, even if he missed the life boats, Jack could at least swim. If his plane dropped out of the sky from 35,000 feet, there was nothing that Jack could do to prevent it—or to change the inevitable outcome. It was this feeling of being potentially powerless in a crisis that bothered him. He didn't like it. Ryan actually felt flattered that Jack would subject himself to this anxiety just for her.

The waitress returned after a few minutes. "Ready to order?" she asked.

Ryan was feeling adventuresome. "I'll have the chili relleno with the Spanish rice and refried beans."

Both women looked at Jack expectantly; he was still studying his menu. He glanced from one to the other self-consciously. "I guess I'll just have the burrito and—"

Ryan interrupted, "Make that two orders of the chili rellenos."

Jack opened his mouth to protest but Ryan cut him off again. "You can get a burrito at a Taco Bell, Jack. If you're going on this trip, it's time to get authentic and order something appropriate. You know, 'When in Rome...'." Ryan pulled the menu from his hand and gave them both back to the waitress who was attempting to stifle a laugh.

"A very good choice; the rellenos are excellent," the waitress said. The young woman headed off towards the kitchen with their orders.

"I don't even know what a relleno is," Jack grumbled, frowning.

"It's a poblano pepper, stuffed with melted cheese and diced pork, covered in an egg batter and deep fried. Or so the menu said," Ryan explained.

"Damn, there goes my cholesterol. I can feel my arteries hardening already," Jack griped.

"Relax and get used to it," Ryan said. "From what I understand, the Hispanics deep fry everything in New Mexico. Lonnie, who is younger than you, is dating Maria now. If he sticks with her, I bet his arteries turn to cement before yours do."

"Maria?"

"Yeah, the hot little Latina number that fights out of our gym. Lonnie is going to make her an MMA superstar. She's good enough, too. Maria's mastered Brazilian Jujitsu and Muay Thai and she's as quick as a cobra."

"You're pretty good yourself," Jack volunteered.

"Thanks, pal. But, assuming I had the talent, I don't have the desire or the heart to devote the time necessary to make a career out of it. Besides, I wouldn't want to take the chance of having my pretty face messed up or my body scarred. You never know when I might have to fall back on them. I don't think I'd look good with a crooked nose or cauliflower ears."

Ryan noticed his expression. "I was joking, Jack, I'm not going back to the old days. That's not what I want. I'm satisfied with where I am now."

"Where is your head at Ryan, and what is it you want?" he asked quietly.

Jack's question caught her off guard, so she mulled it over for several long seconds. She guessed he could be referring to her state of mind in general, future life goals, or wants and desires. But more likely his concern was with the current state of affairs. Ryan decided it was time to be a little more pragmatic and upfront. They needed to keep focused on the task at hand. Jack deserved that.

"I'm sorry for not telling you I was leaving, and even sorrier that I used you to get information," she replied after several long seconds. "I don't want to cause you any trouble, and I don't want you any more involved than you already are." They paused as the waitress placed a bowl of tortilla chips and salsa on the table along with their drinks. Ryan took a chip and dipped up a scoop of salsa and managed to get it into her mouth without dripping any on the table. Ryan paused and wiped her mouth deftly with her napkin.

She decided to be blunt. "I will find the bastard who killed my sister and those other women. And then I will kill him. Slowly. I know that's not how a cop would handle it, preferring to arrest the bad guy, bring him before a judge and jury of his peers, and have him sentenced to prison. Or in this case, probably a psychiatric institution for the rest of his life, not because he's a depraved, homicidal maniac but—according to some smartass attorney—an unfortunate victim of parental abuse, and therefore couldn't be blamed for his actions. Sorry, my friend, that's not what I have planned."

As she talked she had leaned forward, voice rising, eyes catching fire. Several people nearby had turned to look. "Revenge.

That's where I'm at and that's what I want," she finished, glaring at him.

Jack just looked at her, waiting for the steam to run out of his friend. When Ryan leaned back, slightly flushed, he decided it was his turn. "For my part, I'm sorry that I pulled that little last minute charade, but you deserved it. Besides, I'm not letting you run off cross country on your own looking for a killer, no matter how tough you think you are. And I won't let you ruin your life by taking the law into your own hands and executing him in revenge, no matter how much the monster deserves it."

They both had another chip and salsa. "We'll be at an impasse—a Mexican standoff—when the time comes, I guess," Ryan said. She looked at Jack thoughtfully. "Like you said, we'll have to cross that bridge when we come to it, assuming we ever find this guy."

They were sitting at a table in Diego's with a view of the North Terminal Concourse of the Detroit Metropolitan Airport. If Ryan and Jack had glanced out the window at that moment they would have seen a handsome, dark-haired young man walking by with his carryon, heading for the baggage claim area. Jack would have noticed that he greatly resembled the police sketch that Officer Adams had drawn. Ryan would have recognized him as the brutal killer of her visions and dreams.

"These rolleno thingies are pretty good," Jack said between bites.

Ryan smiled. "See Jack, you just have to get out of your comfort zone once in a while and try something new."

He finished and pushed his plate to the side, making more room for his pint-sized glass of Bud Lite. "I should have gotten a shot of whiskey to go with this."

"Relax, Jack, you'll be fine."

"So where are we going to be staying in Albuquerque?" he asked, changing the subject.

"I don't know where you'll be staying, but I'm booked at a Comfort Inn near the airport."

Jack just stared at her with raised eyebrows.

Ryan rummaged in her purse and pulled out her IPhone. A few taps on the screen and she handed it to Jack. "Go ahead, you can call from my phone. You know, of course, that this last minute stuff is going to be more expensive."

Jack frowned and took the phone. She had pulled up information on her motel, including its toll-free phone number. He punched in the digits and several long seconds later had someone from the motel on the line. "I need a room, a single, for..." he gave Ryan a questioning look, and she responded by raising two raised fingers... "two weeks, please. Arriving tonight, and I'd prefer my room next to, or near, room number..." again he looked across at Ryan.

Ryan laughed. "Room 117, Jack."

He relayed the information, paused for several seconds, waiting. "Room 119 would be fine, thank you. Hold on..." Jack pulled out his wallet and fumbled for a credit card. As he recited the information necessary for the reservation, Ryan's mind wandered.

They had to switch planes in Chicago, a short one hour delay, then on to Albuquerque. They were scheduled to arrive at 10:25

pm. After picking up their rental car and checking in at the motel, it would be too late to do any reconnoitering. Ryan glanced up at a wall clock tucked between two gaudy sombreros. The décor of the restaurant left a lot to be desired. They still had a good forty-five minutes before their flight boarded, and their terminal was only a five-minute walk away. It wouldn't hurt to go over their plan of attack for the next few days.

Jack had finished and disconnected, pushing Ryan's phone back across the table to her. "There, all set."

"Okay, let's go over our game plan," she said.

Jack wasn't smiling. "It's your gig. At least for now."

Ryan chose to ignore his somber demeanor. "Since we'll be in Albuquerque—the largest city on our list—we might as well start there. If we strike out, we'll move on to Las Cruces and Santa Fe, the next largest cities. I figure by the time we get checked in tonight we'll be pretty whipped. Tomorrow, after a good night's sleep we'll do what you suggested before, and dig through the records for an unusual event occurring ten to fifteen years ago; something that could conceivably be tied to the specific types of murders you've found in surrounding states. Does that about cover it? Time frame about right?"

"Yes. Hopefully, that would allow for the time between the event and the beginning of the homicides," Jack replied. "But determining the onset could be a problem, depending on how many bodies, if any, were never discovered during that initial period. Our timeline could really be thrown off."

Ryan frowned. "You're a real joy. Think positive. It will be difficult enough just going through that five year time period looking for... well... I'm not sure what we're looking for, but we'll find it. Tomorrow, you can drop me off at the main library, and you can go over to the County and Federal courthouses. A fun day of research."

She forced a smile as a busboy came and cleared their table. No sooner had he departed than their waitress appeared. "Anything else I can get you folks?" she added cheerily.

"I'm all set," Ryan replied. She eyed Jack and then his beer.

He held up his hand. "I'm good."

Their waitress placed their bill on the table. "I'll take it to the register whenever you're ready."

"We're ready," Ryan said.

# CHAPTER 21

Their scheduled layover in Chicago morphed from an hour into almost two, due to an unknown maintenance snafu with the plane. Ryan took this minor setback stoically; better safe than sorry, she figured. For Jack, the delay was a little more problematic. He had made it through the first leg of their journey—a one hour hop from Detroit to Chicago—with only one further fortifying shot of alcohol. Unfortunately, the connecting plane's mechanical glitch turned him into a nervous wreck. He continued to stew over what the problem might be and what mid-air disaster it might cause if not properly repaired. Ryan figured her friend would be blotto by the time they arrived in Albuquerque. She thought it was kind of cute, a big macho man reduced to a fidgeting, powerless bystander.

American Airlines flight 1116 finally passed inspection and Jack and Ryan boarded along with the other passengers, many of whom were in various stages of righteous indignation. The jet taxied down the runway, abruptly shot forward and accelerated towards liftoff speed until its wheels gently parted ways with terra firma.

Jack had a death grip on the armrests—head back, eyes closed. Ryan no longer thought it was so cute. In fact, an unexpected wave of concern and empathy washed over her. She covered his hand with hers and squeezed gently. He opened his eyes and turned his head, smiling at her weakly before returning to his former position. But he released his hold on the armrest and clasped her hand tightly in exchange. Ryan just hoped he didn't squeeze suddenly in his anxiety; he would probably crush her hand.

Much to Ryan's surprise Jack rose to the occasion, surviving the remainder of his white-knuckle flight without drinking himself completely into oblivion, although she decided that she'd be the one driving the rental car when they landed.

It was after sundown when they finally made their approach to the Albuquerque Sunport. The lights of the city spread out below them, thousands of twinkling diamonds scattered by the haphazard hand of a giant. To the east of the city the horizon was blocked by the darker shadow of the Sandia Mountains rising from the desert floor.

As they swooped in for the landing Jack was back to holding Ryan's hand in a death grip. Fortunately, a couple of stiff whiskey and waters in route had eased his stress to the point where he wasn't crushing any of her bones.

They deplaned and made their way into the airport. Although Ryan was carrying her purse in one hand and Jack had a small duffle bag in his, their free hands were still clasped together. She was surprised at the pleasant feeling the simple act of holding hands brought her.

Ryan couldn't remember the last time she had just held hands with a man. There was that boy, Henry McIntyre, back in the ninth grade at La Mirada High who liked to hold hands. Ryan remembered the secure feeling that this unpretentious gesture had engendered, and the pride she felt showing everyone around school she had a boyfriend as they sauntered around together hand in hand. Of course, it wasn't long before Ryan realized that boys, and men for that matter, were drawn to her like metal to a magnet. She wondered whatever had happened to Henry....

Jack stopped and was looking around the immediate area. He found what he was searching for and released her hand. "I have to use the restroom; I've been holding it ever since we left Chicago. I'll be right back."

Ryan watched him go, smiling and shaking her head in wonder. The big guy wasn't even comfortable using the cramped restroom on the plane. She was even more flattered that he had insisted on coming with her. She looked at her now freed hand, frowning....

When he returned, they made their way to the baggage carousel, gathered their luggage, and headed over to the Avis counter to pick up their rental car. It was after 10:45 p.m., and the young man at the service desk was on the home stretch of his shift. He appeared bored and tired, but when he saw Ryan stroll up, his expression changed and he managed a smile. "Yes, may I help you?" And he was, indeed, a professional. When Jack brought up the rear a second later with their luggage, his expression dimmed only slightly.

Ryan glanced at the man's name tag. "Yes, Richard, I'm Ryan Sanders. I have a reservation for a Ford Escape SUV." Despite the long day, she still looked fresh and dazzling, her expression warm and appealing.

The clerk's gaze lingered on her appreciatively for a second longer before he began tapping away on the keyboard of his computer. Richard's face lit up as he scanned the screen. "Ah, yes, Ms. Sanders, just a little paperwork and you'll be good to go." He was grinning like an underpaid employee who had just received an unexpected bonus. He pulled out several forms from behind the counter.

Jack had been watching with a wry expression. "An SUV? I would think a Vette, BMW or something else sporty would be more your speed or, considering your thriftiness, maybe a Cooper, or some other compact. And you got one with a GPS, right?"

Ryan grimaced, deciding to ignore his slightly sarcastic and condescending tone. "You must be getting tired, Jack. Use the ol' noggin; we're in the desert now. I think the Escape might be a little more practical. And yes on the GPS."

Richard chuckled. "A wise choice, Ms. Sanders, very good. I can see you're—"

Both Ryan and Jack turned and stared at him.

The man's eyes retreated and looked down, suddenly interested in the paperwork on the counter. "Er... yes... if you'd just sign a couple of forms here, we'll get you on your way," he said, slightly flustered. He sensed he had crossed an invisible line, and it would be best for him to move on.

With keys and luggage in hand, the two caught the Avis bus over to their car lot. Once settled in for the short hop to the rental area, Jack volunteered, "Ryan, I'm sorry for the comments on the cars. I'm just tired, probably an adrenalin crash from the flight."

Ryan just slid down in her seat, closed her eyes and unconsciously laid her head on his shoulder. "Not to worry big guy. It's been a long day for both of us. We'll be as good as new in the morning."

Once in possession of their rental car and on the road, Ryan plugged the Comfort Inn's address into the vehicle's GPS and within forty-five minutes they had arrived, registered and had rolled their luggage to their rooms on one of the motel's baggage carriers. Their rooms were next to each other on the ground floor. Jack carried Ryan's two modestly sized suit cases into her room, glad she wasn't one of those women who packed half their belongings for a trip, no matter what the duration.

"Okay, breakfast is between six and nine. I'll come and get you around eight?" Jack asked.

"Sounds good." Ryan looked at him gratefully. "And thank you for being here. It means a lot to me." She stepped forward, leaned up and kissed him gently on the cheek. "I'll see you in the morning."

Jack left and wheeled his suitcases down one door. He stopped and looked back at her room. He unconsciously touched his cheek, a bemused look on his face.

# CHAPTER 22

Norman used his trusty Garmin GPS to find Ryan's address. It had accompanied him on his flight from Montana and was now plugged into the power outlet of his 2013 Chevrolet Impala rental—he didn't want to appear too ostentatious in his choice of cars. Of course, it was Nicholas Franklin Bertram who had purchased the airline tickets in Butte and rented the car in Detroit.

Norman had adopted the Nicholas moniker within a year of being released from the Fort Bayard Medical Center back in '02. He had several other bogus identities when the need arose, but Nicholas would do for this trip. Besides, he liked that particular one; it had the same initials as his real name. It never ceased to amaze him at what money could buy. New identities were not that difficult to obtain, once you found the right people for the job. And when you explored the underbelly of society, lifted and looked under rocks to see what crawled out—well, his horizons had expanded and things became even more interesting. Life was good.

Norman Frederick Bartholomew, aka Nicholas Franklin Bertrand, drove by the Sanders residence for the second time since early evening—no lights on, no car in the driveway. He was almost certain she wasn't home. But that was it for the drive-bys, though. Ryan lived on Pine Court, and the same car looping the cul-de-sac too often might arouse suspicion.

He turned onto Saddlewood, drove another two blocks and pulled over to the curb. Norman dialed her number on the disposable Wal-Mart phone he'd purchased that morning. After four rings, her voice mail picked up and Norman disconnected. He donned his custom made blond wig, mustache and horn-rimmed glasses before tugging on his Detroit Tigers baseball cap. He exited his car and walked back to her house.

Boldly walking up her sidewalk to the front door, he rang the doorbell. He could hear its pleasant chimes whispering inside the house. There was no answer. He knocked firmly several more times. Still no answer, and as a welcome bonus no barking dogs either. Norman had a simple and straightforward story should the woman actually be inside the darkened home and answer the door. He'd say he was looking for the Peterson residence at 104 Oak Court and the closest he could find was her 102 address. Of course, Oak Court was two streets north, and after apologizing profusely for his error, he'd thank her for her directions and take his leave. Or maybe, he would just force his way in and take her; his anticipation had been building inexorably.

Norman turned and looked up and down the street. Seeing no one, he started retracing his steps along the walkway, then turned to the right and hurried to the corner of the house—the

Dogwood trees obscuring his route. He stayed next to the wall and carefully made his way in the dark along the side of the house to the chain-link fence surrounding the backyard. The gate was on the opposite side, but Norman easily vaulted over the ineffectual barrier. He paused, the ambient lighting from the street lights and neighboring houses allowing little illumination of Ryan's large backyard. Norman tried to dampen his rising anxiety as he strained to see into the confusing shadows of dark on dark.

He waited a full minute, listening for any breaks in the silence of the evening. Neither the neighbor's houses to the side or the one to the rear bordered too closely. These were nice-sized, older residential spreads, not the small city lots or the newer, get-the-most-bang-for-the-buck cookie cutter suburban developments.

He crouched, his back resting on the brick surface of the home, listening to the night sounds, and trying to detect any change that might be a result of his passage. Several dogs in the distance exchanging their evening barks and yaps, the occasional faint sighing of vehicles on Ridgecrest—the semi-busy thoroughfare to the east—and the gentle rustling of leaves in the trees in Ryan's backyard, remained unchanged.

Norman was distracted by an annoying buzzing around his ear. He waved the mosquito away, swatted at one that had landed on his other hand, followed by the squashing of still another that was drawing blood from his forearm. He wiped the bloody smear off on his dark blue t-shirt. "Fucking mosquitos," he muttered. They were nearly nonexistent in the high, dry climate of his native New Mexico. But the wet, spring breeding grounds common in Michigan made for a flourishing population of the parasitic insects during the summer. The little bloodsuckers were out in droves on this humid August evening, and Ryan's grassy backyard and lush landscaping multiplied their presence.

He stood and made his way to the rear patio, staying in the shadows of the house, and swatting at his torturers as he crept. A sliding glass door, with interior curtains drawn, fronted the patio. Around the corner of the house was another door. Norman quickly checked this one, assuming it lead to a utility room. Norman's luck held—the storm door was unlocked. He surveyed the interior door: solid wood and dead-bolted, but with four small panes of glass at eye height. Not very security conscious, he mused.

Out "jogging" yesterday morning, he had looped the court and couldn't see any alarm boxes on either side of the house. And no cameras. There were no signs or decals on or around the home warning: "This house protected by…" It was an older house in an older neighborhood, but if he found an alarm keypad mounted inside, he'd be beating a hasty retreat.

He surveyed the rear wall of the home in the faint ambient light—no alarm box. He smiled in the darkness; the residents must figure it to be a safe suburban neighborhood, he concluded. That perception would change dramatically after tonight, of course.

Norman located the requisite domestic gas barbeque not far from a nearby patio table and chairs and, after a little searching in the dimness, located a thick oven mitt. He completed his search by grabbing a cushion off a chair before returning to the side door. He carefully placed the seat cushion over the glass panes and gave a sharp punch in the lower right corner, listening with satisfaction at the faint sounds of broken glass shattering on the interior floor. Norman threw the pad aside and cleaned off the glass shards still lodged in the pane's sill with his gloved hand. He discarded the mitt, stood on his toes and reached in and down with his long arm, fumbling, finding and unlatching the deadbolt.

Norman stood for several seconds listening to the night. Satisfied that nothing had changed in the neighborhood's audible flow of the evening, he opened the door and entered. Again he paused. The house, insulated from the exterior lights and sound, was darker and more silent than the night that surrounded it. He waited, listening, as the seconds passed, but could detect nothing moving in the home except him. As the silence deepened, he removed a small penlight from his pocket and turned it on, careful not to inadvertently point it at any windows. He noticed that the drapes and blinds were all drawn.

Norman made his way carefully and silently through the kitchen and small dining alcove, a larger dining room and adjoining living area, and finally to a hallway leading to the bedrooms and bathroom. A cursory look into the large spare bedroom on the left revealed that it had been converted into a combination office/exercise room. A treadmill and a Bowflex exercise machine sat opposite a large, roll-top desk and two small wooden file cabinets. Farther along the hall on the left was another, smaller bedroom. Norman concluded that its neatness and sparse furnishings pointed to its use as a guest bedroom. A bathroom was at the end of the hallway.

The only room on the right was the expansive master bedroom and bath. Nothing too much out of the ordinary here—a bureau, dresser with mirror, a bookcase, curio cabinet, and a king-sized bed with two nightstands, made up the primary décor. There were paintings hanging on the walls, but Norman was more interested in rummaging through the bureau drawers. In short order he had found what he was looking for—Ryan's lingerie. One whole drawer, filled with her bras, panties, nylons and garter belts. His heart thundered in his chest as he explored the lacy items, running their sheer fabric over his face, breathing in their memories....

So engrossed was Norman with his sordid fantasies he failed to hear the car pull into the driveway. But fortunately for him he heard the slam of the car doors. In two long strides he was at the widow and, with his finger creating a slit in the curtains to peek, tried to see the car in question. He glimpsed two shadows disappearing from sight in route to the front door. Damn, he thought; he had been so fixated on his plans for Ryan that he hadn't even considered that she might not be alone.

Norman ducked out into the hallway and slid along the wall until he came to the living room. He stopped; the front door had not yet opened. Back pressed to the wall, he mentally ran through his options. If he acted quickly, he could get out the back door and make good his escape. If he stayed he would have to kill whoever had accompanied Ryan. Norman knew cutting his losses and leaving was his safest option, but his blood was boiling and hammering in his veins, his thoughts ricocheting in his head like a pinball machine. Thoughts of what he'd soon be doing to Nicole... er... Ryan, he amended, were overpowering his common sense. He grinned maniacally in the dark—they were all one and the same. Norman stood rooted to the spot, waiting.

There was the sound of the front door opening, and a woman's voice speaking to someone. "I'll see you tomorrow at the gym, Lonnie. And yes, dinner Friday night at Scallos' is definitely a go." A male voice replied from farther away, but Norman couldn't make out the words. Laughter in response from the woman. Then, "Patience, Lonnie, patience. Play your cards right and there just might be a breakfast in bed for you Saturday morning." Another light, feminine laugh from the woman. "Maybe even a little food later on." More fading, unintelligible words followed by more laughter from both of them. Norman gritted his teeth, his jaw muscles working. He was glad he'd soon be punching Ryan's ticket. The man-eating bitch wouldn't be screwing any more men after tonight.

He started at the sound of the front door shutting and the deadbolt being thrown. A second later the living room flooded with light, and Norman inched back from the corner into the still sheltering dimness of the hallway, waiting to see in which direction Ryan would go. There was the sound of keys jangling as they were thrown on a table top. Finally, his prey came into view for a second as she headed for the kitchen—

Norman gaped in surprise at the woman—it wasn't Ryan. Although dark-haired like Ryan, this woman was much shorter. She turned the kitchen light on and began singing something in Spanish. Every few seconds she'd come into view momentarily as she busied herself making a snack. Norman inched back along the wall in the shadows towards the master bedroom. He was trapped; he'd never be able to get to either door without being noticed. But, then again, Norman wasn't in the least bit interested in leaving. He had no idea why the young Hispanic woman was in Ryan's house; maybe Ryan no longer lived here, or he had erred on the address. Mentally and emotionally he was too far gone to abort this opportunity. He was past the point of caution, or even of choice. Norman just hoped the woman didn't go into the utility room and see the broken glass on the floor.

When this didn't appear to be the case, he crept back to the master bedroom. Silent as a shadow, he entered and made his way to its adjoining bathroom where he waited, his back to the wall, the door left ajar. Less than five minutes had elapsed when he heard the woman coming along the hallway, still singing softly to herself. The bedroom lights came on causing Norman to blink from his vantage point in the dimness of the bathroom. The woman passed by his view with a plate and sandwich in one hand, and a glass of milk in the other. He heard the faint clink of glass as she set them on the nightstand.

Long seconds passed before she came back into view, now clad only in powder blue bra and panties as she walked up to the dresser. Norman stifled a groan of anticipation as he readied himself. The woman stopped. She was staring at the partially open drawer and the undergarments strewn across the surface of the dresser.

Norman bolted from his hiding place and was across the room in three flying strides. Too late, Maria looked up into the dresser mirror at the wild-eyed visage of the killer bearing down on her. A split second later Norman's two hundred twenty-five pounds crashed into the slim body of the woman, slamming her into the dresser and crushing the breath from her. Still behind her bent and slumping body, he deftly slipped his forearm under her chin and across her throat as he yanked her upright, lifting her off the floor as he applied a strangling pressure on her neck. Norman was so maniacally frenzied he couldn't slow the kill, wanting to get her to the final four minutes and beyond as fast as possible. To savor the taste of her ultimate terror, her total and complete vulnerability, the slow passing of her trapped mind—

The struggling woman brought her legs up, planted her feet on the edge of the dresser and pushed with all her strength. Norman, caught by surprise, staggered backward. His squirming prey was still in his grip, but his hold on her neck had involuntarily loosened. Maria jerked her head forward and brought it back sharply, catching Norman in the mouth and splitting his lip against his teeth. He held on, although her body slipped slightly in his grasp, her feet now back on the floor. Maria immediately brought her leg up, her knee to her chest, and brought her foot down with all the strength she could muster, her heel slamming into the arch of his foot. Norman let out a yelp of pain, and his grip loosened even more. Maria extended her arm out and brought it back violently, her elbow punching into Norman's stomach just below his ribcage. Out and back her elbow pistoned—a second, then a third time.

Surprised and stunned by the small woman's vicious resistance, Norman made the error of remaining stationary. Her heel slammed downward again on his damaged arch, and her head clubbed back into his sternum painfully. Norman faltered back a step, and Maria let her weight quickly sag while simultaneously wrenching her head to the side. Norman's weakened grip failed—Maria was suddenly free.

Choking and gagging from her abused windpipe, Maria staggered forward and braced herself on the dresser to keep from falling. She turned to face her attacker just as he charged forward with a growl of rage. Maria's leg flashed out in a rushed side-kick, but still connected just above his kneecap. Off balance and with pain exploding in his leg, Norman careened into Maria, knocking them both onto the dresser. Silently, grimly, the two fought on in a deadly dance. Norman's seething mind could still not comprehend that the petite, brown skinned woman was hurting him like this.

Maria knew that the big man only needed to land a solid punch and it would be over for her. Pinned on the dresser and grunting with each blow she threw, Maria repeatedly slammed her elbow into the side of Norman's head. Norman, with his arms wrapped around her waist and his face buried in her chest, picked her up and tried to throw her to the floor. But Maria's legs gripped him tightly in a lover's embrace, while her arms clasped his head firmly to her breast. This lover's illusion was ruined as Maria threw short elbow chops to the top of Norman's head. Unable to dislodge Maria and staggering from her weight and elbow throws, Norman rammed her backward into the wall, again and again. On the third collision, Maria finally released her hold and slumped to the floor.

Sensing victory, Norman backed up a step, preparing to kick his surprising adversary into oblivion. But she was gone, having rolled away and was even now rising to her feet. He went after her, swinging at the bobbing and weaving phantom with fists that could only find air, as she continued to elude her bigger and heavier attacker. But Norman stayed between her and the door and slowly bisected the room in his assault, constantly diminishing the area and limiting her freedom of movement. It wouldn't be long now; there was no escape for her. Maria's dark eyes reflected the same thoughts with the same conclusions.

She faked left, and Norman unconsciously leaned that way. Maria dashed to the right and, using the bed as a launching pad, leapt up and grabbed the idle ceiling fan. The fan held under her weight. As Norman turned towards her she pulled herself upward, swung her legs up and out, wrapping them around Norman's head from the side. She released the ceiling fan while simultaneously throwing her weight to the right. Norman, with a hundred and ten pounds draped around his neck, staggered several steps backward before crashing to the floor with Maria still wrapped around him. Before he could recover, the young Latino captured his arm and applied an arm bar hold, using his wrist and hand to apply twisting pressure. Her strong legs continued to exert a lethal force on his neck.

Norman's mind, a boiling, raging caldron of emotion, was laced with the cold and sobering thought that this small woman was on the verge of killing him. His muscled arm fought to counter the painful pressure as Maria continued applying it. Norman grimaced at the agony in his arm and the strangling grip of her legs around his neck, but managed to get to his knees, Maria still locked onto him in a lethal clinch. Finally, with consciousness wavering, he somehow struggled unsteadily to his feet, Maria hanging tightly from his head by her legs, still clutching and twisting at his arm.

Norman marshaled his waning strength and swung Maria out like a pendulum, crashing her upper body and head into the bureau. She hung on, desperation fueling her attack. Norman swung her again into the hardwood. This time, Maria's boa-like grip released, and she dropped to the floor with a muffled thud. Face down and moaning, she attempted to push herself up with her hands. Norman fell to his knees next to her and hammered her with his fist. Maria slumped back to the floor and lay silent.

Norman leaned back against the bureau, panting, waiting for his head to clear. He rubbed his tender neck, swallowing with effort, and inventoried the pain in his foot, knee and head. He figured a limp and a headache for a few days were small prices to pay for narrowly escaping being done in by the ferocious little woman. He reached out next to him and stroked the back of one of Maria's smooth, motionless legs. Who would have guessed something so beautiful could be so lethal? That they had almost been his downfall was a lesson he would remember in the future.

Norman ran his hand up her leg until it rested on her lacey, nylon clad buttocks. He winced as he swallowed again, but retrieved a smile from somewhere within him. He would enjoy taking the life from this little bitch. There was nothing she could do then; she would be totally vulnerable, defenseless and compliant. Norman could already taste the terror of her trapped mind in her dead body. As conditioned as the little whore appeared to be, he bet the time between her death and her final journey would be longer than four minutes, maybe even double, allowing him even more time to make her trip as abhorrent as possible—and he was an expert on that.

But before Norman started her on that short journey through those last evaporating minutes, this woman was going to answer a few questions for him.

# Chapter 23

Ryan was knocking on Jack's door at 7:55 the next morning. He was already showered, dressed and had just finished his first cup of coffee, compliments of the little coffee maker sitting on the vanity. You simply had to drop the prepackaged combo coffee and filter into the little pull out holder, add water, turn it on and presto—four cups of coffee dripping through in just a few minutes. And not bad tasting, either. He'd have a couple more cups over breakfast. Jack was still groggy from yesterday, and it would take large doses of caffeine to get things back on an even keel. But all in all, he was feeling pretty chipper.

Another rap on his door. "Hold on Ryan, I'm coming," he yelled. He grabbed his .38 snub-nose out of the nightstand drawer, pulled up his pant leg and secured it in his ankle holster. Large strides carried him across the room to the door.

Ryan stood there, beaming at him, looking as fresh as the early morning dew, hair curled and makeup in place, although Jack had an idea she didn't use much. She didn't need it. Her eye shadow was the faintest shade of amber, matching her nail polish and complimenting her pale yellow, lightweight summer dress—the scoop neckline enhanced by the unsecured top two buttons.

"Jesus, Ryan, did you start getting ready at 3:00 this morning, or what?" Jack asked, visibly fascinated. "And you're only going to the library. Who are you trying to impress?"

"Nobody, except for you of course. And I always like to look my best; a habit from the old days, I guess." Ryan spun around, the light fabric swirling out from her bare legs provocatively. She had sacrificed her usual high heels for open, platform sandals. Finishing her twirl, she gave him a coy smile with one finger under her chin in a Betty Boop gesture.

Jack shook his head and smiled. "Ryan, I'm always in awe of you." He pulled the door shut behind them as they headed out. "Well, let's head on over to breakfast. Anybody who still needs a little wake-me-up this morning will get a pleasant eye opener when they see you." Jack was still shaking his head as they walked down the hall.

The breakfast buffet choices were arrayed along one wall. Jack went for the waffles. He poured the small cup of batter in the waffle maker, flipped the closed griddle over on its axis and waited. The little digital timer counted down from two-and-a-half minutes. While Jack waited Ryan ferried their coffee and juice over to a table by the window, and went back for her breakfast, which consisted of a bagel and a packet of cream cheese.

Jack suppressed a grin as he discreetly scanned the fairly large eating area. There were over a dozen people at various stages of their breakfast seated at the polished, circular wood tables, ages ranging from senior citizens down to young marrieds. Several children scurried around the room checking out the food offerings. Everyone was dressed in "early morning casual," most looking as if they had just crawled out of bed. As Ryan fluttered about the room like a butterfly in a gentle breeze, the men—young and old alike—attempted tactful peeks while the women frowned icily at them. The stares directed at Ryan were critical and on the cold side, as well. Jack wondered what the hell he'd do if they ever needed to go somewhere where unobtrusiveness was a requirement. Ryan wasn't very good at "dressing down."

Waffle gone, Jack was working on a big sesame seed muffin and another coffee and O.J. Ryan had settled for a second cup of coffee. "So, Ryan, what's the game plan for today?" Jack asked.

"I checked Google Maps last night, and I have the addresses for Albuquerque's main library and the Bernalillo County Courthouse," she answered. "Actually, they're fairly close to each other; both of them are downtown. I'll drop you off at the courthouse, and I'll hit the library. If we find anything, we'll just call. We'll take a break at one, and I'll pick you up for lunch. How does that sound?"

"Works for me," Jack replied. He gulped down the last of his orange juice. "Let's hit it."

The Albuquerque Public Library's Microfilm Reading Room was located in the basement of the sprawling, two-story building on the corner of 5th and Roma. Before being allowed access to the room, Ryan had to register at the main desk, furnish identification, and give the reasons for her study. Researching past homicides in New Mexico for a forthcoming novel seemed a reasonable, and partially true, explanation. The short, pleasingly plump lady with the neatly coifed gray hair furnished Ryan with an I.D. badge, which Ryan clipped at the bottom of the scooped neckline of her dress.

The woman—Doris Kenzie, according to her nametag—wore a slight frown and was somewhat abrupt. Ryan had an idea that writing a book concerning murders in her beloved Albuquerque did not sit well with the matronly Doris. Or maybe she harbored a general resentment towards the library for not having scanned and computerized the old newspaper files.

"Ms. Sanders, take the hallway to the right," she said. "You'll come to a stairwell about halfway down the hall. Follow the signs at the bottom of the stairs, the Microfilm Reading room is to the left. The room closes at 5:00 pm. Once you've found what you're looking for in the computer, Mrs. Williams will pull the microfilm for you and have you sign for it."

There were two young women, likely college students, in the room when Ryan arrived. Busy with their individual microfilm readers, neither looked up as Ryan entered and sat at a desk with a computer terminal. She looked around the room. There were a half dozen desks with two micro readers and chairs in the open area, plus the three desks with computer terminals against one wall. One long wall of the room had six cubicles for those who wished to research in privacy. The opposite side of the room was divided between small drawers built into the wall, identified by letters and numbers, and a desk and chair occupied by a middle-aged woman, probably the aforementioned Ms. Williams, currently engrossed in her computer screen.

Ryan returned her attention to the monitor and quickly found the Home Page with the fill-in-the-blank request/search form. She paused momentarily, scanning her options. There was a list of New Mexico Newspapers, the cities they represented, the number of editions and the dates covered and stored on microfilm—actually microfiche—whatever the hell difference that was, Ryan mused. There was also a long list of magazines, periodicals, and other publications available on microfiche. Ryan ignored these and decided to start with the big one, the *Albuquerque Journal*.

She typed in the name and paused for a few seconds while she went over the time frame she and Jack had decided on. Fifteen years, 1998 would be the starting date she'd use. But what month? Why not start off clean with January 1, 1998? End date? The necro-murders started somewhere around ten years ago, so Ryan went with January 1, 2003. She typed it in and hit ENTER. The identifiers J-8 through J-13 came back; the location of that particular microfiche file on the far wall.

Ryan approached Regina Williams—according to her nametag—a rather plain and tired, washed out woman who, nevertheless, looked up from her desk with a pleasant smile. "Did you find what you were looking for?" Ms. Williams asked.

"Yes, Ms. Williams, I'd like to take a look at J-8 through J-13."

The woman rose, giving Ryan a benevolent smile as she did so. "That's five years of the *Albuquerque Journal*. Each microfiche contains 365 editions of the *Journal*, plus extra editions for holidays and events. That's a lot of reading. You'll be lucky to get through one. I hope you can narrow your search somehow. Should I pull a couple for you to start with?"

Ryan's buoyant mood began to deflate like a leaking balloon. Even knowing what types of articles she was seeking... this might take a while. She nodded numbly in reply.

The woman produced a small key and opened a drawer and removed two small, numbered white 4x6 envelopes, then re-locked the drawer. She returned to her desk, retrieved a clipboard and wrote several numbers on it. "Just sign next to the numbers. This is just to show you've checked them out."

Ryan signed.

Ms. Williams handed Ryan the envelopes and glanced at the clipboard and continued. "Ms. Sanders, the disk fits in the slot in the left rear of the reader. If you are unsure of anything, directions are printed on a card next to each reader. If you need to print something, the three cubicles on the far side of the room have printers."

Ryan thanked the woman and within minutes had one of the readers in the cubicles fired up, scanning through articles from early 1998. As the newspaper pages appeared on the screen, Ryan quickly skimmed through them. As she became more adept, her speed increased. She bypassed the sports, business and financial sections, as well as the holiday and most special edition inserts. Ryan concentrated on Sections A and B of each edition, which covered international, national, state and local news. She skimmed the headlines looking for anything in the ballpark of murder and necrophilia, no matter how tenuous.

The problem was that Albuquerque, with a population of nearly 600,000, had its fair share of homicides, suspicious accidents, felony assaults, domestic disputes and just generally weird cases. And since the *Albuquerque Journal* was the largest newspaper in the state, it carried news stories from other New Mexico cities, albeit to a much lesser degree and in less detail.

Ryan was forced to stop and read much more often than she would have liked. She also found herself making notes on a pad she'd brought to research crimes reported in other papers, but only mentioned briefly in the *Journal*. She already had jotted down two for the *Santa Fe Reporter* and another for the *Los Cruces Sun-Times*, along with the dates of the edition in question.

After three hours a headache was well on its way, and Ryan was becoming increasingly depressed. There were several horrendous crimes, but none that put her on red alert. She hoped Jack was having better luck at the courthouse. She guessed not since she hadn't heard from him yet. Ryan glanced at her watch; it was a little after twelve and she was hungry. Time for a lunch break.

Ryan must have accrued a dash of good karma from somewhere because it was at this point it reared its beautiful head in the form of Regina Williams. As Ryan paused, trying to gently rub life back into her closed eyes, the diminutive lady tentatively approached her. The two young women had departed, and Ryan and Ms. Williams were the only ones left in the room.

"Excuse me, Ms. Sanders, five years of the *Journal* is a lot of newspaper to go through. I'm a native Albuquerquean. If it's something specific you're looking for, it's possible I can narrow it down for you. You seem a little tired."

Ryan smiled at her appreciatively. "Unfortunately, it's not something specific. I'm… ah… writing a book on a specific type of crime, or more to the point, a crime that has a particular causal foundation. So, I'm researching articles in larger cities that may have crimes of that caliber, or possibly articles on events that may be related to the pre or post commission of the crime." That sounded plausible and professional to Ryan, and it was actually the truth.

Ms. Williams stood waiting patiently, apparently expecting Ryan to continue.

"Necrophilia, Ms. Williams. Possible necro-homicides, grave robberies, mortuary investigations or anything similar, and anything related to the act before, during or after the crime, or attempted crime, or even the investigation of a possible crime." The librarian was still silent, staring pensively at her. She didn't seem too upset concerning the deviant subject matter of Ryan's research. Maybe she didn't know what Ryan was talking about. Ryan continued, "Necrophilia is the attraction of—"

"I know what it is, Ms. Sanders," the woman interrupted. "I was just trying to remember if anything along those lines rang a bell. It's not exactly a common crime, as I'm sure you are aware."

If she only knew the rest of it, Ryan thought.

"I seem to remember something that might be related. It was a few years ago… let me check on it." With brows knit together thoughtfully, the librarian walked slowly back to her desk.

Ryan decided to scan through another week or two of papers while she waited before heading out for lunch. She was unaware when, several minutes later, Ms. Williams went to the file drawers and removed another microfiche envelope and approached Ryan's desk.

"Excuse me Ms. Sanders," she interrupted.

Ryan looked up.

The librarian continued. "The initial article appeared on August 2, 2001. There were several other follow-up articles. It was somewhat sensational at the time which was why I remembered it, even though it occurred in Socorro—a couple of hours south of here. It was eventually ruled an accidental death, but the child abuse aspect was noteworthy. When they found the mother and son, well, you can read the article; maybe it'll fit in with your research somehow. It's the only article I can think of offhand." She handed Ryan the file envelope.

Ryan debated on whether to view it right then or after lunch. She decided a quick peek couldn't hurt. She replaced the '98 disk with the '01, and quickly forwarded to August 2. It wasn't the lead story, but still made the front page below the fold—the caption: Foul Play Suspected in Mother's Death. Ryan skimmed through the article, but saw nothing of interest until she found references concerning the discovery of the body.

Ryan forwarded through several other issues and found two more follow-up articles on the incident. Interesting, but disturbing. Following the third article, she carefully scanned through several more weeks before discovering a related op-ed piece, discussing the pros and cons of the State custody hearing on the juvenile suspect—the son in this case—and whether his rights had been violated, possible guilt or innocence, his mental condition… blah, blah, blah. But the dates were right, and it was the only thing she'd discovered, so far. Of course, she had a good four years plus yet to cover. Still—

Ryan looked at her watch, it was almost 1:30, and Jack was probably starving. She and Ms. Williams were still alone in the Reading Room. She removed the microfiche disk from the reader and moved to a booth with a reader/printer combo. It was a shame there were no photographs included with the articles. Ryan guessed it had something to do with the son being a juvenile at the time.

Before she started the printer she called Jack's cell. He answered on the third ring. "Jack speaking."

"Jack, this is Ryan, as soon as I print—"

"Jesus, Ryan, I'm starving. I was just about ready to walk down to the corner and get me a couple of hot dogs from the street vendor."

"I'm sorry, Jack, I'm just going to print out copies of several articles from old newspapers, then I'll pick you up. But while you're waiting, check out court cases, grand jury or custody hearings, or anything related for August, and possibly September, 2001, involving a sixteen year old juvenile, Norman Frederick Bartholomew...."

# CHAPTER 24

Ryan looped around the block twice looking for Jack in front of the courthouse. After the second failed attempt she looked for a place to park. She didn't want to pay and park, either in the parking structure or in one of the private run lots. The big lug would never find her. The third time around she found a metered parking spot near the corner where a hot dog vendor was plying his trade. Ryan put two quarters in the meter, pulled out her cell and called Jack. It rang several times before he answered. "Where the hell are you, Jack?" she asked.

"Just finishing up making my own copies," he replied. "I found some interesting stuff on that Norman character. I'll be right down and we can compare notes over lunch. Where are you?"

"I'm near the corner where the hot dog vendor is."

"Grab us a couple chili dogs and cokes and meet me outside in the courtyard at the north end of the building."

"What am I, your servant or something? What kind of lunch is a chili dog, anyway?" she asked. "I should rate more than that.

Plus, you're expecting me to pay?" She could have been mistaken, but it sounded like Jack was laughing.

"And add a bag of chips to my order," he managed between chuckles. "I'll see you in a few minutes." Jack disconnected before she could think up a witty retort.

Ryan fed the parking meter another quarter and walked over to the hotdog pushcart, proudly identified in red block letters on the side as "Freddy's Fantastic Franks." A large umbrella attached to the wagon provided a brief respite from the heat and bright sunshine. The portable business was manned by a gray-haired, sixtyish-looking man with a neatly trimmed mustache and goatee, wearing a Dodgers' baseball cap. He looked at Ryan appreciatively as she sashayed up in her sundress.

The man's face creased with a smile, "Well, aren't you a pretty sight for these tired old eyes." He tipped his ball cap to her in greeting. "What can I get you, young miss?"

"My, my, aren't you the flatterer..." she looked at him questioningly "... Freddy?"

"Yes ma'am, Freddy at your service. It's your lucky day. I'm glad I stayed open a little longer; the lunch hour rush is pretty much over. What kind of Fantastic Hot Dog would you like on this fine, sunny day?" he asked.

"How about three chili dogs, two bags of chips and a couple cokes?" she asked

"Chopped onions with those? Maybe a little green chili?"

Ryan grimaced. "I'll pass on those."

With an economy of motion Freddy put together Ryan's order, opening his stainless steel tubs and containers, combining this and that, and in less than thirty seconds was handing Ryan a cardboard container with her request. He smiled at her. "That'll be $5.00, miss."

Ryan had added up the cost from the price list posted on the side of the cart and had already pulled a twenty out of her purse. She looked at him, her head cocked to the side.

"Discount for the prettiest customer I've had all day," he replied to her unspoken question.

Ryan laughed. "Why thank you, Freddy." She handed him the twenty. "Keep the change; I'm a big tipper." Freddy doffed his cap and bowed as Ryan headed back to the courthouse. It was a beautiful day, and she was feeling good. Farther up on the next corner was a vagrant with a small cardboard sign, she assumed with a scrawled message about being homeless and asking for help, or a similar missive of need. She frowned, hesitated, but continued on her way.

Ryan made the turn into the large piazza of the Bernalillo County Courthouse with her load of food. It was already after two o'clock and the quad was nearly deserted. She spied Jack sitting at a patio table in the shade of a small tree, studiously reading from several sheets of paper spread out before him.

"Ta-dah, lunch is served," Ryan said with a flourish. She set the carryall on the table and unloaded its contents.

Jack looked up at her in mock relief. "About time, Ryan, I was getting faint from hunger."

"Yeah, right. I'd hate to have to foot your food bill. And besides, you're getting a free lunch out of me." She pulled the folded sheets from the library out of her purse and handed them to Jack. "Here's the newspaper articles I was telling you about."

"And here's a nice manila folder for you to put your discoveries in. I got one for me, too. Yes, I sweet-talked one of the court clerks into donating them to the cause, plus make copies for me. I think she likes 'yours truly'."

Ryan looked back out to the street. "Listen, Jack, go ahead and start without me. I'll be just a minute."

Jack grimaced and shook his head. "Let me guess, you're going to make a donation to the homeless guy down on the corner. I don't know why you continue to throw your money away." He was still shaking his head in disapproval as he unwrapped the aluminum foil from his first chili dog.

Ryan stuck her tongue out at him and headed back to the sidewalk. She turned left, a minute later approaching the shabbily dressed hobo on the corner. Thick beard, ratty hair and haunted eyes greeted her, along with a dose of strong body odor. Ryan always kept small bills in one pocket of her purse for just such occasions, although the occasions were usually handing money out via her car window at intersections. She guessed this man was well into his sixties although it was difficult to determine.

"What's your name?" Ryan asked.

"Michael, young Missy," he replied in a raspy voice. "But all my friends call me Mike." These comments were delivered with a bobbing head and gap-toothed smile.

Ryan handed him a twenty-dollar bill, fighting back the sudden urge to cry. "My name is Ryan, and it's been a pleasure meeting you, Mike. You take care, okay?"

His cataract afflicted eyes bounced from Ryan's face to the money in his trembling hand and back. "God bless you, Missy,

God bless you, God bless you, God bless you...." He kept repeating this mantra over and over as his cloudy eyes brimmed with tears.

Ryan kept her own tears at bay, attempting to clamp down on her errant emotions. She picked up the pace on the way back to the bricked courtyard; her stomach was growling, the morning bagel long gone. Jack was still sitting at the table, a half-eaten chili dog abandoned in front of him. His shoulders were slumped and his head hanging—something was wrong. "Jack, what is it? Did you find something, what...?"

Her friend looked up at her with an expression so desolate, so forlorn that a bolt of fear shot through her, clutching at her heart, almost choking her. Jack cleared his throat, but even so, there was a catch in his voice when he spoke. "Ryan, sit down... I just got a call from the Detroit P.D...."

She opened her mouth to say something, but nothing came out. She was afraid to say anything, wanted everything to stop, wanted Jack to stop.

But he didn't. When he stood, his normally ruddy complexion had paled several shades. Worse, his eyes had blurred with tears. "Ryan, someone broke into your house last night. Maria was there. There was a struggle. She's dead. My God, Ryan, I'm so... so very sorry."

Nothing was registering for Ryan. "No, Maria was just house sitting for me. It couldn't be. There was no reason... no... Maria..." Her throat constricted, her voice faltered "... she was just helping me... oh my God, what have I done?" Then she thought of Lonnie. "Oh, my God," she repeated. "Lonnie.

Where's Lonnie?" she cried. Ryan had taken two unsteady steps backwards.

"Lonnie's okay, he wasn't there." Jack came around the table, and attempted to take Ryan in his arms to console her, but she pulled away.

"No… no, I'm okay… please…" she stammered. Ryan took another step back, bumped into a chair and sat heavily.

Jack wasn't sure what to say or do and didn't know how she would react. Ryan had been pushed to the limit by Dana's informational blitzkrieg, but normally she was stoic and unflappable, even in the early years when she had been smacked around by a couple of her "escortees." But this? Jack just didn't know how to proceed.

Ryan took a long drink from her coke and set it down carefully and deliberately. She inhaled deeply, exhaled and looked up at Jack, her jaw muscles clenching. It took two more measured breaths before she spoke, her dark brown eyes now refocused. "Tell me what happened, Jack."

Jack returned to his seat, studying the woman before him. "It happened sometime last night. They haven't determined whether the perp broke in while she was home or before and was waiting for her. Maria put up quite a struggle from the looks of it. She was strangled, possibly tortured. She was supposed to be at the gym this afternoon and, when she didn't show, Lonnie called. When there was no answer, he drove over and… well… ah…"

Ryan was listening without expression. "What else, Jack?"

"An autopsy still needs to be done, but it appears that things might have been done… possibly post mortem…."

Ryan pulled her cell phone out of her purse. Several seconds later she had Southwest Airlines on the phone. "Yes, I need to change the return dates on two..." she looked at Jack, who nodded "... the return dates on two round-trip tickets."

# Chapter 25

"**Mierda!" Hector jumped** when the cell phone went off in his pocket. It didn't ring often, but when it did he jumped. He used the phone exclusively for communicating with Mr. Bartholomew.

Hector was sitting at the kitchen table with Chico, taking care of some paperwork and finishing their lunch. Despite looking and acting the part, he and his crew were not the typical cholos associated with Mexico and the southwest United States. They preferred lurking in the shadows and dabbled in the legit, business realm of the gringos. Being "two faced," they could straddle the gangster and straight worlds to their advantage.

"Mr. Bertrand, I haven't heard from you in a while. What can I do for you?" It was best to keep things short and sweet with his employer—it was how the strange man preferred it. Hector wasn't about to argue; his "retainer" appeared in his bank account like clockwork. And Hector was careful to never use Mr. Bartholomew's real name when in the presence of others. The man had several aliases and wanted no one other than Hector to know his real name or where he lived. And he paid very well for his anonymity.

Chico had taken off his reading glasses and was staring at Hector absently. He only wore them when absolutely necessary; he didn't think they were very flattering for his macho image.

Hector was listening intently. "Yes, we could do it ourselves, but I agree, it would be better to shop this job out. I have several contacts in Detroit that should be able to take care of the problem." He paused, listening, his eyes growing wide. "Two of them, and one a cop? That will be expensive." Another pause. "Okay, I'll get on it as soon as I get the info." Hector hung up, blowing out a tamale scented gust of air through pursed lips.

"What is it?" Chico asked.

"That crazy Nicholas wants me to set up a hit on two people in Detroit, and one of them is a damn cop." Hector pushed his plate aside and reviewed the drug sales figures for the past month, the upcoming shipment dates, a few payoffs that still needed to be taken care of, as well as a proposed new supply route. Plus, the Los Zetas Cartel was pushing for new outlets in the U.S. He had to use kid gloves when dealing with them. They were a dangerous outfit, but the profit potential was great. And he still had to review his and his group's investment portfolios; the market had been a little shaky lately. It was time to dump some of those oil stocks—

"You gonna do it?" his lieutenant prodded.

Hector chuckled. "For the money he pays, I'd fly out and do it myself. Ah, but a cop; I'm glad we'll be contracting this one out. It could get messy. Now, amigo, what about that new supply route?"

Norman overnighted the photographs, addresses and information on Ryan and the cop to Hector's P.O. Box. He regretted having to pass up his planned get together with the Sanders bitch, but after what he had learned from that little spic cunt—with a fair amount of coaxing—he didn't want to take any chances. Norman smiled to himself. He had enjoyed persuading her, almost as much as what followed. He grimaced slightly as he left the post office. His foot and knee still hurt, and his shoulder still ached.

He had no idea how the Sanders broad had learned about him. It seemed impossible. Yet, according to the spic, she and her cop friend were in New Mexico looking for him. Ten years and twenty-six successful "eradications" with never a sniff from law enforcement, and now this woman and some rogue cop were actually on his tail? Time to nip this in the bud. As much as he had been looking forward to her, there were so many other man-eaters out there that needed tending to. Norman hoped when the two returned for the funeral, somebody would be in place to take care of the two pests.

Although he had obtained quite a bit of info on Ryan Sanders, things were a little skimpy on this Sergeant Jack Kroner. The little cunt hadn't been able to furnish much more than his name and that he worked for the Detroit Police Department. But it had been enough for Norman to surf through the Department's public website and obtain the Kroner cop's graduation class picture and basic info. Norman debated on whether to stick around for a few days to see what he could come up with when the two returned. He dismissed the idea almost as soon as it occurred to him. Norman would pay good money for this job; he didn't need to do their work for them.

Hector picked up the envelope from Norman at his post office box, but didn't open it until he was back in his car. After he looked through its meager contents, he pulled out his cell phone and punched in a number to a contact in Detroit.

His contact answered on the third ring. "Hola, Marty. It's Hector, Hector Ramirez," he said. He listened, smiling. "Yeah, Marty, everything's fine in the Land of Enchantment. How are things going in Detroit?" He listened for a minute before it was his turn. "Listen, amigo, I have a friend who needs a couple of people taken care of, a man and a woman… no, no… not a jealous wife deal…" Hector paused to laugh "… just a plain, old fashioned 'no-questions-asked' hit. But the man is a cop," he added.

Hector listened patiently for almost a full minute. "I know, I know Marty. But how does $100,000 sound? Fifty upfront, and fifty upon completion. You set up the deal, decide what you'll pay your boys, and the rest is yours. Better?" Hector grinned at the answer. "I'll send the pictures and info on the targets to you via Express Mail."

Hector smiled smugly. Marty's boys were good; that was one less problem to worry about.

# Chapter 26

Ryan knocked gently on the door of the modest ranch style home on W. Jefferson.

Lonnie had been renting a room with kitchen privileges from a widow, Nancy Carpenter, and her two teenage children, Samantha, age 15, and Jake, age 13. Nancy, a non-working mother in her late forties, had lost her husband to a brain aneurism two years prior. There had been no life insurance or appreciable savings. And although there was no large outstanding debt, other than their home mortgage, Nancy had trouble making ends meet, despite her returning to work as a paralegal for the law firm of Steinman and Humphrey.

At the time, Lonnie had been scraping together the money and the hours to get Madigan's financed and refurbished. Renting the spare room in the Carpenter home was a godsend for both Lonnie and Nancy. Lonnie literally became part of the family in short order. But now that Madigan's was on the verge of becoming a burgeoning success, and having been brought to earth by Maria, the two lovers had been looking for something more suitable for their future. They would look together no more.

Ryan's gentle rapping on the front door was answered by an exhausted looking woman with premature threads of gray in her auburn hair. She had become acquainted with Nancy through her association with Lonnie. Ryan managed a smile for the woman. "Hello, Nancy."

"Hi, Ryan," the woman sighed. From the looks of her eyes, she had been doing a fair amount of crying recently.

Ryan's mouth was dry, she was having trouble swallowing. "I've been trying to call Lonnie, but he hasn't been answering his phone," she managed.

The woman's gray eyes started to fill with tears. "Lonnie has taken it pretty hard. He's at the morgue with Maria's parents. The police are releasing the body to the funeral home, and they're making arrangements and… oh, my…" Nancy's hand went up to her quivering lips, the tears overflowing again "… such a terrible, terrible thing… I'm sorry, please come in, Ryan."

The funeral for Maria Mercado was held at the Swanson Funeral Home on McNichols in Detroit, with interment at the St. Lawrence Catholic Cemetery in Utica, followed by a reception at her parent's home in Utica.

As was the case with many Hispanics, Maria was part of a large, extended family. Added to the mix were friends of the siblings—three brothers and two sisters—as well as aunts, uncles, nieces and nephews. Maria's and Lonnie's friends, including those from Madigan's and the University, turned out en masse And there seemed to be small children everywhere, oblivious to the gravity of the event.

Lonnie's mother, Dolores Allemande, and his sister and her husband, Carolyn and Miles Davis, both attended. They had all known Maria and had driven in from Grosse Point. Lonnie's father had passed away when he was in high school.

Somehow, Ryan made it through the day. Jack was by her side the whole time, stoic and grim faced, occasionally guiding her by the arm when she faltered in the crowd of mingling, talkative people. She had been on emotional autopilot, mechanically working her way through the afternoon, and the throngs of the Mercado and Allemande well-wishers. As much as it was a gut wrenching ordeal for her, she couldn't imagine how awful it was for Maria's parents and Lonnie. She tried talking to her friend briefly before the service, and more at length at the Mercado's reception. Lonnie was inconsolable. Ryan and Jack did their best, but it would be some time before he came to terms with Maria's death. Not just her death, but her murder and the few gruesome details the police were willing to give out to the public.

But Ryan was not so handicapped in obtaining the information. Later that same evening, Jack was sitting across from her at her kitchen table, a manila folder in his hands. "I made copies of the police reports and the medical examiner's findings. I could lose my job for this, but like they say, 'in for an inch, in for a mile.'"

Ryan was expressionless. "I'm guessing I may already know a few of the details of her murder. Let's see... AFTER he killed her the murderer ejaculated in and on her, violently shoved something into every orifice of her body, plugged every hole—not just vaginally and anally, but throat, ears and nose as well. Then he urinated and/or defecated in her mouth. Since it was an open casket funeral, he obviously didn't have time or opportunity to skin her. But did he have time to cut off a breast for a souvenir? Maybe to suckle or eat? He has cured and tanned several in the past, like animal hides; he uses them for change purses. The sicko probably thinks the nipples on the bottoms make them cute. Does that about cover the basics, Jack?" Her voice was rising and tears were threatening. "Or has the monster become more creative in his depredations?" Ryan paused for a breath, fighting tears.

Jack was speechless. He reached across and covered her hand with his. "Yes, that pretty well covers it, except for the mutilations. There was evidence of torture, but before her death, not after. That differs from the others as far as I can tell. I'm sorry, Ryan, but how do you know it was the same guy?"

Ryan pulled her hand away and put it in her lap with the other. "It's not too hard to figure out, Jack. He abducted and killed Dana. He had her belongings, which would include her purse, probably containing my picture and address. It would be just like the sick fucker to want to 'double his pleasure' when he realized Dana had a twin. That would appeal to his twisted mind. Except I wasn't here when he came to visit. Maria was. It should have been me, not Maria." With the back of her hand she wiped the last of her tears from her eyes. "I already called Elizabeth and Bernie at the gym. The two of them will hold things together until Lonnie returns. I'm going back to Albuquerque to track this guy down."

Ryan decided not to tell him of her conversation with Lonnie. Lonnie believed, as Ryan did, that the killers of Dana and Maria were one and the same. Yes, Lonnie was distraught, but he had no qualms when he made Ryan promise to find the killer and take care of him. Of course, Lonnie graphically elaborated on exactly what he meant by "taking care of him." Ryan had promised.

"When?" Jack asked.

"Tomorrow, or as soon as I can get a flight back to Albuquerque."

"I'm going with you, Ryan."

She debated arguing with him, but decided against it—he was a big boy. "If you can get the time off, fine, but I'm staying there until I find him."

"I'll call you tomorrow. Don't leave until you hear from me," he warned.

Ryan didn't answer.

Jack rose and left without another word.

It was almost midnight and Ryan was beat. It had been a long day—indeed, a long week. Tomorrow was soon enough to check on flights. She rose, double-checked the locked, repaired back door, and switched off the kitchen light. Ryan shut down the remaining lights as she made her way through dining room and living room on her way to her bedroom, detouring and checking the locked front door as she passed. She wasn't really worried. Ryan was sure the sick bastard was hiding in his hole somewhere in New Mexico.

Of that, Ryan was correct. But the fact that Ryan was still awake at 3:00 a.m. because of her nervous, over-exhaustion turned out to be what saved her life.

That, and a cricket.

# Chapter 27

The overcast skies blanketed the crescent moon, and the nearest streetlight was on Saddlewood. The two bronze coach lights on Ryan's garage were equipped with light sensors and came on automatically as the light waned at sundown. Of course, if someone was not averse to hopping fences from backyard to backyard...

If anyone had been up at 3:05 a.m. on this dark and eerily silent night, stood near the northeast corner of Ryan's house, and stared long and hard at that side of the house, they might have noticed a slightly darker area of shadows midway along the brick wall. And if they had listened closely, they might have overheard the shadows whispering.

"What's the rush on this job? Marty said the order for the hit was out of Mexico. What's up with that? Drug deal gone bad, you think?" This from the shadow on the left.

The response from the darkness next to him was tinged with scorn. "New Mexico, stupid, not Mexico. New Mexico is a state. And Marty put a rush on it cause some guy's afraid the broad and her friend are heading to New Mexico real quick and could be a big problem. Don't know why they didn't contract the hit there though. Probably not enough time, but not our problem anyway."

There was a pause as the man adjusted his cramped sitting position against the wall before continuing, "Money in the bank for us; we're getting five grand each, plus expenses, to snuff this broad. So, stop the whining. Marty said if we can make it look like an accident, it'll be another ten grand. So, we stick to the plan—knock her out, break her neck, put her in her car and drive her and it off that steep embankment we scouted out a couple of miles from here. It's a back road and there won't be any traffic at this hour, anyway. Tragic accident, too bad, so sad." The shadow glanced at his watch, the dial faintly luminous in the darkness—3:12 a.m. "Then we'll take care of the cop when he's in mourning and be up another twenty grand."

"Whatever you say, and I can't argue about the money, but we've been here a long time. The lights went out hours ago," his partner replied. "We're stretching our luck camping out here all this time."

"Yeah, especially with all this yakking. Time to get this show on the road," his shadowy friend murmured.

Ryan stared at the ceiling through the darkness of her room. She'd been tossing and turning, her legs twisted in the sheets, sleep continuing to elude her. Over-tired, yes, but maybe she was afraid that Maria's murder, and its circumstances, would continue to trigger more Dana type nightmares. She had the feeling she would never completely be rid of them until she found the killer.

She glanced over at her nightstand and the faint luminescence of her alarm clock—almost 3:15 a.m. If she didn't get to sleep soon, she'd be a zombie all day tomorrow, and she certainly couldn't blame it on excess noise. Living on a cul-de-sac, there was no traffic. And at this hour the silence was almost deafening—to cite a classic oxymoron—not even the distant barking of a dog disturbed the night. Joining this conspiracy of silence was the pendulum wall clock in the living room. Normally tolling its melodic chimes every hour, it remained mute between 10:00 p.m. and 6:00 a.m. A very civilized idea, Ryan mused. She just hoped to God she wasn't still awake when it began its morning chimes.

The silence was so total she could even hear the chirping of the cricket coming from somewhere in the kitchen at the far end of the house. The invader had snuck in when she'd taken out the trash earlier in the evening. Ryan had made several half-hearted attempts to locate him, but the little bugger stayed silent whenever she moved near. Currently, it was hiding behind the stove, she thought. She'd worry about the little pest tomorrow if he was still around.

She sighed resignedly. Ryan had read somewhere that the chirping was a characteristic of the males, and could be either a mating call or used to repel other males. In this case he was out of luck. Her little friend was marooned alone in her kitchen with no one to answer his calls. Ryan's mind drifted as sleep began to overtake her. She kind of commiserated with the cricket, being alone and all. She'd have to help him get back outside tomorrow... not his fault... there... finally... her nighttime friend fell silent. Now, only the occasional, distant creaking of the house in the wind—

Ryan's eyes snapped open. Earlier, the cricket had stopped its chirping whenever she was nearby. Why had it quieted now? And it had been a hot and muggy day—no wind. Wide awake with her senses on red alert, she untangled herself from the sheets and eased out of bed.

Shadow number one may have been geographically challenged, but he was an expert at jimmying locks, especially older ones. Once they gained entry, the two men inched along the hallway, one to each wall and spaced several feet apart. Marty had provided them with a layout of the house. How he had obtained it the men had no idea, but it made their job a whole lot easier.

They were making their way silently towards the master bedroom at the end of the hallway. The first man was carrying a blackjack in his right hand. The leather covered baton would put the woman out, but hopefully not kill her. Hitman number two, several feet back and along the opposite wall, was the backup. If things went south, he'd take the woman out by knife, or as a last resort—shoot her. Neither man thought that was going to be necessary. Those thoughts were still running through their minds when the hall light came on.

Accustomed to the dark, the two men were temporarily blinded, as was Ryan facing them at the end of the hallway. The would-be assassins—surprised by the sudden appearance of the tall woman in the short nightshirt—hesitated, expecting their startled, half asleep prey to freeze in shock, or to turn and try to run. She did neither.

Their second surprise was when the woman charged down the hall towards them, her legs covering the distance in three long strides. Behind the curve in reaction time, the pair still acted quickly, number one bringing the blackjack up and number two managing to clear the knife from its sheath before the woman was upon them.

Their third and final surprise was the late realization of just how fast the woman really was. The lead killer's arm had not even started its downward arc with the blackjack before Ryan— capitalizing on her forward momentum—launched a vicious side-kick, her right leg pistoning out, the edge of her bare foot battering into his sternum like a hammer. With a grunt he staggered back off balance, his heart suffering a temporary arrhythmia from the force of the impact. He tripped over his accomplice and fell heavily on his behind with a stunned look on his face.

The second hitman advanced on Ryan, a slashing backhand with the knife slicing through the air and the front of her nightshirt as she jumped back. A few more inches and she would have been gutted. He advanced another step towards her, and the returning forehand arced again, slashing at her.

Again he missed, but this time as the man's arm flashed by her, Ryan darted forward, her left hand pushing on his elbow in the same direction as the thrust, her right hand simultaneously grabbing his wrist while pushing. He was suddenly off balance. Ryan pressed forward with all her weight and strength, and managed to drive him face first into the wall, his knife arm imprisoned shoulder-high ahead of him. Ryan continued her thrust and the knife slide smoothly into the side of his neck. The blood spurted as she held on and hammered a knee repeatedly into his side.

Number one managed to make it back to his knees. He had abandoned the blackjack, instead opting for a small, snub-nosed revolver drawn from the pancake holster on his belt. He swung it around towards a suddenly moving Ryan and fired. The bullet missed and struck his partner. As he tried to re-aim in the narrow hallway Ryan's leg lashed out, her kick sending the gun flying. Her second kick—catching him under the chin—put him back down on the floor, unconscious.

She turned her attention back to the knife-welder. The threat from that sad-sack had passed; he was gently sliding down the blood smeared wall, the surprised look on his face slowly morphing into the vacant stare of death.

Ryan stared at the blood on her hands and shirt. She made her way to the kitchen table and sat down heavily. She began to shake as the adrenalin from the "fight or flight" reaction dissipated. Ryan realized she was inhaling raggedly, almost panting. She struggled to control her breathing and the shaking, gradually bringing them under control.

Ryan glanced back towards the hallway where one man lay unconscious, the other cooling in a growing pool of blood. She needed to call the police. And Jack. Obviously, their return trip to New Mexico was going to be delayed. She looked again towards the hall at the two bodies. Ryan decided that before she made those calls, she needed to have a little talk with Mr.

Blackjack guy. She took a deep breath, clenched her teeth and stood….

Jack disconnected and set the phone on the table. No sense rushing over to Ryan's now. She had already called the Precinct, and the first squad car arrived while they were still on the phone. Ryan had sounded remarkably calm for someone who had just had a go-round with two killers, one of whom was now dead. He thought about the possibility of her being in shock, but dismissed it; he'd already seen what her response was to overwhelming events. Jack was still uneasy though. Ryan had referenced her having a "talk" with the injured hit man and said she had obtained information she and Jack could discuss at a later date. Plus, she still planned on heading back to New Mexico.

Jack made a decision. Ryan would not be doing this alone, no matter how long it took, or how far she traveled. He punched in numbers on his cell phone; it was time to collect on his accumulated P.O.D.'s. The practice of "payable on demand" was a non-contractual, unofficial practice among the Department's officers. If an officer did not have, or want to use, his vacation or sick time, he could have another officer work for him "off the books," the unspoken agreement being they would pay the time back when the working officer "demanded" it. Management looked the other way as long as staffing levels were maintained and all the shifts covered. It kept everyone happy.

In the past, Jack had worked for several officers and kept the hours owed him in a small notebook. It was time to collect. He figured he could get a number of his shifts covered while he filed the necessary paperwork for the Retirement Board and the Department. And if he used his banked vacation and personal leave time—

"Hello, Sammy, it's Jack. Sorry to bother you this early in the morning… yeah, everything's fine… you know the P.O.D. time you owe me? Yup, it's twenty-four hours total… time to pay the piper, buddy. A few things have come up; let's see what you can do for me.…"

Six more phone calls over the next hour and he had the next three weeks covered. He'd start his retirement paperwork later and face a sure to be irate Lieutenant Bocher tomorrow. Jack glanced at his watch. Time to get over to Ryan's and check on her and the crime scene; the techs would be swarming the place by now. The gray dawn had just begun to encroach on Jack's world as he hopped into his car and headed towards his friend's house.

First Maria, and now this. The killer knew they were looking for him.

# Chapter 28

Ryan checked into the Days Inn near her home while her house was being refurbished with new carpet and new paint—especially in the hallway. Only two more days, and then off to the high deserts of New Mexico to resume her search. The police report had been filed and her statement taken. The investigation was ongoing, but since the surviving attacker wasn't talking and Ryan was playing dumb, it was being classified as a breaking and entering gone bad. There was nothing keeping her in Detroit; if the cops needed her, they could call her. She'd check in with Lonnie and see how he was doing before she left.

Right at the moment though, she was sitting and having a cup of coffee at the Burger King next door to the motel, waiting for Jack. It was 10:00 a.m. and the complimentary breakfast at the Days Inn ended at 9:00, so this was as good as Jack was going to get. Since the attack the opportunities for them to talk at length had been limited, what with the whirlwind police investigation and all. This morning they would bring each the other up to speed on their ideas.

When Ryan had mentioned to Jack that she was checking into a motel while they re-carpeted and repainted her home, she half expected her friend to invite her to stay at his apartment for the two days. He hadn't. She was vaguely disappointed at this omission, but she guessed he might have been uncomfortable with that setup, temporary as it was. Ryan didn't know what his current romantic status was. Hell, for all she knew he might be shacking up with someone. Jack was pretty tight-lipped when it came to his female acquaintances, but Ryan was still a little miffed. She and Jack had been friends for a long time—

Ryan's musings were interrupted as the door to the fast-food restaurant opened and Jack lumbered in. As he walked across to her table, he threw a shadow over her as he blocked out the sunlight from the window behind him. She couldn't keep from grinning and shaking her head. "Jack, if we painted you green you could pass for the Incredible Hulk." This elicited a scowl from the big man, making him look even more menacing. If strangers only knew what a gentle giant he was, Ryan thought.

"Nice to see you, too, Ryan," he rumbled. "And if we put rabbit ears and a tail on you, you could pass for a Playboy Bunny." Realizing this was a pretty lame comeback, his frown melted away as he slid into the booth across from her. Now, he just looked sheepish.

She pushed a large coffee over to him. "Black, no sugar. If you want something to eat, I'll get it for you."

"Thanks, but I already ate, although I do appreciate the coffee." Jack took a sip from his cup, appraising her. "I have some information on your two attackers. Both were originally from Compton, California where they had rap-sheets as long as your legs…" Jack gave her a wink, the comment resulting in a sugar packet bouncing off his chest, compliments of Ryan "… but both relocated to Detroit several years ago with no major dustups with the law. The autopsy on the dead perp is done. The DOA was a Robert Nichols, and the cause of death was a bullet to the chest, puncturing his lung and aorta, before exiting his back and lodging in your wall. Even if it hadn't killed him, he would have bled out from the neck wound, which nicked his juggler. The second guy, the one who survived his assault on you…" now Jack was unable to suppress a grin "… was a Marvin Ziegler. He faired pretty well—a little bruising, a dislocated jaw, but no broken bones—except for the three fingers on his gun hand. Oh, yeah, and he's not talking."

Jack's smile grew a little lopsided. "I don't suppose you know how those fingers got broken, do you?"

Ryan's polished nails clicked on the tabletop as her fingers drummed slowly, her lips compressed to a thin line as she studied Jack for several seconds. Finally, "Mr. Ziegler, didn't want to answer my questions, so I encouraged him to be a bit more forthcoming." Ryan expected her friend to be upset, or to at least protest her actions. But he did neither. If anything, he looked resigned, almost as if he had made a decision, or crossed some imaginary line—

"So, what did he say?" Jack asked.

Ryan was caught off guard by his acceptance. She searched his face, his eyes, but couldn't read anything. The man was inscrutable when he wanted to be. "I don't think he knew much, Jack. Some guy named Marty hired him and his buddy. He didn't have an address or any other names, and the monetary transactions were convoluted, making it impossible to trace back to Marty or the original payer. The contract for the hit on me—and you, by the way—apparently came from someone in New Mexico. Mr. Ziegler had the impression it was a third party deal. Plus, they were furnished with the layout of my house, meaning it would have to have come from somebody who had been inside. It appears someone doesn't like us looking for them."

Jack took a gulp of his coffee and sighed deeply. "Well, at least you got more out of him than we did."

"Only because you're limited in your interrogation techniques."

"You should turn this information over to the investigators," Jack replied.

"Not gonna happen. And if you say anything, I'll deny it."

Jack didn't seem too surprised. "So what's your take on this?"

The early fast-food lunch crowd was filtering in. Ryan people-watched for several seconds before returning her attention to Jack. "Well, Mr. Policeman, it should be obvious. A madman kills Dana and somehow, post-mortem, she passes information on to me. With those clues, we begin nosing around New Mexico. But the killer has discovered Dana has a twin sister and, armed with my address, travels to Detroit to have a little more fun. He runs into Maria instead and, after torturing her for information, kills her. From Maria he's learned that you and I are looking for Dana's killer—that would be him—in Albuquerque. He also now knows the layout of my house. He doesn't know how we've tracked him to New Mexico, but he decided to reduce the odds of us discovering his identity by hiring two thugs to eliminate us. They started with me, figuring I'd be the easiest." Ryan looked at him with raised eyebrows.

"Sounds about right," Jack replied. "And all this pretty well confirms New Mexico as the correct state to be looking in." His face settled into grim fault lines. "But I do have something else to add."

Ryan waited patiently.

Jack continued, "Considering the killer's M.O., he is completely bananas. Or to put it more delicately, he has deep psychological issues. But despite his manic obsessions and compulsive behavior, he is intelligent enough to control it—up to a point—and to hide and protect himself from others. And he will take rather elaborate measures to do so as his efforts to eliminate us before we discover his identity illustrates. A reasoning, intelligent homicidal maniac is a rarity, and makes him extremely dangerous."

Ryan was looking at him blankly as if he were relaying the weather report.

Jack sighed and shrugged his massive shoulders. "Okay, so when do we leave?"

"I'm leaving the day after tomorrow."

Jack opened his mouth to say something, but Ryan cut him off. "Jack, you've already jeopardized your career for me—unauthorized investigations, disclosing classified police reports, withholding information, and I don't know what else. Hell, Jack, if you were to stick around to the end they could probably nail you with hindering and obstructing a police investigation and aiding and abetting a criminal. I don't want you to ruin your career. And now I've even put you in danger from this maniac."

Jack grimaced. "I'm a big boy, capable of taking care of myself and making my own decisions."

"I'll go along with the big boy thing, but I'm not so sure about the decision capability," Ryan smirked. "Besides, how could you get any more leave time?"

"Leave that to me. I'm supposed to see Lieutenant Bocher tomorrow, anyway. I'll get the time off." Jack decided not to mention his retirement plans.

"It wouldn't make any difference if I kept objecting, would it?" she asked. Ryan's stomach roiled with conflicting emotions. She didn't want to cause any trouble for her friend, but the thought of Jack being there was reassuring—

"Nope, no difference at all, you're stuck with me." Jack looked around and pushed himself away from the table. "It's getting crowded; I think I'll get me a Double Whopper and fries."

Ryan watched him walk up to the counter. She smiled ruefully, shaking her head. The big guy's arteries would turn into cement at this rate. She needed to have a little talk with him about his diet and nutrition.

# Chapter 29

Southwest Airlines flight #236 was at a cruising altitude of 37,000 feet, and now over the state of Nebraska, its contrail a white thread in the blue afternoon sky as it passed high above the world below. With their short layover in Chicago out of the way, Jack and Ryan were comparing notes as their jet roared towards their destination in New Mexico. Ryan was scanning the old newspaper stories she had made copies of while on their previous trip to Albuquerque. Jack was doing the same with the information he had obtained from the Bernalillo County courthouse.

Ryan was proud of the big guy. His bug-eyed, white-knuckled demeanor during takeoff had slowly dissolved once they had leveled off. Jack had finally released his death grip on her hand, and Ryan was pretty sure he hadn't crushed any bones. The feeling in her fingers had gradually returned.

Jack feigned a look of studious indifference. "So, what's the game plan, boss? Do we continue our research looking for more possible suspects, or follow up on the one we've come up with so far… this Norman fellow?"

Ryan glanced at the papers on the fold-down table in front of Jack. "Did you find anything at the courthouse on the Norman kid before… before you got the call about Maria?"

"Actually, your newspaper articles had a lot more information in them. Of course, you never know how accurate the info is when they start quoting 'inside sources,' and begin speculating and writing op-ed pieces. Since the kid was a juvenile, most of the police reports and investigations were sealed. You'd need a court order to get them opened. Still, the court proceedings corroborated some of the newspaper reporting and gives us a starting point—the mental institution where he received treatment."

"Let me see," Ryan said. She took his notes and scanned through them. She shook her head, suppressing a smile. "Your penmanship is atrocious, Jack. Did you flunk cursive in school, or what?"

He snorted. "Do you need me to read them to you?"

Ryan grinned and kept reading. While she did so, Jack flagged down the stewardess and ordered another whiskey and water—his third. By the time she returned with his drink, Ryan had finished. "I think we stick with this one until we hit a dead end, or things stop fitting the clues."

She put the sheets back together, tapping them on the fold down tray to align the edges. "A single mother dies in an accident at home—electrocuted in the bathtub by an errant portable radio. There was evidence of prostitution, alcohol and drug use by the mother, and probable abuse from an early age—including suspected sexual abuse—of the sixteen year old son, Norman. Abuse that may have gone on for a long time. In any case, the State found there was enough psychological trauma for the boy to be committed to an institution for court ordered treatment until he was twenty-one. And there was a disturbing interview in the *Journal* with the guy who discovered the body of the mother. It seems the son was with mom in bed—after she was dead. He had removed her from the tub and put her in the bed. They surmised it was from the shock and grief of the accident. And the timeline of all this fits the working framework we've set up."

Jack looked pensive. "The kid may have had a mental breakdown from the tragic loss of his mother, resulting in his temporary aberrant behavior, but the possible necrophilia connection is certainly of interest. And the court hearings confirm the psychiatric facility he was confined to— the Fort Bayard Medical Center. He had no living relatives, so in effect, he was a ward of the State. I also found public records of a court hearing on his behalf concerning lottery winnings and their future allocation—"

"Got it right here, Jack," Ryan interrupted. She quickly leafed through the sheaf of papers in front of her and pulled out one from near the bottom, a copy of an article from the *Albuquerque Journal*. "It seems Nicole Bartholomew was a habitual player in the New Mexico State Lottery. As luck would have it, mom bought the winner in a New Mexico Mega-Game jackpot just six weeks before her untimely death—to the tune of twelve million dollars. The court ruled that the money—which had not been allocated as yet—be put into a trust for young Norman, until his release from the hospital and attaining the age of twenty-one."

Jack reclined his seat and lay back. "Well, I'd say we start with the Fort Bayard Medical Center and see what happened to the young lad," he said. "Twelve million dollars... go figure... the lucky s.o.b.," Jack muttered, sipping his drink.

"Take it easy on the booze; you're too big for me to carry," Ryan chided.

"Just fortifying my spirits for the eventual landing of this flying coffin."

Ryan took his big hand in hers and gave it a squeeze. "And thanks again for coming along and keeping me company."

"Someone has to keep you out of trouble."

But as fate ordained, trouble found them. For some convoluted reasoning, airlines seldom made nonstop flights cross-country. Ryan supposed the reasons were economic somehow. Their current flight from Detroit to Albuquerque made one stop in Denver, a city that wasn't even on a direct flight path. Here they switched planes for the final leg. Jack hated these extra stops. They entailed landing and taking off a second time and, as far as he could see it was a needless exercise, since the jets were capable of flying nonstop. The economic reasons—extra connections enabling the airlines to have full passenger loads—were completely irrelevant for Jack.

They boarded their connecting flight and were readying for takeoff when the captain announced over the PA that they would be delayed briefly while the ground crew checked a mechanical problem. Twenty minutes later they received the advisory to disembark. Another hour passed, and the plane was taken out of service.

"You've got to be kidding me," Jack said. He was looking at the digital display next to Gate C-20, now with CANCELED in red next to their flight number.

"Relax, I'll just check with the gate attendant about getting an alternate flight. I'll take care of everything. Keep an eye on my carry-on bag." With that, Ryan was off to see the attendant.

Ryan was at the counter for a good ten minutes. When she came back she was carrying what looked like several boarding passes. She was gazing at Jack with an expression somewhere between a smile and a smirk.

"All set? How long do we have to wait for another flight?" Jack asked.

"Tomorrow morning, 8:55 a.m.," she answered.

"What?" Jack gaped, wide-eyed.

Ryan continued, "There aren't any more flights leaving for Albuquerque until then. But not to worry, they gave us a voucher for a room at the Holiday Inn tonight and meal tickets for dinner and breakfast."

"You mean rooms, as in two?" Now Jack was sure her expression was a smirk.

"No, my bashful friend, just one. Seems we aren't the only ones stranded for the night. Apparently several other flights were canceled because of bad weather. But it has two queen beds, and I promise not to look—unless, of course, you want to search around for other accommodations in the area." Ryan managed to reign in her grin as she looked at the big man inquisitively. She wasn't positive, but she thought Jack was blushing.

Jack cleared his throat, composing himself. "No, one room will be fine. We'll manage; it's only for one night." He broke eye contact and looked around self-consciously. "So, where do we go from here?"

"Come on, follow me." Ryan strode off purposefully.

Like a large freighter caught and swept away by an overpowering ocean current, Jack followed in her wake. He decided to set his male ego aside and let her take care of the airport stuff; he wasn't very knowledgeable about those things. Jack lumbered forward to keep up, Ryan's long legs were setting a ground eating pace through the airport.

Ryan was talking over her shoulder as Jack finally closed the gap. "Our luggage will transfer directly from our plane to the new one. So, now we go to the Southwest Service Desk and pick up our complimentary overnight kits—things like toothpaste and brush, mouthwash, combs, razor, soap, shampoo and their kin—and call the hotel for a ride. Unfortunately, we'll be stuck with the clothes we're wearing."

As he gazed at the tall woman in the black skirt and red silk blouse leading the way, Jack was sure of one thing. When the morning dawned, and they caught the shuttle back, Ryan would look as good then as she did now, no matter what the circumstances. She was one of those women who'd look beautiful dressed in a burlap sack, or could fall in a pile of shit and come out smelling like a rose.

The Holiday Inn shuttle picked them up and transported them to the hotel. After checking in and depositing their carry-ons in Room 363, they had a leisurely dinner in the hotel lounge, quaintly called Benny's Bar and Grill, before heading back to their room—Jack now fortified with three large mugs of something called "Augie's Pale Ale."

Ryan threw her purse on one of the beds and headed for the bathroom "I'll take that one and I get the shower first."

Jack sat on the other bed and bounced on it a couple of times absentmindedly. No complimentary robes, so Ryan would soon emerge wrapped only in a towel. And she'd probably sleep in her bra and panties, or maybe even—he swallowed convulsively, rose quickly from the bed and walked to the bathroom door. Ryan hadn't started the shower yet. He called through the closed door, "Ryan, I'm going back down to the lounge for another drink."

He heard the shower start as she yelled back. "Okay, but go easy on the booze. I have no idea how I'd drag your sorry ass back up here if you didn't."

Jack went through three more Pale Ale's at Benny's, giving Ryan plenty of time to finish up with her shower and whatever nightly rituals women often went through. When he returned to their room Ryan was sitting up in bed watching TV, the covers pulled up to her armpits, her dark hair still curled and damp from the shower. And no bra straps, Jack noticed, meaning it was the "maybe even" alternative to her nighttime clothing attire—or lack thereof, he nervously mused.

Ryan smiled up at him. "I see you're still walking, which is a good thing. You don't need a hangover tomorrow morning; we have to get up at 6:00 to catch the shuttle back to the airport at 7:00. If you want more than coffee for breakfast, you'll have to get up even earlier."

"Works for me," he replied. "I won't miss breakfast. I'm going to take a quick shower and then it's lights out. A good night's sleep, and I'll be able to tackle another plane ride tomorrow."

Several hours later Jack was still awake, lying in bed and staring at the ceiling in the quiet of their third floor room. He glanced over at Ryan, a silent, nebulous shadow in the ambient light filtering in through the partially open curtains.

He realized a good night's sleep was out of the question. His thoughts were in a continuous loop, revolving around the woman sleeping in the other bed. He knew what Ryan's intentions were if she found the killer. And Jack would have to stop her, not only for her own safety, but to protect her from the possible legal ramifications. Jack would bring the murderer in alive, which wouldn't make Ryan happy—or himself for that matter. He didn't want her to have to live with her conscience should she fulfill her goal of revenge. As much as Ryan felt her actions justified, he knew that final act would haunt her for the rest of her life.

But thoughts of Ryan, unrelated to the hunt for the killer, kept intruding; feelings he had been consciously suppressing for... years... if he was honest with himself. And now she was sleeping just several feet away from him, soft and warm and clothed only in the bed covers. With mixed emotions he realized he was growing hard. Jack groaned softly and rolled over and buried his face in the pillow. Ryan was a beautiful, vibrant twenty-eight-year old woman, and he was a hulking, brutish looking cop, fourteen years her senior. He was not even remotely in her league. With clenched teeth, Jack pushed that line of thought back into the shadowed recesses of his mind. He'd have to be content with helping and protecting his young friend as best he could, for as long as he could—however he could. It was hard to believe, but Jack eventually fell asleep—a restless, image filled slumber....

*He was wandering along an unknown, fog-filled roadway. The mists swirled around him and, peering as he might, he was unable to see more than a few feet in any direction. City or countryside, he knew not.*

*A scream from somewhere to his right caught his attention, filling him with panic and an overwhelming dread. It was Ryan. He didn't know how he knew this, he just did. He flailed at the swirling whiteness enveloping him and floundered towards the harrowing sound as another scream fractured the eerie stillness. In a panic he started running, oblivious to any danger. Jack almost ran into the side of a building as it magically appeared before him.*

*A door. Jack flung it open and faced a dimly lit staircase leading upward. Without hesitation he bounded up the stairs towards the agonized moaning now echoing inside his head. The staircase went on endlessly, disappearing in a distant horizon. He took the stairs two at a time, heart pounding and lungs gasping.*

*After countless steps and an eternity of exhaustion, Jack stumbled and fell to his knees on a small landing in front of a heavy wooden door. He could hear Ryan moaning and crying from somewhere inside the room. He pulled himself up and pounded and kicked at the barrier, screaming at Ryan to open the door. No response. The door held, and the sobbing continued—*

Jack's eyes flew open in the dimness of the motel room. In the ambient lighting from the street lights and neon sign leaking in through their window's partially opened curtains, he could see the lighter color of the room's stucco ceiling, even the sprinkler head located in the middle of the room. Although still slightly disorientated from the dream, the all too real images were rapidly fading. Except for the distant crying and occasional sniffle. They didn't fade.

He looked over at Ryan's bed. She was sitting up and facing the wall on the far side, her head hanging. The faint sounds of distress were coming from her. He stared at the long, pale expanse of her exposed backside, its paleness a refreshing shadow in the darkness. A corner of Jack's mind recognized the contrast as a kind of oxymoron.

Jack sat up. "Ryan, are you okay?" he asked.

There was a sudden hitch in her subdued sobbing, followed by a hiccup. Ryan pulled her rumpled bedspread up and around her, covering her nakedness. "I'm sorry, Jack, I just had a bad dream. I didn't mean to wake you. I'm okay." He heard another hiccup in the darkness.

Jack got up and walked around to her, thankful that he had worn his tee shirt and boxer shorts to bed. He sat next to his bedspread-clad friend. "I don't think I have to guess what your nightmare was about," he whispered.

"Sometimes the memories haunt me in the night," she mumbled. "I'm just afraid the dreams won't ever end until I find him." She gazed up at him, her expression unreadable in the night. Slowly, she leaned against him and laid her head on his shoulder. He put his arm around her. Another hiccup in the darkness.

"Hold your breath," Jack advised.

Ryan did, the silence lengthening until she let out the imprisoned air in a whoosh. Several minutes passed in the quiet, Jack's suggested cure seemingly doing the trick. "Thank you for being here, Jack," she sighed.

"Just call me Dr. Jack," he replied, smiling.

Ryan gave his bare leg a playful punch. "No silly. I mean thank you for always being there for me. You've never judged me or questioned me... well, except maybe back in college." She giggled girlishly before continuing, "You're always there when I need you."

Jack could feel the heat rushing to his face. "It's always been a pleasure, ma'am," he answered.

Ryan punched him again in the leg. "Stop with the ma'am stuff, you old fart; it makes me feel old."

Jack gave her a gentle squeeze. Ryan was a strong, independent woman, her life a roller coaster of ups and downs often requiring a resiliency lacking in most people. But beneath her seemingly tough, disciplined veneer was an endearing vulnerability, a tenderness that was all too rarely revealed. Jack had cherished those infrequent appearances over the years. If he only knew how to peel off her protective layers of emotional insulation.

Not only had Ryan's hiccups ceased, but her breathing had deepened, becoming slow and regular. She had fallen asleep on his shoulder. Supporting her, Jack laid her head gently on the pillow. Careful to keep her bedspread toga in place, Jack lifted her legs onto the bed and carefully straightened her, fearful that she might awaken. But Ryan was exhausted from wrestling with her nightmare and slept on undisturbed.

Jack crawled back into his own bed. He stared up at the ceiling, realizing his sleep was over for the night.

# Chapter 30

Somehow they survived their layover in Denver, and the last leg of their flight to Albuquerque proved uneventful—which was always a good thing. By the time they picked up their rental car and checked into their motel—separate rooms this time—it was too late to do much of anything, other than to have dinner and discuss their plans.

For this excursion they had opted for a four-wheel-drive vehicle and were on the road in their Jeep Grand Cherokee rental by 9:00 the following morning. Both Jack and Ryan were city dwellers and had no idea what to expect driving in the high desert countryside of New Mexico. Albuquerque was a sizable city and gave no hint of what to expect once you left its urban confines. Jack had volunteered to take this leg of the driving, and Ryan occupied herself by studying the countryside as it slid past her window.

Ryan was amazed at the change once they left the city—wide open spaces, gently rolling hills, occasional alligator juniper trees, dusty looking plants, and a whole lot of barren, multi-hued brown landscape. Too much space; it didn't appeal to Ryan. And the way Jack kept frowning as he scanned the sweeping countryside, he didn't care for it much either. They had lived most of their lives among the tall buildings, housing developments, strip malls, shopping centers, and the constant hubbub of cars and people. The highway they were traveling passed through none of that, just miles and miles of barren countryside.

Occasionally, they would see clusters of trees and greenery some distance from the roadway. As they drew nearer Jack and Ryan realized they were the sites of homes, with well-water irrigated vegetation in the areas surrounding the houses and outbuildings. The same with arroyos. Although dry, the banks of these arid waterways sported occasional vegetation and stunted trees, albeit scraggly looking. Water must have been close enough to the surface for the root systems, Ryan theorized. Given enough water, she guessed that you could grow anything anywhere.

After three hours of traveling south on the I-25 Interstate they turned off onto Route 180 and headed west. But before doing so they stopped for gas and switched seats; Ryan was now the driver and Jack the passenger. It was a wise move.

Jack sighed and slouched in the passenger seat trying to find a comfortable position. Through eyes weary from lack of sleep, he surveyed the gently rising terrain ahead of them. He glanced over at Ryan. "Are you sure about this shortcut?" he asked.

This new route would take them into the Gila National Forest and the Black Mountains, as opposed to continuing south until they hit I-10, which would bypass the southern edge of the forest and mountain range while heading west towards Bayard. "The roads may be a little slower and the terrain a little rougher, but it should cut a good hour off our driving time. I guess you could call it the scenic route," she laughed.

The elevation gradually increased as evidenced by the higher number of trees and flora in the area. Alligator juniper commingled with pinon and the occasional cottonwood. The only town they traveled through was the quaint burg of Hillsboro—no traffic lights or stop signs—just a few buildings, a small post office and one rustic looking saloon/restaurant—which garnered a wistful look from Jack as they drove by.

By the time they reached an elevation of 9,000 feet, the transformation was complete and forests of pine trees surrounded them. There was little traffic, and the reason for this soon became apparent. Ryan had to reduce their speed drastically as she traversed switchbacks, S-curves, and hairpins—many severe enough to justify the posted speeds of 10 and 15 m.p.h. Even at these lower speeds the effect on Jack was nearly traumatic.

The views were majestic as she navigated the edges of the mountains, often on roadways separated from sheer drop-offs by flimsy looking guard rails, wooden posts, or in many cases—nothing. Although the vistas were breathtaking, Ryan could only manage occasional glances as she concentrated on the winding road ahead of her. She spared a few peeks at Jack and had to suppress a grin at his discomfort.

Jack was wide eyed, his right hand had a white-knuckled grip on the passenger door armrest, and his left was balled into a fist. Every time the roadway neared the rim of the mountain and afforded Jack a good view of the drop off into the valleys and rocks far below, his eyes would widen even more, his lips compress and his teeth clench. Ryan's grin faded as she sensed her friend's continued distress. She now wished they had opted for the longer route to the south around the mountains. "Are you okay, Jack?" she asked.

Without breaking his trance-like stare at the sheer drop off into the nearby scenic abyss, he answered her question with one of his own. "Could you slow down a little on these curves?" he croaked.

As if in answer, she braked again as they entered the next hairpin turn. She thought she heard Jack groan in response. "Jack, you could walk faster than I'm driving. Try to stop looking out the window at the drop-offs and the distant horizon. Concentrate on something else," she advised.

With an effort Jack pulled his trance-like gaze away from the window and refocused on Ryan. Over the last several miles the hem of Ryan's brightly colored, red sundress had slowly inched up as she continued to alternate between the gas pedal and the brake, the thin material now resting well above mid-thigh on her smooth, slightly parted legs. His eyes involuntarily succumbed to the provocative sight, traveling downward from her face to her exposed legs, as if in response to an overpowering magnet.

Oblivious, Ryan was still talking. "Besides, it shouldn't be much longer now before we're heading down the other side of the mountain and—"

Ryan stopped mid-sentence, finally noticing the new direction of Jack's mesmerized stare. The heat rushed to her face as she blushed. She nervously tugged at the hem of her dress in an attempt to pull it back down to her knees. She was flustered, a reaction to which she was unaccustomed. Chagrined, Ryan couldn't remember the last time anyone or anything had made her blush... maybe back in her freshman year of high school with that boy, Tommy... but now, with Jack... after her years as a—

Ryan severed those thoughts, and with her dress properly readjusted, looked over at Jack, now tight lipped and studiously watching the winding road ahead of them. It was hard to tell, but it looked as if Jack was a little flushed himself beneath his dark complexion. Ryan returned her attention to the road. "Anyway, it shouldn't be long before we're out of the mountains," she mumbled into the stillness of the car.

In less than an hour they descended out of the mountains and onto a more manageable and less dramatic highway, eventually turning onto the well maintained, graveled and graded, Fort Bayard Road. It wasn't long before they spied the Medical Center in the distance. A right turn past several large cottonwoods, and they had arrived. The Medical Center was part of a larger complex, the Center itself expanded and renovated as it usage increased. In the mid-80s a secure, psychiatric ward had been added.

They parked in front of the two-story, white-washed limestone administration building, entered and confronted the bespectacled, middle-aged female receptionist. Jack took charge. "I'm Sergeant Jack Kroner, and we'd like to talk to the Hospital Administrator. It's concerning an ongoing police investigation into several homicides. We're on a multi-state task force gathering information."

The receptionist who introduced herself as Dolores Winkle, was duly impressed with Jack's gruff voice and professional, authoritarian demeanor. His rugged good looks hadn't been lost on the woman, either. He pulled his police I.D. badge out of his Levi's and flashed it at the woman, sealing the deal. The awed woman was too flustered by the broad shouldered man in the denim shirt to notice he was slightly outside his jurisdiction. She made a quick phone call, and after a short conversation with someone in subdued tones, had the two of them heading for the Administrator's office.

Fortunately, the Center's Administrator, Andrew Parsons—a thin, dapper looking man with a thinning thatch of gray hair—didn't resent Jack and Ryan barging in without an appointment in the middle of the day, especially when he saw Ryan. It was obvious that Mr. Parsons considered Ryan a very pleasant interruption in the warm day, as his appreciative glances demonstrated.

Jack and Ryan took the offered chairs across from Mr. Parsons' desk. Ryan eased onto her seat and crossed her legs casually, allowing her skirt to inch higher. Jack again flashed his I.D. and began his spiel. Distracted, Andrew leaned forward on his desk, discreetly attempting to get a better look at Ryan as he listened.

Stifling a grin, Jack again explained that he and Ryan were part of an inter-agency task force investigating a series of possibly related serial killings. As for Ryan, she managed not to gawk at Jack as he calmly rattled off the police investigation explanation—one that was potentially putting himself way out on a limb, as far as his police career was concerned.

Still, the results of their conversation bore fruit. Ryan interceded early in the conversation when it became apparent that Andrew was quite taken with her, and she had judiciously added a few details concerning the homicides. The Administrator had paled at several of the descriptions. "So, as you can see, Mr. Parsons, any information you could give us on our person of interest, Norman Bartholomew, would be extremely helpful," Ryan concluded.

Andrew smiled, but was apologetic. "I'm sorry that I can't divulge patient details or treatment without a court order, Officer Sanders, but I'll give you what I can," he replied with a tinge of regret.

Outwardly, Ryan beamed a warm and appreciative smile his way. Inwardly, she grinned at the man's acceptance of her being a police officer. If he only knew, she thought grimly.

Andrew slid out a computer drawer and typed on a keyboard for several seconds. He studied the results on the desk monitor for a long minute before looking back at Ryan. Jack looked a bit rueful, having been relegated to a spectator in the proceedings.

Andrew smiled hopefully at Ryan. "I can confirm that a Norman Fredrick Bartholomew was a patient at this facility from May 14th of 1998 to March 30th of 2003, at which time he was released upon the recommendation of the Center's Board of Directors. Further, the doctors in charge of Mr. Bartholomew's treatment were a Dr. Susan Belmont and Dr. Benjamin Tolliver, both of whom are no longer with the Center. Dr. Belmont has a private practice in Denver, Colorado. Dr. Tolliver retired in 2008 and is now residing in Santa Fe, New Mexico." Considering the circumstances, the Administrator didn't see a problem with furnishing Officer Sanders and Sgt. Kroner with the doctors' addresses, since they were now in the public sector. Plus, it was a police investigation after all....

Although it was getting late in the afternoon, they decided to make the five hour drive back to Albuquerque. It was Jack's turn to drive, which meant it would be more like a six hour trek because, without a word, Jack headed south away from the mountains towards the I-10 freeway and the longer route home. Ryan smiled and remained mute, absently tugging at the hem of her dress.

She continued in silent mode as they headed back towards Albuquerque, watching the landscape flash by as Jack navigated the desert throughways. But eventually, Ryan couldn't help herself. She stared at Mr. Inscrutable next to her, his stony visage centered on the road ahead. "What the hell do you think you're doing spewing all that bullshit about task forces, official police investigations and serial killings?" she asked.

Jack looked at her without expression. "It got results, didn't it? And you managed a few pretty graphic contributions yourself."

Ryan could only shake her head, confused, dismayed and a little angry. "Don't play stupid. You're comparing apples and oranges, Jack. I'm just a wronged civilian searching for the killer of her sister. But you? You're putting your head on the chopping block. If the Department finds out what you're doing, the shit's going to hit the fan. Why the hell are you doing this? When we find this maniac, you know what I intend to do with him. I don't think I've made that a secret. And when that happens, your involvement will become obvious, if it doesn't even sooner. I think you should cut your losses and go back to Detroit."

Jack had been staring straight ahead, slightly hunched forward. His grip was white-knuckled on the steering wheel. He turned and looked at her, his lips a crevice through the rocky, but gentle, terrain of his face. "I'm a big boy Ryan. I'm your friend, and intend to help you and, at least try, to keep you out of trouble. If…" he looked at her, the black agates of his eyes boring into hers "… no, not if… when we find him, I'm hoping you'll see reason and let the law handle it. That would be me—at least for now. However this ends, I'm not going to let anything happen to you." He pulled his eyes away from her and back to the road, his death grip on the wheel and his tense posture relaxing.

Ryan was speechless, unable to respond. The look in his eyes just before he turned away… in all the years she'd known him… she couldn't remember the big cop looking so vulnerable. Ryan was on a mission of revenge, and Jack was willing to take the chance of throwing his career away just to help and protect her—not only from harm, but from doing something that might ruin her life. On the one hand, it strengthened her resolve to let nothing dissuade her from her goal. On the other, his sincere and overwhelming concern was causing a churning, unfamiliar feeling in her stomach.

She pushed the feelings and thoughts aside and changed the subject. "So, I'm thinking we head up to Santa Fe tomorrow morning and talk to this Dr. Tolliver," she said.

Jack kept his eyes on the road. "Sounds like a plan to me," he replied.

Ryan turned her face back to the side window and resumed gazing out at the passing scenery—this time her vision of the desert landscape blurred by tears.

# Chapter 31

**D**r. Benjamin Tolliver's residence in Santa Fe was a beautiful, older adobe home, completely restored and furnished in traditional Southwestern décor. From the enclosed flagstone courtyard with its desert flower landscaping, to the Spanish Saltillo tiles of the foyer and hallway, then on into the open, spacious living area with its eclectic mix of Pueblo Indian and Mexican paintings, pottery and sculptures, the doctor's home was strangely homey in a way that neither Ryan nor Jack were accustomed to.

They had called ahead and, once they had explained who they were and the seriousness of their inquiry, the retired psychiatrist had agreed to see them. Dr. Tolliver, a slightly overweight, gray-haired man of sixty-five, greeted them at the door and ushered them into his home. He soon had them seated on a plush, subdued multi-colored sofa, and placed a tray filled with coffee, tea, and an assortment of cookies on the coffee table in front of them. The table itself was mesmerizing, wrought iron legs supporting a rough, gray, rectangular faux stone slab, engraved with alien looking Indian symbols. Ryan guessed that one symbolized the sun, another—a spiral, maybe representing time, another—

"I see you like my coffee table, Ms. Sanders." Dr. Tolliver was sitting in a dark leather chair across from them, sipping his tea and gazing from Jack to Ryan appraisingly.

"Please, just call me Ryan, Dr. Tolliver," she replied. "And yes the table is beautiful." She gazed around the large, tastefully furnished room, then up at the open-beamed ceiling. "Your whole house is absolutely gorgeous; I've never seen anything similar. The hotel where we're staying has a little Southwest decor, but nothing like this."

"I've been decorating it ever since I retired five years ago. The table I found on Capital Street in the art district right here in Santa Fe. They have many fine artisans in this city. And just call me Ben; I'm out of the psychiatry business." He looked over at Jack.

Taking his cue, Jack finally spoke. "Since everyone else has gone informal, you can drop the Sgt. Kroner and just call me Jack."

Ryan took a sip of her coffee. The good Dr. Tolliver might be retired, but ingrained habits were hard to break. While Ryan and Jack were seated on the couch, Ben had the dominate position facing them in the large chair, and he had steered Jack effortlessly into the conversation.

Dr. Tolliver was smiling. With his khaki pants, loose fitting linen shirt and slightly mussed gray hair, he exuded a warm paternal air about him—a person one would feel comfortable confiding in. "So, Ryan..." he directed his gaze to her "... and

Jack…" now shifting his hazel eyes to him "… I can only assume your visit, and the urgency you conveyed on the phone, would have to concern one of my former patients."

Jack took the lead. "Yes, it does Dr. Tol… I mean, Ben. We have information that leads us to believe a former patient of yours, a Norman Bartholomew, might be responsible for a series of brutal murders in several states over the last ten years."

Ryan was studying the doctor. At the mention of Norman's name, Dr. Tolliver's smile imperceptibly dimmed, the corners of his mouth fractionally dipped, his intelligent eyes narrowed ever so slightly. But the changes were so minute that it could have been Ryan's imagination.

The doctor set his saucer and teacup back on the table. "Jack, even though I'm retired, I'm still bound by a 'doctor/patient confidentiality.' Besides that inviolable trust, Mr. Bartholomew was a juvenile for two of his five years under my care. Another layer of legal confidentiality. I can't directly discuss any of my former patient's cases. You must know that from your law enforcement career."

Ryan immediately homed in on the word "directly" in the doctor's comments. And judging from the slight widening of Jack's eyes, he had caught the adverb as well.

"Yes, I know that," Jack replied. "And as I explained on the phone, this is an informal investigation and Ryan is a relative of one of the victims. In my current capacity, I'm off duty and more of a private investigator. Should I come up with any concrete evidence I'll be turning things over to the proper jurisdictional authorities."

Ryan smiled benignly through this give and take between the two. Jack was being honest about it all, but Ryan figured that if the good doctor could read her mind and realize her intentions, he would not be so forthcoming in conceding any information.

Jack was still talking "… but, Ben, maybe you can help us with general psychiatric observations so we might better understand what we're dealing with here. And if there's anything you can legally and ethically divulge, please do so. First, let me describe what our killer's M.O. is. By M.O. I mean—"

"Modus operandi—method of operation. I know what M.O. means, Jack."

"Sorry, Dr. Tolliver… Ben… of course you do." He continued, "In the Western states the bodies of fifteen women were found in various states of decomposition—six of them buried, the others secreted in different and imaginative places. Given time, the killer buries the bodies, so there may be other related, unsolved homicides the police are not aware of yet. We're only looking at any unsolved killings bearing specific, distinct similarities." Jack pulled a folder out of the slim, leather briefcase he had brought with him, removed several photographs, leaned across the table, and handed them to Dr. Tolliver.

"Those are police and forensic photographs of the victims," Jack continued. "I've scribbled notes on the bottoms of the photos. There is forensic evidence of necrophilia being committed on most of the subjects, so I've dubbed these homicides as 'necro-killings.'" He didn't mention the non-forensic evidence—Ryan's detailed description of the post-death mental information and images she had received from her sister concerning the killer.

Dr. Tolliver took the photographs. "Sergeant, the proper term is necrophilic homicide— murder to obtain a corpse, not necro-killings," he added quietly. Seconds ticked by as Dr. Tolliver slowly leafed through the photographs, his eyes traveling from the images to Jack's notes in the margins. They watched in silence as the doctor's smile ebbed like a receding tide, leaving in its wake a desolate beach. His brows knitted as his eyes grew darker. At one point he mumbled, "Oh, my…"

He sighed and returned the photos to Jack. "I'm guessing you may be out of bounds legally in this investigation…" he nodded at the police photographs "…but I can see the urgency in finding the killer of these women—I'm sure the murderer will not cease his depredations anytime soon." He looked at Ryan. "Are you okay, my dear? You look a little pale," he queried.

"I'm okay; I guess I was just wondering… why anyone would kill them first, then after they were dead… do… and then do those things…" Ryan stopped, a brief tremor coursing through her. She forced herself to swallow and take a deep, shuddering breath. "I'm okay, really."

Dr. Tolliver looked doubtful, but continued. "Jack used the term necrophilia. The simple definition is 'sexual attraction to corpses'—"

Seeing Ryan grimace, Dr. Tolliver paused.

Ryan closed her eyes for a long second and shook her head. "Please, go on."

Dr. Tolliver looked concerned, but resumed. "There are references to the practice dating back to ancient Egypt, but I don't think you're here for a history lesson. More to the point:

In 1989, Rosman and Resnick gathered and reviewed information on dozens of cases of necrophilia, interviewing the subjects as to the motivations for their behavior. Surprisingly, only 15% professed an actual sexual attraction to a corpse as their primary desire. The vast majority, 68%, reported an obsession to 'possess an unresisting and un-rejecting partner.' Besides 'unresisting and un-rejecting,' I would add the desire to dominate a totally 'vulnerable and helpless' partner as a strong motivational desire for the necrophiliac. In fact—"

Ryan couldn't stop herself and interrupted. "I find the whole idea absolutely obscene and disgusting... sex with a cold, discolored, stiff cadaver... I can't even imagine..." She shuddered again.

Dr. Tolliver smiled in agreement. "Obscene and disgusting, yes, but not entirely for the reasons you just gave. Your friend Jack could fill you in on a lot of this, I'm sure, but since we're on the topic, I'll continue. You said cold, discolored, stiff? Not necessarily. After death, the body cools—called algor mortis—only two degrees in the first hour and one degree each hour after that. Between one and two hours after death, livor mortis begins to set in—the purplish discoloration at the low points of the immobile body—as gravity exerts its force on the non-circulating blood, and it begins to pool. The onset of rigor mortis—the stiffening of the muscles and the resulting rigidity of the body—begins two to three hours after death. All of those things are subject to variations in the environment, of course—temperature, humidity, body composition, to name a few."

Ryan was listening raptly as he continued. "So, Ryan, let's say you enter a room and find an unresponsive person lying on the floor. The body is warm, pale and completely supple. Since they would be in that state for over an hour before any outward physiological changes occurred, how would you know if they were dead or not?"

Ryan blurted, "By checking to see if they were breathing, and had a pulse or heartbeat."

"But, you don't know if the person 'died' a few minutes prior, or an hour ago," Dr. Tolliver replied. "Drugs, heart-attack, drowning, electric shock, smoke inhalation, suffocation, complications during surgery, any number of occurrences can stop the heart and breathing. And we know of instances where many of those victims have been revived successfully. Imagine, if you will, pulling a drowning victim out of a swimming pool and finding no respiration or heartbeat. But you have no idea when they drowned. A minute? An hour? So, are they irretrievably dead? You're not going to attempt CPR? What if they had drowned just prior to your arrival? One minute or one hour, at that point there's no way of knowing for sure."

The doctor took a sip of his tea before continuing. "The brain can survive for several minutes after death on the residual oxygen in its tissue before cerebral hypoxia sets in. If you can restore a heartbeat and restart the circulation of blood and oxygen to the brain within a few minutes, the subject can be revived undamaged. But in as little as four minutes, the brain cells can begin to die and the likelihood of brain damage increases as the minutes continue to elapse. Again, the time for this damage to occur would vary somewhat based on temperature, environment, blood oxygenation, and the physical condition of the deceased before their death, among other factors. How long before the brain completely dies is unknown—maybe as long as ten minutes, I'm guessing—but permanent brain damage may have started before then, sometime between four and ten minutes."

Dr. Tolliver had been looking at Jack during this last part, but glanced back at Ryan when he heard a small gasp. He noticed Ryan had paled even more and her eyes had grown wide as if she'd seen the proverbial ghost. "Oh my, Ryan, something is wrong. What is it, what can I get you?" he asked.

Jack was looking at Ryan in alarm, but he addressed Dr. Tolliver. "Ben, if you could get her some water, I think she'll be okay. Her sister was murdered recently and all this talk of death has upset her; I shouldn't have brought her with me."

"Yes, yes, of course," the doctor replied. "I'm so sorry, I'll be right back." He rose, leaned over and patted Ryan's arm before scurrying off to the kitchen.

Jack put his arm around Ryan and pulled her head to his shoulder and whispered over her head. "I'm sorry for bringing you, I shouldn't have—"

With a catch in her voice, Ryan muttered, "That part about the brain not dying after death and all… it just caught me by surprise and brought everything back… I'll be okay in a minute."

Dr. Tolliver was returning with the water. Ryan sat back up and Jack removed his arm. The doctor handed the glass of water to Ryan. "Here, my dear, are you going to be okay?"

Grateful, Ryan took a sip. "I'll be fine, Ben, thank you."

Dr. Tolliver returned to his seat, still looking concerned. Jack decided to speed things along. "So, Ben, was Norman Bartholomew a necrophiliac?"

The doctor's expression turned from concern to dismay. "Jack, you know I can't discuss Norman's particular case."

"Ben, from the public records and newspaper articles we've managed to dig up, it would seem that Norman's mother, Nicole, a prostitute who sexually abused her son for years, died in a suspicious accident in their home—electrocution, if I remember correctly. There was also a rumor that one her 'johns' came to the home and found Norman in bed with his dead mother—"

Dr. Tolliver, expressionless, interjected. "A lot of media sensationalism and unsubstantiated reports. Norman was never charged with anything."

Jack pressed on. "True, and many of the facts were sealed because Norman was a juvenile. Ten years ago, a year after his release from your care, the murders started. Dr. Tolliver... Ben... you saw the photographs. These killings will continue, and if Norman is the psychopath..." Jack let the statement hang in the air.

The doctor closed his eyes and seemed to shrink in his chair. An almost inaudible whisper escaped him. "I told the hospital board he shouldn't be released."

Jack remained silent. Ryan was holding her breath.

Dr. Tolliver looked from Jack to Ryan, then to some far away point between them, a forlorn look on his face. He began in a measured tone. "Let's suppose someone, from a very young age, was sexually abused and forced into unnatural acts by their mother. This offspring might well develop a love/hate relationship with that parent, a potentially devastating psychological division."

Dr. Tolliver paused before continuing, his eyes moving from Jack to Ryan and back, thoughtful and measuring. "If the victim was a son, the abuser the mother, and this scenario was carried to the limit, the victim might well transfer his schizophrenic mania to other women—if his mother was no longer available. If this occurred—say his mother died, for example—and the psychosis was profound and permanent, the cycle might never stop. He would love, hate, and if it had reached the catastrophic extreme, kill his mother over and over again—substituting all women for his mother."

Dr. Tolliver paused again, gathering his thoughts before continuing. "This hypothetical person would have a fundamental problem in dealing with women in any normal setting. Having been abused and subjugated his entire life by a dominant female—his mother—his severe feelings of inadequacy, and an unrelenting, underlying terror, might well render him incapable of dealing with women—unless they were dead, and therefor powerless. This would occur in the most extreme cases, of course."

The doctor managed a humorless grin. "He would never consider necrophilia as applying to himself. His primary goal would be to permanently subjugate his mother—or any female surrogate— to make them totally and completely vulnerable and submissive, permanently subservient to his needs and wants, without fear of rejection or criticism—for ever and ever, so to speak. It would, of course, have to be within the first hour or so after death before true signs of their passing became apparent, when the illusion of life—"

Jack interrupted. "And if he knew the mind of his victim was still alive and believed it was aware of what was happening to its body?"

Dr. Tolliver peered thoughtfully at Jack. "It would be the perfect scenario for Nor... for the killer. He could exact both love and hate on his victim, knowing that his helpless prey, trapped inside, was at his complete mercy—he could exact both love and vengeance, reveling in the imagined terror—at least as long as he believed that their brain was living on for a few more minutes."

Jack was sitting close enough to Ryan to hear a small groan escape her. He glanced quickly at her and decided to wrap things up. "And if this person had a choice of where to live, where might that that be?"

"It could be near where the childhood atrocities occurred, and if the mother was deceased, probably not too far from where she was buried."

Jack rose and helped Ryan to her feet. "We want to thank you, Ben, for your hospitality."

"One other thing," added Dr. Tolliver. "Initially, another psychiatrist was assigned to Norman Bartholomew after his mother's death, a Dr. Susan Belmont. I believe she has a private practice in Denver now. But I doubt she could help you much with his case; she only had him for three months before he was transferred."

"Any particular reason?" quizzed Jack.

Dr. Tolliver frowned. "It seems that Norman couldn't 'relate' to Dr. Belmont. He was either morbidly timid and self-conscious, or fearful and terrified in her presence. Either way, it was almost impossible for him to interact with her. Since it appeared he had a problem with women, they reassigned him to my care."

Ryan managed to refocus and rejoined the conversation. "Almost forgot something, Ben." She opened her purse, retrieved Officer Adams' sketch of Norman, unfolded it and handed it to Dr. Tolliver. "Ben, is this Norman?" she asked.

The doctor studied it thoughtfully for several seconds. "Hmmmm… I haven't seen Norman in ten years… but this certainly could be him." Dr. Tolliver's fatherly smile returned as he handed it back.

At the door he shook both of their hands. "Good luck in your search." His smile widened. "And I'm sorry I couldn't discuss Norman's case with you."

# Chapter 32

**"What?" Norman yelled.** His grip on the cell phone tightened danger-ously; it wouldn't be the first one he'd broken. "You mean to tell me that Ryan bitch took out two of your men and killed one of them?" Norman's teeth were grinding as he listened in-tently, his face a mask of barely controlled rage. "I don't care if they weren't your men, Hector..." he paused and listened for a few seconds before interrupting, "... and for your sake they better not have known where their marching orders originated. I pay you good money, amigo, to do what I say—no questions asked. Those two will be back here looking for me. And if so, they'd better not find me—I would be more than a little upset with you. I gave you their pictures. Make sure you and your thugs keep an eye out for her and her friend around the Socorro area." Norman's usually pleasant voice had degenerated into a growl. He disconnected without another word.

Norman went to his bedroom, donned his shorts and sleeve-less t-shirt and stomped off to his weight room. After warming up, he started circuit training—moving from one apparatus to another with only a fifteen second break between them—hitting every muscle group. Finally, after an hour he finished with the bench press, doing three sets of twelve reps at 210 pounds, the last few accompanied by howls of exertion.

Norman sat on the edge of the bench breathing heavily, leaning on his knees, sweat dripping on the green, rubberized padding on the floor. Although his rage had been dampened by the exercise and fatigue was setting in, he worked out on the heavy bag hanging in the corner. For the next fifteen minutes he pummeled it mercilessly until his arms became leaden. No way was he going to let a woman hurt him again like that little spic had in Detroit. And if he ever got his hands on that cunt, Ryan… Norman finally allowed himself a sardonic smile as he visualized the outcome of that meeting and its glorious four minute ending. He grew hard during his musings, but instead of a quick trip to the shower to take care of himself, nagging thoughts kept derailing his fantasy. Soon, he was as limp as overcooked spaghetti. Norman growled in frustration, his rage simmering again.

How in the hell had the woman traced him to New Mexico? He was meticulous in his killings although his temporary fugues had become a bit unnerving. But the sisters lived over 1800 miles apart and Norman had removed all traces of the one he'd killed. He had checked her out of the motel. Her car was in a chop shop in Mexico. He had checked her cell phone and there had been no outgoing calls for over 48 hours. And she had just arrived at the motel the day before Norman had the good fortune of finding her. Or possibly misfortune... Norman ignored the ridiculous thought.

Maybe Ryan knew her sister was visiting New Mexico. Even if this were true, Norman realized he might be overreacting. New Mexico was the fifth largest state at over 21,000 square miles. Other than the actual records at the motel, there was no evidence of her in Socorro, and certainly none in Magdalena. And the bottom line, of course, was that there was absolutely no connection between Dana and Norman for Ryan to find.

Even if the impossible happened and the Sanders whore somehow made a connection between her cunt sister and him... well, Norman would just have to keep an eye out for her and her cop friend for a while. He had gotten a pretty good description of the pig from the spic broad before he killed her, plus he had the picture of the Ryan woman. Hector and his boys would be keeping an eye out for them. He was worrying needlessly. Still, better safe than sorry. And when the two finally tired of looking for him and went home... well... another trip to Detroit just might be in order.

Norman strode off to the shower. Standing under the near scalding water, he felt the familiar urges stirring, and began playing with himself. He knew he needed and deserved the real thing... but it was too soon... way too soon, he warned himself. And he needed to plan it out; it might be stretching his luck to take another one in-state, let alone near home.

Maybe he'd calm himself by working on the new "Dana" change purses. Too bad he couldn't use them in public or sell them on eBay. Norman grinned at the thought. The cunt's tits were perfect—now cured and tanned— and ready for him to trim, punch holes around the outer edges and insert the leather drawstrings. And her long nipples were ideal; they would look so provocative protruding from the bottom of the purses. They reminded him of Nicole's. Her nipples and breasts that had been a forced part of his life—among many other things—right up until the day he killed her.

Although killing women on his home turf was dangerous and to be avoided, it had one advantage. When he was out of state, cutting off and transporting their tits back home posed a few inherent and dangerous problems. After scooping out the fat and tissue, a messy proposition to begin with, he needed to cure the skins by salting or keeping them on ice—a temporary process to prevent bacterial decomposition—while he transported them home where he could do the permanent tanning procedure. The out of state locations of his attacks normally prevented the dismemberment and curing. When you added to that the absurdity of trying to transport the skins by plane or the potential danger of discovery—however unlikely—of transporting by car, taking victims at home had a distinct advantage in those areas.

His first victim—Amanda, if he remembered the name correctly—was dispatched in his basement over ten years ago and provided his first experiments in tanning. Norman was just learning back then, and those first change purses didn't last very long. A few years later he chanced transporting a hastily removed bounty, cut from the Phoenix teenager he abducted and worked on in the desert. Norman was getting better at the tanning process, but even so, those purses degraded faster than animal hides.

Human skin—even when painstakingly cured and tanned—seemed to have a shorter life expectancy than other animal skins. It was time for new ones.

Norman frowned in the bright lights of the basement. The breasts, rawhide strings and various instruments were now laid out on the workbench before him. He stared at the tanned breast skin, their erect nipples taunting him—much like Nicole's had. But the disquieting thoughts again snaked their way into his mind.

All his kills—or "cleansings" as he liked to call them—over the prior ten years were accomplished with no major problems, essentially "flying under the radar." This Ryan woman, the sister, was becoming a nuisance, a thorn in his side. Norman shook his head and picked up the skins, trying to push thoughts of her out of his mind. She couldn't know anything, and she certainly didn't have any information on him. He smiled, picked up the awl and one breast skin and began punching holes around the edges. When he finished he'd run the rawhide drawstring through the holes, completing his new change purse. He paused and lovingly stroked the nipple. Norman hummed to himself as thoughts of Ryan and Jack slowly faded from his mind and he began to suckle on the breast.

# CHAPTER 33

Ryan and Jack spent the night in Santa Fe before making the three-hour drive south to Socorro, Norman's old stomping grounds. Norman's mother, Nicole Anna Bartholomew, had died and was buried there and, based on Dr. Tolliver's comments concerning the possibility of Norman living somewhere nearby, it was a logical place to start. Plus, it was possible that if Dana had traveled that way, memories of the area might have been passed on immediately after her death to Ryan, and could provide further clues aiding their search.

But first, the two had time to drop a chunk of money on souvenirs, primarily jewelry for Ryan, at the plaza in Old Town Santa Fe. As with the older cities and towns settled by the Spanish in New Mexico, they were built around a central plaza—the cultural and social center of the early, fledging settlements—and from which the original streets radiated.

Jack and Ryan browsed through several of the quaint shops surrounding the rectangular plaza, enjoying the shade of several large cottonwoods and the green, tranquil setting of the old town square, complete with a white band shell. It was a beautiful area often used as the venue for weddings. Ryan dropped the bulk of her souvenir money on several handmade pieces of turquoise and silver jewelry sold by Native Americans, their wares spread out on brightly colored blankets along the walkways under the wooden awnings of several of the shops.

Later, as they ate dinner at the Hacienda Cafe—a rustic, Spanish themed restaurant on one of the narrow side streets— Ryan noticed that her friend was even quieter than his usual taciturn self. "So, Jack, what did you spend your hard earned money on?" she asked.

Jack roused himself from his reverie, picked up a bag he had set on the floor next to his chair, and took out a feathered object and handed it to Ryan. "I bought a couple of Dream Catchers, one for each of us."

Ryan took the object and held it up in front of her by the rawhide strap. It was a circular, leather covered hoop approximately four inches in diameter. An intricate pattern of interconnected catgut filled the hoop, very much resembling a spider web. From the hoop hung several foot long strands of leather, interspersed with beads, feathers and silver.

The rocky terrain of Jack's face succumbed to a hesitant smile as he gazed at Ryan's intent inspection of the object. "It's a handmade Native American Dream Catcher," he said. "Tradition and Indian lore dictates you hang it in the corner of your bedroom. During the night when dreams come, the web inside the hoop lets the good dreams in, but keeps the bad dreams out. Sort of

like a spiritual filter, I guess. I figured we could both use one...
wouldn't hurt, anyway."

"Thank you, Jack." She paused, studying him. "I keep forgetting, your great-grandmother was from one of the tribes here in New Mexico, wasn't she? Any of the Native American vendors here from—?"

"No," he interjected. "She was from the Acoma Pueblo, a good hour's drive west of Albuquerque. The Sky Pueblo they call it, built atop a large mesa and billed as 'the oldest, continually inhabited city in America.' I'll have to give you a history lesson on it someday." He paused, frowning. "I guess I'm feeling a little guilty about never visiting, never exploring my Indian heritage."

"Maybe when this is all over we can visit the reservation," Ryan replied. To herself she wondered—considering the different outcomes she and Jack envisioned for their quest's resolution— what exactly each of their futures might hold. She pushed the dismaying thought aside. "Your great-grandfather was Russian. How in the world did he and your great-grandmother meet?" she asked.

Jack shook his head, seemingly bemused by his mixed heritage. "Viktor Kronin immigrated to America in the late 1800s from a small town in the Crimean Peninsula. He landed in San Francisco, worked his way across the country, eventually ending up in Detroit. When he passed through New Mexico, he stopped at the Acoma Pueblo looking for food and lodging. It just so happened a wedding ceremony was taking place, and the friendly inhabitants invited him to join in the post-ceremony celebration. My great-grandmother, Moema—which means 'sweet' in the

Tupi language—was a member of the bridal party; a bridesmaid I guess you would say. It was love at first sight." Jack shook his head again. "A Russian and a Pueblo Indian; go figure. Now, that's a mixed up lineage."

Ryan sighed. "Actually, that's a pretty romantic story, pal." She flashed a huge grin at him, gesturing with both hands palms up, towards him. "And ta-dah! Look what an impressive hunk their combined gene pool eventually turned out," she added. She wasn't positive, but she thought a tinge of blush accompanied his flustered look.

Jack cleared his throat self-consciously. "Okay, enough of the history lessons. Let's finish up here and get back to the motel. We have a long day ahead of us tomorrow."

Later that night in her room, Ryan took her Dream Catcher out of the bag and hung it from the ceiling sprinkler head in the center of the room. She watched it slowly turn to and fro in the invisible air currents. She would take all the help she could get in filtering out the bad dreams. Ryan glanced at the door, wondering if Jack had hung up his Dream Catcher in his room.

Ryan undressed and slipped under the covers; she'd take her shower in the morning. Her thoughts swirled around as she lay staring at the ceiling in the dark. Assuming this Norman Bartholomew was their guy and assuming they were able to track the animal down—somehow Ryan was confident they would— she would part ways with Jack before the final showdown. No way was she going to have him involved when she enacted her payback. Her friend had already gone way out on a limb for her, as he had done several times over the years.

When they found the serial killer, Jack would want to arrest him and turn him over to the "proper authorities." That would not happen—it wasn't in her plans. She would have to decide how to handle her and Jack's separation when the time came. Ryan's last thoughts as sleep overtook her were... how in the world did Jack... get so much time off... to go traipsing... around the country... with her...?

They left Santa Fe at 9:00 in the morning and arrived in Socorro less than four hours later. Ryan was driving when they approached the city limits. Mentally on autopilot, she looked to the west at the stretch of nearby mountains. She reflexively jerked the steering wheel when she saw the first "memory landmark." There was a large white "M" painted high in the mountains to the west. Ryan wasn't sure what it stood for, but it was something Dana must have seen from the I-25 Freeway. Dana had been in Socorro, or had at least passed through the city.

Jack had felt the slight pull of the vehicle. "What is it; you tired or what?" Jack questioned

"No, just daydreaming I guess. Sorry." Ryan managed a smile, keeping her excitement in check. After they exited onto California Street, the main drag through Socorro, she spied a McDonald's coming up on the right. "Let's grab a Big Mac and find out how many cemeteries this town has and where they're located."

As it turned out, Socorro had two cemeteries within the city limits. One was the old Socorro Mission Cemetery, the final resting place for a number of the older Spanish and Mexican families, but had been closed to new burials for over fifty years. The other was the San Miguel Cemetery. There were three others within easy driving distance, but they started with the one still operating in town.

As they pulled into the shaded grounds of the San Miguel churchyard, it took all of Ryan's willpower to maintain her composure and suppress a shudder as she "recognized" the cemetery. This was where Dana had first seen her killer.

Ryan wheeled their Jeep into a parking space in front of the cemetery office. She continued with the charade, "We'll start by finding out if this Nicole Bartholomew is buried here."

"Have you recognized anything from Dana's memories?" Jack questioned.

"Nothing yet," she lied, without expression. Ryan could have shown Jack exactly where the grave was.

"Okay, I'll be right back." Jack exited the car and ambled over to the building. He was back in less than ten minutes. "It's down that way," he said, nodding to their left. "They gave me a map of the grounds."

Minutes later they were standing and looking at the bronze marker of Nicole Anna Bartholomew. The only inscriptions were her name and the dates of her birth and death. There was a plastic, bronze-imitation flower vase nearby with dead flowers in it.

"The grounds-crew picks up the vases and dead flowers from the graves weekly," Jack mused. "But the clerk has no idea how often or who brings flowers to the individual graves. The plastic vases are always available in the office for everyone. I suppose we could always stake out the cemetery and hope he shows up soon."

Ryan knew the man she "remembered" standing by this same gravesite and the one that had kidnapped and killed Dana were one and the same. And unless someone other than Nicole's son was visiting this particular grave, that person was indeed Norman.

Ryan managed to quell the rising emotions within her. She had to feign ignorance and continue the charade. "Well, we've already tried directory assistance, and there's no listing for a Norman Bartholomew in Socorro, or anywhere in the county for that matter. Probably changed his name a long time ago. With luck, he might show up here, and I'd identify him from Dana's memories. If it is Norman, we could follow him, see where he lives and possibly come up with something definitive, something incriminating. Then again, we could be waiting here for weeks, maybe forever."

Jack was looking at her, studying her. Finally, he sighed and looked away. "Well, let's drive around town for a while. Maybe you'll see something that you remember. Or Dana remembered," he corrected.

They meandered through Socorro for the next two hours, Ryan carefully denying recognition of anything when questioned. She was glad she was gazing out the window when they passed Little Anita's Restaurant. She covered her gasp of shock with a cough and clearing of the throat. Dana had been at that restaurant and, worse, was attacked and kidnapped in the parking lot.

Jack glanced at her, but didn't comment on her throat clearing. "Maybe this Norman character isn't the guy we're looking for, as promising as it appears," he said. He sounded resigned to failure. "If Dana was here, you'd have recognized something by now. We might as well head back and figure out where we go from here. We could always backtrack to Albuquerque tomorrow, do a little more research; it's quite possible we missed something, or didn't look hard enough." Even so, Jack tried several of the dirt roads surrounding Socorro before admitting defeat.

Ryan was pondering on how to follow-up on a few of Dana's memories, especially Little Anita's, without tipping off her friend. A nagging, unrelated thought from the prior night resurfaced and intruded. "Jack, when do you have to go back? How did you get so much time off from the Department?" Ryan asked.

Jack glanced at her, then back at the road, peering intently over the steering wheel. He looked uncomfortable. "Ah... I had vacation time... and... you know... that P.O.D. payback stuff between officers—"

"I'm guessing not this much, Jack," she interrupted. "And now you're talking about going back and starting over with the search. You know I won't stop until I find him. There's no telling how long that may take, and yet you haven't mentioned going back to Detroit."

Her stoic companion's hands had a death grip on the steering wheel, his muscled arms tense, his broad chest stretching the fabric of his white polo shirt. "Ryan, I won't leave you. You might actually find this maniac... I'm not going to let you do something stupid... or get hurt...." He paused, almost as if he were stalling.

"And?" she pressed.

Jack cleared his throat and continued to stare ahead for several long seconds. He finally continued. "Technically… it's not official yet… not until my accrued vacation time runs out, that is… but, Ryan, I retired from the Department."

Ryan was incredulous. Eyes wide, she stared at him, her mouth hanging open. "You what?" she questioned.

"I'm… um… retired."

"Jack, that's your career you're talking about. What in the world were you thinking?"

"Ryan, the Department's minimum retirement age with full benefits is 20 years of service. I'm 41; I started on the Department when I was 21, so I qualify. As for my career… I've been thinking about going into the private sector as an investigator… maybe starting my own business…." Jack's voice trailed off as he fixedly continued to stare straight ahead.

Bullshit, Ryan thought. She had known Jack for a long time—she wasn't stupid, he was doing it for her. She couldn't believe it, couldn't wrap her head around the idea. Quit his job, his career, just to tag along with her and her personal quest of revenge? If she hadn't been in turmoil from the eerie familiarity of Socorro, she certainly was now with this new knowledge.

Ryan spied a small bar sitting forlorn and alone off the roadway among the cacti and sagebrush. They had wandered several miles to the west of Socorro. "Pull in there, Jack, I need a drink."

"Sounds good to me," he replied, sounding relieved. Jack wheeled up the short drive in a cloud of dust and parked near a restored, maroon '63 Chevrolet Impala low-rider with chrome wheels. It was flanked by two rather decrepit, dust covered pick-up trucks. A weathered sign over the entrance of the sagging adobe building identified it as the Chollo Cantina.

# Chapter 34

Ryan had read somewhere that New Mexico averaged 320 days of sunshine each year. She had no idea how they compiled their statistics. How long did the sun have to be shining during the day for it to be considered sunny, she wondered? There would be no question about this day though. The sky, a striking cobalt blue, was without the blemish of a cloud anywhere; a flawless, sapphire dome placed over a dry, arid world. Ryan grimaced as they headed towards the entrance. Her thoughts were bouncing around like ping-pong balls.

Jack pushed open the rough wooden door of the tired-looking cantina. After the brilliance of the early afternoon, the change to the dimness of the bar was startling. Jack slowly took off his sunglasses and waited for his eyes to adjust. He stood just inside the doorway, a formidable silhouette framed against the backdrop of the day, casting a long and searching shadow into the dusty room.

A gravelly voice sounded from his right, behind the bar. "Hey, asshole, shut the fucking door. Let's keep the heat on the outside."

Ryan, standing to the left of Jack, had to admit the interior was measurably cooler. A tired ceiling fan labored sluggishly in the center of the room, wobbling slightly on its axis as its dust encrusted blades stirred the tepid air. A swamp cooler clunked away somewhere on the roof, wheezing marginally fresher air through dirty vents.

The place needed a good scouring and fumigating; the smell of grease, sour beer and old cigarette smoke permeated the room. Ryan gently closed the door behind them. They approached the acne-scarred bartender in the dirty white t-shirt and sat down gingerly on two of the wobbly bar stools. Several scratched and chipped Formica tables with battered chairs and torn upholstery, a forlorn-looking pool table in the rear, two tobacco-stained neon beer signs on the wall, and a few requisite liquor bottles on shelves behind the bar pretty well summed up the shadowy dive. There was a small grill at one end of the room behind the bar, obviously as neglected as the dish towel slung over the stocky barman's shoulder. Ryan wrinkled her nose at the fetid odors. The place was definitely a health hazard.

Jack pulled the folded police sketch of the killer out of his back pocket and slid it across the worn surface of the bar towards the man. "Have you ever seen this guy before? He ever been in here?"

Ryan didn't know if she wanted the barkeep to recognize the picture or not.

The potbellied Hispanic didn't even bother to glance at the photograph. "Nope, never seen him." He pushed the drawing back across the bar and continued to wipe at a beer mug with a dishtowel that didn't appear to have seen the inside of a washing machine in several weeks.

From her perch atop her barstool, Ryan looked around the Chollo Cantina, a dingy, hole-in-the-wall dive in the middle of nowhere. It appeared to have been furnished by a bipolar interior designer with access limited to garage sales and junkyards. The walls were stucco, but the furnishings were wood, except for several chipped Formica tables and the old pool table in the back. Dust, grease and time had reduced the interior colors to several shades of brown, almost as if the colors of the surrounding desert had seeped in over the years and bleached the inside. Ryan couldn't believe the ceiling fan could still rotate under the accumulated sludge; it obviously hadn't been cleaned in forever.

Other than Jack, herself and the grungy, middle-aged bartender, the place was inhabited by a half dozen other patrons. Besides a nondescript drunk at the far end of the bar, there were two older men with weathered faces and gray hair talking in low tones at one of the tables. Three younger, Hispanic men were at another table, talking and laughing among themselves, their voices often raised as they frequently leered and ogled in Ryan's direction. She was the only woman in the place. Ryan's manicured nails were gently drumming on the police drawing. She glanced at her passive friend sitting on the stool next to her. "Well, what do you think?" she asked.

Jack frowned. "We stopped for a drink, I'm still thirsty, so let's do it." He peered at the grease encrusted grill. "But, although it's almost five o'clock, I think I'll wait till we get back to the motel to have something to eat." He looked back at the bartender. "So, pal, since we're here we'll have a beer." Jack grinned at his rhyme, but grimaced again at the foggy mug in the barkeep's hand. "Bottled beer, of course."

Ryan really needed a cigarette. She took a pack of Marlboros out of her small red handbag, shook one out, lit the cigarette between her slender fingers and inhaled deeply. She exhaled several perfectly formed smoke rings from between her pursed, red lips, and smiled sweetly at the man behind the bar. "You heard him, two Coors—bottles, please."

The greasy looking barman had been fixated on Ryan in her tight jeans and clingy, red blouse, but managed to stop his own ogling, left and returned with the two requested bottles. Ryan slid a fifty across the bar along with the picture. "Are you sure you haven't seen this guy?" she asked.

Now he glanced down, staring blankly for several seconds. "Nope, never saw him." He took the fifty and ambled away towards the drunk at the far end of the bar.

Jack was staring at the smoldering cigarette in her hand. "I thought you quit. That wouldn't be setting a good example if they found out at the gym."

"Dammit, Jack, give me a break. It's only been since this all started, and it's only once in a while. And I never smoke around Madigan's, let alone before or after my workouts. I'll quit again when this is all over." Ryan took one more drag, then stubbed it out angrily in a small aluminum tin that might have once have held a chicken-pot-pie, but now subbed as an ash tray. A second later she was grinning and continued, "Just imagine what they'd think if they knew how I worked my way through college and came up with the money to go into business with Lonnie. Then again—"

Ryan sensed someone approach from behind and swiveled around on the stool. It was the three el tipos from the corner table, all clad in low-slung blue jeans and white, muscle tank-tops, the kind she affectionately called "grandpa" tees. It was the short, stocky tattooed guy who was speaking, apparently the spokes-man for their little group. "Hey, querida mia, how about us buy-ing you a drink? Maybe we can have a little party."

All three of the men laughed. They ignored Jack.

Ryan looked the leader up and down, then sized up his bigger, taller, companions. One featured a shaved, bald head, the other a jagged scar bisecting his left cheek. "Sorry, Poncho, not interested. And I'm not your sweetheart," she replied tonelessly.

The man's smirk disappeared. "Listen, my little puta, maybe you need a little of this." He grabbed his crotch and gave it a cou-ple of suggestive shakes. "And my name is Miguel," he growled.

Ryan held up a hand; she couldn't feel too upset about the whore reference. "Sorry, Miguel, I'm just having a bad day. I re-ally don't have the time to party, and I don't want any trouble."

She turned to Jack, who had been quietly taking it all in. "I have to pee. Let me hit the john, then we're outta here," she said. Ryan took a long swig of her beer, got up and walked around the slightly startled Miguel and his friends and headed for the restroom.

Everyone watched her stroll away and disappear into the women's lav. Miguel stared and licked his lips. He looked at his companions and the barman, gave a nod towards Jack and headed after her. "Baldy" grinned at Jack and took Ryan's vacant seat. "Scarface" scowled, spread his feet and crossed his arms, blocking the path toward the john.

The smirking barman had returned to the group, leaving the oblivious drunk to his stupor. An old, Colt .38 revolver had appeared in his hand and was now pointed in the general direction of Jack. The two senior citizens quickly and quietly called it a day and disappeared out the door.

Jack smiled sheepishly and put up his hands, palms out in a "hold it" gesture towards the man. "No problem from me boss, but you might want to call 911 and get an ambulance over here," he suggested.

Scarface sneered at him and snickered. "Miguel's not going to hurt her. Not too much anyway, just gonna have a little fun."

Jack frowned and shook his head resignedly. "The ambulance isn't for her. It's for your buddy, Miguel."

The men's uncomprehending stares were interrupted by a loud yell from the bathroom, followed by an equally loud crash. More yelling, several smaller bangs and crashes, then silence. Everyone was staring open-mouthed at the door once marked "Dolls," the euphuism crossed out and the more appropriate Hispanic word Mujeres now written next to the standard silhouette-picture of a female. Even the semi-conscious drunk's attention was aroused.

Seconds later a smiling Ryan walked out, approached the bar, reached around Baldy and took another swig of her beer while inspecting a broken finger nail. She looked at Jack and asked, "Ready?"

Jack nodded in the direction of ol' Potbelly behind the bar with the gun.

Baldy and Scarface were both standing now, looking at each other in confusion, waiting for their leader to emerge from the bathroom. When that didn't happen, Scarface reached for Ryan's arm. In one fluid motion she brought her beer bottle up and around in a wide arc, smashing it into the side of his head. For a split second he stood stunned, a vacant expression in his eyes before he slumped to the floor in an unconscious pile.

His partner managed one step forward before Ryan's arm pistoned out, the heel of her hand crunching the cartilage of his nose as it flattened. The man let out a roar of pain a second before her long, jean-clad leg jack-knifed up—her knee catching him flush in the groin—reducing him to a moaning, writhing heap on the floor.

For a big man Jack was fast. When Ryan moved, he reacted. He stood, reached across the bar and grabbed the gun from the distracted barman, gripping the cylinder so the trigger couldn't be pulled. With the other hand he grabbed a handful of hair, and slammed his head on the bar, face first. The man's stunned expression slowly disappeared below the counter as he slumped to the floor.

Ryan had one more sip of her beer, briefly considered having another cigarette before regretfully rejecting the idea. She picked up her purse and turned to Jack. "Are you ready yet?"

Jack was writing on the back of a 'Madigan's MMA Gym' business card. From the floor behind the counter, the bartender had managed to grip the edge and pull himself back up to an unsteady, standing position, his nose bloody and eyes glazed. Jack, who was now holding the man's gun, opened the cylinder and emptied the bullets into his palm.

He threw the slugs across the room and handed the gun back to the dazed man, followed by the business card. "If you do see the guy in the picture, just give us a call," he said, nodding at Ryan. He glanced towards the silent restroom, down at the two moaning men on the floor and back to the bloody, befuddled face of the barman. "As you can imagine, it would probably be a good idea," he added.

They both quickly donned their sunglasses as they headed back out into the bright sunshine. Jack glanced at Ryan, grinning and shaking his head. "I'll drive. You had a much more strenuous workout than I did." His smile dimmed somewhat. "Are you okay, Ryan?" he asked.

"I'm fine, except for this broken nail." She held her hand out in front of her, fingers spread, and stared at the damaged nail ruefully.

Jack hopped into the driver's seat of the Jeep. "I just hope you never get pissed off at me," he added.

"Not to worry, Jack. I know you're just a big teddy bear deep down inside that gruff exterior." Ryan folded into the passenger seat and buckled up. "Let's get back to the motel; I'm hungry, and I need a shower after tangoing with those slime balls."

They drove in silence for several minutes, each lost in their own thoughts. Ryan turned on the radio and found a soft rock station. "Okay with you?" she asked, glancing over at Jack.

He smiled lopsidedly at her. "Fine with me. But we need to get something to eat; I'm starving. Most of the places are along the main drag in town. I remember several fast- food places, a Domino's Pizza and a couple of restaurants. There's a number of drinking establishments that probably serve bar food, like the one—"

"No thanks, the 'Chollo' was enough bar for me today," she interrupted. "Let's get back to the motel, get cleaned up and we can order in, or I'll run out and pick us up something. Then we can map out what the hell we're going to do tomorrow."

"Good enough," Jack replied.

Besides, Ryan mused as they continued driving, she already knew what restaurant she was going to visit. Alone. As if in answer, they passed Little Anita's a short while later. She had noticed it when they passed it yesterday and earlier today. It had to be the one. The adobe, Southwestern styling reminded her of the same Spanish architecture she remembered from growing up in Southern California. But it was more than a familiarity with the design. Ryan was sure Dana had seen it and possibly had eaten there. Fragments and pieces of her memories were floating just out of focus in Ryan's mind. She would check it out, but without Jack shadowing her.

They pulled into the motel parking lot. As they headed for their respective, but adjacent rooms, Ryan spoke to the broad shouldered back moving away from her. "A quick shower, Jack, and I'll head out and pick us up dinner. Clean up your room and I'll be over with the food."

Jack glanced back over his shoulder. "What's on the menu—pizza?" he asked.

"I'll surprise you," she answered. She quickly let herself into her room and began stripping as she headed for the shower. It would indeed be a hasty shower. She wanted to get to Little Anita's as quickly as possible.

# Chapter 35

In less than an hour Ryan showered, dressed, and was on the road heading south on California Street. Five minutes later she was parking in the lot at Little Anita's. She slowed as she walked towards the entrance, gazing at the Sandia Mountains to the east. The early evening had cooled, and the setting sun had cast the distant mountain range in watermelon hued tones. It was beautiful. But it was the nearby San Mateo Mountains to the west that struck the chord of familiarity.

If Ryan thought the alien memory of the mountains odd, she was jarred from her contemplative mood when she pulled open the wooden entry door of Little Anita's. An overwhelming sense of Déjà vu overcame her—Dana had definitely been there. She was sure of it.

Ryan was greeted by a hostess clad in a loose black maxi-skirt and white peasant blouse with puffed sleeves, obviously an outfit to compliment the eclectic Spanish décor. The young woman smiled at Ryan. "How many in your party, senorita?" she queried.

Ryan couldn't help but smile. "Just myself," she answered.

The woman led Ryan to a small table nearby and waited for her to be seated before adding, "Your waitress will be with you momentarily."

Ryan thanked her, settled in and looked around, admiring the restaurant's furnishings. Seconds later she was interrupted by a pretty brunette, similarly dressed like the hostess in peasant attire.

"Hello, my name is Belinda and I'll be your waitress today. What—"

Ryan had glanced up as the young woman began her spiel, then looked at her a little more closely. The waitress seemed strangely familiar. The woman was staring back with a mildly surprised expression of her own—a look of recognition.

Belinda recovered quickly. "It's nice to see you again. So you decided to stick around for a while, do a little sightseeing, and enjoy our 'Land of Enchantment'? Been having fun…" she paused, wrinkling her nose as she scanned her memory "… Dana?" Her grin widened as she mentally patted herself on the back for recalling a customer's name.

Ryan had been gazing in puzzlement at the young waitress— until the mention of Dana's name. Her eyes widened perceptively, but she managed to keep from gaping. Dana had been in the restaurant and had actually talked to this waitress. Her mind raced on ahead. "Yes, I decided to check out your beautiful state a little longer. I've been up to Albuquerque and Santa Fe and just yesterday got back to this area. Thought maybe I'd get down to…" her mind stalled for a second as she recalled her geography

"… Las Cruces, and check out that area. I've lost track of time touring around. How long has it been since I was here?"

Belinda pursed her lips, her eyes thoughtful. "I'd say at least a month or so. Still have that big appetite? You want the combo plate again?" She laughed and said proudly, "I even remember what you had to drink. I think it was that 'Sleeping Dog Stout' from the Chama Brewery. Want a bottle?"

"Actually, Belinda, I'll take two of those combo plates to-go, plus a couple bottles of that 'Sleeping Dog' stuff. And a bottle right now while I'm waiting."

"Coming right up."

Ryan was running over options in her mind. After the little scuffle in the restroom at the cantina, Miguel had—with a little persuasion from Ryan—coughed up the name of the guy who headed their gang; the one who had alerted them to be on the lookout for Ryan and furnished them with pictures of her. It seemed her restroom buddy had a low tolerance for pain.

When the waitress returned with her drink, she was ready. "Belinda, I have a friend I'm traveling with now. He's been looking for someone he knew back in school he thinks lives in this area, a guy named Hector Ramirez. There's not that many restaurants in Socorro. Do you know of anybody by that name that may have—"

The young woman was scowling. "I don't know what he was like when he was younger and in school—I'm surprised he even finished—but your friend would probably be disappointed in how Hector turned out."

Ryan paused, wondering if she had said too much, or if she should have said anything at all. She gave the woman her best "trust-me-you-can-tell-me-anything" smile. She leaned forward, lowered her voice and whispered, "Go ahead, Belinda, my friend hasn't seen him in years. He'd appreciate an update, even if it was bad."

Reassured, the waitress continued, unconsciously lowering her voice. "Yes, Hector eats in here occasionally, usually accompanied by some of his posse. He imagines he's a big shot, and he probably is when it comes to the local drug trade. Or so rumor has it. Mostly, he and his gang like to push people around. I'm sure he's into a lot of other shady stuff, but I really don't want to know about it. I've adopted the popular attitudes of 'ignorance is bliss' and 'what you don't know won't hurt you.'"

Ryan was glad Belinda was a talker. She decided to push her luck and began rummaging through her purse. She pulled out and unfolded a copy of the police sketch of Norman Bartholomew and handed it to the waitress. "Was this guy ever here with Hector? Maybe he's been a bad influence on him."

Belinda pursed her lips and squinted at the drawing. "Come to think of it, a guy resembling this drawing has been in with Hector a couple of times. He's good looking, but something about him—his eyes especially—give me the creeps. Just the way he looks at you… he's kind of hard to forget." She was now looking at Ryan suspiciously. "Say, what's this all about?" she asked.

Time for half-truths, Ryan figured. "Actually, my friend is a cop, and he's looking for the 'handsome, creepy guy' in the drawing for cross-border drug dealings. I don't suppose you know where either of them lives?" Ryan mentally crossed her fingers.

That was good enough for the chatty young woman; she obviously harbored no fondness for either of the men. "Can't help you there, but I think Hector hangs out at the Chollo Cantina north of here on Route 60, and I overheard those two mention the village of Magdalena a couple of times. That's a sleepy little burg another twenty miles farther north on the mesa."

Ryan smiled. "That's what the big M painted on the mountain stands for?"

"Geez, Dana, that's what I told you when you were in here last time."

Ryan winced. "Sorry, I forgot." She pulled a pen out of her purse and wrote her cell phone number on a napkin and handed it to the woman. "If either of the men stop in again, would you give me a call?"

Belinda folded up the napkin and put it in her apron pocket. "No problem. Both those guys are creeps, and should be put away for smuggling drugs. Your to-go order should be done; let me get it for you."

Later, after Ryan had returned to the motel and fed Jack, she sat in her room pondering her next move. It was time to cut her friend loose from the chase. He had already gambled way too much by helping her, and she didn't want him to take any more risks that might get him into hot water. Of course, she didn't want Jack to interfere with her in any way either, she admitted guiltily. His retiring from the Department really bothered her, but she shoved the creeping remorse from her mind. Ryan didn't want to brood about it now; she had too much to do.

She'd get up early, leave a message at the motel desk for Jack and head out in the Jeep. He'd just have to get himself another rental. He'd be pissed for sure, but she was determined to finish this journey alone. Ryan was surprised at the sadness she felt, but she refused to dwell on the reasons.

Ryan's first course of action would be to stake out the Cantina. By now Hector would have heard about his friends' getting roughed up, and just might stop in. If so, she would have a little chat with the gang leader concerning Norman. But, in case her vigil took a little longer, she'd stop at the local K-Mart and pick up a few camping supplies.

Ryan stripped and padded to the bathroom. She would take her shower tonight, pack her things, and write the letter to Jack before bedding down for the night. She'd check out around 5:00 am while it was still dark; Jack wasn't expecting her until 9:00.

As it turned out, Ryan didn't have to spend a single night camping in the desert.

# Chapter 36

After reconnoitering the area around the Chollo Cantina, Ryan pulled off the roadway a half mile north of the bar, and drove several hundred yards out into the desert until she came to a north/south running arroyo. She soon became adept at dodging the cacti, sagebrush and occasional alligator juniper that grew near the wash.

As Ryan navigated parallel to the ravine, she sought a gentler downward slope and drove the Jeep into the arroyo itself, which was nearly fifty yards wide at this point. She backtracked south and continued on until she estimated she was within range of the Cantina. Ryan parked near the arroyo's bank. The sides were steeper here and, after exiting, she was forced to search for a more manageable assent nearby before scrambling up and out of the ravine.

Her Jeep would be out of sight to anyone on Route 60, and because the ground sloped up gently from the roadway to the arroyo, it would be invisible to anyone until they were on top of the wash itself. The Cantina was on the other side of the road, over a quarter mile away.

Ryan hunkered down near a scrub juniper that was somehow surviving in the arid climate. She guessed the vegetation was sustained by the rains and storm sewer discharges the arroyo was infrequently called upon to channel to the Rio Grande River, nearly three miles to the east. Ryan had read about the dangers of the arroyos. Thunderstorms could turn these dry conduits into raging white water rapids. Although the "rainy season" of June through August had passed, Ryan had always harbored a secret belief in Murphy's Law. She wouldn't be surprised if an errant thunderstorm caused a flash flood and washed her Jeep down to the Rio Grande.

Ryan pulled the Bushnell PowerView binoculars she had purchased at the Target store out of the carrying case dangling from the strap around her neck. She scanned the front of the building in the distance, confirming they would do the job. There were two cars parked out front. During her little talk in the john with Miguel the day before, he had volunteered a description of Hector's vehicle—albeit under duress—a 2013 copper colored Buick 300 with chrome spinners. He had rattled on with a physical description of Hector, but to Ryan it sounded like a thousand other Hispanics she had seen over the last couple of weeks. The thought seemed racist somehow, but she wasn't exactly sure why. It was too bad Hector's buddy had no idea where Hector lived. It sure would have made things easier.

The juniper provided a minimum amount of shade, but Ryan figured it would help mitigate the projected eighty-eight degree day. She'd do her surveillance from the cover of the tree and set up camp a few yards down-slope from there. She hoped nobody would stumble upon her makeshift camp. The odds were pretty slim considering the desolate area. She had purchased a sleeping bag, camping paraphernalia and stocked a cooler with food and water. Ryan imagined she could hold out for three days before having to restock, but had her fingers crossed that Hector would show up before then.

Ryan hadn't done any camping since she and Dana had pitched a tent in their backyard in San Diego when they were kids. Ryan doubted that it qualified as camping; she would just have to learn on the fly. She gazed around her at the endless sand. But surprisingly, besides the cacti and sagebrush, there were actually other small patches of vegetation scattered about.

Even in the shade it was uncomfortably hot. A trickle of sweat coursed its way downward between her breasts, tickling her stomach. She sighed and scooted downhill on her butt before rising and heading back to the Jeep to unload her supplies. It was lunch time, and she was hungry.

Hector had arrived at the restaurant several minutes before and was sitting in Marilyn Bronson's section. Marilyn was one of the older waitresses and had trouble keeping up with the clientele during peak hours. Belinda glanced up at the decorative, wrought-iron wall clock behind the bar—12:47 p.m.—still the lunch rush hour, and Marilyn was looking a little frazzled.

Belinda fell in step with Marilyn as the harried waitress headed for the kitchen area with several more orders. "Marilyn, let me take care of the two tables in your section over by the window. You can keep the tips," she volunteered.

Her gray haired co-worker looked at her with a mixture of surprise and hope. "Belinda, you're working a double shift; you're not even supposed to be here. You should be conserving your energy, not volunteering more. And keep the tips? That really doesn't seem fair—"

"Don't worry about it," Belinda interrupted. "You can owe me one. Someday, I might need your help."

Marilyn smiled gratefully. "I doubt that, but okay, and if you're sure... I could really use the help."

Belinda touched base with several of her own tables on the way over, then took the orders of the middle-aged couple at one of Marilyn's tables before finally approaching Hector and handing him a menu. "Good afternoon, sir. My name is Belinda, and I'll be your waitress. May I get you something to drink to start out?"

"It's about time. Bring me a Tecate and leave another menu, I'm expecting someone any minute." He looked away, dismissing her.

What a prick, Belinda thought.

She put the couple's order in at the kitchen pass through and walked over to the bar, pulling out her cell phone as she did. She ordered the Tecate, plus two margaritas, a glass of red wine and a whiskey sour for several of her other patrons. Belinda pulled out the folded napkin with Ryan's phone number on it and punched in the numbers.

After receiving the unexpected call from Belinda, Ryan threw her phone back in her purse and scrambled out from under the tree, down the incline, then the embankment, abandoning the remnants of her picnic lunch. Damn, she had to hurry. If she could get back to Little Anita's before that Hector character took off, she could follow and maybe have one of her little talks with him, possibly obtaining information on where Norman lived.

Belinda said she'd try to stall as much as possible to give Ryan a chance to get there. Ryan grimaced at the irritating discomfort of the sand sticking to her perspiring body; sand that had somehow materialized through some form of magical osmosis inside her jeans and blouse. And she planned to camp in the desert for a few days? Right now she couldn't help but think of a nice, long shower....

Ryan pulled into Little Anita's parking lot a half hour later and found a spot which allowed her to observe the entrance/exit to the restaurant. She squirmed in her seat and turned the air conditioning on high. She undid her blouse and reached inside her bra in an attempt to wipe away the offending sand with Kleenex from her purse. Her jeans would just have to wait.

Less than fifteen minutes later Belinda called again, advising her that Hector and a cohort who had met him there, were heading out.

Seconds later two Hispanic males came out and briskly walked over to a bronze colored Buick 300 on the other side of the parking lot. So, the blabber mouth at the Cantina had been telling the truth about Hector's car. But Ryan noted with disappointment that the male with Hector looked nothing like the sketch of Norman.

The Buick pulled out onto N. California St. and headed north. Ryan followed discreetly, several car lengths behind. Traffic was heavy for a midafternoon weekday and Ryan didn't want to lose him. She wasn't surprised when he turned west on Route 60 towards Magdalena. She slowed, allowing the distance between them to increase. Traffic was much lighter along this highway; there were only a few small villages between Socorro and the resort towns of Pinetop-Lakeside in northeastern Arizona, almost 200 miles distant.

Ryan's next guess also proved correct. Ten minutes later the Buick pulled off the roadway and into the dusty lot of the Chollo Cantina. She cruised on by and retraced her route of earlier that day—off the roadway and into the parallel running arroyo. She backtracked quickly, pushed the Jeep hard on the packed sand of the wash, and arrived back at her makeshift camp in less than two minutes. Ryan scrambled out of the car and up the embankment with her binoculars. She noticed the remnants of her lunch had disappeared, compliments of the local wildlife she assumed. Shielded by the tree, she took up her former surveillance post. Ryan breathed a sigh of relief; the Buick was still parked out front.

Ryan managed to work up enough saliva in her mouth to spit—she even had sand in her mouth. She stood, moved behind the tree, and scanned the desolate area around her. If anybody hiked by in the next couple of minutes they were in for an unexpected treat.

Ryan hastily removed her tennis shoes and socks and shook the sand out of them and set them carefully aside. Next, she stripped off her blue jeans and panties and shook them out.

Quickly putting them back on, she repeated the process with her blouse and bra. Finally, leaning back against the tree, she brushed off her feet and put her socks and shoes back on. She was already perspiring again in the late afternoon heat. But it would have to do until she managed a shower somewhere. The strip show over, she resumed her post.

Hector emerged from the bar twenty minutes later, alone, and got into his car. Ryan waited until he pulled out of the lot and back onto the roadway to see which direction he would go. He headed west, away from Socorro towards Magdalena. Ryan sprinted—running and sliding—down the embankment to her waiting Jeep. So much for getting the sand out of her clothing, she thought bleakly.

Ryan gunned her car into a U-turn, fishtailing in the sand as she floored the gas pedal. When she reemerged onto Route 60, Hector's car was almost a mile ahead. She tried to put a damper on her adrenalin rush, resisting the urge to speed up and close the gap too quickly.

Ryan stayed a half mile behind the Buick, and tried to let the occasional west bound vehicles pass her in an effort to be less obvious, but Hector was clipping along at a good pace. They drove through Magdalena until Route 60 intersected Route 107. Hector turned south on 107.

Ryan drove past the intersection and slowly counted to five before hanging a U-turn on the now deserted road, backtracking and turning south on 107. The Buick was only a dot in the distance. She fought a rising panic that she might lose him and increased her speed. Ryan was closing the gap on the speeding bronze dot when it suddenly disappeared in a dusty haze in the distance.

Ryan slowed when she came to the approximate area where the Buick had disappeared off the roadway. The sun was sitting low in the west, but a faint veil of dust still hung in the hot, still air of the high desert. She spied a narrow, graded dirt road winding up a gentle slope, gradually disappearing among the trees scattered along the drive. A large NO TRESSPASSING sign block-printed in large red letters, was posted to the left of the driveway near the road. There was a nondescript mailbox on the right.

Ryan wondered if there was a motel in Magdalena, or if she'd have to drive the 25 miles back to Socorro. Either way, she was going to take a bath before she returned and explored the area after dark. She sighed resignedly. Of course, the simplest thing would be to wait for Hector to leave, follow him, and have a little chat about who lived out here in the boondocks. With her luck, Hector probably lived here, and she might be waiting for a long time before he left home again.

But one way or the other, she would find out who lived at this "No Trespassing" residence.

# Chapter 37

Jack was fuming. When Ryan hadn't shown up at 9:00 a.m. as planned he called her room and, receiving no answer, was pounding on her locked door within minutes. He immediately called her cell phone, only to have her generic voice mail answer. He tried a second and third time, with the same result. A quick trip to the front desk revealed that Ryan had checked out at 5:23 a.m. Jack couldn't believe it.

Ryan must have seen or heard something that had triggered a memory. She had kept it from him. It must have been something that confirmed the killer was Norman, and worse, was the possibility she had found out where Norman lived. Ryan had hidden any revelations about Norman very well. Still, he should have been more alert, more observant of her demeanor. Ryan had been on a mission of vengeance, and she wasn't going to let a minor thing like the law—which Jack represented—interfere with her execution of the killer when she found him.

Despite the fact that Ryan had used Jack and then dumped him when she no longer needed him, he found fear to be the predominate emotion roiling to the surface. Ryan the prostitute, the businesswoman, the fighter... and his friend. Jack should have felt resentment and anger, but the only emotion gripping him was fear. Fear that something could happen to Ryan, that she could be injured... or worse.

After Jack found the Jeep missing, he had made a call and was now sitting on the edge of the bed, waiting for Enterprise Rent-A-Car to deliver his new rental vehicle. He glanced at his watch—10:20 a.m. He wasn't sure where to start his search for Ryan, Norman, or anything else. He had to calm down and think. Jack glanced over at the trash receptacle by the writing desk. The top of the plastic bag containing last night's dinner was peeking out the top.

Jack walked over, pulled it out, and rummaged through the Styrofoam containers, used napkins and... yes, the receipt from the restaurant—Little Anita's. The receipt had the restaurant's address on it, and to the best of Jack's recollection, was the only place that Ryan had gone where he hadn't accompanied her. Maybe there was a connection somehow; at least it was a place for him to start. He certainly didn't have any better ideas.

It was after 3:00 p.m. when Jack pulled into the parking lot at Little Anita's with his newly rented Chevy Impala. He briefly debated on trying Ryan's cell phone number again, but since all his other calls had ended up going to her voice mail, it was obvious she wasn't going to answer.

Jack selected a booth near a window overlooking the parking lot while still affording a descent view of the interior. Oblivious to the esthetically pleasing Southwestern décor, he surveyed the sparsely occupied restaurant; it was between the lunch and dinner hours. A short, stocky waitress—one of only two working at the moment—was at his table within minutes of his arrival, giving him ample time to scan through the menu.

"Hello, my name is Nancy. Could I get you something to drink to start?" she asked.

"No thank you, Nancy."

"Are you ready to order, or do you need more time?"

"I'm ready. I'll have the combination plate and a Diet Coke… plus, the onion ring appetizer while I'm waiting," he added as an afterthought.

As Nancy was jotting his order down on her pad, Jack retrieved two pictures from his wallet. One was a folded up copy of the drawing of Norman. The other was a picture of Ryan, taken in front of Madigan's Gym the day they signed the closing papers, making her and Lonnie owners of the business. Originally, Lonnie had been in the picture, but Jack had cut the photo in half, leaving just Ryan smiling at the camera. Jack laid the pictures on the table. "Nancy, I'm a police officer, and I'm looking for these two people. Have either been in here recently?"

The waitress glanced at the pictures, then suspiciously at Jack. He pulled out his police I.D. and showed her his Sergeant's badge.

Apparently satisfied, she said, "I don't recognize the man, but the woman looks familiar. I think she was in yesterday afternoon and again earlier today. But I didn't talk to her either time, Belinda waited on her." She gestured at the other waitress over her shoulder.

"Could you please send Belinda over when you get the chance?"

Soon, a smiling Belinda was at his table. "You must be Dana's cop friend, investigating Hector and his gang. You didn't miss her by much; she was in earlier."

"Dana? You mean Ry—" Jack caught himself in time. "Yes, Dana... she took off on her own without me, and I'm just worried about her."

Belinda put her hands on her hips and frowned. "I don't blame you for being worried. She wanted me to call her if Hector or the guy in the drawing came in." She glanced at the picture of Norman lying on the table, "Yeah, him. He wasn't in..." she said nodding at the picture, "... but Hector met one of his pals here, so I called her. She wanted me to stall if I could until she got here so she could follow him. That was at least three hours ago."

"Do you have any idea where this Hector character was going?"

"I think the Chollo Cantina. I heard him mention it. It's on Route 60, about half-way to Magdalena and—"

"I know where it's at," Jack interrupted. He pocketed the pictures. "You've been a great help, Belinda. Could you make my order to go? I'd better get after... ah... Dana, before she gets herself into trouble." Really big trouble, he added mentally. "Can you give me a description of this Hector guy...?"

Jack ate while he drove, which proved a bit difficult—but doable—since the traffic on Route 60 was light. He pulled into the

Chollo a little after 5:00. There were only three cars in the dusty parking area out front; a sparse crowd for Happy Hour, Jack thought grimly. Without hesitation, he parked and was through the roughhewn front door in seconds. He stopped just inside the doorway, removed his sunglasses and let his eyes adjust to the dim interior as he surveyed the room. There were two patrons sitting at a table by a dingy window off to the side— plus the bartender. Neither triggered a memory from Ryan and Jack's previous visit.

But the barkeep was a different story. The man did a double take when he saw the massive cop in the doorway. He never took his eyes off Jack as he sidled to his right and reached for something behind the counter. Jack waved his forefinger back and forth while shaking his head, a subtle warning that whatever the man was up to was a bad idea.

The man was as grubby and unkempt as he had been the first time around. Jack figured his food stained t-shirt hadn't been removed, let alone washed, since then. But his movements had ceased—his face a frozen mask of apprehension. The swelling and discoloration from his broken nose was still visible.

Jack wasn't taking any chances and closed the distance between them in three long strides. The barkeep unconsciously took a step back. Jack crooked a forefinger at him in a "come hither" gesture. He made sure he kept the two men at the table within his peripheral vision. To the nervous, pock-marked man behind the bar he said, "Relax, amigo, I just need a little information."

"I don't want no more trouble, mister," the man replied. He was nervous and moved no closer to Jack.

Jack's smile disappeared. "I said come here," he growled.

The man inched back to the counter and placed his hands palms down on the smooth surface in an obvious placating gesture towards Jack. The two patrons at the table had stopped talking and were looking their way, but neither made any effort to interfere. Jack hooked a thumb at them and gestured towards the door—a clear indication it was time for them to leave.

The two looked at each other, then back at the big gringo at the bar, indecision etched on their faces. Jack glanced at the barman and uttered two words. "Stay put." He heaved his bulk off the rickety barstool, hitched up his pants, and took a step towards the men.

Both patrons made their decision, rising and heading out the door—their unfinished drinks warming on the dusty table.

Jack reseated himself and turned his attention back to the barkeep. "What's your name, amigo?" he asked.

"Pedro," the man replied. Wisely, he had remained immobile behind the bar.

"It's like this, Pedro. I'm having a bad day, and I'm on a very short fuse; so don't fuck with me. Now, where can I find a Hector Ramirez?"

"I don't know nobody by the name of—"

Jack covered the man's hand with his, squeezed and savagely twisted it towards him.

Pedro let out a howl of pain, his height diminishing as his knees buckled.

"Let's try that again, my friend. Where is Hector Ramirez? If I don't get a satisfactory answer, I'm going to start breaking your fingers."

The man's eyes were squeezed shut in pain, and he was actually whimpering. "Please, please, I don't know where Hector lives; he just comes in once in a while, sometimes with friends. He was in a few hours ago with somebody, but left after one drink."

Jack maintained pressure on the man's thumb. "Did the woman I was here with the other day come in?"

"No... didn't see her."

With his free hand Jack pulled the drawing of Norman out of his back pocket and placed it on the counter. "I showed you this to you yesterday. Was he in?"

Pedro squinted at the drawing through pain-filled eyes. "No, no, I haven't seen him, really I haven't," he wheezed.

Jack released the quivering man. He grabbed a dingy napkin off the bar and wrote his cell number on it. "Pedro, please believe me when I say this to you. If Hector, the man in the picture, or my lady friend come into the bar, I want you to call me immediately. If you don't, I will find out, and you will be tending bar from a wheelchair. That is a promise. Do you understand me?"

Pedro was cradling his injured hand to his chest, nodding, eyes downcast. "Yes, senior."

"Repeat my instructions."

"If the woman, or Hector, or the other man come into the bar, I'm to call you right away."

"Very good, Pedro." Jack slapped a ten-dollar bill on the counter. "Buy yourself a drink." He stared at the man grimly. "And, amigo, you best hope you never have to see me again."

Jack walked out into the bright New Mexico sunshine and over to his car, now the only one parked out front. It appeared to be sitting lower in the dusty hardpan of the makeshift parking lot. The reason was obvious—the sidewalls of all four tires were punctured. He sighed and shook his head. Maybe he shouldn't have kicked those two guys out of the bar.

He retrieved the rental paperwork from the car, called Enterprise, and arranged for a wrecker and new tires to be brought to the scene. Unfortunately, it would take at least two hours. Disconnecting from the call, he stared at the front of the rundown cantina. Resigned to his temporary fate, he headed back inside.

Pedro was still behind the bar. He gaped wide-eyed as Jack reentered and ambled up to the bar. It was obvious he was expecting the worst.

"Relax, Pedro. I have a flat tire and have to wait for a wrecker. I guess I'll have a beer while I wait—make it a Corona in a bottle."

The bartender looked relieved, still favoring his tender wrist. "You want something to eat, senor?" he asked.

Jack looked again at the derelict grill at the end of the bar and grimaced. "Nah, I'll pass, not hungry." Jack waited, took the proffered beer, and went to a table in the corner to wait. He stared at the wheezing ceiling fan laboring in the still air, wondering where Ryan was and trying to calm a rising dread.

# Chapter 38

Norman walked up to his henchman, placed a hand gently on his shoulder, and gazed dispassionately into the nervous brown eyes before him with an icy blue intensity. "Hector, my friend, we've gone over this before. I pay you good money to protect my interests and do my bidding. Do you know what those interests are?"

Hector had managed to keep from flinching under the touch of the big man, but was struggling mightily to meet his gaze. "To keep other drug dealers from interfering with your business interests and to eliminate the competition if you feel it necessary?" he replied. Hector felt the grip on his shoulder tighten.

"With no questions asked and without my direct involvement. True?" Norman prodded.

"Yes, sir, Mr. Bartholomew, just you and me. You direct and I follow."

"And while we are on the subject of 'you and me'—what is my requirement concerning anyone knowing anything about me?"

"Other than me, no none is to know anything about you," Hector answered. Norman's grip on his shoulder was becoming painful. He clenched his teeth in his effort to keep himself from moving; pulling away didn't seem like a good idea.

"So, I give you an assignment to eliminate a woman and her friend in Detroit, but you fail," Norman continued. "You maintain the men you hired were out of the information loop and wouldn't talk anyway, at least the one who lived. But somehow that woman shows up here in New Mexico asking questions—with a cop, no less—looking for me. And busts up some of your gang at the Chollo in the process. You maintain your boys know nothing about me other than our business relationship. But she and her cop friend are still out there somewhere nosing around. Something is wrong with this picture, Hector. I'm beginning to wonder if this bitch could be psychic or something. But no, my friend, I don't believe in that crap." Norman's voice was flat and dispassionate, the grip on Hector's shoulder tightening even more. "So, you can see why I'm starting to get a little nervous. And when I get nervous, I get a little… erratic… you might say. Do you understand?"

"Yes, sir, I understand," Hector said, his eyes focused on the floor. And indeed, Hector did understand. Two years earlier, Hector's then second in command, Julio Sanchez, and a cocky young guy, Donnie something-or-other—and new to the Loko Krew gang—had allowed curiosity to get the better of them. Contrary to Hector's standing orders that Noman's total anonymity was of the utmost importance, the two began following Hector in an attempt to learn the "Numero Uno's" real identity.

Eventually, they learned of Norman's ranch, and even began following him. Who knows, greed may have had something to do with it, figuring that Norman would pay to keep his secrets, whatever they might have been.

The two had disappeared without a trace. Well, not exactly, Hector mentally corrected. One day Norman called Hector in. Norman told him that he, Hector, needed to tighten up discipline within his posse; a couple of his group had been nosing around and asking questions—a violation of Norman's 'need-to-know' cardinal rule. And that made him nervous. Norman had wanted to stress his absolute need for anonymity, and to reemphasize the point, handed Hector a small, metal cash box. In it were two bloody penises and two sets of testicles. Norman reminded him that, as the boss of Loko Krew, Hector was responsible for any problem along those lines. Hector made sure his boys got the word—along with the graphic reminder.

Satisfied that he had made his point about Ryan and the cop, Norman released his grip and walked over to the kitchen counter and picked up his tall glass of orange juice and took a long swig, his muscled arm flexing with the movement. He'd just finished working out and needed to hydrate. He returned, favoring Hector with an icy grin and asked, "You and your compadres have connections all over Socorro, true?"

"Yes," Hector managed.

"So, it would be safe to assume that someone might be acquainted with someone in the car rental business?" Norman asked.

Hector still sported a blank look. "Yes, that's probably true. Or somebody who knows somebody. Why?"

Norman sighed, his dark eyes boring into Hector. "The bitch and her sidekick are from Detroit. I doubt they drove all this way. So, it would be a fair assumption they rented a car upon their arrival, wouldn't it?"

Hector shifted his weight from foot to foot nervously. "But that would probably be in Albuquerque, not—"

"This is the age of technology," Norman growled. "All these dealers are interconnected one way or the other. A few keystrokes, and you can find who rented what, and where. You have both of their names and their pictures..." Norman walked over to the mahogany dining room table, picked up two photographs and handed them to Hector, "... but just in case you've lost them..." Norman threw Hector a hard look "... here's two more. I know the pictures are dated, but they're better than nothing."

Hector appeared mesmerized and rooted to the floor.

Norman smiled, a smile as cold and bleak as the Antarctic sun. He slapped Hector on the back. "Well, my friend, get a move on and get the word out. I want to know who's seen them, where, and what they're driving. And I want results."

"Yes, sir, Mr. Bartholomew; I'm on it." Hector turned and headed for the door, consciously slowing his pace. He didn't want his strange employer thinking he was cowed or anything. But those icy blue eyes gave him the creeps. As soon as he was out the door he was on his cell phone and making his first call.

By the time he'd walked the fifty yards to his car, Hector had completed two terse phone calls: Miguel would work the rental car angle, and Angel was going to meet him at the Chollo. He would make sure Angel had copies of the photographs and had passed them out to everyone in the Krew. Between the pictures and the hoped for identification of a rental car, they should be able to locate the two gringos—if they were still in town.

Hector assumed it was a drug deal problem of some sort although Hector was beginning to wonder. His boss was one weird dude. The volume of drugs that Norman dealt didn't seem to warrant the extreme measures he sometimes went to. The contract he'd put out on the Ryan woman, for example. But Norman paid him big bucks to take care of his business—whatever it might be—and Hector wasn't about to kill the golden goose.

Hector opened the car door but paused, looking back at the sprawling hacienda in the late afternoon sunlight. Maybe he should have mentioned something to the boss about the Jeep that might have been following him. Hector had noticed it tagging along some distance behind earlier in route to Norman's house. He was probably just being paranoid. There hadn't been any problems or contacts with any of the rival drug dealers, and there was no reason to believe the mystery woman and her cop friend would be out here in the middle of nowhere following him. Hector shook his head and got in the car. Besides, he really didn't want to go back in and face his creepy boss again.

Hector was heading back on Route 60 through Magdalena when he passed the Alameda Motel. It was nearing sundown and, had it been any darker, he might have missed the tan Jeep Cherokee in the lot a short distance off the highway. As it was, the gathering twilight reflecting off the vehicle was enough to give Hector pause; the nagging question of that Jeep behind him earlier in the day resurfaced.

Hector made a U-turn and headed back, while at the same time calling Angel and redirecting their meeting place to the Alameda Motel. A heart to heart talk with the motel clerk, along with a few bucks, should be enough to find out who belonged to the Jeep. He also had a picture of Ryan to show the clerk. Should good fortune smile upon him—and the owner turned out to be the Ryan broad—he would find out which room she was in. Then he and Angel would hog tie the bitch, and Hector would hand deliver her to Norman.

Considering his boss's keen interest in the woman, there would probably be a bonus in it for him. He put the cell phone back in his shirt pocket with a lopsided grin. If all this came to be, he had an idea Norman would dispose of the woman himself, relieving him of the duty.

Hector parked on the opposite side of the lot from the Jeep and walked towards the motel office. He might as well take care of a few of the preliminaries prior to Angel's arrival. Besides, he didn't want any of the boys to know any more than was necessary. Norman had always been pretty clear on that.

# CHAPTER 39

Ryan finished toweling off her jet black hair and threw her head back to get it out of her face. She stared into the ebony eyes glaring back at her from the bathroom mirror. She had managed to keep her remorse for leaving Jack behind on the back burner of her mind during the busy day, but ever since she had checked into the motel and caught her breath, it had resurfaced with a vengeance.

Jack was her best friend, even more so than Lonnie. Jack had been with her, one way or the other, ever since her college days when he had first busted her for prostitution—or tried to, anyway. When she needed someone he had always been there. When she had told him the incredible tale of Dana's death at the hands of a killer, he never questioned it. He had taken time off from the Department—putting his career on the line with his actions—to help her in her search. And now he was quitting the force. Jack wasn't fooling her. He hadn't merely retired, but had abandoned his career to follow her, protect her and to prevent her from possibly ruining her life in her quest for revenge.

Ryan inhaled deeply, her breasts rising. She exhaled, reached up and ran her hands slowly down from her breasts, following the inward curve to her narrow waist, and ending at the swell of her hips. The man was acting like he was in love with her. But Ryan was a prostitute, a whore—albeit a high class one—or had been, anyway. She had used her body to get what she wanted. Could a moral man like Jack really love her after what she had been and done? And as for Ryan, what did she know about love? She had never loved any man, only used them for her own ends, her own needs. Even Jack.

Hands resting on the sink, Ryan leaned toward the mirror and stared at the face that had entranced many men—a modern day Medusa. She clenched her teeth. Enough self-pity. Whatever she felt towards Jack wasn't going to stop her in her quest. He was out of the equation. She wasn't—

A loud knocking interrupted her reverie. A muffled voice sounded through the motel room door, "This is the management Miss Sanders. We seem to have a problem with your credit card. I'm sure it will only take a moment to straighten out."

*Damn, what now?* Ryan thought. She grabbed one of the over-sized bath towels and wrapped it around herself, tucking in the ends at her breasts, the bottom barely covering her ass—one of the unexpected downsides of being tall. The manager would get an unforeseen bonus—an eyeful of Ryan. "Hold on a sec, I'll be right there," she called out. She wondered why they hadn't just called her from the office.

As she headed for the door, she grabbed her purse off the dresser and retrieved her wallet. The knock came again. "I said

I'll be right there," she said in response. Ryan flipped open the lock and slid off the safety chain and—

The door slammed open, smashing into Ryan. She instinctively brought the hand up holding her purse, which prevented her face from being flattened by the metal clad door. As it was, the violent crash sent her pin-wheeling off balance back into the room before falling to the floor on her rear end. Hector and Angel were inside with the door shut behind them before she ever hit the floor.

As Lonnie had always marveled in the past, Ryan had eerily fast reflexes. As she hit the ground, she continued her backward momentum, turning her fall into a back somersault and regaining her feet almost immediately—sans the bath towel, which was left puddled on the floor.

It was probably this result that prevented the two men from getting the best of Ryan. As they faced their quarry, they momentarily froze at the sight of the nude, dark haired woman before them. Both were holding old fashioned, lead-weighted saps in their hands; they didn't want to kill Ryan, only render her unconscious. Hector planned to deliver her to Norman—maybe a little worse for wear—but all in one piece and still breathing.

Unfortunately for them, their initial delay at the sight of a nude Ryan was their downfall. As both men paused for that split second, eyes gaping at her, she reacted without hesitation, charging forward.

Angel was the nearest. As his eyes refocused on the danger hurtling towards him, he tried to bring the sap up to ward off the threat. It was too little, too late. Ryan launched herself into a flying sidekick—her leg a beautiful lance, her foot a lethal club. Her momentum and her strength, coupled with the jackknifing extension of her leg just as the edge of her foot connected with the man's chest over the arm attempting to block it, sent him hurtling back into the door with a heavy thud. His eyes bulged in shock—not male admiration—as he slid to the floor, his face contorting into a mask of pain. Ryan's kick had been off center, and instead of connecting with his sternum it was his ribs that bore the brunt of her vicious kick. The man would be dealing with a couple of broken ribs in his immediate future.

Hector was quicker and less distracted, lunging towards her while swinging the sap in a vicious arc. Ryan instinctively tried to duck away but was only partially successful; the sap missed her head but thudded painfully into her collarbone. Hector swung a second time as Ryan attempted to backpedal. He again missed her head, striking a glancing blow to the same collarbone and the side of the neck, just above her shoulder. Stunned, she continued to stagger backward, little black dots dancing across her vision, her gag reflex cutting off her air. Her left arm dangled numbly in response to her severely bruised clavicle.

Ryan's retreat ended when she backed into the wall. Hector moved in for the kill. He swung again at her head, but she managed to parry the blow, blocking his forearm with her own. She threw her weight forward into Hector, her good shoulder catching the man high in the chest and forcing him back. Ryan's thrust didn't do any damage to her assailant, but managed to create space between them as he was pushed back.

Hector quickly regained his balance and charged again, raising the sap for another swing. Ryan spun, her right leg lashing out, the side of her foot slamming into the man's kneecap. There was a faint, but audible crunch from the abused ligaments as the knee hyper-extended. Hector let out a pained roar and listed heavily to his damaged side but stayed upright, his momentum carrying him into Ryan and slamming her into the wall. Ryan pushed with both hands, her aggrieved shoulder shooting a bolt of pain down her tingling arm, but managed to force her attacker back—back far enough for her to savagely piston her knee up into his groin.

Hector grunted, groaned and dropped to his hands and knees. Ryan, leaning and falling forward like a felled tree, lead with her elbow as she plunged downward with all her weight. Her elbow—backed by her weight and momentum—struck the stunned man in the back of the head with sledgehammer force. Hector collapsed face first onto the floor, silent and unconscious.

Ryan rolled over and pushed herself to her feet with a groan. Panting, she stood with her hands on her knees, calming herself and bringing her breathing under control. She straightened and slowly lifted her injured left arm. She winced in pain, but the very fact that she could raise it at all was proof that her clavicle wasn't broken. But it would be one hell of a sore bone bruise.

Ryan looked at her reflection in the dresser mirror and realized she had been fighting in the buff, *au natural*. She quickly dressed in jeans and a t-shirt and evaluated the situation. From the waitress' description and her own long distance observation from outside the bar, she assumed the unconscious man was

Hector. His partner, now groaning and slumped against the wall, was conscious but in obvious pain, shallow breaths wheezing in and out from, what she suspected, was a punctured lung. The blood on his lips was undoubtable from internal bleeding resulting from that puncture.

Ryan would have to take the injured man to the hospital. She checked Hector to make sure he was still breathing. Assured that the man was still alive, she went to her car where she had her various supplies stored and retrieved a roll of duct tape—in her opinion one of the most versatile products ever invented.

She secured Hector hand and foot; the maid would have a surprise when she came to clean the room in the morning. Glancing at the prone man on the floor, Ryan decided she would pay for another night when she left. If Norman wasn't up to speed, there was no sense in letting Hector inform him of their little meeting. It was too late to worry about the small stuff now. She was close, but somehow Norman was onto her, otherwise why the surprise visit from Hector and company?

She knelt by the injured man sitting against the wall. "What's your name?" she asked.

He winced at her with pain-filled eyes. "Angel," he replied.

"Well, Angel, I think you are a little busted up inside. Let's get you to your feet." Ryan managed to get him up without using her sore shoulder. "I'm going to put you in my car and drop you off at the hospital in Socorro. But I have a few questions for you, and if you give me any trouble, I'll bust you up some more. Do you understand?"

Now standing, Angel glanced down at the inert Hector. He coughed, swallowed and replied through clenched teeth, "I understand; no problems from me, lady."

Ryan paid for another night at the motel and headed out into the early evening with her injured passenger, still trying to formulate exactly what she was going to do after she dropped him off at the hospital.

# Chapter 40

The following morning Jack wolfed down his free continental breakfast at the motel and headed back out. He could either stake out Little Anita's Restaurant or the Chollo bar hoping Norman, Hector, or one of their cohorts wandered in. He didn't know what else to do and had to consciously keep from grinding his teeth in frustration. His fear for Ryan's safety and what she might do, or try to do, was mounting—his forced impotence in the face of the unknown was driving him crazy.

Jack decided the Chollo Cantina was the logical choice. It seemed to be the watering hole for all the local scumbags. Pedro, the bartender, had been properly cowed by Jack, and was sure to be amenable to pointing out Hector, or any of his comrades, should they happen to visit.

Jack pulled into the dusty lot of the bar a little after 10:00 a.m. There was no one in the saloon except Pedro when Jack entered. The barman was sitting at a table watching an old black and white 19" TV sitting on a wooden stool against the nearby wall. The old set had an equally ancient set of rabbit ears sitting atop it, bringing in a slightly snowy picture.

Pedro scowled when he saw Jack and stood and faced him.

"Relax, amigo," Jack said amiably. "Get me a Coke, in a bottle please, and I'll tell you what we're going to do." Jack followed the man with his eyes as he went behind the bar to get his soda. Jack continued, "I'm going to be in your joint here for a good chunk of the day, I'm guessing."

Pedro was staring at him now, still silent.

"I'm looking for the guy named Hector, or anyone in his gang for that matter," Jack said, still grinning. "And you'll let me know when they come in. Okay with you, Pedro?"

"And if I don't?" Pedro questioned.

"I'll burn this dive to the ground with you in it." Jack's smile had disappeared.

"You wouldn't. You're a cop."

"I'm retired. And believe me, I would."

Pedro stared at the smoldering eyes of the hulking man for several seconds before breaking his gaze, looking away as he set the bottled Coke on the counter top. His eyes still averted, the man mumbled, "Your being here is bad for my business."

Jack pulled his wallet from his hip pocket, counted out fifty dollars, and placed the bills next to the Coke. "That's to cover your potential loss of revenue. And there will be another hundred if I find anyone who can help me with information. I'll just sit over there in the corner, and you let me know if anyone comes in I might be interested in talking to."

Pedro scooped the money off the counter, but remained silent.

Jack picked up his Coke and started to turn away, but paused. "Amigo, you're here in the morning and afternoon. Who else works—?"

"Just me," the grubby barman interrupted. "I have a room in the back. I live here."

Jack just shook his head, his smile returning. He grabbed his soda, took a seat against the far wall facing the door, and began his vigil.

Jack was in a foul mood several hours later. He had obviously not thought his plan through, at least not concerning where and what he was going to eat, should his prey not stop in during the day or evening. He wasn't eating anything served in this place. That's all he needed, to come this far just to end up dying of food poisoning. For lunch he munched down two bags of potato chips. Jack didn't bother to check the expiration date; he would just have to trust in good ol' American preservatives.

A few customers wandered in, mostly crusty, older Hispanics and several cowboys complete with boots and hats. None of them stayed long, apparently uncomfortable with the big gringo sitting silently in the back watching them.

It was 3:30 p.m. and there was no one else in the cantina. Jack was weakening, actually considering having Pedro cook up something on the dirty grill at the end of the bar. But he spied the barman taking out a brown bag from the under-counter fridge and removing something wrapped in aluminum foil. He got up and walked over. "What do you have there, Pedro?"

"Two bean and chicken burritos," was the answer.

Jack fished out his wallet. "Five bucks for one of them."

Pedro looked from Jack to the burritos in his hand. "Ten dollars, gringo—you are bad for my business."

Although Jack had heard that line before, he couldn't argue with the logic. He swapped a ten for one of the fat burritos, picked up another bottle of Coke that the barman had so graciously added, and returned to his vigil at his table.

Jack wolfed down his dinner and was half way through his soda when a man hobbled in through the door. Younger than any of the earlier clientele, he had a pronounced limp, winced with each step he took, and was using a crooked, four-foot-long tree limb as a crutch. The man shuffled up to the counter and, with a grimace, maneuvered onto a bar stool. He didn't notice Jack sitting in the shadows.

Pedro glanced at Jack in the dimness, then quickly back to his new customer. Silently, he poured a liberal shot of tequila into a water glass and set it in front of the new patron.

Hector downed it in one gulp. "Pedro, give me your cell phone. That puta bitch stole mine after she tied me up last night. I need to call someone." Hector took the proffered phone from the barman. "Have you seen Angel? I think she hurt him good, but he wasn't there when I woke up."

Hector made it to the fourth number on the keypad before his breathing came to a temporary halt from the impact of Jack's rock hard fist slamming into his kidney. The cell phone clattered to the floor as Hector sat looking like a fish out of water, his mouth opening and shutting as he sought air. Jack grabbed him by the back of the shirt to keep him from slumping forward off his stool.

Jack looked at the very nervous barman. "Remember what I said I'd do to you and your bar?"

Pedro's eyes kept darting back and forth between the gulping Hector and the big cop. "Si, Senor, I remember."

Jack continued, "Now me and Hector are going to the john and have a little confab about a few things. I suggest you put a closed sign on the door. Figure out how much that will cost you in business revenue, and I will reimburse you for your losses."

Pedro's face was a blank.

"Do it now," Jack growled.

As the nervous man scurried towards the front door, Jack jerked Hector up off the stool and half dragged, half walked the gimpy man to the restroom.

# Chapter 41

The new, Ford F-150 pickup lead a cloud of dust along the rutted dirt drive as Norman navigated from his home to the county road, almost three miles distant. It was a long driveway, but that suited him just fine. Norman had purchased the land with a chunk of his Mega-Lottery winnings—Nicole's actually, he mentally amended. He chuckled humorously; he probably should get the road graded.

Norman was a man of leisure now and had been for over ten years. His main interests were traveling and, needless to say, torturing, mutilating and raping beautiful, man-eating women—after their deaths, of course. And there were, oh, so many of them. So far, he had made twenty-six of them pay—twenty-eight counting Montana and that spic bitch—in six different states over the course of the last ten years. And the inept police were no closer to catching up with him than they had been a decade ago.

Norman turned up the radio. It was an oldies station and Norman hummed along with "Baby, baby, can't you hear my heart beat…"

He was almost past the last turnoff when he saw a tan Jeep Cherokee with its hood up, near a stand of trees fifty yards off the roadway. It was unusual to see any vehicles along his lengthy driveway. Norman had posted "No Trespassing" signs out by the main drag and along the private drive. But what really caught his eye was the tall, leggy blonde in the Daisy Duke shorts, leaning in and looking under the hood.

Norman stopped, backed up, and pulled in behind the Jeep. He glanced in the rearview mirror at his tanned and handsome face and pasted on his most engaging smile. He ran a hand through his thick, dark hair and got out. With a forced swagger he approached the young woman.

The slim, attractive blonde turned and smiled as he approached. "This piece of junk started sputtering and coughing; I just managed to get it off the road before it died completely," she sighed.

Norman licked his lips nervously. Besides the Daisy Dukes, she had on a pale green blouse, tied in a knot below ample breasts, exposing a bare midriff. The blouse matched the green of her eyes. He managed to keep his smile in place. "I'm sorry about the car, Miss, but this is private land. Didn't you see the 'No Trespassing' sign out by the road?"

The blonde's smile disappeared, replaced by a forlorn look. "I'm sorry, I was in a hurry to get to my friend's birthday party over in Hillsboro. I was looking for a shortcut and must have missed the signs." Now she was smiling again. "I can't get any cell phone reception here. Do you live nearby? Maybe I could use your land-line to call a wrecker?"

Norman's mind was racing. He avoided finding victims in New Mexico, let alone bringing them to his ranch. He had only disposed of two at his house over the last ten years; he liked to spread things around. It was less risky, much safer that way. And it had only been a few months since he'd brought the last one here... that Dana cunt... the one who had caused all these problems somehow. Besides, his agenda for the following month called for a trip to Idaho for his next go-round—a state that would soon have another unsolved murder on the books. He didn't need to take the added risk... plus, he'd have to get rid of her car....

Reeled in like a hooked fish, Norman's eyes refocused on the woman's body before him, Nicole's body...

The perspiring woman was back to looking under the hood, leaning in, bent over. Her body was mocking, taunting, a forbidden fruit luring him. Norman hated her, despised her, loved her. He clenched and unclenched his hands, his mouth dry... Nicole... he looked around at the isolated, secluded area. No way could he wait to get back to the house. Not now; he was on the verge of losing it. He'd take her here.

Norman kept his boyish smile etched on his face and managed to keep his voice even and steady. "Certainly, I only live a mile or so from here; I'll give you a lift. But first let me take a look under the hood for you." Confident now, he strode toward her.

The woman stood, faced him and grinned as he neared. "Sure, look all you want. Give it your best shot."

Norman's head and balls were throbbing, but his throat was the worst; he could hardly swallow—it felt like a golf ball was lodged there. He opened his eyes and, even in the gray dimness, it took several seconds for his eyes to adjust, then several more seconds for them to register where he was. "What the hell...?" he rasped. He was in his own basement, bare-assed naked, sitting in a chair, completely immobile.

Then his mind began to clear. Norman remembered the blonde and that beaming smile. He had been ready to take her when she unexpectedly lashed out and caught him in the throat with her fist. As he staggered, choking, she had kicked him in the balls. Then she had hit him over the head with something, and now he was in his own basement, tied to his favorite chair. Even his head was immobilized.

Although he couldn't move his head left or right, up or down, his eyes could see his forearms duct-taped to the chair arms and his thighs duck-tapped to the chair bottom. It didn't take much imagination to figure out that his lower legs, torso and head were duct-taped to the chair legs and back. He allowed himself an ironic, self-congratulatory moment; the extension he had added to the chair back for securing their heads worked well. Norman didn't even try to struggle. He had built the chair himself and bolted it to the cement floor and knew it wasn't going to move or break.

Norman winced as light flooded the basement. The blonde was sitting on the leather couch smoking a cigarette, the remote control for the overhead lights in her hand. "I was getting worried. I thought I might have whacked you too hard with my Louisville Slugger," she said.

Norman had a splitting headache, and it hurt to talk, but he managed to bark, "What is this? What are you doing and why in hell did you attack me? You can't get away with this—"

"Stow it, Norman, I don't have time for your bullshit; I have some serious work to do."

The blonde unwound from the couch, stood and ground her cigarette out on the cement floor with a sneakered foot.

Norman stared at her. "How do you know my name? Who are you?"

She walked over, bent down hands on her knees, and stared Norman in the eyes. "My name is Ryan. I'm the bitch who's going to introduce you to those four minutes you were talking about."

Norman's eyes widened. "What... how... how... why did you say that...?" His mind was trying to grapple with everything. Ryan... Ryan, he knew that name from somewhere. The name ricocheted through his throbbing and addled mind.

Norman tried to follow her with his eyes as she went to retrieve something outside his range of vision. Seconds later she was back, wheeling a portable hospital tray he sometimes used as a table when he ate in the basement. But, instead of food, it now had several other items on it: vise-grips, clamps, screw driver, several knives, a box cutter, and a number of other things on the edge of his vision.

"Let's see... Norman Frederick Bartholomew, serial killer of... ummm... two dozen women and counting, right? This may take a while, since you'll be atoning for all of their deaths—slowly," Ryan said. She picked up a teaspoon off the tray. "I've read of a novel use for this. Just insert it under someone's eye, maybe an inch into the orbital cavity, then a quick flick up—like shooting peas—and presto; the eyeball just pops right out." She put the spoon down and picked up a small knife. "But personally I liked the one where you cut off the eyelids; you'd have to watch everything. Plus, they say the pain—as the eyeballs dry out—is excruciating."

Norman's eyes jerked left, then right, attempting to track her as she deliberately walked back and forth in front of him. Panic, like a welling tsunami, was growing in his darting eyes. He literally screamed, his voice reduced to coarse sandpaper, "Who are you? Why the hell do you care? Why don't you just call the cops?"

Ryan stopped her slow pacing. "You know, your theory on that 'four minute' thing was pretty accurate. The brain does retain enough oxygen after death to last four or five minutes, or in Dana's case, well over eight before it started to fade. Of course, she was a cross-country and marathon runner; her body was a little more efficient than average in utilizing oxygen. She was still hanging in there when you started shoveling dirt over her."

Confusion had now joined his panic. "That's impossible; you can't know that!"

Ryan cupped a palm below her eyes and removed her contacts. When she finished, her green blouse no longer matched her dark eyes. "And you were right. Our parents wanted a boy, instead they got a double whammy, twin girls—Ryan Dana Sanders and my sister, Dana Ryan Sanders. Our parents were pretty slick, huh?"

She pulled off her blonde wig, shaking her head vigorously as her dark tresses fell to her shoulders. "There, that's better." Ryan picked up and leisurely began tugging on a pair of blue latex gloves, snapping the thin rubber with an ominous finality as she finished.

Norman was speechless. He opened his mouth, but nothing came out. His mind was reeling.

"Dana and I never had any of that 'twin-telepathy' stuff, no paranormal, psychic connection. We couldn't 'feel' what was happening to each other in adjoining rooms, let alone over great distances... until those few minutes after you killed her, that is. I don't know why, but it is what it is, and very unfortunate for you."

Eyes wide, Norman was still staring, his mouth agape.

Ryan smiled. "You'll be catching flies if you don't close your mouth."

Norman's eyes widened even more and a choking, groaning sound escaped him.

She slipped a white plastic bib-apron over her head and tied it around her waist. "For most people, the last four-plus minutes after death is a peaceful transition—a gentle going-to-sleep as the oxygen fades away. But for others it can be a horrendous final experience, residual memories of terror, a wraith-like sense perception of the outer world," Ryan explained.

She pulled up a chair and sat facing Norman, their knees almost touching. Ryan leaned forward, staring into his eyes, her smile long gone. "I can't explain it, Normie—some kind of seventh sense from her dying, oxygen starved mind, reaching out to me in terror 1800 miles away, somehow giving me ethereal, hazy images of things in that gray area between black and white—a sense of your house, of you, of your truck, of things seen and heard in those last minutes, as well as a flood of images from her past life. Fortunately, I was able to cull out enough information about her trip and you to bring us to this moment."

Ryan picked up a roll of duct-tape from the tray and ripped off a strip. "It didn't hurt that I have a cop friend willing to assist me." Ryan's smile faltered as she thought of Jack and her betrayal. What would he think when this was all over? Why did this bother her so much now? With an effort she pushed thoughts of him from her mind and refocused on the monster before her. "Just a matter of research, planning, reconnoitering and bingo, here we are." Her eyes had darkened, and the sharp edge of vengeance was in her voice, righteous retribution strengthening its timbre.

Ryan wandered over to the wall dominated by a corkboard display, her eyes traveling over the pictures of Norman's twenty-eight victims displayed there. They narrowed as they reached the end and found Dana and Maria, sandwiched around a once attractive blonde. Ryan gritted her teeth and breathed deeply through her nose several times, attempting to maintain her composure.

She returned to her silent captive, continuing in a voice growing stronger as she warmed to the task. "The police will really appreciate those pictures..." Ryan gazed around the basement "... among all the other evidence I'm sure they'll find in and around your home. Of course you won't be around to appreciate it."

Ryan pulled a small notebook out of her back pocket. Jack's research had been as thorough as was possible. "Let's see now... your first victim... Brenda Lee Anderson, October

2001 We'll start with a little payback for her." The strip of duct-tape she'd torn off, and still dangling from her fingers, she now pressed over Norman's mouth, grinning at the bulging terror in the eyes above. "I know we're out in the middle of nowhere, Norman, but your screaming will get on my nerves."

She picked up the box cutters and slid out the blade. "Be patient, Normie, this will take a while, but we'll eventually get you to those final four minutes. And I promise to make it as painful as I can."

Norman's eyes were wide with fear, the snuffling sounds of his panicked breathing through his nose growing louder, the tape covering his mouth crinkling slightly as his mouth worked beneath it.

Ryan leaned forward to begin. She paused and licked her lips, not in anticipation, but in indecision. Seconds passed. Ryan continued to hesitate, her eyes moving from the blade in her hand back to Norman. With an effort she lowered her hand.

Norman's breathing slowed and his eyes narrowed as he gauged the woman before him, realizing his executioner was having second thoughts—an apparent attack of conscience he hoped. His thoughts were confirmed when the woman abruptly stood, her teeth clenched and her jaws working.

Ryan glared at Norman, turned and threw the box cutters against the far wall. She grabbed the medical tray next to her and violently upended it. Almost panting, she glowered at the bound man before her. If looks could indeed kill, Norman would have been incinerated on the spot.

With effort Ryan brought her emotions under control, walked back to the couch and removed the cell phone from her purse. Jack had been right; better to let the justice system do its thing—as slow as that sometimes was. Despite the illegality of her actions, she figured that there was enough evidence—especially if Hector flipped on his boss—to get a search warrant. They could also get Norman's juvenile records unsealed and released, hopefully including DNA from his youthful incarceration. And, if so, those results could eventually be matched with a number of his homicides over the ensuing ten years.

Ryan stared at the cell phone and the fact that there was no reception in the cement block basement. She walked around slowly, moving the phone through the air as she walked—still no reception bars on the phone's face.

She glanced back at the tightly bound man and the piercing eyes that had been following her every move. Ryan headed for the stairs. Once out of the basement she'd be able to call Jack, fill him in on the situation, and let him take it from there. As she ascended the stairs, she felt oddly calm. Revenge had driven her to this point, but she had been unable to complete the last step. She just didn't have it in her as much as Norman deserved it. Ryan felt a perverse disappointment in the outcome, but felt relieved in her failure. She smiled as she thought how pleased Jack would be when he found out she could not do it.

When Norman could no longer hear Ryan on the stairs, he quickly evaluated his situation: it wasn't good, and he didn't have much time. He was sure the bitch was calling the cops or her cop friend. At best, the police would soon end his winning streak. At worst, the long-legged cunt might overcome her attack of conscience and return for her revenge before finishing him. With his head immobile, he couldn't see what she had been throwing around, but guessed from the sound it was the hospital tray with its array of instruments. They would be on the floor now.

Because of his height his feet were flat on the floor and his legs bent because of their length. Norman guessed she had taped his legs to the chair last and had been in a hurry because she had bound them at the shins instead of the more efficient and secure position of the ankles.

Norman pushed with his feet and felt the chair move backward slightly. The bolts securing the chair's front legs to the floor were loose. The struggles of his past victims must have loosened them. It might have been secure enough for the women, but not for the man now bound in the chair. He'd have to tighten the bolts up when this was all over, Norman mused.

After several hard yanks to the right, the left front and rear bolts surrendered their hold on the cement floor. The right side held temporarily as he violently thrust his 225 pounds back and forth and from side to side. The chair finally listed to the right on its last pendulum swing before toppling over with a bone jarring crash to the floor.

The violent landing briefly winded Norman, but he managed to keep his head from bouncing off the floor. He was grinning as he wiggled and yanked his right arm back and forth; the sharp crack from the chair's armrest upon landing confirming the wood had fractured when striking the ground. Within seconds

Norman had his right arm free. A little more wiggling and he had reached the scalpel lying nearby. He cut through the tape binding his other arm, legs and feet. Norman staggered upright, his head throbbing.

At first he didn't even consider looking for a weapon. But by the time he reached the foot of the stairs common sense made a brief appearance. Norman detoured to a bureau against the far wall and pulled out the bottom drawer. From beneath several sweatshirts he retrieved a snub-nosed .38 Smith and Wesson revolver he secreted there in case of emergencies. And this qualified as an emergency. He suddenly realized he was still nude and had nowhere to stash the gun. Norman spied his clothing heaped in a pile at the end of the couch. He kept an eye on the doorway as he quickly dressed and stuck the gun in his waistband.

With a growl deep in his throat, Norman headed for the stairs. He would kill the bitch with his bare hands.

# CHAPTER 42

Hector lay crumpled in the corner of the bathroom, Jack towering over him. The man's eyes were squeezed shut in pain, a low moaning sound escaping his lips as he clutched his damaged leg. Thanks to Jack's savage kick of a few seconds before, the man's knee was now in even worse shape than when he had entered the bar.

Jack unfolded the drawing of Norman from his back pocket and held it in front of Hector's face. "No time for games, asshole," he rumbled. "I need to know where this Norman Bartholomew guy lives, and I need to know now. Fuck with me and I'll bust you up bad; they'll have to feed you through tubes for the rest of your life. And if anything happens to my friend before I get there, well, what I just described to you will be the least of your worries."

Hector sat up with an effort, his back braced against the bathroom wall. Teeth clenched, he glared up at the man looming over him. "Fuck you, pendejo," he wheezed. "I don't know any Norman Bartholomew." In a show of misguided bravado, Hector spit at his tormentor, the combination of blood and phlegm landing on one of Jack's new cowboy boots.

The offended boot lashed out and struck Hector in the face, bouncing his head off the bathroom wall. Norman's henchman might have slipped into blessed unconsciousness if it were not for the heel of that same boot coming down on his supporting hand splayed on the cement floor. The excruciating pain of the bones in his hand being crushed by Jack's full weight snapped him back to a tortured awareness. His face contorted in agony, Hector's former bluster now morphed into a mewling whimper.

"No time for this friendly give and take, Hector," Jack intoned. "I'm going to work my way up your arms, then start on your legs—"

It could have been the agonizing pain, or the icy, dispassionate tone of the big cop's voice, but Hector decided that discretion was the better part of valor. As much as he feared his employer, Hector whole heartedly believed the crazy cop would carry out his threats. He didn't relish the idea of being in a wheelchair for the rest of his life.

"Wait, wait… I'll tell you, I'll tell you," Hector gasped. Wincing, he pulled his damaged hand onto his lap.

"Where does he live?" Jack growled. He took a step towards the broken man.

Hector's eyes widened in fear. "426 Route 107, about ten miles south of Magdalena," Hector rattled on in panic. "There's a long dirt driveway, a 'No Trespassing' sign, and—"

"You'd better be right," Jack interrupted. "If not, I will be back to finish things."

Before Hector could reply, Jack had spun around and left the bathroom.

A full minute passed before Pedro opened the door and peeked in timidly. His eyes widened at the sight of Hector slumped against the far wall, breathing heavily, his face bleeding, a swollen, misshapen hand cradled in his lap.

Hector looked up at the barman. "Give me your phone again," he slurred through puffy lips.

Pedro quickly walked over and did so.

With his good hand, Hector keyed in Norman's number. There was no answer. There was a brief pause, then a beep. Hector left a terse message, "The two know where you live, and they are coming for you. I'll try to get help." He dialed a second number. Several seconds passed as it rang, but this time his call was answered. "Felipe, are you and Mateo anywhere near Magdalena?" Hector wheezed into the phone.

The two were scheduled to make a drug delivery to the small town of Quemado, fifteen miles to the west of Magdalena. They were the only members of the Loko Krew gang Hector could think of who might conceivably be close enough to do any good. For the first time that day, lady luck smiled on Hector. They had finished their business in Quemado, were returning to Socorro, and were currently only three miles west of Magdalena.

"Listen very closely, Felipe, and don't ask questions," Hector managed. He struggled to speak clearly, hampered by his newly loosened teeth and swelling lips. "I'm going to give you an address and directions to a ranch on Route 107. The owner of the ranch is very important to Loko Krew. The big cop we've been looking for, driving a…" Hector paused, remembering the car in the Chollo parking lot… "dark blue Chevy, is on his way to kill him. The woman we've been searching for may be heading that way too, or might already be there. You might be close enough to intercept them. Kill both of them and you will be rewarded, big time. Now, here are the directions…"

When he finished, Hector groaned and leaned back against the wall. Maybe Norman would kill him for divulging the location of his ranch to others… or maybe he would be rewarded for stopping the two gringos before they could harm him… or maybe the cop would kill Norman and come back and kill him… or maybe Hector would be going to prison. Hector was having trouble concentrating; the pain was excruciating. With effort, he slid the phone across the tile towards Pedro, who was still standing near the door and gaping at the broken gang leader on the floor.

"You'd better call me an ambulance," Hector wheezed through bloody lips.

Jack peeled out of the sandy parking lot, clouds of dust spewing out behind the car as he fishtailed onto Route 60 and gunned the rental westward towards the village of Magdalena. The Cantina was maybe halfway between Socorro and Magdalena. He guessed he was only ten minutes away from the remote little burg, less if he abused the 55 mph speed limit. But how far outside of the town was Norman's place?

He roared in frustration as his fist pounded the steering wheel repeatedly. How could Ryan go after this maniac by herself? Jack knew an all-consuming revenge was behind her actions, but she had to realize that there could only be two outcomes: she would either get herself killed or go to prison for killing Noman—no matter how justified she or anyone else might view her actions. Jack had to stop her. He'd better call the local police, or this far from Socorro, the county sheriff's office. He was guessing law enforcement patrols were thinly spread across such a large and sparsely populated desert area. Jack prayed there was a patrol car somewhere nearby. He couldn't just let—

Jack's cell phone vibrated in his pocket, the ring muffled by the thick denim of his Levis. With the car now rocketing forward at over 80 miles per hour and weaving slightly on the roadway, he fumbled awkwardly as he retrieved his phone from his front pocket and looked at the Caller-ID. It was Ryan. The car swerved dangerously as he hit the brakes, but Jack managed to pull off the roadway without rolling the car, a brown fog of dust enveloping the vehicle as it came to rest.

Jack roared into the small cell phone, "Ryan, are you okay? Where the hell are you? What do you think you're doing? Tell me where you're at and don't do anything, I'll be right there. Please, don't go after—"

Jack's world stopped spinning as Ryan's familiar voice interrupted from the small speaker. "Stop… stop… hold on big guy. Listen to me. I'm okay, everything's okay. Please calm down. Please, just listen—"

"Thank God, Ryan. Okay, okay, I'm listening." Jack realized he was breathing heavily as if he had just raced up a steep flight of stairs. He inhaled deeply, trying to calm his roiling emotions.

"I'm out on Route 107, south of Magda—"

"You're at Norman's," Jack accused. "I know where that's at. I just had a mano-a-mano talk with Hector. Don't do anything until I get there. Stay away from—"

It was Ryan's turn to interrupt. She actually laughed although there was little humor in the sound. "You and Hector?" She chuckled again. "All in all, I'm guessing Hector isn't feeling too well. I'm also guessing he's wishing he stayed at the motel for the extra day. As for Norman, not to worry. I got the drop on him, and I have him trussed up in the basement, taped and tied up like a Christmas present."

Jack was overwhelmed with relief that she was not only safe, but hadn't taken the law into her own hands and done anything to Norman. But he had no idea what she was referring to with Hector. "Hector? What the hell are you talking about?" he asked.

Ryan's humorless laugh again issued from the phone. "I had a little run-in with him and a friend last night. Let's just say I left Hector sleeping and figured he'd be spending another night on vacation. He must have gotten loose. I'll fill you in later."

The conversation shifted back to Norman as Ryan seemingly read his mind. "I couldn't kill him, Jack. As much as the bastard deserves it, I just couldn't do it. Go ahead and call the Sheriff and I'll wait for you and—"

This time the interruption came from her end—a loud, breathless grunt—followed by a loud crash. A deep, guttural growl of rage emitted from the phone. It wasn't Ryan's voice. There were echoes of a struggle—muffled groans, grunts, thuds and scuffling sounds, followed by a louder shattering crash of breaking glass. Another alien roar and Ryan's shrill scream, climaxed by a sharp clink—and the connection was broken. The sounds were a spear piercing Jack's heart, pinning him to the seat. Uncomprehending, he stared at the phone wide-eyed.

Reality came crashing in like an avalanche. He jammed the shift into drive and slammed the gas pedal to the floor, the car spewing dust and gravel as it fishtailed back onto the pavement. Jack howled and rocked back and forth violently in the seat in an unconscious attempt to force the car to go faster. The car rocketed down the highway towards Ryan, thoughts of calling the Sheriff's Department momentarily forgotten in his panic.

Minutes later Jack was racing through the quiet streets of Magdalena, fervently praying that no pedestrians, cyclists, animals or cars wandered out onto the roadway; at his speed he'd never be able to avoid them. Seconds later, his prayers answered, he was through the village and heading southwest racing along Route 107 with the accelerator pressed to the floor.

Although the area was desolate and sparsely populated, Jack forced himself to reign in the speed of the car as he neared the ten mile mark. He didn't want to miss the driveway to the killer's house. Minutes later Jack spied the inconspicuous dirt road sandwiched between the decrepit 426 mailbox and a bold "No Trespassing" sign.

Jack turned onto the uneven washboard track, and within a quarter mile saw an unoccupied Ford F-150 parked just off the roadway. There was no sign of the Jeep Cherokee rental. Jack forced himself to continue driving slowly as he punched in 911 on his phone.

The Sheriff's Office answered, Jack identified himself and gave a concise, abbreviated description of his location and the situation. He also requested an ambulance be dispatched to the address. The dispatcher advised that she would have the EMT and nearest patrol car respond, but it might be 10 -15 minutes since the nearest car was in Socorro, the nearest State Police cruiser another 15 minutes south.

For the third time during their brief conversation, the dispatcher advised Jack to stay on the line, and not confront the suspect. He was to wait for the Sheriff or State Police to arrive—

Jack hung up.

# Chapter 43

"I couldn't kill him, Jack. As much as the bastard deserves it, I just couldn't do it. Go ahead and call the Sheriff and I'll wait for you and—"

As silent as a shadow, but as forceful as a freight train, Norman plowed into Ryan—a football player making an open field tackle—head lowered, shoulder ramming into the middle of her back. The all-out assault almost broke Ryan in two, the force of his impact carrying them both into a side table on the near wall, vases and glassware crashing to the floor. Norman roared incoherently at her, the feral sounds seemingly coming from afar.

Ryan couldn't breathe, the air forced from her lungs. Her ears were ringing as if they were stuffed with cotton. The pain in her lower back reassured her that her spine was still intact. Despite her disorientation and physical pain, one thought repeated itself over and over in her stunned mind like a run-amok metronome—*Move! Move! Move!* If Norman managed to pin her down in her present condition, she would be dead.

Ignoring the pain, Ryan rolled to her left in the broken glass and debris from the overturned table. Norman had temporarily stunned himself in the collision with the wall and lost contact with her when they crashed to the floor. She rose to her feet unsteadily, Norman scrambled to his like a praying mantis, several feet away.

Ryan labored to get her lungs working and turned to face her attacker, her face etched with pain. Pain radiated down her left arm from her shoulder, the injury from Hector's blackjack aggravated by the violent impact with Norman, the wall and the floor. She ignored the pain, but her uncanny speed and reflexes were gone, and the killer was upon her before she could even raise her arms.

They again crashed to the floor, rolling and grappling in desperate silence for several seconds. Norman's superior strength and weight won the battle as he mounted her, his weight a crushing force, his hands around her throat with devastating pressure. Ryan glared up into the face of the homicidal maniac above her as she continued to struggle.

Although her eyes were blinded by tears and her throat was constricted in agony, her mind was still working, and she realized she was still gripping her cell phone in her right hand. Ryan rolled against his suffocating weight and brought her arm up in a short, vicious arc, striking Norman in the side of the head. A second and third time she struck, each time eliciting a grunt from him.

The fourth blow was a direct hit to the temple, and Norman's death grip on her throat loosened.

The ache was excruciating, but Ryan arched her back, bucking upward and again twisting to the side. Off balance and stunned from the violent attack with the cell phone, Norman released his grip, and Ryan managed to throw him off and roll away. She staggered to her feet, choking and gagging from her damaged throat, her body racked by pain. She knew she had little chance against Norman and had to escape until Jack arrived—as she knew he would.

Through blurred vision she looked around frantically and spied the sliding doors leading to the rear patio. Ryan limped across the room trailing blood from a gash in her right thigh, apparently sustained from a broken shard of glass. As she reached the door, she glanced over her shoulder. Norman was up and advancing towards her, his face a mask of hatred.

Through the door and out on the sparsely furnished covered patio, Ryan squinted into the western sun and the scenic vista of the high desert terrain. With a sinking heart she realized she'd never be able to out distance Norman in her wounded condition. She had to make her last stand here. Ryan calmed and steeled her mind, turned and faced the house as Norman burst through the doorway and charged towards her.

Enveloped in a cloud of dust, Jack pulled his car into the paved, circular driveway and saw Ryan's Jeep already parked there. He pulled the Glock .45 from his belt beneath his shirt and racked a shell into the chamber. Jack had forgone the snub-nosed S&W

he usually carried in an ankle holster in lieu of the higher caliber semi-automatic. He quickly checked the interior of the Jeep to make sure it was unoccupied.

Jack crouched to lower his profile, hurried to the entrance of the enclosed courtyard, and invested several precious seconds scanning the front of the large adobe ranch. All was quiet; nothing appeared amiss. With gun drawn and at the ready, he crept across the flagstone courtyard and approached the front door looking for any telltale movement from inside or outside.

So intent was Jack's focus and need to maintain control of his panic, he failed to notice the hazy cloud of dust in the near distance behind him; a sign that another vehicle was rapidly approaching along the three mile, unpaved driveway.

The windows in the front of the hacienda had the decorative wrought iron security bars protecting them, and the front door appeared to be of heavy solid wood and, as Jack soon confirmed, was securely locked. He would have to expend time, effort, and undoubtedly have to shoot his way in—not exactly a discreet way to gain access. Jack decided to check the sides and rear of the ranch before he chanced blasting his way through a door. He did it as quickly as possible, checking each barred window as he went.

He was almost to the rear of the home when he heard a noise from somewhere behind him. It sounded like car doors slamming. Jack hesitated in his controlled haste, indecisive whether to continue to find access to the home, or to waste time checking out the commotion from behind him. He continued forward. If he didn't find a way in soon, he would shoot the hell out of something, and worry about things later. There must be a way into Norman's fortress. He would—

The first bullet ripped into the side of Jack's lower back and spun him around. He staggered backward, but managed to stay upright. Years of training took over, and Jack instinctively brought his gun to bear on the two assailants standing at the front corner of the house. Jack began squeezing off rounds as another bullet whizzed by his ear with an angry whooshing sound, another burying itself in the heavy adobe wall next to him.

The gunfire was deafening as the bullets danced through the air in a deadly ballet. One of his attackers let out a yelp, staggered backward, and fell heavily to the ground. His partner continued advancing and firing. Jack grunted as a shell tore into his upper thigh. Still, he remained standing. He steadied himself and fired a last round, striking the surviving man in the forehead, dropping him where he stood.

Jack wobbled back against the cool adobe wall and slid to the ground. He had no idea how serious the wound in his back was, but it didn't appear that the bullet in his thigh had hit the femoral artery; the blood was oozing as opposed to pumping out. He dropped the magazine from his .45 and quickly checked it. There was one remaining in the clip and, including the one still in the chamber, he had two final shots, if necessary.

Jack regained his feet and limped painfully to the rear of the house where he was greeted by a large, tiled veranda, occupied by an assortment of patio furniture and decorative pottery and plants. The far side of the patio was dedicated to a large, in-ground hot tub.

Something was floating in the pool. As Jack staggered across the veranda to investigate, Norman appeared in the open doorway, gun drawn.

# CHAPTER 44

**Norman found out** the hard way the injured woman was far from incapacitated. When she limped out onto the patio and turned to face him, he could see the grimace of pain masking her face, and she was having difficulty lifting her left arm up into a defensive posture. His rage overcame caution, and he charged towards her.

Despite her injuries, Ryan landed three vicious kicks, stopping Norman in his tracks. He backed away and circled her more warily—limping, nursing bruised ribs and a charlie-horse in one leg. He grinned at Ryan malevolently. "You fucking cunt, you're going to die, you know. Then you'll be able to watch from the inside for another four minutes…" Norman gazed at her critically "… probably a little longer, I'm guessing, considering the excellent shape you're in." He snickered. "Kiss that pretty ass of yours good-by—then you can watch what I do with it."

Ryan didn't reply, eyes focused on him as she stumbled back across the veranda, blood trailing behind her from the gash in her leg, her full lips reduced to a slim line of determination.

Norman advanced again, a little more cautiously this time. Ryan's leg lashed out again. This time Norman managed to block it with his muscled arms. The woman was still fast, but pain had reduced her reflexes to those of a mere mortal. She kept kicking from every angle, grunting with each. Norman blocked three more, closed, and swung a looping right hand, determined to permanently extinguish the light in the dark eyes focused on him. This would be Nicole's last hurrah.

Somehow Ryan blocked the punch with her injured arm. A split second later a sharp jolt of pain erupted in Norman's lower jaw as Ryan's right hand clipped him. Fortunately for Norman the blow had missed its intended target—his neck and throat. But the shock of the errant punch was enough to temporarily halt Norman's advance. Ryan continued to retreat across the patio.

Norman yelled in frustration and charged again. Ryan spun around in a 360 degree pinwheel kick, her leg flashing out in a beautiful arc, her sneaker clad foot a club aimed at his head. But her kick was slower than normal and Norman caught her leg and heaved upward in one motion. Ryan fell heavily on her back, her head bouncing painfully off the flagstone. She rolled to her hands and knees and attempted to rise, but Norman was there in two steps, and kicked her viciously in the ribs—a football player kicking a game-winning field goal.

The force of the kick rolled Ryan completely over and back onto her stomach. Groaning, she attempted to rise again, but she was moving in slow motion. Norman's shadow hovered over her. She made it to one knee before looking up at the menacing shadow. Norman's fist clubbed downward in a powerful blow, snapping her head sharply to the side. Ryan crumpled to the ground.

With a roar of triumph Norman grabbed the semi-conscious woman's hair, and dragged her the remaining distance to the hot tub despite her feeble, albeit surprising, continued resistance. At the edge of the hot tub Norman released her, stepped back, and administered two more vicious kicks to her torso. It was probably just his imagination, but he fancied that he could actually feel her ribs break.

With his foot Norman pushed the groaning woman over the edge into the calm, four-foot deep water. The water seemed to revive her, and she began to make weak, flopping motions—managing to get her head above water. Norman had to admit the woman was one tough bitch. He would enjoy the next few minutes even more.

Norman jumped into the hot tub on top of the sputtering whore, driving her to the bottom and letting his weight pin her. The body beneath him increased its thrashing and floundering in a futile attempt to extricate itself. The woman attempted to push herself up with her arms, but his weight was too great. He forced the woman's head against the bottom of the pool.

As the seconds multiplied and morphed towards a minute, the squirming beneath him continued to wane. It seemed to take forever, but all movement under him eventually ceased, and a steady stream of bubbles broke the surface as the woman's autonomic nervous system forced her to exhale the pent up carbon monoxide. Several more seconds passed. Suddenly the body beneath him convulsed violently as it conceded to the overwhelming need to inhale. As the water aspirated into the lungs, the body futilely attempted to expel it. Finally, movement again ended, and the surface of the water once more grew calm.

Norman sat on the inert body and counted to ten before he pulled himself out of the hot tub. He sat on the edge and watched as the dead woman floated to the surface of the still water, face down and spread eagled, her stretch jeans and cotton blouse plastered to her body provocatively. It was time for fun, and he would relish this one more than all the others. He reached for the body to pull it to the side, but jerked back at the sounds of gunfire coming from somewhere nearby, around the north side of the house it seemed.

Norman instinctively reached for the gun he had stuck in his belt earlier and found it missing. He stood and quickly scanned the patio and, not seeing it anywhere, realized it must have fallen out somewhere in the house during the struggle with the woman. He dashed through the sliding door to find it, resenting being cheated out of the grand finale with Ryan—those last few minutes before her trapped mind fled in terror from this world forever.

Ryan wasn't surprised that she died, only the process and the thoughts that domino'ed through her mind during it. Her injuries and Norman's oppressive weight atop her made her death a foregone conclusion, but the instinct for survival was strong. She continued to resist the inevitable.

The pain in her chest had grown inexorably as she forced her lungs to retain the last breath she had inhaled. As the oxygen diminished and the carbon monoxide grew, the threat of the next imminent inhalation increased. Her body would be unwilling to concede asphyxiation, and soon she would have to breathe.

*Oh, Jack, I am so sorry. This is all my fault. I should never have done this, never have involved you, never have left you. Please forgive me. You have been there for me from that first day you arrested me back in college.* Her mind's eye cried as it flashed through the halls of her memories; her remorse almost as overwhelming as the vise-like pressure in her chest. *I have caused you worry, grief, and even your career. I have hurt you, and you were the last person in this world I would ever want to suffer that. You are coming for me—but I will be gone, and Norman will be waiting. Please forgive me.* Now, she would never be able to tell him how she felt. And to never ever see Jack again—

Ryan's trachea convulsed as she swallowed reflexively, an involuntary attempt to find another molecule of oxygen from somewhere, anywhere. But oddly, there was no panic. Instead she was filled with waves of remorse and regret for the pain her death would cause Jack. A dark whirlpool engulfed her, an intense melancholy and longing for something she had never had—and now, never would. *I love you, Jack. I love you, and I will miss you wherever I am going. More than I ever realized.* Finally, Ryan understood, admitting to an emotion she had thought impossible for her—love for someone other than herself. *Oh, dearest Jack...*

Unable to survive another second without air, her oxygen starved body overrode her survival instinct, her mouth opened, and she inhaled. There was a split second of intense pain as water abruptly filled her lungs in lieu of life giving air. Asphyxia was almost instant, her body convulsing violently, her mind exploding in kaleidoscopic flashes of disjointed colors. As death embraced her in its arms, a blank world of dark shadows and vibrant light engulfed her in a slow, swirling dance of shapes—heralding in a slowly approaching, unknown eternity.

# Chapter 45

For a big man Jack was fast, but with two bullets in him his reflexes were sluggish. The Glock had gained weight, and he was slow to bring it to bear on the figure in the doorway. Years of training served him in good stead as he instinctively adopted the Weaver Stance: left foot forward ahead of the right, right arm thrust towards the target at eye level, right hand steadied by the left, offering a diminished profile to his adversary.

Jack attempted to calm his hand as he concentrated on the rear sights of the .45, and the figure of Norman beyond. There was an angry buzzing as a shell nearly took his ear off. Just as he squeezed the trigger for his first shot, he felt a sting in his upper left arm as a bullet ripped into his flesh. Jack fired his second, and last shot, a split second before another .38 slug slammed into his chest with the force of a sledgehammer, shattering a rib. He staggered and fell heavily on his backside. Some cop he was, Jack thought. He'd gotten himself shot four times, was sitting on his ass in some desert courtyard with an empty gun, bleeding out while waiting for the killer to finish him.

Weary, his head heavy, he looked towards the house awaiting the inevitable. But Jack's final two shots had run straight and true and had found Norman, his body now lying motionless just inside the doorway.

But Ryan... Jack still had to find Ryan....

Jack steeled himself and pushed his body up and out of the growing pool of blood on the ground and stood. Lightheaded, he weaved unsteadily as he took a step towards the house. He glanced over at the hot tub and the floating object in the calm water. He stopped and focused.

The realization it was Ryan's body in the water hit Jack like an electric shock. His head cleared as he hobbled over to the pool, his wounded left arm cradled against his broken rib, blood from his wounds soaking his clothing red.

Jack ignored everything. He jumped into the water, grabbed Ryan with his good arm, and pulled her to the side. Gasping and groaning, the water turning pinkish from their commingled blood, he managed to maneuver her limp body out of the water and onto the deck. With weakening effort, he pulled himself out behind her.

Jack rolled her onto her back. Ryan's normally pale complexion was suffused with a bluish tinge; a sure sign of cyanosis. She was not breathing, and he couldn't find a pulse. He turned her head to the side, opened her mouth and pulled out her tongue, checking her airway for obstructions. Finding none, he ran his fingers down the front of her chest until he found the bottom of her sternum. He overlapped his palms at that point and forcefully applied rhythmic pressure in five measured thrusts. Jack quickly repositioned her head, pinched her nostrils shut, covered her open mouth with his and breathed deeply into her—once, twice, three times. He then went back to the chest compressions.

Jack continued with the C.P.R. in the eerily silent desert, as if the world was waiting with bated breath to see the outcome of his frantic efforts.

After a minute he checked her pulse again. There was none. He went back to work on her still, lifeless body. How long had she been in the water? Jack remembered Dr. Tolliver's words concerning irreversible brain damage occurring within four to ten minutes after oxygen deprivation. How long had it been for Ryan? He had to bring her back. He prayed silently to God for the first time in a long time. *Please bring her back. I'll take care of her, nurse her, love her. Don't let her die! I'm begging you....*

Jack was weakening from blood loss and the continued C.P.R. His world was starting a slow spin as his head filled with its own deoxygenated sludge. It was if he was viewing the world through undulating waves of water. With an effort, Jack concentrated and continued: five compressions, three breaths, five and three... *He would not stop until all the blood drained from his body, until he was dead and God came for him, until—*

Ryan's body convulsed beneath his hands and she gagged repeatedly, water spewing from her mouth. Jack rolled her onto her side as she continued to cough and aspirate fluid from her lungs. Finally, her shuddering ceased, and she rolled weakly onto her back and stared up at Jack with the most beautiful, bloodshot brown eyes he had ever seen.

Ryan managed a smile. "Jack, if you had wanted to kiss me that badly you should have just done so. You didn't have to wait until I drowned."

With a strength he thought had abandoned him, Jack reached down, grabbed a fistful of Ryan's blouse and pulled her up into his arms. He held her close, ignoring the pain in his damaged shoulder and ribs. He buried his face in her wet hair. He realized he might be dying, and all reticence left him.

"Thank God you're okay," Jack whispered. "I don't know what I would have done if you had died. I love you Ryan, I have from the first day I ever set eyes on you. I love you, I love you, I love you. I always have and I always will," he murmured. "Please, don't ever leave me again." His eyes were squeezed shut, but his tears escaped and traced down his cheeks, mingling with the dark tresses against which they were pressed.

Jack's strength was ebbing. He had been kneeling next to Ryan, holding her. His arms slowly slipped away from their embrace and he listed to the side. Ryan, still weak from her ordeal with death, sat up and managed to hang onto him and help him to the ground, his head resting in her lap. She maintained her sitting position by bracing herself with her other arm, ignoring the throbbing of her own injuries.

It was only now that she became aware of the blood soaking Jack's shirt and pants, and their causes—the bullet holes in his arm, leg and chest. "Oh my God, Jack, you've been shot," she cried. The tears flowed from her eyes as her free hand sought out each injury, frantically indecisive as to which oozing wound might need direct pressure more.

A siren sounded in the distance.

Jack's eyes fluttered open, and he smiled at her weakly. "And that's not counting the hole in my back. They got me pretty good. Some cop I am." He coughed and wheezed wetly. Ryan noticed blood on his lips and the corner of his mouth.

"I think a busted rib may have punctured my lung," he breathed, reading her mind. His eyes closed.

Fear and panic was a tide rising uncontrolled within Ryan. Her hand caressed Jack's cheek and forehead. She brushed his wet hair back from his pale brow. "You're the finest person I've ever known. Don't you dare leave me now, Jack. You can't die. I love you. I came back for you. Do you hear me? I love you. Stay with me, stay with me...." Her hand tracked across his face, tracing every curve, wrinkle, nook and cranny, memorizing the feel and texture of his skin—as if by her touch she could transfer life from her to him.

The sirens were nearer, now having morphed from one into a chorus of several. She willed them to go faster. *Please, please hurry*, her mind screamed.

Jack's eyes were still closed. Ryan's throat, raw from its recent abuse, constricted in fear. She gulped twice before whispering, "Did you mean it, Jack? Can you... do you... do you... can you really love someone like me?" she asked.

Ryan winced at the inanity of the thought. The man had been there for her from their beginning, whenever she needed him, however she needed him. Not only had he saved her, he was willing to die for her... might be dying right now in her arms... "Jack, Jack, I'm so sorry," she sobbed. "This is all my fault." Ryan grabbed his hair, entwining her fingers in the thick mop and shaking his head back and forth. "Wake up, Jack, wake up," she begged, her voice rising painfully from her throat. "I love you. Do you hear me? I love you. Don't you dare leave me. I love you," she whispered vehemently. "You can't leave me. You can't—"

Jack's eyes flicked open. "Hey, go easy on the hair. I'm not going anywhere. Someone's got to stick around and take care of you."

Between the two of them they marshaled enough strength to get Jack into an upright sitting position. They sat wrapped in each other's arms, precariously balanced.

"Jack, do you know what was going through my mind after I died?" Ryan asked, murmuring into his ear.

Jack's head was buried in her neck, but she felt his head move slightly in denial. Ryan continued, "All I could see was you. And me with you. Every minute we had ever been together, every word spoken. All I could see and hear was us together," she repeated. "I had to come back."

Ryan's eyes grew wide as a sudden realization exploded in her wounded mind. Her arms tightened around Jack possessively, her fingers digging into his body in fear. "Where's Norman? What happened to Norman? Where is he?" She was almost hyperventilating as her eyes darted around the patio in fear.

"Ouch, Ryan, take it easy with those talons of yours. Relax, I shot him. He went down inside the doorway." Jack squinted over

Ryan's shoulder at Norman's motionless form just visible inside the house. "It's over, Ryan. The police will be here any minute."

Too weak to continue sitting, they eased back and lay prone on the cool tile. For a moment the stillness was complete. The strident sounds of sirens no longer disturbed the dry desert air. Soon, the sounds of voices, doors slamming, yelling....

The police and the EMTs found the man and woman on the rear lanai lying motionless on their backs, the man's head on the woman's stomach, her hand resting on his chest—two lovers in serene repose.

Jack regained consciousness as they loaded him onto the stretcher. His face was distorted by an oxygen mask, and an oxygen tank was strapped to the stretcher. An IV tube ran from his arm to a saline bag held aloft by an EMT next to him, the sharp pain of his injuries reduced to distant throbs. Jack's mind was a little fuzzy, but he guessed they had packed his wounds to stem the bleeding, and injected him with pain killers. Jack turned his head and saw Ryan on a stretcher nearby, a matching oxygen mask marring her beautiful face. She smiled at him. Jack felt wonderful.

There were several uniformed police officers milling around on the patio and two plain-clothes detectives. Jack pulled off his plastic mask and yelled at the nearest one, "Hey, detective, over here." The yell came out as more of a croak, but the nearest detective heard him.

The technician had grabbed the oxygen mask and was trying to get it back over Jack's mouth and nose—a difficult task since Jack kept swatting his hand away. Two techs wheeled his stretcher towards the patio door. Ryan was similarly attired, her gurney trundling along right behind his.

The detective, gray haired and sporting a decent pot belly, walked next to his stretcher, a comforting hand on Jack's arm. "Take it easy Sergeant Kroner; you were shot up pretty good. We can talk at the hospital once they get all the holes plugged. The young lady filled in a few of the blanks for us. She'll be okay."

What about the others? Jack asked. "Alive or dead?"

"Both dead."

"Both?"

"Yeah, the two guys on the north side of the house. Shot by you, I assume," the detective replied, more of a statement than a question.

They were at the patio door. "The one inside the doorway? What about him?" Jack asked.

The detective glanced over at two techs standing near a sheet covered mound. One shook his head, the other spoke. "We couldn't save him, Detective Morrison. We tried, but he'd already lost too much blood."

Detective Morrison returned his gaze to Jack, his smile grim. "Well, I guess that makes you three for three. Good riddance, I'd say," he muttered under his breath.

They wheeled Jack past Norman's motionless, covered body, Ryan's gurney close behind. Ryan's voice, strong and imperative pierced the stillness. "Stop!"

Jack looked back at Ryan. The EMTs, caught off guard, had halted next to Norman's body. Ryan propped herself up on one elbow, reached down and threw the sheet off of Norman's face.

The techs looked in confusion at Morrison, who in turn started back towards Ryan. Jack reached up and grabbed him by the arm. Their eyes met. "Please, she needs this, just give her a minute." The detective hesitated. "Please," Jack repeated.

Oblivious to this exchange, Ryan leaned farther over, grabbed Norman by the chin and turned his head toward her to better look into his lifeless, staring eyes. His irises, dwarfed by the whites surrounding them, made his death mask hard to define. Was his final expression one of pain, or fear?

"I just wanted to say goodbye, Norman," Ryan cooed. "Yes, I know you're still in there, suffering the last four minutes you always relished in your victims." Ryan squeezed his forearm. "Of course, you've really taken care of your body, so I'm guessing you'll be able to hold on in that twisted mind of yours for several extra minutes." Ryan smiled conspiratorially. "I figure you might want to hang around as long as you can, I'm sure your mother is waiting for you in the great abyss, and I bet she has a few things planned for you, some catching up to do. Then again, maybe she's in there with you already. In any event, you'll have an eternity to spend together."

Ryan was sure it was her imagination, because there was no way his glassy, dead eyes could reflect the terror she knew he was experiencing. Or was there? She smiled at the possibility. "Well, Normie, goodbye and say hello to Mommy Nicole for me. You two have fun." She patted him on the cheek before pulling the sheet back over his face. Her adrenalin having run its course, Ryan fell back onto the gurney with a groan surrounded by a smile.

Detective Morrison looked from Ryan to Jack, confused. "What the hell was that all about?" he asked.

Jack was grinning. "Let's just chalk it up to shock, detective. You wouldn't believe me if I told you."

Made in the USA
Charleston, SC
23 January 2017